An author of mo[...] [...] [...] [...] [...] [...]
adults with more [...] [...] [...] [...]
Janice Kay John[...] [...] [...] [...] [...]
pens books of g[...] [...] [...] USA
TODAY bestselling [...] and an eight-time finalist for
the Romance Writers of America *RITA®* Award, she won
a *RITA®* Award in 2008. A former librarian, Janice
raised two daughters in a small town north of Seattle,
Washington.

Karen Whiddon started weaving fanciful tales for her
younger brothers at the age of eleven. Amid the gorgeous
Catskill Mountains, then the majestic Rocky Mountains,
she fuelled her imagination with the natural beauty
surrounding her. Karen now lives in north Texas, writes
full-time and volunteers for a boxer dog rescue. She
shares her life with her hero of a husband and four to five
dogs, depending on if she is fostering. You can email
Karen at kwhiddon1@aol.com. Fans can also check out
her website, karenwhiddon.com

Discover more at millsandboon.co.uk

WHAT IS HIDDEN

JANICE KAY JOHNSON

SECRET ALASKAN HIDEAWAY

KAREN WHIDDON

MILLS & BOON

First Published in Great Britain 2022
by Mills & Boon, an imprint of HarperCollins*Publishers* Ltd
1 London Bridge Street, London, SE1 9GF

www.harpercollins.co.uk

HarperCollins*Publishers*
Macken House, 39/40 Mayor Street Upper,
Dublin 1, D01 C9W8

What Is Hidden © 2022 Janice Kay Johnson
Secret Alaskan Hideaway © 2022 Karen Whiddon

ISBN: 978-0-263-30372-8

1222

MIX
Paper | Supporting
responsible forestry
FSC™ C007454

This book is produced from independently certified FSC™ paper
to ensure responsible forest management.

For more information visit: www.harpercollins.co.uk/green

Printed and Bound in Spain using 100% Renewable electricity at
CPI Black Print, Barcelona

WHAT IS HIDDEN

JANICE KAY JOHNSON

Prologue

The lighting in this parking lot sucked. She hadn't noticed on her way into the tavern. *Then* she'd been feeling sophisticated, a grown woman confident enough to saunter into a bar on her own. Now her forehead crinkled in puzzlement as she tried to remember where she'd left her car. Wow—she had to be a little bit drunk.

Oh, wait. Her keys were in her hand. *Press button on fob.* And—taillights flashed off to one side. Who knew? She was a genius, right? Or not really drunk. Or…

Of course, she fumbled with the keys as she opened her car door, and they fell to the ground. Wonderful. It was so blasted *dark* over here. Why hadn't she picked a tavern that planned for somewhat pickled customers to be able to find dropped keys? But there they were, and she got in behind the wheel. Then it took her a minute to insert the key in the ignition and to lay her hand on the seatbelt clip. It was important to wear a seatbelt, she told herself with a serious nod. Especially when she'd been drinking.

Which was totally all right, since this was her twenty-first birthday. Her friends at school had held a party for her yesterday, and her parents were expecting her tomorrow and would undoubtedly "surprise" her with a cake, candles and gifts. They didn't know she'd decided to head home this afternoon. *She'd* surprise them. Home wasn't even an hour away.

As she sat there, a weird feeling came over her, the fingers tiptoeing down her back kind, making her look around uneasily. Well, no wonder; with the overhead light on and that damned dark parking lot, she was on display. If somebody was watching, they were probably just trying to decide why she was just sitting there.

She fired up the engine and heard all the locks *snick*. A moment later, she pulled out on the narrow highway, so familiar from drives to the big city—Springfield. She giggled at the thought, then noticed she'd crossed the center line. Oops! Fortunately, there was hardly any other traffic, only headlights that had appeared quite a way behind her.

She'd like to think she'd sobered up some by the time she turned off the highway onto a narrower one, more a country road, even though it, too, had a yellow stripe down the middle. Hardly any shoulder, though, and awfully dark. Not like she wasn't used to it; her parents had acreage several miles outside town, and she'd been taught to drive super carefully, especially at night, because deer and coyotes and other wildlife often crossed the road right in front of a car without realizing the danger.

On her dashboard, a red light caught her eye. When had *that* come on? She had no idea what it was trying to tell her, but it probably wasn't good. She might be imagining a faint burning smell, but… Yes, she should pull over and call her dad to come and get her.

There wasn't any way to really get off the road, but she braked anyway, and was proud of herself when she managed to switch on the warning lights. Oh, and she should probably turn off the engine, in case the oil was perilously low or something like that.

She groped in her purse on the passenger side. Her

phone wasn't in the outside pocket where she usually carried it. "*Where, oh, where,*" she half sang as her searching fingers found her wallet, a small cosmetics bag, receipts, a tissue packet. Something hard…no, that was her electronic reader. *Where, oh, where...*

A picture appeared before her. Her sitting on a barstool, chatting with several guys, including the kind of cute bartender. Phone lying there; she'd almost decided to text her parents instead of surprising them. Then she'd accepted another refill, and… Couldn't remember another thing.

Oh, God—had she left her phone behind at the tavern? Once she was home, she could call and they'd surely have it, but…unless someone came along to give her a lift, she'd have to hoof it. Which wouldn't kill her—it probably wasn't more than a couple miles to go, but the near-complete darkness gave her the creeps. None of the local wildlife attacked *people*, as far as she knew, except maybe a mama black bear with cubs, and it *was* spring.

And then—oh, thank you, God—headlights appeared in her rearview mirror. Given how remote this was, the driver just about had to be a neighbor. Someone she knew. The lights were high, almost blinding her in the mirror, which meant it was a pickup. Practically everybody hereabouts drove pickups.

A turn signal came on, and the truck pulled up behind her. Its flashers came on, too, and she watched in her side mirror as the driver's side door opened and someone—a man—got out and walked forward.

Bulky shoulders in a well-worn jean jacket. She couldn't really see his face even when he stopped beside her door and made a twirling motion with one finger. Only she couldn't roll down the window without turning the engine back on, so maybe it would be better if she just opened the door.

She had it open, and he'd gripped the top of it and leaned down before she did see him…and recognized him. He'd been at the tavern, on the barstool right beside her. He'd flirted with her, but not in a way that scared her. It had to be just chance that he lived out this way, too, didn't it?

But then he smiled, and dread filled her.

"You got a little farther down the road than I expected before your engine conked out," he remarked, "but practice makes perfect. And since you didn't get all the way home…"

His hand fisted and he swung at her. Pain exploded in her cheek and temple. As she slammed into the steering wheel and true darkness engulfed her, her last thought was a desperate plea.

Mommy. Daddy.

Chapter One

"We need you."

Thanks to the memory of her stepfather's plea, guilt rode along with Jo Summerlin during the entire drive from her home in Illinois to southern Missouri where she'd grown up. She might as well have buckled it into the passenger seat beside her. And however she tried to justify herself, that sense of guilt wouldn't shut up.

As if this internal argument/justification was anything new.

Still, she couldn't help thinking, *This is my fault. I was practically Lucy's mother, and I abandoned her.*

Except, she *wasn't* her half sister's mother. Yes, Jo had stepped in when their mother walked out on them all: her husband and three children. Jo hadn't had any choice, though she'd been a kid herself, only thirteen.

Still, would it have killed her to stay closer for college? Gotten a job locally? Even lived at home for a few more years?

She left the freeway for a highway, then another one. Roads became narrower; this last one had a yellow stripe down the middle, but nobody with any common sense would exceed the forty-mile-an-hour speed limit.

Jo hadn't passed a single other car since she began the climb that took the road along the steep hillside above the river. The water was running especially high, she couldn't help noting, not surprising after the unusually wet spring. To her left, just on the other side of the guardrail, the land dropped precipitously. To her right, trees cloaked in the vivid green of new leaves somehow clung to the rocky, equally steep hillside.

Spring. Well, technically summer, but still. For the first time all day, Jo felt genuine anticipation. The countryside in the Ozarks was gorgeous, only the vivid fall foliage eclipsing springtime.

The sight of the garish billboard ahead that read SUM-MERLIN CAVERN had her making a face without even thinking about it. She'd argued for using the billboards on state highways but going for something more tasteful in this wooded setting. She'd lost. As always.

Taking the familiar turnoff, Jo ordered herself to think positive. Being home for the summer might be fun. And she really would be glad to spend more time with Brody and Lucy, if it wasn't too late. Teenage Lucy and Brody, almost twenty-one, might be too busy with friends to care if Jo was around or not.

Time to quit beating herself up. She'd stayed in close touch with her siblings; the three of them texted regularly, shared photos and occasionally talked on the phone. Lucy had come to stay with her a few times—when her dad could "spare" her. Jo came home for most major holidays. No, she hadn't made it since Christmas, six months ago, but Lucy hadn't gone off the rails now because big sister wasn't around. She might have been quiet lately. Caught up in the final weeks of the school year; Jo hadn't noticed any new distance, though—not until Jo's stepfather had called to beg her to come home to "do something about" Lucy, his frustration and bewilderment bleeding through every word of that phone conversation.

She'd teased him by saying, "You know, I spoiled you. I was such an angel."

A brief silence. Then he burst into laughter. "You're right. Never a moment of defiance."

That might be putting it a *little* too strongly. She laughed, too, although it's true that she'd been an exceptionally well-behaved teenager, too afraid of abandonment after losing her mother to be anything else.

The last thing her stepfather said was, "Whatever is going on with Lucy isn't rebellion. It's—" he hesitated for a long moment before finishing "—anger. Or fear."

What could have happened? At Christmas everything had been...well, not smooth, there were always undercurrents with this family, but fine. Normal. Brody was a jerk, but probably no more so than most guys strutting into new adulthood. Lucy had been given to rolling her eyes and mumbling lines she refused to repeat loud enough for Rod to hear, but wasn't that normal for a teenage girl who had to defy her dad somehow?

Well, Jo was determined to get to the bottom of this. She hadn't been home for an entire summer since she'd graduated from college. Rod had somehow conned her into agreeing not just to a visit, but to work, just as she had during high school and college breaks. Really, what else would she do with herself? At least there'd be no learning curve since she'd worked in the family business most of her weekends and after-school hours since she was twelve or so.

But this time, it was for her sister's sake.

A final curve, and a stunning vista opened in front of her. More stunning if an extensive parking lot hadn't been blasted out of the hillside, but at least the building that housed the gift and coffee shop had been built of the same gray stone that formed the bones of the hill and tumbled into the river.

The enormous half-open mouth of the cavern yawned in the hillside. Summerlin Cavern, open six days a week for tours. Jo had led hundreds—no, thousands of them. She'd been the barista; she'd operated the cash register in the gift shop where tourists also bought tickets for the tours. Her stepfather kept the cavern profitable by hiring help as little as possible, and as young as Jo had been after the divorce, she'd already been a useful part of the operation.

Which was maybe a slightly cynical way to look at the truth that Rod had stepped up to raise her as his own.

There were enough cars parked in the lot to suggest a tour was underway, but her experienced eye told her there couldn't be many people waiting for the next tour. That wouldn't please Rod. She'd have to remind him that school had barely let out for some districts—including the one in Illinois where she taught—and probably some had yet to finish for the year. Business would pick up drastically by July.

She drove on by the parking lot, taking a narrow road, marked No Trespassing. Around a last curve, just out of sight of the cavern entrance, a white-painted two-story house clung to a patch of ground barely wide enough for the foundation and a garage. From this narrow perch on a cliff, plank stairs led down to a dock on the river. Home since she was a kid, when her mother married Rodney Summerlin.

Jo made a face. Her six-year-old self had been okay with a stepfather, but she remembered all too well her first sight of the cavern opening. It had terrified her. She'd had nightmares about that cave for months. Rod's exasperation wasn't surprising. He loved the cavern named for his family. Other well-known show caverns in Missouri had names like Fantastic Caverns, Devil's Well, Talking Rocks Cavern, Bridal Cave. Forget that. Rod Summerlin had inherited the land and everything that lay beneath the ground from his father, who had inherited it from *his* father. Part of the tour spiel included family history, somewhat exaggerated. He wouldn't have it any other way.

When, at about Lucy's age, Jo got enthusiastic plotting how they could raise interest in the cavern, she'd announced they needed more highway billboards, and a new name. Something spectacular. Rod had not reacted well.

Braking in front of the house, Jo realized she was rolling her eyes, but also grinning at the memory.

Rusty, the family dog, raced around from the back barking furiously. A stray who'd showed up a couple of years ago, he was maybe part Labrador but had a scruffy rust-brown coat and eyes of two different colors. Jo found him endearing, but no one could call him handsome.

Once she got out of her car, Rusty must have recognized her from her last visit, because he jumped at her trying to lick her face. After some petting, she slung her purse and laptop bag over her shoulder, and lifted a sizeable suitcase from the trunk. Why hadn't Rusty's racket brought Lucy out? She was surely home by now. Wasn't this the last week of school locally? There weren't likely to be any after-school activities this late in the year.

Jo outright snorted. She couldn't remember Lucy ever doing theater or yearbook or whatever. Rod had always favored his son. Brody had been permitted to play high school sports—football in the fall and baseball in the spring—but Jo had managed one season of volleyball as a freshman only by begging rides home from other parents. She'd given up after that. Even though she wasn't his real daughter, Jo was supposed to be as dedicated to promoting the great and glorious Summerlin Cavern as Rod was.

Well, she'd do her part this summer, for Lucy, but also because she did admire Rod's dedication. This was among the most extensive and impressive caverns in a state that boasted well over seven thousand of them. Tour guides were top-notch, and people never left feeling anything less than awestruck.

Also, Jo had to admit, she owed her stepfather. After Mom ditched the family, he hadn't been obligated to keep Jo and raise her as his own, but he had. There was no question of whether she'd help now that he needed it.

Heck, it occurred to her, Lucy was probably leading the current tour or stuck in the gift shop behind the espresso machine or the cash register.

Jo hauled her stuff up the steps onto the porch that stretched the width of the house and let herself in with her key, shutting the door on a woeful dog.

"Anyone home?" she called, just in case.

"Jo?" The voice floated from the bedrooms above. "Is that you?"

"Who else?"

The pretty teenager came rushing downstairs and cast herself into her big sister's arms. "You're here! I didn't believe Dad when he said you were coming! You're not really staying all summer, are you?"

Laughing, Jo said, "I'm afraid so. He didn't see why I should laze around for three months when I could be making myself useful here."

Lucy pulled back, her delight having vanished into resentment. The change was shockingly abrupt. "Babysitting *me*, you mean."

"I'm excited to spend time with you." Jo didn't want to directly lie and say, *No, he didn't say anything about you.*

"Sure. Well, I'm *fine*!" she exclaimed. "He just doesn't

like me doing stuff with friends. *Brody* can go out and party whenever *he* wants, but *me*? *I* have a *curfew*."

Since she was sixteen while her brother was just short of his twenty-first birthday, Jo could sympathize with Rod even if she, too, had been mad at him half the time until she escaped to college. Still, the drama seemed excessive.

Jo smiled. "The two of us can flee when we feel like it and go do stuff."

"You mean, you'll keep me busy so I don't have *time* for my friends." Lucy backed up, her expression ugly. "I'm not *dumb*, you know, and I don't have to listen to *you*." She whirled and tore up the stairs as fast as she'd come down. A moment later, a door slammed.

Jo gaped at the empty hall above. She hadn't forgotten her own tumultuous moods, mostly around the time she turned thirteen, although she had had plenty of excuses. But Lucy had turned sixteen in April. She should be past the stage of excessive hormones, shouldn't she? She *was* past it. She and Jo had had fun during Christmas break.

Why blast me, Jo wondered, *if Lucy was mostly mad at her dad? Please don't let her be pregnant. Or...*

Getting into drugs?

Mood squelched, Jo dragged her suitcase upstairs to her old bedroom, unchanged from when she left for college at eighteen. Maybe if she updated it this summer, she wouldn't so easily slip into feeling like the kid she'd been then.

But she shrugged off the idea. Maybe she'd walk over to the gift shop and say hi to Rod and Brody when they had a free moment. To Austin, too—he'd worked full-time for the Summerlins for the entire ten years since she left for college. Would he hit on her again this summer?

THREE DAYS LATER, Jo regretted her ready agreement to come home. It felt...strange, to be back, sleeping in her childhood bedroom. Her sleep wasn't easy. The mattress had been a cheap one to start with, and now sagged enough that she kept catching herself just before she rolled off the bed. Then, last night, Rusty got excited about something and barked up a storm. The barking receded, as if he was chasing something, then gained in volume. What, did he want one of them to boost him up a cliff to convince that squirrel to descend within reach? Brody yelled out the window, to no effect. Rod must have gone downstairs, because she'd heard him swearing at the "damn dog" before letting him in.

She'd discovered that Rod and Brody believed she had assumed all household tasks, starting with cooking and cleaning the kitchen. That might be her fault, because she'd been so eager to contribute during her previous, much shorter visits. But for three months? No.

To top it all off, she was getting absolutely nowhere with Lucy. The most open communication they'd had was yesterday when Lucy had cried, "Things have just been weird, okay?" Of course, she'd immediately raced upstairs and slammed her bedroom door.

Weird *how*?

The question still on her mind, Jo asked her brother when they both happened to be in the gift shop this afternoon at a rare, quiet moment. Brody walked with a swagger and looked a lot like his dad: just under six feet, stocky and strong, with sandy-colored hair and brown eyes. He had wandered over to her cash register.

"Weird?" he repeated. "I don't know what she's talking about. She's just flipped out lately." He sneered. "Maybe it's a guy or something."

The fact that he didn't seem to want to meet Jo's eyes gave her a stir of unease.

Brody was *sounding* more like his father every day,

too. She hoped she was imagining the way he treated his sister, as if she wasn't worth much. So far, he at least pretended to respect Jo.

"Rusty was sure worked up about something last night."

"Still was this morning. I had to lock him up at home. He's not the sharpest knife in the drawer."

Probably not.

"You didn't say whether you're planning to go back to school in the fall," she commented, as much to change the subject as anything. He'd finished his second year at Missouri State University in Springfield, commuting from home, but then decided to take a year off. She felt sure he'd have had a lot more fun and been more engaged if he'd roomed on campus, but he hadn't fought that battle as successfully as Jo had. In retrospect, she suspected he hadn't cared one way or the other.

He gave a careless shrug. "Probably not. We're so busy here. I have to learn the business since it'll be mine someday."

"Is that what you want?" she asked.

He looked at her like she was nuts. "Why wouldn't I?"

Oh, because there was a big, wide world out there? But she smiled. "Just asking."

"I probably wouldn't have gone at all if it weren't for you," he said, and he wasn't thanking her. "It was a waste of time, just like Dad said."

She kept her voice mild. "Depends on what you want out of life."

"I want to open more of the cave to tours," he burst out. "Advertise. Why shouldn't Summerlin be as well known as Meramec or Onondage? Have you heard about the wild tour the Smallin Civil War Cave offers? They take people adventuring in some of the passages that don't have paved paths and lights. Why can't we do that, too? Some of the best chambers are—"

They paused so Jo could ring up the purchase of a handful of polished multicolored minerals and poured them into a small brown paper bag that said Summerlin Cavern beneath a curving line that suggested the arch of the mouth. The mother and girl—ten or eleven, maybe?—beamed when she asked if they'd enjoyed the tour.

"It was amazing," the mother declared.

Jo waited until the double glass doors closed behind them before she resumed the conversation with her brother. "Did you ask Rod about it?"

"He said it was too dangerous." Brody got the sullen look that she particularly disliked. "I said I'd lead them. I know what I'm doing!"

"You do. Have you done any more exploring?"

The shrug was sulky, too. "He doesn't want me to."

There was speculation that many, if not most, of the caves in Missouri were linked. She knew for a fact that passages in the Summerlin Cavern exited at a somewhat smaller opening on neighboring property. The water that had formed the limestone caverns would have found many crevices to eventually join the streams and river. As a girl, she'd made the trip from that opening to exit at their own end of the cavern, as well as venturing into a few other passages, some opening into spectacular rooms with high ceilings and distinctive formations. Back then, Rod had argued that a one-hour tour was the standard, and most people wouldn't want more than that. She hadn't been able to argue, but she also had some sympathy for Brody's schemes. At least he knew he'd eventually inherit the cavern from his father and be able to do whatever he wanted.

Maybe the assumption it would one day all be his

had something to do with Lucy's anger. Rod's belief that women and girls were second-class citizens was pretty obvious.

"I hear voices," Jo said.

Brody pulled out his phone and glanced at it. "Yeah, tour should be letting out. Here come some people from the parking lot, too."

Jo got busy selling tickets for the next tour even as she was aware of the group that had been on the last one spreading out through the extensive gift shop, some talking excitedly, all oohing and aahing at the available merchandise.

Rod's marketing here was effective, from T-shirts and sweatshirts as well as postcards that said Summerlin Cavern with a close-up of one of the extraordinary columns, stalactites, stalagmites and flowstones that were such wondrous sights deep in the cave, to a huge selection of polished and raw rocks and minerals as well as some carved into bookends, boxes and beads and pennants for jewelry. Local crafts did well here, too: hand-woven baskets, carved wood, artwork and pottery. She did a brisk business ringing up purchases, wrapping them carefully and handing them over with a smile in between selling tickets.

Austin, who had led the most recent tour, grinned the moment he saw Jo. Yes, he'd already asked her out, but shrugged blithely when she said, "Gee, no thanks."

From what Brody and Rod had told her, the lanky guy in his thirties never suffered from lack of female companionship. She smiled wryly in return before greeting the next customer.

Rod had been back in the offices doing his bookkeeping or ordering or whatever. Now he began to circulate with a geniality and pride that drew people to him.

The next tour was to be led by Brody, with Austin probably slated for the following one. He was the only full-time employee right now. Besides, of course, Rod, Jo and Brody, with Lucy slated to be full-time, too, for the summer. Jo hadn't been here twenty-four hours when Rod started including her in the tour rotation. A couple of college students usually worked here summers, too, and part-timers filled in as he grudgingly needed them.

Brody edged over to her again. "Do you know where Lucy is? Dad has that slitty-eyed look."

Jo glanced his way. Yes, indeed, he was rotating in place to scan the room with barely veiled irritation.

"No, is she even home from school?"

"She's supposed to be."

Jo smiled at the next person in line just as she saw her sister rush in from the outside, cell phone clutched in her hand.

Spotting Brody and Jo, she hurried to them, her expression distraught. "Autumn just called! Did you hear?"

"You'd better hide that phone and get to work," her brother said. "Dad wants you to take over the espresso—"

"Listen to me!" she cried, voice shrill enough to carry. People started to turn. "It's Amy Kendall this time! She's gone, and the police don't even care!"

Gone? This time? Jo wondered what nobody in the family had bothered to tell her about.

Rod bulled his way through the gathering cluster as Jo hastily boxed a gorgeous pair of earrings.

"We don't have time to stand around gossiping," he said, keeping his own voice down. "This is a bad time—"

"You never listen," Lucy spat. "Amy Kendall has disappeared, and everyone is saying something bad has to have happened. She'd never take off on her own."

"Am I supposed to know who this girl is?" Rod asked, with ill-concealed impatience.

"Yes!" Lucy dashed at tears that had started to run down her cheeks. "She was Brody's girlfriend."

Jo saw the shock on her brother's face even as she absorbed her own dose. "I used to babysit her," she heard herself say slowly. "Remember? Amy and her sister Caroline." Amy had been a year ahead of Brody in school, if she remembered right, which would make her almost twenty-two. She was a beauty the last time Jo saw her—dark, straight, shiny hair that practically reached her butt and swayed with her every move, long legs and slender body, and startling eyes that had made Jo think of amber.

"Excuse me," a man said loudly. "We don't want to miss the tour. Can we buy our tickets?"

Rod shook himself. "We'll talk about this later. The police know what they're doing. We need to concentrate on *our* jobs right now."

He was right, Jo thought, although she was shaken enough that she wouldn't be able to think about anything but the young woman she'd known, who might be in deep trouble.

And…*this time*? Was Amy not the first young woman to go missing?

Chapter Two

Alan Burke drove the last nail into the back porch step he was replacing. Both the sweltering-hot Missouri sun and bitterly cold Missouri winters were hard on wood. This house had sat empty for too many years now. The interior needed a lot of work, too—more than he might bother to do—but fixing up the exterior was essential if he intended to sell the place. The exertion quieted the unrest inside him, too.

No matter what, he had to do something with his days besides work out in the weight room he'd set up in what had once been a dining room in the house where he'd lived until his mother sent him away. Giving himself too much time to brood wasn't healthy. He'd done his job as well as he could. Trusting that he could ever rely on others in the same way again, though, that was something else.

He bounced experimentally on all three steps, feeling no give. Good enough. Might as well stain them this afternoon—

The growl of an engine—pickup truck or SUV, he thought—coming up the nearly mile-long gravel driveway made his muscles tighten in an instinctive need to be combat ready. *Dial it down*, he told himself. What he should be was irritated; he hadn't ordered anything lately, so this couldn't be a postal worker or delivery service. On the few occasions he'd been recognized in town he hadn't been subtle about his preference not to be bothered.

Alan gave thought to staying where he was, or even going inside and ignoring any knock on the front door, but finally growled under his breath and stalked around the house, hammer still in his hand.

Being completely unarmed didn't sit well with him.

SUV—navy blue with a white and red insignia on the side as well as a rack of lights on the roof. Sheriff's deputy. What, someone was checking to be sure he hadn't taken up his old man's trade?

The driver's side door slammed closed, and a cop appeared around the front, eyes on Alan. Lean guy, light brown hair, dark glasses. And familiar, although it took Alan a minute.

"Drew?"

Andrew Frazier had been his best friend when they were boys, but after so many years, he didn't think he'd have recognized the guy if they'd happened to pass anywhere else in the world. But here? Had to be.

The deputy took off the dark glasses and grinned. "Damn. It really is you."

Alan made a noncommittal sound in his throat. He wasn't so sure the man hiding out in the backwoods of Missouri was anyone even he knew, much less a grown version of the outwardly cocky boy he'd been, the one who never let anyone see how bad things were at home.

"Didn't know you were still around," he said, grudgingly polite.

The two of them had had good times, both a little wild for different reasons. They'd been driven to explore the extensive cave systems rife in this part of Missouri. Not that either had mentioned their hobby to their parents.

"I did an enlistment in the army, then college." Drew's

shoulders moved. "Came home for a visit, ran into my high school girlfriend, *bam*. Have two kids now. Take it you're not married?"

"I don't think there's a woman alive who'd put up with me these days." He hesitated. He wouldn't have even considered inviting anyone else to come into the house, but this seemed unavoidable. "Can I offer you a beer? Or a cup of coffee?"

Drew's face tightened. "Not a beer. I'm on the clock. I'd have made it out here to say hi one of these days anyway, but I'm here now because I'm hoping you can help out tomorrow, as close to first light as we can make it."

Alan didn't like the sound of that, but only dipped his head and led the way up onto the front porch he'd replaced last week, and inside. Drew's head turned as they passed the weight room, but Alan didn't stop until he reached the kitchen. It was ugly as hell—*dated* didn't even begin to describe a room caught in a major time warp—but at least it was clean.

Alan had made a pitcher of lemonade earlier, and poured them both glasses instead of brewing coffee. They sat at the battered kitchen table on the only two chairs—picked up at a thrift store—and looked at each other.

"Your grandmother came back to bury your mom," Drew said after a minute. "Told me you'd gone into the navy."

"That's right."

"Later, there was talk you'd become a SEAL."

"I suppose Grandma stayed in touch with someone in town." He let his tone become sardonic. "I'm surprised anyone believed that story, everybody being so sure I'd end up no better than my father." Dad had manufactured meth, sometimes using the caves to hide his operation.

"You really were a SEAL?"

The urgency in the question made Alan curious. "Yeah. I stayed in until I didn't make it back far enough from an injury to return to active duty." He hid his disquiet. "What's this about?"

His friend let out a long breath and scrubbed a hand over his face. "We've got a young woman missing."

Shocked, Alan rocked forward, his chair scraping. "Are you looking at *me*?"

"No, no! We need manpower to search, and I'm thinking you might have skills we can use. You know what it's like. In a county as rural as this one, we don't have anywhere near the numbers we need for any serious search and rescue. We're organizing volunteers, but they're not always as useful as they want to think they are."

Settling back into the chair, Alan nodded his understanding. "What makes you think this woman didn't just take off?"

"Sheriff thinks that's what happened, but I'm pushing hard for us to take this seriously." He paused. "Thing is, turns out several other young women have gone missing in the past few years. Might be some even earlier, but that's harder to determine. Nobody tied them together, because this was over a three-county area. And you know how it is. They were all at least twenty-one. With adults, law enforcement wants to believe they'll come home on their own when they're ready."

Alan nodded. He knew.

"Only none of them ever did. I didn't like what I heard about the one who vanished from Douglas County three years ago, but she wasn't in our jurisdiction."

And cops were usually too busy to follow up when the crime wasn't their responsibility. Too much else usually was.

"Nagged at me, you know? Her friends and family all

said she wouldn't have done anything like that. She had a boyfriend and a summer job lined up." He shook his head. "Then we got the call this morning. Girl named Amy Kendall, almost twenty-two, left a kegger last night. She'd driven herself, set off for home by herself. Never arrived."

"Car?"

"No trace of it. We put out a BOLO and have been doing a rudimentary search along her route home, but so far nothing. Her family is having some Missing posters made up. Nobody who knows the girl believes she'd take off like this. She had lots of friends, was smart enough, but didn't want to go away to college. Father owns several appliance stores, and she was doing bookkeeping for him."

"No blowups?"

"I haven't heard even a whisper that there was anything wrong." Drew's tone was downright grim.

Alan would have said no to just about anyone coming out here to ask anything of him, but this… Crap. He'd spent his entire adult life serving and protecting, in one way or another. Grimacing, he asked, "So what is it you think I can do for you?"

"Supervise a group of volunteers doing a search, to start. We plan to fan out every direction from the site of the party—which was in the woods, by the way. Couple of miles from here. If you held on to your dive gear, you might be able to investigate lakes or sinkholes in the area if it comes to that. You know we have a bunch of them, and some are deep."

The two of them had gone swimming in forbidden places, too, reckless as only kids that age could be. Then, he hadn't had the gear to explore flooded caves, but he'd wanted to.

Ignoring his reluctance to get involved, Alan nodded.

"I can do that." His hand explored his jaw. "I might even shave so I don't scare anyone. Where do we meet?"

They would gather not two miles away, where a dirt road led into a dense stretch of woodland perfect for groups of teens to hide their activities from parents and patrolling sheriff's deputies.

"Thank you." Drew pushed himself to his feet, lines scoring his forehead. He started toward the front door but stopped. "You get out of the navy recently?"

"No, five years ago."

"Just out of curiosity, what have you been doing the past five years?"

Alan's mouth curved into a smile, rare for him these days, at the irony of all this. "I became a cop, what else?"

"THIS IS *SO* CREEPY!" one of Lucy's friends exclaimed—and she or one of the others had said more or less the same thing half a dozen times. Despite the early hour, they were all frenetic, Lucy most of all.

Lucy's melodrama might be normal for her age under the circumstances, but it unsettled Jo as it had since her sister made the big announcement yesterday. The sixteen-year-old was wired, as if she'd taken an upper. She was in constant motion, jittery, her voice edging into shrill.

On the other hand, well, her friends seemed to be acting the part of shock and horror as if they were auditioning in Hollywood.

Maybe I'm overthinking this, Jo thought, and made an effort to look around instead.

A good-sized crowd had showed up to search for Amy, which shouldn't be a surprise. This was a small enough town, people knew each other. A couple of clipboards with a headshot photo of Amy were being passed around. Seeing it a few minutes ago had made all this more frighteningly real.

A question nagged at the back of Jo's mind, though. Did walking the woods really make sense? People were saying that all the kids who'd been at the party agreed she'd left in her car. If, say, it had broken down and she'd had to get out and walk, where was the car? Could authorities have planned this search just to look as if they were doing something meaningful? Or did they have a reason to believe someone had lied?

Maybe cops *always* took into account the likelihood they'd been lied to.

Naturally, Amy was all anyone could talk about. In fact, right behind Jo now, a man said, "I hear no one else leaving the party drove the same way she did." He sounded knowledgeable, although who knew? What if one of the other partygoers had, in fact, left ahead of Amy and then waited beside the road until he saw her car?

"Where'd you hear that?" a woman asked, just as Jo turned to see who the guy was.

No one she recognized, but he replied, "Deputy Frazier told me when I asked."

"Oh."

Several people made shushing sounds.

Her gaze went to the three men standing together, apparently prepared to start organizing the milling group now that there were almost no new arrivals. Two were in uniform, both sheriff's deputies. One was a stranger to Jo, the other vaguely familiar. He'd been so far ahead of her in school she wouldn't have recognized him if she hadn't seen him a few times around town when she was home visiting. Brody had known who she was describing and said his name was Andrew Frazier. He was a good-looking guy with sandy hair and an athletic build. She'd passed him once coming out of the grocery store in town with a three-or four-year-old boy riding his shoulders, accompanying a woman who also looked familiar pushing a cart that held an even younger child.

The second deputy was shorter, chunky. Thick neck, square face. Obviously trying to appear authoritative, he had the shaved-head thing going she hated, and now stood with his feet braced apart and his hands resting on the wide leather belt, one really close to his holstered weapon. He had his eye on the guy who wasn't in uniform, and his expression verged on hostile.

Even if she weren't wondering what that was about, the third man was the one to command Jo's attention. Uniform or not, something about the way he carried himself said he was a cop, too. Tall, as much as six foot three or four, he would dominate any crowd with those broad shoulders and long, lean body. Not quite handsome, his face could better be described as craggy, with a strong jaw and chin, and a gaze that swept the crowd as if he expected gunfire to break out at any minute.

That gaze met hers as she watched him and paused. In fact, they stared at each other just a little too long considering they were strangers. From this distance she couldn't tell what color his eyes were, but felt an odd cramp inside before he continued to scan the faces of the volunteers.

Maybe their hands, too, she speculated. His expression wasn't trusting.

Who the heck was he?

Deputy Frazier spoke up then, overriding other voices. He introduced himself, Deputy Hudson and Alan Burke, who he said had a military and law enforcement background, without being specific.

Wait. The Burkes had owned the property neighboring the Summerlin land for as long as she could remember. Rod used to grumble about the piece of scum over there. Not this Alan, who was too young, but hadn't there been a son who lived somewhere else? If so, he'd made Rod mad over the years, too, by refusing to sell his place to her stepfather.

She tuned in to learn the group was being divided into four groups—a khaki-clad man had joined the other three. Apparently he was head of the local search and rescue group.

Without any such intention, Jo found herself under Alan Burke's authority. Brody had wandered away a few minutes ago to talk to friends and would be with Deputy Hudson. Lucy—Jo looked around. There she was, hanging back, but apparently joining yet a third group with several of her friends. She gave Jo one defiant look.

Rod hadn't been happy about his family ditching their duties at the cavern to join the search, insisting girls Amy's age were known for being unreliable, but after Jo had spoken up, had irritably conceded it might be the right thing to do. Austin was there, and Rod had called in two of the summer help who'd arrived this week, neither locals who would have known the missing woman, to keep tours going. He had full bookings today, so she understood. It was only fair to people who'd bought tickets in advance.

She was abruptly recalled to her purpose here when Burke spread a local topographical map open against a tree trunk and had everyone in his group study the area delineated by a red marker. A couple of people seemed to be having trouble making out landmarks, but most of them knew the area well enough to nod. He directed them to walk as far apart as they could without losing sight of the people on each side of them. His gaze moved from one face to the next.

"Call out to those folks if you need to leave the line

to check out a heavy clump of shrubbery or a break in the land," he said, in a calm, deep voice. "We ended up with the most challenging terrain, including a rugged side slope. All we can do is our best. I see some of you brought walking sticks. They're good to use to poke around. Keep an eye out for snakes, especially those of you who aren't wearing boots."

Jo glanced around to see that some wore athletic shoes that left ankles exposed.

"The left side of our line will meet up with the river in half a mile or so."

Maybe a mile downriver from the Summerlin land, Jo calculated.

"That will keep us oriented," he continued. "There is a sinkhole here—" He tapped the almost round blue spot on the map. "We'll split to circle it. I want to know if anything catches your attention: a shoe or any other sign a person was here, some broken branches, scuffed ground, tire tracks. *Anything.* Got that?"

Heads bobbed, including Jo's. Riveting blue eyes compelled attention.

"I'll be at the uphill end because that's the hardest walking, and I have the experience. I'll also do some moving around to stay in contact with all of you. Okay?"

More nods.

Saying, "You, you, you," he got them in line. Jo was more than disconcerted to find herself directly to his left. Did he see her as a weak link he had to watch over? Or know somehow who she was and assume she must have done some hiking and scrambling in the area?

Theirs was the first of the four groups to start out. A married couple Jo knew vaguely had been positioned on one end; she could just make out their voices. Otherwise… she became aware of a heaviness in the air, the beginning of summer humidity, and a quiet that didn't seem quite natural. Birds and small animals had probably hunkered down at the sight of these humans intruding in a mostly deciduous forest that made it easy to imagine Indigenous hunters slipping from tree to tree. She could hear herself breathing, every rustle and crunch underfoot.

The guy to her left made more noise than seemed necessary. She had to keep turning her head to be sure Alan Burke was still there, though, so quietly did he move through the wooded landscape. It wasn't as if they had any reason to avoid making noise, she reminded herself. In fact…the hush here in the dappled light beneath the tangle of trees felt eerie today.

As if in response to her thought, a shriek made her heartbeat leap. She heard a sharp oath from the man to her right just before a flicker of bright blue settled her nerves. Blue jays did *not* like intruders in their woodlands.

Burke muttered, "I'd forgotten that sound."

"Shortened my lifespan," she mumbled.

A surprising, crooked grin told her he'd heard her.

His eyes were almost as bright a blue as the wings of the jay.

Twice he left his place in the line to take a look at something that caught someone's attention; both times he shook his head at the others as he returned.

She was sweating and scratched up by the time he called, "Spread the word down the line. We'll take a short break."

Jo spotted a newly downed tree and headed for it. The guy to the left gravitated the other direction, probably to join a friend. Alan Burke walked right to her and sat only a couple of feet away, stretching out his long legs.

"Hope everyone is up to the steep terrain."

"They all look fit." She hesitated. "I'm Jo Summerlin. I have a feeling we might be neighbors."

"Jo?"

"Short for Josephine." She took her water bottle out of the day pack she carried.

He did the same. "Ah. I keep hearing from a Rod Summerlin. He your father?"

"Stepfather."

Those sharp eyes watched her with more intensity than seemed natural. Was he hyperalert, or was it something about her?

"Rod is all about the cavern. He wants to own the whole thing."

"It might go on for miles," he pointed out. "Some of them do. The whole region may sit on top of a complicated interconnected labyrinth."

"But there's another opening on your land. At least… assuming you do live near us?"

He took a long drink of water without taking his gaze from her. "I'm one of those Burkes."

At his dry tone, she frowned, only vaguely recalling the talk about his father. Like he was the town drunk? Or…no, he manufactured and sold methamphetamine. That was it.

"I don't remember you from when I was a kid."

"I have to be older than you are," he said shortly. "I left to live with my grandparents before we'd likely have met in school."

She nodded. When he stayed silent, she asked, "Why this search? I mean, Amy left that party in a car, right?"

"So I'm told." His head tipped. "Do you know her?"

Thank goodness he hadn't said *did*, as if he believed Amy was dead.

"I babysat her and her sister sometimes. I hadn't seen

her as an adult until, oh, two or three years ago. She and my brother were dating at the time."

"Your brother?"

"Brody? He volunteered today, too. He's with Deputy Hudson."

Alan seemed to mull that over. "They weren't still together?"

"No, it's been a while. A year or two? He might know who she's seeing now."

"I'll pass that on."

What did he mean by that?

"Wait. Are you suggesting *Brody* would be a suspect if Amy really was abducted or attacked?" *Murdered.* That's what she really meant.

Dark eyebrows rose. "I'm not the investigator. Whoever it is would likely want to talk to any of Ms. Kendall's...friends."

Guys Amy had been involved with. *And I just set Brody up for that*, Jo thought. Except...had she? Any of Amy's friends would know she and Brody had been an item at one time. There'd undoubtedly been other boys since.

Alan watched her while she fussed before he finally sighed, tucked his water bottle back in a pack that was more sizeable than hers, then rose to his feet with effortless grace. He put two fingers in his mouth and let out a piercing whistle. "Let's get moving!"

Rising herself, Jo studied the steep slope of exposed rock, stunted trees and tangled undergrowth ahead, then the woods stretching into the distance with a high canopy and deep shade. She pictured it in the middle of the night, when even a nearly full moon wouldn't have penetrated the darkness.

This woodland would have been prettier earlier in the spring, with the redbud, pawpaw, serviceberry and dogwood trees in bloom. Now... Goose bumps rose on Jo's arms as she imagined Amy, terrified, running, stumbling, looking desperately for a place to hide, even as her pursuer gained on her.

She shuddered, aware that the man beside her had noticed. But, after a moment, he gave a brief nod and walked away.

Other volunteers she could see were spreading out in readiness to resume the search. She shouldn't hold them up, but... To Alan Burke's broad back, she asked, "Do you think we'll find Amy today? Out here?"

He stopped, turned, his expression enigmatic. Muscles flexed in his jaw. "No. I don't expect to find her."

With a lump in her throat, Jo wondered whether he meant today, in the grid they'd been assigned to search... or whether he didn't expect Amy to be found at all. Ever.

Chapter Three

An hour later, Alan had dropped down the hillside, speaking briefly to each of the volunteers to be sure no one was struggling, when a piercing scream rang out. This one was from a human throat.

He spun and scrambled at a near run uphill, having to catch himself with a hand to the ground a few times. Damn, that had to have been Jo Summerlin. Could he have been wrong? Had she been unlucky enough to stumble across the body of a young woman she knew?

The last guy before her position in line was staring up. Sweat dripped down his red face. "I think she's all right," he said uncertainly.

Alan ignored him. Even given his level of conditioning, his heart beat viciously against his chest wall by the time he finally saw her, on her hands and knees.

The sight shook him, although he didn't understand why any more than he understood why she'd riveted him earlier, at first sight. Yeah, she was a looker, but nothing like the women who swarmed SEALs in any bar near a base. Jo Summerlin wasn't so much voluptuous as delicate, despite an above-average height for a woman. Dark haired and dark-eyed, her slim hips and leggy, lithe body consistent with the fine bones. Athletic, he'd thought.

Now twigs had tangled in the long hair that was sagging

from a formerly smooth ponytail. Blood beaded a scratch across one cheek, and others decorated her forearms. Like all of them, she was sweating, but she didn't look hurt.

He lowered himself to a crouch in front of her. "What is it?"

"Oh." She blew air upward in obvious, if futile, hopes of shifting sweaty strands of hair from her forehead. "I'm sorry about the scream. I...was startled."

"What—?" And then he saw it, too. In fact, if he hadn't been so focused on getting to her, he'd have already noticed a faint trail leading to a rock face—and the dark opening into a cave that would have been obscured by the vegetation around it if they hadn't happened right on it. Water trickled out of one side, enough to have turned the first tumble of rocks below the cave mouth slick. Earlier in the spring, that might have been a real stream.

"A bobcat burst out," Jo explained. "I think he must live here. He brushed right against me and took off."

"That would do it," he conceded. Bobcats were shy and seldom seen.

"I...noticed what looks like a trail."

"I see it. It's probably made by animals, you know."

"I do, but..."

He frowned. The cool air from the opening reached him, carrying the familiar musty, heavy smell, in this case tainted by notes of blood, if he wasn't mistaken. Again—probably that was thanks to the predator that lived here, but the only way to be sure was to take a look.

"Why here?" He was arguing as much with himself as with her. "Can you imagine carrying an unconscious woman up this hillside?"

"Have you seen a picture of her?"

"Face only."

"She's petite," Jo told him. "Five foot one, maybe? And slender. I'll bet she doesn't weigh over a hundred pounds."

That might make her particularly appealing as a target for abduction, he couldn't help thinking.

"Is there a road into the sinkhole?" Jo asked.

He turned, seeing a glint of water over the tops of the trees. "If this track goes down to there…"

She was right. It would be doable. And hell, why was he dragging his feet? He'd been asked to ensure that every square foot of his area was examined, and that included this unappealing hole in the hillside. He had to check this out, whether he had brought the basic equipment with him or not, but he wasn't excited about it.

"I need to go in."

"Not alone," she said firmly.

"Have you done any caving?"

"Are you kidding? It's the family business."

He let his eyebrows climb. "This—" he jerked his head toward the opening that wasn't more than three feet high by three or four wide "—doesn't have much in common with a cavern that could stand in for a ballroom."

"I don't love wriggling through chokes," she admitted, with a dignity he had to admire, "but I've done some of it."

He sighed. *He* didn't love trying to rearrange his very bones to squirm through an extremely narrow passage. "Okay. We won't go far—we don't dare without equipment. If this is navigable, I'll probably have to come back later, but maybe we can tell right away if anyone who is two-legged has ever been in there." He rose to his feet. "At least we can take one basic precaution. I'll pass the word so people know why we've disappeared."

JO IMMEDIATELY REGRETTED her offer—okay, *demand*—that she accompany him. She didn't even enjoy passages that meant she had to crawl, and thus far in her life had balked at anything that would have required her to squirm like a snake and chance getting stuck. The fact that this cave had likely never been explored, and that she and Alan might be the first people who'd ever stepped foot in it...

Well.

Chickening out wasn't an option, though. She pictured Amy Kendall, first as a silly girl, then a pretty almost adult, and her spine stiffened.

Alan rejoined her, setting down his pack and rummaging inside. She did the same with hers, and both produced gloves and flashlights.

His mouth quirked. "You're not completely surprised."

"Around here, dogs uncover cave openings every time they try to bury a bone. Highway crews find new ones. Like you said, there's a subterranean maze under us."

"Maybe your stepfather would like to buy this piece of property," Alan said drily.

She let herself grin. "Who knows?"

He studied her boots and heavy jeans with a critical eye, then slung a coil of rope around his shoulders. All right," he said. "Here we go."

"Maybe I should go first—"

"Let's just take a look inside before we make any decisions."

He had to duck while straddling a barrier of rocks to get through the opening. She followed his example, feeling a momentary rush of relief from the cooler air. Right before she gagged.

All caves she'd been in had the smell of a house that had been shut up for decades. She'd already gotten used to it anew in the time she'd been home, but this was way worse, almost putrid, probably because the space was so much tighter.

Plus, bones and some bloody shreds of an animal—a
rabbit, she thought queasily—gave evidence of the bobcat's residence. Now Jo was able to stand upright, but Alan
had to stoop. One side of the cave gleamed wet, the wall
glittery calcite. The single passage immediately narrowed
again.

Alan frowned at it. "I wish we had helmets."

She didn't comment, and a moment later he seemed to
shake himself. "Ladies first." That still-frowning gaze met
hers. "Anything looks unstable, you stop."

What could she do but nod? It made sense that with
his greater strength he follow her. He'd be a lot more capable of pulling her out of a bind, if it came to that, than
she would be of dragging his much larger body so much
as an inch or two.

She didn't have to squirm—forearms and knees were
fine, and her shoulders and hips didn't touch the sides of
the passage, but the knees of her jeans got wet right away,
and icy water seeped inside her glove. The beam of her
flashlight speared the darkness ahead, revealing nothing
but a curve and...something that scuttled.

Ugh. A salamander, one of the cave denizens that also
spent time outside. Harmless, and she didn't mind them,
but thank goodness she hadn't set a hand down on it. She
might have embarrassed herself by screaming again.

Within what she guessed was five minutes—although
when crawling through the darkness, time began to feel
less definite—she started to shiver. The caves in the Ozark
region stayed at an average sixty degrees, which made
them a temperate retreat for bats and bears and sundry
other creatures that hibernated in Missouri's cold winters.
For a woman who'd been sweating copiously, sixty degrees
was chilly. Never mind the cold water.

A low voice came from behind her. "You okay?"

"Sure. Am I too slow? Sorry."

"No. It's more important to be careful than fast."

Given the bruises she could already feel forming on her knees and forearms from the rough floor of the cave—oh, what she'd give for pads—he was right. She peeked behind to see that his flashlight wasn't on. Smart. They shouldn't waste battery life in case... What? They got trapped in here?

This chill wasn't the same kind, because cave-ins did happen.

People knew where they were, Jo reminded herself, and went back to trying *not* to think about the weight of the earth above them, or the increasingly musty smell, or the fact that she felt as if the air had a weight, too. She hadn't seen any evidence that bats did occupy this cave, but their guano could poison the air.

Thank goodness she could hear the quiet sounds of Alan moving behind her. She wouldn't want to be alone.

Her beam of light was suddenly being swallowed by darkness. She stopped, sweeping the flashlight from side to side. The smaller passage had opened into a room. A good-sized one, she decided, before crawling forward a few more feet and standing. She turned to light the way for Alan, who rose to his feet, too, and switched on his own flashlight to examine a shining cavernous space with stalactites and stalagmites formed by the slow drip of calcite-rich water. These weren't eye-catching like the ones in Summerlin Cavern, but formed in the same crucible.

Here, the water seeped down the walls on all sides, and raking the ceiling with light, she saw wet cracks.

The cave went on, narrowing again, but wide enough Alan took a turn at going first. If they'd been walking, she would probably have been stepping on his heels, so close did she follow. They reached other rooms, beautiful but not spectacular, none showing signs of occupancy by anything but a few salamanders. The constantly seeping water wasn't deep enough for the crayfish that made their lives in the dark streams and pools of some caverns.

She was once again ahead, on her knees and forearms, when she heard a cracking sound. She'd barely begun to hunch, the words "Watch out!" stuck in her throat when something banged into the side of her head and her shoulder. She dropped flat on her belly.

"Jo! Damn it, I knew better! Are you all right?"

At his demand in that gritty voice, she cautiously lifted a hand to her head. With the gloves on, she couldn't tell if she was bleeding, or even if a lump was forming.

"Yes. I don't think it was that big a rock."

"We need to back out. Slowly, carefully. I'll move a foot or two, you move a foot or two. Try not to come in contact with either wall."

"Okay." She worked at regulating her breathing. "I need to get back up on my knees, though."

"I know you do."

His tone of gentle reassurance gave her the confidence to push back up. Resting back on her knees and forearms, her hand came down on a rock she didn't think had been there. She groped it. It was…oh, maybe the size of a baseball or a little bigger. A softball. It hadn't dropped all that far, or she could really have been hurt.

Quiet sounds came from behind her, then a hand closed on her ankle. "Your turn."

That first minute or two of their slow retreat was the most hair-raising. Once a section of the roof began to crack, at least a partial collapse could happen anytime.

They kept squirming backward, Alan murmuring things like, "That's good. Now hold up for a minute."

Then, suddenly, he said, "This space is big enough to sit up and take a rest. We can turn around."

Once she'd gotten up onto her butt, relief left her feeling momentarily weak. "Well, that was fun."

"I should have come back, not brought you in here to do a half-assed exploration with neither of us adequately prepared."

She reached out and closed her hand on his forearm. "A rock grazed me, that's all. If the whole roof had collapsed, you'd have dug me out."

He muttered something probably not meant for her ears before saying, "You're okay to keep going?"

"No problem." She'd have a bruise on her shoulder, she could already tell, and probably a modest lump on her head, not for the first time in her life. She'd hit her head a lot harder when she was learning to ride her bike in the cavern parking lot.

"We've been on our way longer than I meant anyway. Stick close to me."

Turning her head, she saw his face, eerily shadowed by the narrow beams of their flashlights. She guessed she looked owlish instead of mysterious.

"I don't know why anyone would have gone on," she agreed.

"I would have as a kid sure I'd find Spanish gold or pre-Columbian artifacts just a little farther along." Was that a smile in his voice?

"Lose your optimism?" Jo asked.

He was quiet just long enough to make her curious. Then, expressionless, he said, "You could say that."

Subject closed.

Making their way back toward the entrance felt torturously slow, despite the fact that they no longer had to exercise the same caution. She definitely had a headache now and was shivering besides. Plus, she felt the effects of the scrambling that had brought them to the cave opening in the first place. She tried to stay in shape during the school year, but jogging or using the elliptical didn't necessarily translate well to hiking along a rocky side hill.

Jo suppressed a whimper at the sight of daylight, and took pride in her stoicism as she crawled over the rough rocks at the entrance and out into the heat that immediately made her feel as if she'd immersed herself in a steam bath.

Alan looked so much the same as he had before they ventured into the earth, she felt disgruntled. His gaze was keen on her face, but she didn't meet his eyes until he said, "Let me take a look."

Wonderful. She tipped her head and felt his fingers sifting through her hair until he found what was definitely a bump. The bump, she discovered, wasn't the only part of her scalp that was oversensitized beneath his fingertips.

"You're bleeding a little." He didn't sound happy about it. "Okay, rotate your shoulder for me."

When she obliged to his satisfaction, he didn't make her bare her upper body, thank heavens. She had to wonder how bad she looked but didn't want to admit why that mattered.

"Did the others go on?" she thought to ask for the first time.

He grunted agreement. "I told them we'll hold to the same elevation and meet up with them at the sinkhole. Let's take a minute and have a bite to eat."

Jo nodded sturdily, put her flashlight and leather gloves in her day pack, and took out both a bottle of water and a bag of peanuts.

Alan sat down, stretched out those long, muscular legs clad in cargo pants and produced nuts and raisins from his pack.

He seemed disinclined to chat. As much as she'd have liked to ask him what he knew that volunteers like her didn't, she accepted his cue and didn't say a word.

KNOWING A ROCK had fallen onto Jo had given Alan a major scare. He hadn't known how big the damn thing was, whether the ceiling was about to cave in, whether she was unconscious, bleeding, hurt in some way that was *his* responsibility. They'd skated, but he wouldn't soon forget how narrow a miss they'd had even if he also knew he was blowing out of proportion what had been a minor incident. If she'd really been hurt— All he knew was, having *her* the one who'd been injured really ate at him. He'd clamped his mouth shut after checking her out, but those frightening moments kept running on an endless reel in his head.

This had to be an echo of the last disastrous police operation during which two hostages had been killed. Not his fault, but he never entirely let himself off the hook.

The search had otherwise been as pointless as Alan had expected. Didn't mean they wouldn't keep looking, although deciding where next had just become more difficult.

After the discovery of the cave, he'd started looking upslope and down with a different eye. How many other entrances were disguised by rocks or dense vegetation? But that speculation was easily confounded by the same logic that had made him hesitant to enter the cave they'd already penetrated. No woman on the run would climb up here. And why would a man who'd abducted a woman carry or force her this distance from any road? There had to be plenty of vacant houses and cabins in the area. His own house, plenty isolated, had been empty for enough years, it would have made an ideal site to hold a captive.

And, damn it, when looked at objectively, the odds still

were that Amy Kendall had taken off on her own. It happened. Parents and friends didn't always know what was going through someone's head. Maybe she'd gotten on drugs, met a love interest she knew her parents would hate. Or she just wanted to become a free spirit.

Alan didn't believe any of that, not given the disappearances of the other young women in this corner of the state. All in their early twenties, all described as beautiful. Four years ago, in Newton County, a young woman named Christy Dodswell had been driving home after babysitting her nieces and nephew. Neither she nor her car had ever been found. Six months after that, another young woman up in Lawrence County had set out to walk home from a friend's house at one in the morning and never arrived. A couple of years back, Jeannie Kennedy had finished finals at the university in Springfield and decided to surprise her family by starting for home in the late afternoon instead of waiting for morning. She'd made it partway, stopping at a tavern in an apparent impulse to celebrate her twenty-first birthday. Her locked car was left barely over a mile from her house. The fact that her luggage and purse were missing along with the young woman created speculation that she'd gone away with a man, deliberately leaving behind the car that belonged to her parents.

Because the sheriff's department lead detective was refusing to believe the missing women could possibly be linked, or had been abducted rather than taking off on their own, Drew was the one who put in calls to jurisdictions in neighboring states to find out if there was any chance a predator had taken yet more young women than the ones of which they were already aware. It was a miracle that the sheriff had given him the go-ahead.

Alan's gut said they'd eventually find more victims, including runaways or prostitutes no one missed. Or women merely passing through the area who happened to catch a killer's eye when they stopped for gas or lunch at the wrong time and place. When they didn't arrive at their destinations, there was no reason anyone would suspect their journeys might have come to abrupt ends in a rural corner of Missouri.

After his group had reached the sinkhole and worked their way carefully around it—they found that, indeed, a track led up to a wide dirt area where cars could be parked, and that not all the people who swam here had picked up their trash before leaving.

He climbed up on a rock and looked down into water he suspected was very deep. He couldn't swear this was one he and Drew had dove into but had a suspicion it was. It sure as hell would be a good place to make a body vanish, were it tied to a concrete block or the like.

"Climbing back up here after a swim wouldn't be easy," a soft voice said from beside him.

He started. Jo Summerlin, of course. Maybe his radar had dismissed her as a threat. He couldn't imagine how else he had failed to hear her approach.

"That's part of the fun."

"You'd dive off here?"

His shoulders moved. "Probably have. Ten years old, I thought I was capable of anything." Except, on some level, he'd known that wasn't true. He couldn't keep his father from battering his mother or him, or her from growing less and less present, physically and in every other way, once she too became addicted to the methamphetamine that was the livelihood and curse of Alan's father.

Too bad it hadn't killed him sooner, Alan thought now, almost dispassionately.

He shook off dark memories, aware of Jo watching him. He still hadn't quite figured out why the sight of her had hit him so hard, but he would have been smart to position her somewhere else down the line of searchers instead of near enough for him to keep an eye on her all day.

What he'd learned was that she was fit, graceful, more observant than he liked, brave and able to laugh at herself. He wasn't likely to see much if anything of her after today, though, and told himself that would be best. He was in no state to start something with a woman, and particularly one as normal as her. She'd come home for the summer to be with her family, a concept that was alien to him.

Still, he was curious about her. "You grew up here. Didn't you let yourself get a little wild sometimes?"

She made a sound that might have been meant to be a laugh, and he'd swear her eyes had darkened. "No." She spoke even more softly. "I…didn't really have the chance."

Because she'd had parents who gave a damn about her?

"What do you do for a living?" he asked.

"I'm a teacher. This past year I had second graders, and will again come fall."

An elementary school teacher. Of course she was.

Not for him, even if he'd been so inclined. Which he wasn't.

"I think I hear our ride coming," he said, and she nodded.

He had absolutely no idea what she was thinking.

Chapter Four

"The missing woman is all the tourists could talk about."
Rod shook his head as he scanned the serving dishes filling the center of the table.

Surprised, Jo paused with her fork halfway to her mouth. "How did they hear about her?"

"Town." He shrugged, stabbing what was at least a third slice of meatloaf from the platter and transferring it to his plate. "Cafés, grocery store, bed-and-breakfast, the lodge."

That made sense. Mayville *was* a small town. Dramatic events like this didn't happen often.

"You'd have said if they found anything." That was Rod again, not even really asking a question. Of course they would have.

"We didn't," Brody said tightly. He'd been withdrawn since coming home.

"It was boring." Lucy bit her lip. "I mean, it was scary, too. I kept thinking—" She broke off.

Jo nodded. "I was as afraid of finding her as I was of not."

Lucy looked grateful. "Yeah."

Brody frowned at Jo. "You got stuck with that Burke guy."

Rod's head came up. "Burke? The neighbor?"

"Yes, Alan Burke," Jo agreed. "Have you met him?"

"I didn't even know he was in town. I've written him half a dozen times." He mumbled something she felt sure was less than complimentary. "What the hell is he doing back here?"

"I don't know. We didn't get personal." They were all staring at her. Jo hesitated, then said, "We came across a cave on that steep hillside south of the highway. A bobcat burst out of it, scaring the daylights out of me."

"A cave?" Rod and Brody echoed in unison.

Two of a kind.

"Nothing that interesting. I went into it with Alan, because I didn't think he should go alone. It was obviously the bobcat's den. It stunk." Her audience didn't care about that. "We followed it for a ways, mostly on hands and knees, found a few rooms but nothing very interesting. I wondered it if might connect to our cavern."

Rod leaned forward. "Where was it exactly?"

She did her best to pinpoint the location for him, wondering if he planned to check it out. If so, he didn't say so.

Once satisfied, Rod asked, "They done with this search nonsense?"

"It's *not* nonsense!" Lucy cried. "Amy has to be *somewhere*."

Rod snorted. "Probably Kansas City or Des Moines by now. I still don't understand why the sheriff's department jumped the gun like this. Girls that age are undependable. We all know that. Her car is missing, right? Where do they think *it* is? Something probably happened at that party. Her boyfriend broke up with her, maybe, and she took off."

Jo raised her eyebrows. Boys were solid as the earth, girls undependable? She didn't think so. "From what I hear," she said, after giving Lucy a tiny shake of her head, "Amy is levelheaded. No one believes she's the kind to get so dramatic, or to scare her parents this way. If she was abducted, the man who did it could have taken her car someplace. Left it in an abandoned barn." She decided not to share the thought she'd had today about the seemingly bottomless depths of the sinkhole people with a lot more courage than she had apparently swam in.

Rod tightened his jaw, evidently realizing he had just been chided, but all he said was a curt, "So what's the plan for tomorrow?"

"As far as I know, no mass searches." Jo looked at her siblings.

"That's what Deputy Hudson told us," Brody agreed. "He seemed to think the whole thing was a waste of time. But *he* didn't know Amy."

"Was she dating anyone recently?" Jo asked.

Brody looked down at his now-cleared plate. "I don't know. I didn't see her very often and we didn't really talk."

Disturbed, Jo wondered if he was lying. Or was it only that he wished Amy Kendall *had* been talking to him? What had broken the two of them up? Just that Brody had gone off to college and Amy felt left behind? That might explain him blaming Jo for him having "wasted" his time these past two years.

The atmosphere subdued, they all finished eating. Whatever their worries, the two men dug into big slices of apple pie topped with ice cream, while Lucy and Jo declined it.

Jo had just opened the dishwasher when, out of the corner of her eye, she saw Lucy sidling toward the hall and the foot of the staircase.

"Stop right there. You're not leaving me with this."

"Why can't Brody help?" her sister asked sulkily.

"He doesn't know it yet, but tomorrow it's his turn. I'm setting up a schedule." Foolishly, she'd assumed that once Lucy and Brody were old enough Rod would have made

Brody help in the kitchen, too. Apparently not. Jo wasn't
about to put up with that, not when she and Lucy worked
just as hard all day at the cavern. Brody had grumbled at
her insistence but fallen in line. Rod hadn't said a word.
"I don't mind doing a lot of the cooking this summer,"
she added now, "but the least you can do is help with the
cleanup."

"Oh, fine." Lucy stomped back into the dining room,
returning a minute later with several nearly empty serving dishes.

Jo started rinsing dishes before putting them in the dishwasher. "Are you as tired as I am?"

"I don't know. Where we were was mostly flat. You really found a new cave?"

"Like that's news around here?"

For once, the teenager grinned. "I guess not. But…a
bobcat?"

"It actually brushed against my leg. I just about had a
heart attack."

Lucy giggled. "I know I would have." She sneaked a
sidelong look at Jo. "He's kind of hot. That Burke guy."

Jo made a face. "Yes, he is hot. Closemouthed, though."
More than that: grim was a better description. Her heart
gave a peculiar jump when she remembered the one grin.
"I don't know anything about him. Do you?"

Lucy grabbed a pan out of the dish drainer and started
to dry it. "Only that he's living out there. The house has
been empty for *years*. Someone said he's been in the navy."

Military. Deputy Frazier had said so, but Jo would have
guessed just from the way he carried himself and the air
of command that appeared to be part of him.

"Do you know why Rod wants that property so bad?"
Jo asked.

A shaken head. "Except… Dad is all about the cavern.

Like that's news. Maybe he's afraid someone will widen that opening and start competing with him. That would have to hurt business."

"I didn't think of that." Jo paused momentarily, shook her head and put the last dinner plate into the dishwasher. "I don't remember that end of the cave being spectacular enough to make him jealous."

"You've been in it?"

"Years ago with Dad and Brody." Curious, she asked, "You know that Brody wants to extend the tours into other passages?"

"Sure." Lucy jerked one shoulder. "Why not? There are other cool rooms out there."

"Rod never seemed interested in expanding, unless that's why he wants to buy the Burke land."

Lucy slipped the damp dish towel through the handle of the refrigerator. "You remember how he used to keep the keys to the gates hanging right inside his office?"

"Sure." Worried, she studied her sister's fine-boned face.

"Brody and I used them a few times, like, the past couple of years."

"You mean, you went exploring?" The idea quickened her pulse. Brody might have the common sense to equip himself for safety and bring along an experienced friend or two, but Lucy had been displaying too much impulsive behavior this summer to make Jo think she'd have done the same.

"I guess Brody did." A purely malicious expression crossed the girl's face. "He had parties back in there a few times, too, when Dad was gone."

"Parties." Inebriated teenagers wandering unfettered in parts of the cavern that were still in their "wild" state. Had they damaged delicate formations? What if there was a shaft somewhere? One wrong step, and a kid could stumble over the edge to his death.

"It was fun!" Lucy said defiantly. "When I saw people leaving and he told me what they'd done, I had one, too!"

Aghast, Jo exclaimed, "You *know* how dangerous that could be."

With an exaggerated shrug, Lucy backed away. Hot color touched her cheekbones, and her jaw was set. "Nobody got hurt. But I had to tell Dad because— It doesn't matter. Now he's hidden the keys. I can't find them anywhere."

Jo appraised her sister, sensing something feverish simmering just below the surface. "Why would you want to?" she asked, going for calm.

"Because…because…" Tears formed in her eyes. "Jesse Phipps found something." She gasped. "I don't know why I'm bothering! You wouldn't believe me, either." Naturally, she turned and bolted.

Jo heard running footsteps on the stairs before she could decide to pursue.

BRODY HAD LEFT immediately after dinner. Jo had no idea whether he had a girlfriend, or what. Lucy stayed closeted in her room. Jo waited a good fifteen minutes to make sure her sister didn't plan to reappear, then rapped her knuckles on the half-open door of her stepfather's office.

"Jo?" He looked away from his computer monitor, peering over a pair of glasses he'd started needing in the past couple of years. "What's up?"

She went in and sat down in the extra chair beside his desk. "Lucy told me something."

An expression of resignation crossed his face. "About the skull."

"The *what*?"

His eyebrows rose. "She didn't tell you."

"She said a friend of hers found 'something.'"

Rod grimaced. "That would be it. Did she admit that she and her brother both threw some wild parties deep in the cavern?"

Jo nodded. "Although she didn't say wild."

"What do you think?"

Of course a bunch of teenagers had been drunk, if not using illegal substances.

Seeing her expression, he grunted. "Just imagine the appeal. Pitch-dark except for a few flashlights, the drip of water, strange formations and shadows, weird echoes. What could be better?"

"Did they do any damage?"

"In a few places. I gave 'em hell, which neither of them appreciated," he growled. "I still can't believe they were so careless with a precious natural resource that's our liveli-hood, on top of everything else!"

"I didn't know you were ever away from home long enough at night for them to do something like that—" She broke off. It wasn't her business where he'd been.

But he said, "Seeing a woman. Thought Lucy and Brody were old enough to be responsible when I was gone for a few hours, or even overnight."

Jo could only bob her head. She'd have thought the same. She also wondered if he'd been "seeing a woman" when she was growing up, too. She'd always assumed his absences in the evening meant he'd gone back to the cavern offices to work. As if that kind of history mattered now.

Chagrined, she said, "I'm not getting anywhere with Lucy. Maybe I'm too much of a mother figure for her."

"Give her time." He sighed and settled deeper into his chair. "She seemed fine early in the fall. I'm not even sure when this hysteria set in."

"When her friend claimed to see bones?"

Her stepfather spread his hands in frustration. "Why would that stir her hormones? For God's sake, I listened! I went so far as to call a sheriff's deputy out to join me and led him to where that kid claimed he'd seen a skull, but we couldn't find a damn thing!" He blew out a breath. "Wish we had. Just think of the publicity if we'd found the skeleton of a nineteenth-century train robber. Better yet, complete with a chest full of gold."

Jo laughed. "We could rewrite the tour narrative."

He grinned, making her feel as if he was relating to her as an adult rather than the kid she'd been. In too many of her memories, he'd been stressed, demanding or flat-out dismissive with his family, in painful contrast to his charm with the tourists. Now he sighed again. "The kids were drunk, that's all, crashing around where they didn't belong, and spooked themselves."

"So now you're hiding the keys to the gates?"

"Damn straight I am! Do you blame me?"

"No," she admitted. "That was…really dumb of them. I'm especially surprised at Brody risking any damage to the cavern."

"He can't seem to understand that his brainstorm about extended tours would do damage, too. I figure as it is, we're protecting huge parts of the cavern while providing access to spectacular rooms and formations. That's enough to give people a good idea of the wonders deep inside the earth."

His argument made sense, Jo couldn't help thinking, sympathetic as she was to Brody's desire to do something more exciting while setting his own stamp on the management of the Summerlin Cavern.

"You think they'd do the same thing if you gave them access again?"

Lines darkened his expression. "I'm hoping not Brody. God knows with Lucy. I can't rely on her at all anymore."

"I can see that."

"Everything is high drama. This thing with the missing young woman. You'd think she'd been Lucy's best friend."

Jo squeezed her fingers together. Tentatively, she suggested, "Maybe it has to do with Mom leaving us the way she did. Just…never coming back. It could be a sore place that Lucy's never acknowledged."

His gaze sharpened. "You took it in stride. Your mother didn't have what it took to stick it out, and you knew it. Young as Lucy was, why would she have missed her?"

He had no clue how hard her mother abandoning her *had* hit her. She still bore the bruises. But Jo said only, "She was two. Well, almost three. Psychologists think a lot that impacts our psyche is introduced by that age."

Rod snorted. He wasn't the most sensitive of men, which probably had something to do with his divorce from Jo's mother, who always cried when movies ended on a sad note. "All I can say is, she better get over it. Summer is when we make most of our income. She needs to get her act in gear. I'm not going to put up with much more of this nonsense."

"It would help if Amy Kendall was found," Jo said, but knew immediately she was wrong. If Amy Kendall was found dead, which seemed increasingly likely whatever Rod said to the contrary, Lucy wasn't the only member of this family who would be traumatized. The whole community would be shaken.

Her stepfather didn't say a word, which made her wonder if he wasn't thinking the same thing. Unless his intense focus on his cavern and family left him entirely indifferent to Amy's fate.

UNOFFICIALLY, ALAN JOINED the next stage of the search, too. The department was too thinly staffed to allow deputies to use much time driving every road and turn up every dirt track, never mind looking inside every derelict structure in the county. Some were volunteering their days off, as was one officer from the Mayville PD, but that was still a drop in the bucket. Alan had no deadline for restoring the house or selling it; truth be told, he didn't mind having a purpose again. A mission, of sorts. His willingness made him wonder if he hadn't turned a corner from the zombie he'd been after walking away from his job and the police department, his ability to believe in his fellow officers broken into rubble. He still had no idea what he could do next with his life.

Today, out of curiosity he took the road leading to the Summerlin Cavern. He hadn't seen more than the billboard out on the highway since he was a kid.

The approach was beautiful, all gray rocks and vivid spring growth, the plunge down to the river. Even the parking lot didn't detract much from the setting. The giant half-moon of the cavern opening would inspire awe and primal uneasiness in almost anybody.

The parking lot was mostly full, some animated people walking back from the gray stone building toward the cars, most carrying bags that presumably held souvenirs bought at the gift shop. A road marked No Trespassing continued around a curve out of sight.

Still driven by curiosity, Alan parked in the lot, then walked down that narrow road. A hundred yards, and there was a two-story farm-style house, a detached garage and little room for anything you could call a yard.

A dog started barking inside the house. Alan could see him through the front window. Homely animal, but he knew his job.

What Alan hadn't expected was the front door to open. A woman appeared, gripping the dog's collar. Jo-for-Josephine Summerlin herself.

Only then did Alan acknowledge that he hadn't been curious about the cavern; he'd speculated about Jo. Wanted to see where she'd grown up, to know whether she was home only for a brief visit or for the summer.

"Alan?" she said, surprise in her voice.

No avoiding this now. He shouldn't have let himself get drawn here in the first place. "Jo. Just being nosy. I haven't been over here since I was nine or ten years old."

"Rusty won't bite," she promised, and released the dog. Still barking, the mutt raced toward him, circled him a couple of times, then succumbed to the lure of an outstretched hand. Fingernails down his back erased his caution and he happily accompanied Alan toward the front porch.

"Would you like some lemonade?" Jo asked, gesturing toward a row of comfortable-looking Adirondack chairs on the broad porch.

Thank you, no. I shouldn't be here.

His mouth opened and he heard himself saying, "Thanks."

She smiled and disappeared inside. Alan went to one end of the porch and peered down at a stretch of river, water tumbling over rocks. Even at a season when the water was high, there wasn't enough channel for boating of any kind, not on this stretch. A dock, probably built for fishing or just dangling feet in the cold water, stretched out from the rocky bank.

When he heard the screen door squeak behind him, he went back to the chairs and sat in one. She set a tray down with a pitcher and two glasses on a small table. Then they gazed at each other.

He was uncomfortably reminded of his first sight of

her when the volunteers gathered for the search. He'd had trouble tearing his gaze from her, even though at the time he'd had no idea why.

He still didn't, not entirely.

"Can you tell me what's happening with the search?" she asked, breaking the too-long silence.

He saw no reason not to share what he knew. Her forehead crinkled at his explanation.

"Is that why you're *here*?"

"No. I might have driven as far as the parking lot and turned around, just to be sure there were no driveways off your road, but I remembered that much. You're clinging to the hillside here."

"No kidding," she said wryly. "Lucky no one in this house sleepwalks."

He laughed, something he hadn't done much of in a while. She seemed to have that effect on him.

"Rusty likes you," she observed.

Alan had hardly noticed that the dog had rested its head on his thigh, and he'd been petting him. Now he scratched the itchy area under the collar. "I've always liked dogs."

"You don't have one?"

He shook his head. "We had a dog when I lived with my grandparents. Since then..." He shrugged. "I was active duty military, then a cop. Not home enough."

Darker striations showed in eyes that were a chocolate brown in the slanting sunlight. "Someone told me you were navy, but not the cop part. No wonder they roped you in for the search."

"Drew Frazier and I were friends as kids." He glanced at her. "Deputy Frazier. He's the one who thought I could help." He kept waiting for her to ask why he was here, but apparently it hadn't occurred to her that he might have reason to stop by that was unrelated to the search. Instead she asked if anybody had found anything.

"Not that I've heard." He took a long drink of lemonade.

"If her car isn't found—" She sounded more strained than he'd expect, given that she wasn't close to the missing young woman. "Will authorities just give up?"

"They'll be talking to everyone who was at the party or friends of Ms. Kendall, here and from college. Try to get a look at her social media accounts, in case she's been in contact with anyone unexpected or hints at a plan she hasn't confided in her local friends about."

Suddenly wary, she said, "Nobody has talked to Brody yet, as far as I know."

"Sheriff's department's single detective isn't convinced police should be involved yet. Even when—if—he gets there, he's one man. Lot of people to talk to."

Jo bit her lip and nodded. She hadn't so much as sipped her lemonade. Instead, her fingers were twined tightly together on her lap.

Not taking his eyes from her, he said, "There comes a time when there won't be anything more the department can do."

She swallowed. "I…understand."

Did she really? He couldn't help speculating on the tension he'd felt in her from their first meeting. Could she suspect her brother? Knew about a recent argument, maybe?

The cop in him had to press. "This Amy isn't related to you or a friend of yours. You seem…more upset than I'd expect." And, damn, his tone sounded clinical.

He got what he deserved. A flash of shock, supplanted by anger. She shot to her feet. "I don't even want to think about what you're suggesting, Mr. Burke. Excuse me, I'm expected at the gift shop."

What could he do but rise, too? He didn't wait for her

to take the lemonade to the kitchen so they could walk together. He was pretty sure he'd just burned any bridge they'd formed between them yesterday, which was probably just as well. Keeping his distance from her would be smart.

Chapter Five

The visit from Alan Burke lingered in Jo's mind as the day dragged on. Why *had* he stopped by, and gone to the trouble of walking as far as the house? He never had said. *My fault*, she acknowledged.

She asked her brother and sister, casually, if he'd also stuck his head into the gift shop. Both had looked surprised.

"Not that I saw," they said in unison.

Did Brody look apprehensive?

Since Alan couldn't possibly consider her, Jo, a suspect, she had to wonder if his goal had been sounding her out about her family. Because that's what he'd done, wasn't it? And if *that* was so, he had to be more involved in the investigation than he'd admitted. Had he been a detective when he was a cop?

How dumb had she been to let her guard down with him. He was an attractive man. Fine, but her loyalty was to her family.

In the midst of straightening a display of T-shirts, she looked down to see that her hands had gone still. Silly. The investigation didn't have anything to do with her family!

Except...she'd imagined Brody looked evasive a couple of times. And then there was the fact that he'd been seriously into Amy, and never said what had broken them up.

Except, that wasn't all. It was Lucy, too. Something had her scared, and Jo had to wonder if it wasn't fear for her brother.

Jo brooded about it for the rest of the day, then followed Lucy up to her bedroom and slipped inside before her sister could slam the door in her face.

The pretty teenager backed up until she bumped into her bed. "This is *my* room! What are you doing here?"

Jo leveled a look at her. "I want to hear what this friend of yours found in the cavern, and why you're so sure I won't believe you. Have I ever let you down?"

"You aren't here enough to do that," her sister retorted.

She'd known right where to slip the blade between Jo's ribs. Everything Jo had tormented herself with was true, then; Lucy did believe her big sister had abandoned her, just as their mother had abandoned them both. Despite the pain, Jo was determined not to let herself get paralyzed by guilt. She *hadn't* abandoned Lucy; she'd been a good big sister. If she should have done more, well…she couldn't go back, but she could help untangle whatever it was that tormented Lucy *now*.

"Dad said your friend—Jesse?—found a skull."

Lucy sagged into a sitting position on the edge of the bed, looking defeated. She crossed her arms as if trying to hug herself. "*He* didn't believe us."

"Us?" Jo edged toward the bed. "Did you see it, too?"

"No, but Jesse started to yell and he came running out of the dark like he'd seen a ghost or something. He was really freaked."

Jo sat down beside the teenager. "Did he have a flashlight with him?"

Lucy nodded. "Everyone did."

One smart decision.

"Didn't anyone go back with him to look?"

She shook her head. "*Everyone* was freaked. You know? I mean, that was part of the fun, but Jesse went off by himself and it was really dark, and even *I* don't know that part of the cavern very well. I should have gone, but—"

She, too, had been scared. And was now ashamed because she hadn't been brave enough to find out whether her friend had told the truth.

"You didn't go very far up any of the passages, did you? I mean, for the party?"

"No, just that room with the shallow pool. You know the one?"

Jo did.

"It's big, and there aren't a lot of stalagmites or stalactites that anyone could damage, and I didn't tell anyone the water isn't really deep, even though it looks like it is. If they stumbled in, they couldn't drown." More common sense. "I didn't think anyone would want to go off by themselves, because the passage gets really narrow after that."

It did. Claustrophobically so. That was one reason the section of the cavern had never been included in tours. It *could* be; the stretch where Jo always felt as if she needed to suck in her stomach to make herself skinny only extended five or ten feet. It could be part of the thrill to the wild tour that Brody was envisioning.

"You told Dad where Jesse saw the skull?"

"Of course I did!" Lucy's eyes were as dark as Jo's, and right now they were huge. "He *said* he searched, but—"

"Why don't you believe him?" Jo asked, puzzled.

"I guess 'cuz he was mostly mad about us using the cavern for drunken parties," she mumbled. "That's what he called them, even though we didn't have *that* much to drink. I could *tell* he didn't really believe me."

Jo had no trouble imagining why he'd been doubtful, assuming that was the case. Young teens having fun getting wasted and scaring themselves silly were likely to have wild imaginations. Say, seeing a round rock shadowed with indentations that could be eye sockets in a brief flare of a flashlight. Not that she'd say as much to Lucy.

"He says he did go back there. He even had a deputy with him. He told me he wishes they had found a skeleton. Like a long-ago train robber."

Lucy let out a watery giggle. "I bet he would like that."

They sat for a minute in silence. Lucy broke it.

"Yesterday, did you really go in a cave nobody had ever explored? Weren't you scared?"

"Not really." Jo smiled. "I had a big, brawny man right behind me. I knew he could pull me out of trouble, no problem."

Lucy giggled again.

Jo frowned. "Is this Jesse especially brave? Was he trying to show off for you or another girl?"

"Show off? Nuh-uh. He's really scrawny, so he fit through the passage without it being a big deal."

"Did he say why he wandered off?"

"Yeah, he heard strange sounds and then Rusty barking—" Expression apprehensive, Lucy grabbed Jo's hand. "I didn't tell Dad Rusty was with us. You won't tell him, will you? He'd be even madder."

Jo hesitated. It wasn't uncommon to hear eerie moans or rattles or other weird sounds. The wind and water moved through cracks, and earth settled. Occasionally, a rock broke off.

The dog's presence, though…that increased the likelihood of Lucy's story being true. Rusty could have smelled human remains, even really old ones. He might have picked something up and brought it partway back, then barked out of excitement. Or just because he enjoyed the echo. Only—

would he have carried the skull away again, dropping it who knew where before he heard Lucy calling for him?

On a shiver, Jo thought, *maybe.*

"I won't tell Dad," she said after a moment.

But apprehension prickled over her skin as she remembered how worked up Rusty had been the night Amy Kendall disappeared. The two things couldn't possibly have anything to do with each other...but the dog hadn't acted like that since. And *other* women had gone missing, ones whose remains could be skeletal by now.

Jo rolled her eyes at her own speculation. *She* was getting spooked like any teenager to even imagine a connection between the family cavern and the women who'd disappeared.

Still, she had to do *something* to verify or discount Jesse's story. If this incident had caused the alienation between Rod and Lucy, there was a chance Jo might be able to bring a close to it.

Except—that meant *she* had to venture into the forbidden part of the cavern on her own. Keeping her intentions secret from Lucy unless she found something...and defying Rod. To whom Jo owed such a debt.

She suddenly wished she could ask Alan to go with her.

ALAN TOOK CALLS while he methodically drove one road at a time across the quarter of the county he'd been allotted. It was slow going, given that he also turned into every driveway that disappeared into the trees, parked and investigated derelict buildings, and stopped at turnouts to be sure a body hadn't been tossed from a vehicle and that there wasn't broken vegetation suggesting anyone had driven deeper into the woods.

His phone rang just as he braked in front of a barn that was one snowfall away from collapse. The double doors hung crookedly, but there were enough cracks between old, dried-up boards forming the siding that he doubted he'd need to get a door open to survey the interior.

Staying behind the wheel, he answered the phone. "Burke."

"Alan, it's Drew. I've found another diver. He thinks he can give you the backup you need."

In other words, a recreational scuba diver had come forward. The guy probably had never descended past fifteen feet, and that in the clear waters of the Caribbean on a cruise ship excursion.

"Let me have his number," Alan said noncommittally. Diving alone was never a good idea, but he'd about resigned himself to doing so. Dropping far enough into the various deeper lakes, quarries and sinkholes in the area was unlikely to present much of a challenge—or risk—to him. Still, complacency wasn't a mistake he'd made since he'd been lucky enough to survive being a reckless kid. Anyone might be better than no one.

Even as he listened to Drew's answer, his gaze followed what looked like movement in the falling-down structure in front of him. An animal? Or had someone taken possession of this place for an unknown reason?

"Name's Edgar Madsen," Drew said. "I've met him before—he's a detective in Marion County across the border in Arkansas. Lots of lakes there." Drew hesitated. "We're striking out otherwise."

No surprise that a rural county in the middle of the country wasn't home to a host of passionate deep-sea divers.

Not taking his eyes from the barn, Alan said, "I'll call and let you know." Then he opened his door and climbed out, dropping the phone in a pocket and reached for the handgun he carried in a holster on his belt. Staying behind the cover of the car door, he called, "Anyone here?"

Wood rattled followed by the crashing sound of someone—or something—running into the woods.

He dashed to the corner of the barn and peered around it. "I don't care if you're trespassing," he yelled. "You don't have to run away."

The sound of someone or something fleeing continued to recede. He grunted, holstered his weapon, and bent to peer between the heavy warped boards that made up the siding. Bands of light let him see the dirt floor, but the bulk of what might have been stalls or equipment left behind blocked his view of the whole space.

Instead of wrestling with the obvious entrance in front, he eased around the back. An ordinary-sized door stood open. He turned on the LED flashlight he'd carried in yet another pocket of his cargo pants, shone it in a wide arc, and stepped inside.

Two rusting pieces of farm equipment sat in the middle: a tractor and what he thought was an old harvester. Both were well past any chance of a second life. In a stall that stretched along one side of the barn, he found a setup that suggested someone was camping out here. An indentation in a heap of old straw; a bundle that he saw, after a nudge of his booted foot, held some sandwich makings, a few soup cans and a couple of battered paperbacks; and a wool blanket prickly with straw slung over the side of the stall.

He poked around the ground floor, found no sign of digging, and climbed partway up the ladder into the loft. Not trusting the brittle rungs, Alan swung himself the rest of the way. There wasn't much up there; using a rusting rake with a broken handle, he pushed the rotting remains of old straw or hay around to be sure no bodies or evidence of any other human presence were there.

Then he swung himself over the edge, landing hard and rolling. He took another look at the nest in the stall before going out to his pickup truck. Pity made him want to let sleeping dogs lie; it was probably a runaway or a homeless person camping out here, but he knew he couldn't not report what he'd discovered. Not with the possibility a serial killer had just abducted an innocent young woman.

After starting the engine, he kept an eye on the barn while he made two calls: one to the detective who turned out to have more diving experience than Alan had guessed, then to Drew himself.

ONCE SHE HAD her hands on the keys—and boy, did she feel like scum after searching Rod's bedroom—Jo's next dilemma was when she could search the gated passage without anyone's knowledge. She seriously considered asking Lucy to accompany her. Jo wasn't crazy about the idea of venturing beyond the tourist area of the cavern entirely alone, but she concluded that she couldn't trust Lucy to keep her mouth shut, and Brody…wasn't an option.

Sneaking out of the house in the middle of the night seemed problematic, plus gates were closed and locked at the mouth of the cavern at night, too. Put dinner on, then slip away while it was cooking? Problem was, Rod often lingered in his office in the gift shop longer than the rest of them, and several nights a week returned there after dinner, too.

So—during the day, Jo concluded, while Rod was leading a tour. She'd make an excuse to Brody and Lucy or anyone else who might wonder at her absence. She'd claim to have a headache, she decided, say she was going to take some prescription medication and lie down for an hour. Instead, she'd slip into the cavern on the heels of the tour. She should be able to get in and out during the hour before the tour returned. If memory served her, it wasn't that far to the spacious room with the shallow pool that Lucy had described.

She led the one o'clock tour herself. Rod was to take the next one.

She walked everyone into the gift shop and was still smiling, answering questions and thanking the people who'd accompanied her through the cavern when Rod approached.

"You okay?" he asked in a low voice.

Her anxiety had to be leaking out even though she hadn't yet had a chance to start acting. Oh, face it—she never had been very good at being sneaky or lying.

"Headache," she murmured back. "I'll be okay."

Eyes sharp on her face, he nodded.

Not ten minutes later, he had gathered the next tour group—a big one, probably twenty-five people—and led them into the maw of the cavern. She saw only Brody near enough to talk to and made her excuses to him, then slipped into the shadowed interior of the cavern close enough behind the tour to hear Rod's strong, confident voice and the group laughter he knew how to arouse.

The lights strung throughout were turned on, section by section, by the tour guide, then turned off as they moved on. At one point, halfway through the experience, those lights were all turned off just long enough to have the tourists squeaking and gasping when they found out what complete darkness looked like.

Jo slipped on her helmet with the headlamp as soon as she was certain no one would see her, and carried a flashlight besides. She just had to be sure Rod didn't catch so much as a glimpse of a beam of light where it didn't belong.

Heart pounding, she crept along the familiar path, smoothly paved but unfamiliar when she was relying only on the edges of the glow from the overhead electric lights well ahead. She had to keep reminding herself that she knew this route like the back of her hand. She ought to have been able to walk it blindfolded.

Nonetheless, she was glad when she reached the magnificent, twisting flow formation that served as an exquisite curtain to hide a metal gate sunk in concrete pilings. A second gate later on the tour was obvious, and that's where the tour guide would explain about the multiple passages that wound in a maze not yet entirely explored. Rod was especially good at talking about the secrets those as yet unseen passages might still guard: Spanish gold, illicit bullion stolen from a train robbery when the crime was common in the days of Jesse James, fossils, even the remnants of a Prohibition era still. He liked to hint that his own family, longtime owners of this land, had been up to some not yet revealed sins.

Jo had to turn on the headlamp to get the key in the lock without doing something dumb like dropping it. Once through the gate, she closed it as quietly as she could—but only after testing several times her ability to let herself *out*.

Once she turned her back on the gate, she faced the stunning darkness that always gave her a tiny frisson of fear even when she was the one to switch off the lights during the tour. Her eyes strained to see anything at all, and failed. She imagined eternal darkness if she went blind, and shuddered. No. She was comfortable in the cavern and caves in general from long experience, but she didn't love being underground the way Rod and Brody did.

A stray thought passed through her mind. Was Alan Burke a dedicated caver, too?

And why was she just *standing* there? Deadline, remember? Jo turned on her headlamp, inexpressibly relieved by the warm, broad beam that revealed the passage in front of her. It was easily ten feet high if somewhat narrower. Walking required dodging several stalactites hanging from the ceiling. She examined them as she passed, glad not to spot any damage.

Rubble covered the floor of this part of the cave, broken pieces of limestone, but nothing new that she could see. She bent to pass below an overhang that shone damply. An icy drop of water hit her neck, of course. She shivered as it trickled down her neck.

Beyond—she'd forgotten, but this was a primary reason Rod hadn't wanted to include any of this passage on the tour. To one side, nestled in a curve of the wall, was what looked for all the world like an undersea garden of coral. A helictite, defying the force of gravity, and perhaps the most fragile of cave formations. God, if Lucy or Brody had let any of their drunk friends damage *this*—

Jo stopped longer than she should have to shine her LED flashlight over the formation, as Rod had certainly done when he passed through here after learning about the parties. No damage, but she sympathized even more with his rage. He was right—protecting the fragile wonders beyond the tourist path was a responsibility she was glad he took seriously.

Deadline.

She moved as fast as she could now, with the limited light and the thick air and silence that wasn't quite silent. Whispers, murmurs, tiny drips, sighs. The cave talked, if you listened carefully enough. To someone unfamiliar with this environment, it would sound like ghosts.

It took her less than fifteen minutes to reach the Mirage Room, so named by Rod, although Jo hadn't thought about it in years until Lucy told her where she'd thrown her parties.

Somewhat like the famous Mirror Room at the Mera-

mec Cavern, the water in a slow-moving stream that had
spread to fill half the floor space appeared to have vast
depths, reflecting the surfaces around it. In truth, it was
only inches deep.

Jo stopped, sweeping her flashlight every direction, all
but holding her breath. She could easily imagine a timid
kid scared out of his wits once he'd been separated from
his friends down here. If she heard the sepulchral barking
of a dog, she'd probably jump out of her skin.

She rolled her eyes, pinpointed the dark outline of what
looked like a skinny doorway and forced herself to continue.

As she'd remembered, the passage narrowed just enough
to induce a hint of claustrophobia, but in something like
fifteen feet it again widened and the ceiling rose, too, although this space was nowhere near as big as the Mirage
Room. As if it was breathing, she could hear the water
that ran through here, although *hear* might not be the right
word, so soft was it. She could *feel* it, then.

A prize exhibition on the tour was a nest of cave pearls
that appeared for all the world to be eggs laid in a nest. Jo
had never heard of one big enough for even a sloshed kid to
mistake for a skull. Yes, some rocks lay around, probably
remnants of long-fallen limestone formations, but really
this room was one that, at least in the beam of her head-
light, seemed tinted orange. Not seemed: orange calcite
wasn't uncommon in these limestone caverns.

Even as she kept an eye on the watch she wore when
leading tours to keep her on schedule, she searched the
periphery of the room. Nothing leaped out at her. Unfortunately, this was one of those spots where multiple passages opened up, and she remembered that one of those
split a hundred yards or so farther along.

Tilting her head and concentrating, she decided she

wasn't mistaken picking out a susurrating sound different than what she'd heard earlier. This seemed to rise and fall, as if someone was crying somewhere in the cavern.

Of course, that was just her brain trying to label a sound created by ancient forces within the earth, but…she had to know.

Gritting her teeth, she started for the first of the several passages.

Chapter Six

Alan splashed backward off the rock into the water of the sinkhole—a long-ago collapsed part of a cave system—as if he was entering from a boat. Persuading a car to drive off the rim would have been a job, but could have been done. And this water looked plenty deep enough to hide almost anything.

There wasn't much hope of finding the Kendall girl alive nearly a week after her disappearance, but Alan would do anything he could to help find the killer. This was the next step.

Exhaling into his regulator, he moved a short distance with easy movements of his ankles as he waited for his dive partner to enter behind him.

Alan had been reassured almost at first meeting with Detective Ed Madsen. Late-thirties, early forties, the guy was five foot ten or so and fit. The equipment he'd unloaded from his pickup looked both well used and well cared for. Decent quality, too; he'd invested some money in his hobby.

They'd shaken hands, evaluating each other as Drew Frazier looked on.

"You were really a navy SEAL?" Madsen asked. He had a noticeable accent, making Alan guess he was originally from a Deep South state.

"I was."

"Damn. I'm not often impressed, but I'll admit I am."

"No need," Alan said with a relaxed smile. "I don't think we'll be doing anything that will require my super-powers."

Madsen laughed. "Don't suppose. I keep up my skills by doing some diving in our local lakes. Used to do cave diving, too, but my partner moved away, and I haven't found anyone else I'd trust to join me."

They eyed each other. "I've done it in other parts of the world," Alan said, "but never locally." He'd missed being in the water, the escape from gravity and sense of solitude even with dive buddies. Yeah, he might enjoy some exploring if he could trust this man as backup.

Halfway through the day, he'd decided he had enough confidence in the detective to join him on an expedition through one of the flooded caverns in the Ozark area.

They'd already gone deep in another sinkhole to find a crack wide enough to have allowed passage that very possibly opened into a cave. The crack wasn't wide enough for a car to have scraped through, though, so they'd turned around and risen at a pace that allowed for a few safety stops back to the surface.

They'd actually located a rusting hulk of a pickup truck in a quarry first thing that morning. Alan had photographed a license plate that barely hung by one screw for Drew to identify the vehicle, but this truck had been down here too many years to be connected to any of the missing women.

In fact, Drew had been irritated, because that had been a favorite spot for teenagers to dive, and no one had ever reported the pickup.

"We'd better haul it out," he grumbled, "before some kid gets snagged exploring."

Alan wholeheartedly agreed. "Let me know if you need help once you get it arranged." Chains would have to be attached to the heap in places where the metal wouldn't just crumble off when any force was applied.

"Ditto," his diving partner agreed.

Now Madsen signaled to Alan and both men pulled the valve on their buoyancy control devices to begin a relaxed descent, shining their main dive lights in front of them. From long practice, he slowed the beating of his heart, leaving behind his stresses. This water was the cloudiest they'd seen yet. It was being fed from another source, Alan diagnosed, and pulled downward, possibly into another flooded cavern. Even so, the lights penetrated plenty far enough for them to move with confidence and reasonable speed.

Now and again, he paused to sweep the lights to each side, visually measuring the width of the sinkhole. It was narrowing, but only slightly, and they were already—he glanced at his dive computer—forty meters deep, and no bottom in sight.

This would be a hell of a place to make a vehicle disappear.

He tapped the computer on his wrist. Madsen looked at his own and nodded his understanding. The only way they'd have time at this depth to evaluate anything was to plan for decompression stops as they surfaced, especially since this was their third dive of the day. No problem if they reached the bottom soon and saw nothing, but he knew of one flooded cave in the area that was considerably deeper than they'd yet gone.

And then his light picked out a shape that didn't belong, and he adjusted the angle of his flippers to take him straight at it.

It was a car, all right, a shiny red Ford Focus. Damn.

Part of him hadn't wanted to find anything, but here it was. He snapped photos of the license plate, although he didn't have to. After getting involved in the hunt for the missing young woman, he'd memorized the plate number on her car.

While he did that, Madsen gestured to him, and he moved enough to see that the car rested atop a second one. He thought gray, but wasn't sure in the cloudy water, and saw signs of rusting. He and Madsen both photographed this license plate, too, before he shone his light at the abruptly narrowed walls of the hole to be sure there wasn't room for yet another vehicle to be down here. Then he took out his writing slate and scribbled a note for his partner to see.

Madsen gave a thumbs-up, and began a slow rise to look inside the windows of the Ford Focus while Alan did the same with this Pontiac. He was taking the greater risk; if Madsen bumped the Focus he could dislodge it.

After sweeps with the light, Alan saw nothing in the car. Not even a lump that might have been a woman's handbag. He was tempted to open the trunk, but decided not to. When he inhaled enough to rise, he saw that Madsen, too, had taken out a slate and written, *Trunk?*

Alan shook his head. The detective didn't argue. Both knew these cars would have to be raised from the water depths. Any remaining questions could be answered then. Alan didn't expect to find any bodies in the car trunks. Odds were that someone trying to ditch a dead woman along with a vehicle would have seat belted her in behind the wheel to confuse the issue of whether she might have chosen this death.

The ascent was slow, his patience with the decompression stops next to nonexistent. His mind worked the entire way, as he felt sure Ed Madsen's did as well. They were both cops, official today or not, and knew what this discovery meant.

He didn't like knowing how scared Jo Summerlin would be to hear what they'd found. She had to be feeling protective where her brother was concerned—but Alan found himself wondering how viable a suspect Brody was. If, as Alan suspected, this second car had belonged to the first woman to disappear, Brody would have been only sixteen years old. Okay, almost seventeen, but that was really young to commit this kind of crime. Foolishly, he wanted to share what they'd found today with Jo—but he had no business undercutting the investigation.

ONCE HE HEARD the news and studied the photos on both men's underwater cameras, Drew had made several calls, starting with the sheriff and ending with the owner-operator of a local tow company that had hauled smashed cars up from deep chasms. Underwater was new to the guy, but once reassured that volunteer divers would hook up the chains, he agreed to give it a try.

Given that he and Madsen shouldn't dive again until morning, Alan wished Drew had held off on making that call. He tended not to trust anyone to keep quiet with juicy news, but he didn't say anything. The very fact that he was again having to remind himself this wasn't his investigation made him conscious of a faint itch that told him he wished it was. Especially since he hadn't been impressed by anything he'd heard about the sheriff's department detective.

He and Madsen waited to one side, both listening to Drew's side of the phone calls. There'd been a time Alan wouldn't have hesitated to go back down again, no problem, but he hadn't done any diving in the past year, and the detective looked spent to Alan's eye.

"We haven't had any women disappear from my county," Madsen said out of the blue. "I was counting my blessings when Frazier first called, but now…"

Alan made a sound of agreement. He'd feel a lot better about this had any of the crimes been conducted in Madsen's backyard. At least he respected his new diving partner. Unfortunately, now that abduction had been confirmed, Detective Jantz would take over lead on the investigation from Drew.

Drew got off the phone and walked over to them. "We're set for nine in the morning."

Both nodded.

Looking grim, Drew added, "I got a hit on the second license plate number. Not a surprise. The car disappeared along with Christy Dodswell four years ago. She's the one from Newton County, the missing woman we tentatively connected with the others."

Not tentative anymore. Finding the two cars dumped in the same place tied those two missing women together despite the lengthy gap between their abductions. And with those two linked—

Ed Madsen said what all three of them were thinking. "We have a serial killer."

"Looks like it." Drew rubbed a hand over his face. "Sheriff wants us to keep it quiet as long as possible so we don't start a panic, but I don't think that's possible."

Madsen gave a sharp laugh. "Who does he think he's kidding? Even if the crew from the tow truck company keeps their mouths shut, you'll be hauling the two vehicles to—what?—department impound? If I remember right, it's in town surrounded by chain link fencing. Anyone going by will see in. You're going to have to notify the two families. The sheriff plans to try to stifle *them*?"

Alan hoped the sheriff's motivation had nothing to do

with his reelection campaign. When nobody commented, Drew shook hands with both Madsen and Alan. "Can't thank you two enough."

"Any way I can contribute," Madsen said, before heading to his pickup.

Alan echoed him. "I think I'll stop for a bite in town. If you want to join me—?"

Drew grimaced. "I'll need to go see the Kendall girl's parents. Don't care what the sheriff thinks. They deserve to know what we've found."

"You wouldn't want them to hear from someone else," Alan agreed. "I'd suggest you try to keep them away in the morning, though. It'll be a long, hard job, and if her body turns out to be in the trunk…"

Drew swore under his breath. "Seeing her like that might kill them."

Privately, Alan couldn't help thinking that might almost be easier on the people who loved the girl than being left wondering what she was enduring—or never knowing what had happened to her. Drew was bound to have the same thoughts, though.

They parted ways, Alan not envying his childhood friend the duty that lay in front of him. He'd given terrified people the same kind of news in the years he'd served on the police force. Had to be the worst part of the job.

THE FIRST JO heard was a voice coming from around the end cap at the grocery store.

"I hear they're diving, looking for her body."

Jo stopped her cart in front of spices, even though she didn't need any.

"It would float right up, wouldn't it?" said another woman. "And why would anyone expect her to have been dumped in a lake?"

It would be Alan Burke doing the diving, wouldn't it? Everyone knew he'd been a SEAL. The sheriff wouldn't hesitate to take advantage of Alan's expertise, would he? She had no reason to know much about the sheriff.

The two women's voices had dropped, and Jo was just about to resume her shopping when a third person evidently joined them.

"Well, *I* heard they found something!" Another woman, and this one sounded triumphant about being in the know. "Not *they*. It was that Burke man, the one whose father sold methamphetamine." Spite infused her voice. "Of all people for our police to trust. If she's dead in the water, who's to say *he* didn't put her there in the first place?"

There might have been a polite rebuke, but if so the hateful woman overrode it. "Anyway, that deputy Frazier called Jed Chapman about him using his equipment to pull something out of the water."

"Why would they need a tow truck if they found a body?" one of the women asked with refreshing common sense.

"Well, her car is missing, too, isn't it?"

Chilled, Jo wondered if there was anything to this new report. If it was true, it was spreading awfully fast. Although, it would surely be better to have any answer as to what had become of Amy than to have none, wouldn't it?

What Jo hated was the tone of what she'd heard. Did that nasty woman think being able to spread news before anyone else could was more important than a local girl's well-being? Or that of her family? Indignant, Jo turned her cart around, grabbed a bottle of olive oil off the shelf, and kept going. She didn't want to see those women's faces. She'd be too tempted to say something scathing and make enemies for the Summerlin family. Rod wouldn't appreciate that.

She rushed through the store despite the risk of forgetting something, and loaded the trunk of her car without so much as turning her head to see who else came out on her heels. With luck, she wouldn't recognize those women, anyway. One of the first two voices had sounded familiar—a friend's mother, maybe, or someone who'd worked at the school?—but the most distinctive didn't ring any bells for her. God—think how horrible it would be if Amy's mother had been shopping and *this* was how she received the news! Jo hoped someone was doing all of the basic chores for the Kendall family, and that they weren't the kind to be determined to follow the routine of their days no matter what.

Jo turned out of the parking lot, intending to make a stop at the hardware store before going home, but the sight of a giant pickup truck parked at the curb in front of Ralph's Café changed her mind. Big black pickups weren't uncommon in these parts, but she'd seen Alan Burke drive away from the search in one just like this. Plus it had—yes!—Virginia license plates. She parallel parked as soon as she saw a spot, grabbed her purse and walked back to the café. In only half a block, she passed two Missing posters, one stapled to a pole, the other in a store window. Would putting Amy's face out there like this help? Jo shivered.

She saw Alan the minute she entered the café. He was the only person sitting alone, having claimed a booth in the back corner. He saw her as quickly.

Waving at the waitress, Jo hurried to Alan's booth. "May I join you?" she asked.

The pause might have been her imagination, but the resignation on his face when he said, "Of course," wasn't. Tough.

"Was it you diving today?"

His expression was well locked down now. "It was."

"I heard at the grocery store—"

Crud, there was Wendy Smith, who'd been a waitress here since Jo was a little girl. She approached the table with a menu for Jo.

"Cup of coffee?" she asked.

"Make it iced tea."

"Okey doke." Wendy nodded at Alan. "Your food will be out any minute, honey."

Alan didn't react to the "honey," saying only "thanks." But he raised his eyebrows at Jo as soon as the waitress was out of earshot. "The grocery store?"

"Three women talking. One said she'd heard that you'd found two cars in, I don't know, a sinkhole or lake."

He scowled. "Damn. Did you see who it was?"

Jo shook her head. "They were out of sight. The woman sounded so hateful, I didn't want to know who she is."

"Hateful? About the missing women?"

Oh, heavens. She shouldn't have said that. But now that she had… She took a deep breath. "She implied you might be responsible for dumping the cars as well as finding them. Because of your father."

He wiped away all expression again, which hurt to see. Jo would wish she hadn't said that, except he'd be bound to hear someone else expressing the same opinions.

"Your father wasn't violent, was he?"

"Nosy, are you?"

She made a face. "I know it's none of my business."

"It isn't," he said. "Yes, he was. Beat the tar out of my mother and me regularly. Cops came out a few times. Never found his meth lab, but they locked him up twice that I remember for fights at the bar, or maybe walloping a customer who didn't pay him. Not sure. Nothing like what's happening now, but if he were still alive, the cops might be looking at him."

She swallowed. "Oh."

Before she could think of anything sympathetic or even halfway intelligent to say, Wendy showed up with his burger and fries as well as Jo's iced tea, refilled his coffee and only nodded when Jo declined to order food.

Alan started eating as if the topic of conversation hadn't been at all disturbing.

Jo dumped a packet of sugar into the iced tea, stirred it and finally said, "I'm sorry."

His big shoulders moved. "Long time ago."

She met his eyes. "Some things never feel as if they happened long enough ago."

A tip of his head conceded her point. He grabbed a fry and dipped it in catsup.

Apparently he wasn't going to volunteer any news. Since word—true or not—was already spreading, Jo wasn't about to go home without finding out what had been found.

"*Did* you find two cars?"

Alan sighed. "We did. I'm sorry, Amy Kendall's was one of them. The other belonged to another of the missing women."

"Oh, God. That means they're both dead, doesn't it?"

"Christy Dodswell, almost certainly yes." He grimaced. "I shouldn't have told you that name. It'll get around soon enough, but I'm asking you not to repeat that to anyone."

Stunned even though this had always been the likely outcome, Jo nodded. It would probably take a while to notify Christy's family, and that was assuming they hadn't moved away.

"Amy…" Alan continued in that gritty voice. "Who knows? We didn't find bodies. She could still be alive."

It might be trite, but wasn't it also true that where there's life, there's hope? At this moment, though, Jo wasn't so sure, not when she could imagine the horrific things Amy might be suffering.

"I don't suppose they can get fingerprints or anything like that off cars that have been immersed in water for any length of time," she heard herself say.

"Unlikely. Unless the guy dropped something that survived…" Alan shook his head. "All finding the cars really tells us is that we have one perpetrator, and when something works, he repeats it."

"But…what about the other missing women's cars?" She couldn't remember details about the other abductions.

"Not all of the women were driving when they disappeared. One vehicle was locked up and left beside the road not far from her house."

Jo leaned forward. "Wouldn't that have been the smart thing to do? I mean, unless he was on foot, it must have taken a long time to make a victim's vehicle disappear."

"Yes, except if someone happened to come along right after he snatched a girl and the police acted fast enough, that would up his risk."

"I…suppose so," Jo said slowly.

"Also, having the car gone clouded the issue. Had people thinking she might have just taken off."

Also true.

Alan chewed and swallowed a bite of his burger before saying, "So, you stopped by just to interrogate me?"

Heat rose to her cheeks. "I…was curious."

"I noticed that about you already."

"What?"

His amusement became apparent. "You weren't about to let me go in that cave by myself. What I saw, you wanted to see, too." Except, suddenly, the smile in his eyes was gone. "Unless you've been thinking like the woman at the grocery store all along. Why wouldn't anyone belonging to the Burke family be a logical suspect? What if I'd stashed the body in that cave?"

Chapter Seven

The shock on Jo Summerlin's face felt like a fist in the gut to Alan. Damn it, why had he said anything like that? He knew better. Even after such a short time, he knew *her* better.

"Jo."

"You think I'm like that?" She scooted fast across the vinyl bench seat to get away from him. "What have I ever said—?"

"Stop." He half rose. "Please. I'm sorry. I…lashed out for no reason." No reason? Or had he been hurt by even a faint possibility she agreed with the common local opinion?

She's not for me, remember?

Instead of getting to her feet, she hesitated, her eyes searching his.

"I came in here looking for you because I was mad about what that woman said." Her voice trembled just a little. "I would never believe something like that. I've always hated the idea that we're predestined to be like our parents. *I* would never—"

She broke off so suddenly he didn't learn what she would never do. Whatever it was, it involved hurting another person, and she was too compassionate to do that if she could help it.

After the things he'd done, whether in theory he'd been on the side of good in the battle with evil or not, he didn't belong at the same table with her. And yet, she drew him powerfully, and he hated knowing that, at the very least, what he'd said had stung.

"I…let myself get sensitive," he made himself admit. "I'm getting a lot of that attitude from townspeople, even ones who knew me as a kid."

Her forehead crinkled. "Were you a delinquent as a child?"

He shook his head. "A little wild, maybe. I didn't like to go home any more than I could help, so I did some trespassing. Got caught sleeping in someone's car or barn a few times. I wasn't the best student back then."

To his astonishment, she reached across the table and laid her hand over his. "Were you glad to go live with your grandparents?"

"Yeah." He had to clear some hoarseness from his throat. "I felt guilty about leaving my mother, but…yeah."

"She was an adult."

"I know." He did. Even then, he'd realized he couldn't do anything for her. She wasn't just terrorized by his dad, she was using by then, probably to dull the reality of her life. Alan would be forever grateful that she'd had the courage to defy his father by sending him away.

To his regret, Jo took her hand back. He wasn't much accustomed to someone expressing sympathy with a physical gesture, especially when that someone was a beautiful woman.

God, he thought; what if the killer had happened on her during one of her visits home these past few years? Alan would never have met her. Not that he could see a relationship with her going anywhere. Except…she was tougher than he'd first imagined, and for whatever reason, she fired up his protective instincts.

Maybe, it occurred to him, because they had at least one quality in common. He had no doubt she'd be fierce in defense of the people she believed in. Or in her case, he should probably say loved. Pure nosiness didn't explain her determination to stay on top of the investigation; no, she was worrying about her brother's connection to the latest victim.

She let out a sigh and scooted back toward the middle of her side of the booth. "You should eat. I'm sorry if I ruined your meal. If you want me to leave…"

Alan shook his head and smiled crookedly. "Having a pretty woman keeping me company never spoils a meal for me."

She wrinkled her nose at him. "Do you have any idea what the police will do next?"

He guessed she was trying to get them back on an even keel. "For starters, pull the cars out of the sinkhole. Go over them with a fine-tooth comb."

"Will you be helping them with that?"

"I and a deputy from Arkansas will dive to hook the chains in place so the tow truck can haul them up. Otherwise…" He hesitated. "I guess I'm out of it, unless any more searches are organized."

Jo nodded her understanding.

"They'll start an investigation," he continued. "Find out if Amy and Christy had anything in common. Who might have known both?" Although there was no saying that the killer had known any of the victims in advance. They might simply have caught his eye when they were vulnerable.

"Christy wasn't local, was she?" Jo asked.

"Another county, but not that far away." He had a vague recollection. "I think she was a cheerleader."

Jo looked dismayed. "Amy was, too."

"There you go."

Come to think of it, he hadn't heard where Christy had been when abducted. Near home? Or was there some chance she'd been around Mayville? Did anybody know, given that her car hadn't been found at the time?

"But…were Amy and Christy close enough in age to have known each other?"

He should quit thinking out loud, Alan realized. He was forced to yet again confront the fact that this investigation wasn't his, despite his certainty he could handle it better than the unimaginative, by-the-books and near-retirement detective for the sheriff's department. The one who'd opposed searching for Amy at all. It was to the sheriff's credit that he'd let Drew run with it.

After the cops Alan had worked with and trusted had failed so badly in his estimation with such tragic consequences, he'd been sure he was done with law enforcement. Could be he'd been wrong. Assuming his boss in his previous department gave a decent recommendation that would give him a shot at a job with a different department, that was.

"There might have been a connection that didn't have anything to do with age," he felt compelled to say. Jo had babysat Amy, for example, knowing the girl well enough to grieve now, despite the span of years between them. "Besides, whether they knew each other or not isn't the point."

"It's who else they both knew," she finished.

"Yes. Maybe. Although these could have been crimes of opportunity."

They looked at each other again in the unguarded way that made him feel naked. Alan didn't know how she did that, or whether he was imagining it. But, damn it, she got to him as no one had in a long time.

"I'm scared," she said quietly. "I mean, this is a small town. I know most people. Or at least, I did. You—"

He arched an eyebrow. "Feel safe?" There was irony, when she felt anything *but* safe to him.

"No-o." Color brushed her cheeks.

Along with the blushing was a shyness that surprised him, even as it stirred his body uncomfortably. So "safe" didn't describe how she felt when she was with him. Well, he didn't feel all that safe with her, either, except in a literal sense. Certainly, in the cave Jo had exuded a confidence and competence that had relaxed him.

"Jo—" He was going to do something foolish. He knew he was. Asking her out wouldn't be good for either of them, but damn, he wanted to get to know this woman.

"I should be going." She slid out of the booth quicker than he could draw a breath. Her eyes wouldn't quite meet his. "I have groceries in the car. I shouldn't have dawdled this long. Anyway, I'm the cook tonight, and it's getting late."

Alan had a feeling she was the cook every night while she was home, but maybe he was wrong.

"Okay," he said, wanting to be glad she was fleeing before he could make a stupid suggestion. "Remember what you promised."

"Promised?" Comprehension had her casting a quick look around her. Even so, she lowered her voice. "You mean Christy. I keep promises."

"I...have no doubt you do," he said, something in his voice he hardly understood. Intimacy? Trust deeper than it should have been? If that was it, he had to shut it down. Now. "I may see you around," he said brusquely.

A flicker in her eyes was Jo's only reaction. Then she dropped a five-dollar bill on the table and walked away.

NONE OF THE rest of the family was home when Jo got there. She carried the groceries in, realized Rod would be annoyed that she'd forgotten to stop at the hardware store and shrugged it off. Too bad. He could grab what he needed the next time he was out. After putting the food away, she started dinner—spaghetti, a perennial favorite.

All three arrived together. Rod grinned at her as he walked into the kitchen. "Smells great."

Lucy wrinkled her nose. "Do we *have* to have broccoli?"

Brody bumped her with his shoulder. "Can it, kid, unless you want to take over cooking duties. And please, God, let that not happen."

"You're a jerk," his sister told him.

Wait until they were all sitting down? Jo asked herself, and decided, *No.* She did dump the spaghetti noodles into the boiling water, then turned to face them.

"I heard something in town."

Her tone killed the good humor on all three faces.

"They found Amy's car today. It was at the bottom of a sinkhole. Or maybe a lake, I'm not sure."

"Damn," her stepfather said, sounding shocked. "I really wanted to think—"

Jo nodded. "We all did."

Lucy was still gaping. Brody's hands closed into tight fists.

"Was…*she* in the car?"

Lucy whimpered.

"Not the way I heard it," Jo said. She turned down the heat under the spaghetti and the broccoli both.

"How did you hear?" Rod asked.

"Some women talking at the grocery store." Tell them about her conversation with Alan? No. Rod would disapprove of her being friendly to this neighbor who was thwarting his ambitions.

"So...someone went diving?" That was Brody again.

"Alan Burke. He was a SEAL, you know. The police were probably grateful to have someone with his diving experience available. I think maybe there was someone else, too." Wasn't that what Alan had implied, mentioning some guy from Arkansas?

Her stepfather snorted. "Burke. Why's *he* so eager to help?"

"He spent years in the military," she said as mildly as she could, considering her reaction to his contempt. "And I understand that he's been a cop since he got out of the navy."

Another sound, this one deeper in his throat, and Rod said, "Let's wash up."

Tears trembled on Lucy's lashes. "But...how can we just *eat*? Amy must be dead!"

Her brother turned on her. "Don't say that! Maybe—" His throat worked. "Maybe..."

In the absence of any help from the rest of the family, Jo stepped forward and hugged him, this solidly built young man she wasn't always sure she knew very well but who was her brother. His arms came around her and he hugged her back, hard. When he stepped away, his expression was tormented and his eyes wet, too.

"Amy...she's—she was—so sweet."

"I know," Jo whispered.

Predictably, Lucy broke out sobbing, whirled and ran for the stairs. A moment later, they all heard her door slam. Rod grumbled under his breath before saying, "She'll get hungry later."

"This is an easy dinner to reheat," Jo agreed, ignoring the lump in her own throat.

Brody stomped to the cupboard and got out dishes to set the table. Typical guy, she thought; he didn't let his emotions get in the way of meals.

She wished she didn't still feel that tiny bit of…oh, not suspicion, call it *apprehension*, when she thought about Brody and Amy, even though Brody couldn't possibly have had anything to do with Christy Dodswell's abduction. He'd been only sixteen, or was it seventeen? Anyway, how could he have met her? He hadn't even had his own car that long ago, had he?

No, she should be ashamed that she'd ever, for one minute, wondered about her own brother.

BRODY LEFT THE house right after dinner, as he so often did. Meeting up with friends, Jo assumed. Rod never commented on it, at least not in her hearing. The one evening she'd announced that everyone could heat up their own choice of leftovers, his irritation was obvious, but he'd managed to use the microwave. Tonight, Rusty excitedly accompanied Brody to his old pickup truck. Jo wished her brother would buy a new muffler for it.

Rod thanked her for cooking, kissed her on the cheek and said, "I still have work to do," and left the house, too. He hadn't gotten past the front porch when she heard yet another excited woof from the dog followed by Rod swearing. The front door opened and closed again, this time emphatically, and Rusty dashed for the kitchen, claws clicking on the worn hardwood floor. Jo hustled to clear the table, not sure she trusted the dog not to plant his paws on one of the chairs and slurp up any leftovers.

Sometimes Rod drove away, too, seeing the lady friend, she assumed, but most often, as he did tonight, he walked back to his office in the gift shop building. Apparently he hadn't wanted company. Rod didn't seem all that fond of the dog. He wasn't much of an animal person; he and her mother both shook their heads at her pleas to have a pet when she was young. Lucy and Brody were lucky he'd agreed to let them keep the young dog when he showed up as a stray.

She enjoyed Rusty's companionship as she cleaned the kitchen—didn't it figure this had been Lucy's night to handle the job—and went so far as to set a plate down with some leftovers before she put a plate for Lucy and the remaining leftovers into the refrigerator. She should have grabbed Brody and asked for help with clean up before he got out the door. Once she started the dishwasher, Jo sighed and headed for the stairs. What she wanted was to take a hot bath and then shut herself into her own room, but Lucy needed her whether she knew it or not.

She knocked on her sister's door.

"Jo?"

"It's me."

The tear-choked voice said, "You can come in."

Rusty had followed Jo, of course, and he pushed in as well and rushed to his girl, who went to her knees on the rug and threw her arms around the dog. Jo sat on the edge of the bed next to them.

"I wanted to be sure you're okay."

Lucy gave her a distraught look. "How can I be?"

"I know you're upset, but you weren't that close to Amy."

"No, but—" Her breath hitched.

"She was part of what should have been a safe world." Jo remembered feeling the same after her mother abandoned her.

Lucy's head bobbed.

When Jo stroked her hair, the teenager kept one arm around the dog but also leaned against Jo's leg. "It's just so awful."

"I know."

"And…and I know that skull didn't have anything to do with Amy, because she was still alive when Jesse found it, but…it's so *creepy*."

Yes, it was. Jo would give a lot to know what had excited Rusty so much the night Amy was abducted. Imagining some kind of connection was probably ridiculous, but the timing niggled at her.

Fortunately, she could at least partially reassure Lucy. Jo hadn't had a chance to talk to her sister yesterday evening. That was part of the reason she'd been determined tonight.

"I got the key and went in the cave," she said.

"What?" Lucy sat up straight and turned to allow herself to see Jo's face.

"I told you I'd try. Yesterday, when I said I had a headache, I slipped in once the tour passed that gate. I went to where Jesse said he saw the skull, and then farther yet. Several passages separate there, you know. I went a little ways into all of them." Hurriedly, but she didn't say that. "I didn't find anything, any more than your dad did. And that deputy he said he took with him," she added. "Was that Drew Frazier?"

"Uh-uh. It was Deputy Hudson. I didn't like him. And I don't think he really wanted to go into the cavern at all, but he wouldn't admit *he* was scared."

Jo hadn't seen enough of the stocky cop to say she didn't like him, but she hadn't been impressed. And he did look like the kind who wouldn't want anyone to suspect he had any weaknesses whatsoever.

"That wouldn't be a shock. A lot of men are like that."

"I guess." Lucy was quiet for a minute. "You're *sure*?"

"I'm sure there was nothing like a skull or any kind of bones when I went looking," she said. "Honestly, not even a rock that looked remotely *like* a skull. I guess Rusty could have carried something off, but he couldn't exactly bury it in a hole back there."

"No." The teenager's face scrunched in thought, even as she studied her big sister. "You think Jesse imagined it, don't you?"

Jo hesitated, but finally said, "I do. *He* could have been spooked by the cave, you know. If he was drunk…"

"Except he wasn't that drunk," Lucy said softly. "And he was totally freaked out. I wish… I should have gone to see for myself, but… I guess I was scared."

"I don't blame you." Jo made a face. "Don't tell anybody, especially Brody, but I didn't enjoy poking around. I don't mind leading the tours, but I've never wanted to go exploring."

"Me, either. Brody's jealous that he's never had the chance to learn to dive, because he wants to be able to go into caves with passages that are underwater. Can you *imagine*?"

Sump diving. In Jo's opinion, exploring that kind of cave was particularly unappealing, if only because it involved dry stretches where you'd have to carry a hundred plus pounds of air tanks and all the other gear required for the underwater parts, and then you had to figure out how to squeeze the tanks through narrow spots. What if you got through, but the tanks wouldn't fit? The idea made her shudder.

She'd bet Alan Burke wouldn't think twice about joining something like the search for the kids and their coach trapped in the flooded cave in Thailand a few years ago.

She needed to quit imagining him as a hero. Who knew, he might have been fired from his last job as a cop. Nobody had said. There had to be a reason he didn't seem to be working.

Bringing herself back to the moment, she said, "I'm sorry to have brought the news about Amy. It's really hard to imagine something like that happening here. We think we know everyone."

Lucy bobbed her head. "It makes me kind of afraid to go anywhere by myself. You know?"

"You should be extra careful." Jo didn't want to terrify a girl who was at an age where she needed to be asserting her independence, but this was a good time for her to stick close to home.

"Why? I don't really fit. The girls that disappeared have all been lots older."

Early twenties didn't seem to be "lots older" than a sixteen-year-old to Jo, but all she said was, "Their ages might be chance. Because the missing women were old enough to do things like drive home alone from college for a school break."

Lucy hugged herself, her eyes huge. She said suddenly, "I'm glad you're here."

Jo gave a shaky smile. "Me, too."

With something that might have been a sob, Lucy pushed herself up to her knees and threw herself at Jo, who closed her arms around this sister whose certainties had been shattered.

She didn't think Lucy cried, but they stayed like that for a couple of minutes.

Finally, she murmured, "What do you say we go downstairs and I'll warm up some spaghetti for you?"

Lucy took a deep breath and slowly separated herself. "Is Dad still here? Or Brody?"

"Neither."

"Oh. Okay. Thanks."

As Jo heated leftovers a few minutes later, she tried to decide whether she dared raise the subject of the tension between Lucy and her father. Her conclusion: no. She'd had a breakthrough with her sister already. Why spoil the one step forward with two back?

Anyway, she understood. She hadn't had an easy relationship with Rod, either. Most of the time, he was brusque and uninterested in talking out any issues. Like a lot of men, he was probably just more comfortable with boys versus girls.

Assailed by renewed guilt, Jo regretted having failed to notice any change in Lucy's emotional state until Rod called asking for help. Well, from here on out, she'd be paying much closer attention, she vowed. Her sister still needed her more than Jo had realized.

Chapter Eight

Alan wasn't worried for himself. He'd made an automatic evaluation of the possibility that a piece of machinery as heavy as a car not resting on a solid foundation would shift at a mere bump, or even because the water around it was disturbed. He'd done a lot more dangerous work underwater than hooking the axle of a car so it could be raised to the surface. His main concern was that Madsen's experience with diving was all recreational. He lacked the experience to judge the risks, and the ability to avoid so much as brushing the car unnecessarily. Alan wished he'd told Ed to leave this part up to him, to stick to providing backup. It was too late now, though.

Amy Kendall's Ford Focus had settled with the back bumper sitting atop the trunk of the vehicle below it, much of the undercarriage seemingly lying on the roof of the other car, so that the nose tipped upward. The position encouraged them to think they had easy access to the front axle. Alan never trusted a promise of easy.

He had his eye on Ed, who was already under there, a hook in his hand, dragging the heavy duty chain behind him. Ed was to secure one side of the axle, Alan the other. Damn, he'd feel better if the car sat solidly on a rocky bed, but as long as they were careful—

The car lurched, brushing his shoulder. Alarm ignited

his instincts. He finned backward. Ed had either come in contact with a fender, or the heavy chain pulling over the front bumper had upset the delicate balance. Had he felt the movement?

Shoving back at an out-of-body instant, Alan dropped his hook and went after his partner. He grabbed Madsen's ankle and yanked backward. Metal was probably squealing, but sound was muffled down here. He felt as if he was moving in slow motion. What if there wasn't enough time to get Ed out?

But at his touch, the other man reacted instantly by curling away from the car and, with a couple of hard flicks of his fins, placing himself at a safe distance. Heart beating a hell of a lot harder than it should be, Alan joined him in watching the small red car slide in slow motion until it lay almost on its side, but still resting against the other car. Given a ten-or twenty-second difference in reaction time, Ed could have been crushed by metal on each side.

Damn, Alan thought. He was breathing harder than was safe at this depth. He knew better. The movement had stirred up increased debris in the water, too, impairing his ability to tell whether Ed was shaken up. Grimly, Alan set about slowing his own breathing, taking control of the speed of his pulse. Madsen did have enough experience to be doing the same thing himself.

Finally, Alan drifted closer to the car again, aware that the detective was with him.

He flattened a hand on the roof and shoved. The bottom was far from flat, but he felt no new movement. Ed tried the same by pushing on the bumper. He looked toward Alan, who gestured toward the dangling hooks.

He took hold of his again, this time maneuvering into position to use the self-locking hook to secure the chain around the low side of the axle. Once he'd backed out, Ed swam close and got the second hook in place.

This time, they eased over to the guide rope they were using to communicate with the people above. Knowing how likely screwups were, Alan had insisted on a way to send signals. Good thing, because the initial chains dropped had come up short despite Alan having shared the exact depth yesterday.

He and Ed had been forced to hover down here waiting, trusting that Drew Frazier, at least, was monitoring the rope and remembered that an emphatic two yanks translated to *doesn't reach the car*.

Now he gave one hard pull. *We're coming up.*

Their ascent would be slower than the car's, given the decompression stops they had to make, but he wasn't taking the chance of the damn thing being raised ahead of them. What if it broke free from the chains? The sinkhole was too narrow for them to be sure they could get out of the way. This wasn't the kind of thing Alan left to chance.

A good long while later, he hauled himself out of the water and signaled the go-ahead to Drew Frazier and the tow truck operator. Creaking, cranking noises began as the winch turned, and the chains grew taut. He'd been impressed earlier to see how hefty this tow truck was. It included a good-sized boom and a flatbed that was hydraulically operated so that a car could be pulled right onto it and lifted for transport. The whole setup wasn't all that different from ones used by the military, although those tended to be armored, too.

Ed Madsen crawled right up beside Alan. He wrestled free of his tanks, flopped onto his back and tore his mask off his head. "Son of a bitch. That was fun, and we get to do it again tomorrow."

Alan shared the sentiment. Even assuming all went well

now, bringing the first car up had eaten up too much time. He had no intention of taking a relatively inexperienced diver back down again today.

Wrestling the tanks with all the attached gear off his back, Alan watched Jed Chapman, a bulky, balding guy, operate the winch while his assistant leaned over the sinkhole waiting for the car to come into sight. Drew and the sheriff's department detective hovered right beside him.

The lip of the sinkhole was rocky. The boom was adjustable, allowing them to winch the car almost straight up so it hung like a mighty big fish on a line before it was slowly maneuvered over the flatbed of the truck. Metal screamed. Water ran off the car and out of it, spilling in every direction. Jed and the assistant stayed intensely focused, adjusting it in the air, until it landed with a thud and some final rocking on the flatbed, tire side down.

They produced tie-down straps, but waited for Drew to open the unlocked driver's side door of the little red car and find the lever to release the trunk latch. They'd all waited for this moment. Detective Jantz was the first to position himself at the back to get a good look inside the trunk.

Figured.

Jantz looked irritated when Ed and Alan stepped forward as the trunk lid rose, but even he must have decided he couldn't say much after the work they'd put in to find and bring the missing girl's car to the surface.

There was a kind of belching noise before the trunk lid lifted high enough to let them see in. The space was full of water. Something blue floated on the surface, obscuring their view. Drew fished it out with one gloved hand. A raincoat. Below that, there wasn't anything but the bump of a spare tire.

No dead girl. No obvious weapons. No clue.

Alan might have been disappointed at the whole lot of

nothing, except he hadn't expected anything else, and he assumed Drew and even Jantz weren't any more surprised.

Amy Kendall, alive or dead, was somewhere else.

He turned to Drew. "This took too long. We can't go back down until morning."

His friend looked disappointed but nodded his understanding, while Jantz said, "What the hell? We've got the whole day ahead of us! Maybe we can get some other divers."

Alan just looked at him. "Good luck with that. If I don't hear from you to the contrary, I'll see you all at the same time tomorrow morning."

Without waiting for a response, he walked over to pick up his tanks, light, flippers and weights. Out of the corner of his eye, he saw Ed was doing the same. Within minutes, both peeled off their black neoprene wetsuits, scrubbed wet hair with towels they'd brought, and pulled on jeans and sweatshirts. Neither spared so much as a glance toward Detective Jantz, who shared some intense words with Drew before stomping over to his official vehicle, getting in and taking off with a spurt of dirt and gravel.

Probably wanted to be the first to share what little they'd gleaned with the sheriff.

"I had a close call down there," Ed remarked as he finished tossing his gear into the back of his SUV and slammed the hatch. "Thanks for the quick warning."

"You're welcome."

The Arkansas detective opened the door and got in. "Let's hope tomorrow goes more smoothly."

"Amen. But hey, today could have been worse."

Ed grinned crookedly. Yeah, he could have been crushed. "You suppose Jantz will bother getting up early tomorrow morning?"

Alan glanced toward Drew, who was now talking to the tow truck operator. "I'm betting not."

"You and me both." Ed shut his door, fired up the engine and lifted a hand to Alan, who guessed he ought to exchange a few words with Drew before he took off, too.

He didn't like that he wished he had an excuse to see Jo today. What would she have said yesterday if he'd suggested meeting for lunch again instead of shutting her down the way he had?

Jo DIDN'T SEE much of her sister as the day went on. She assumed that was by chance; they both took turns as tour guide, barista, gift store clerk and just wandering, indoors and out, to answer questions. Business had accelerated this week, with most school districts out. Rod was in a good mood all day, so he must be happy with the take from tickets and sales.

Jo was somewhat distracted, too, thinking about the operation to raise the two cars from the bottom of the sinkhole. Was the job done? Had they found anything in either car? She didn't want to think about what would happen to a body immersed in water for close to a week, never mind one down there for several years. If the body was trapped in the trunk, at least there wouldn't be damage from fish or who knows what nibbling—

That was as far as she let herself get. She didn't *want* to know how a dead person decomposed in water or anywhere else.

She did want to know whether either victim had been found, though.

A little bit of uneasiness kept giving her moments of pause, too. Her talk with Lucy had gone well. Right? Lucy seemed relieved that Jo had verified Rod's insistence that there was nothing to be found in the area where the teen parties had been held. But…had Jo really convinced her sister? What was it Lucy said?

You think he imagined it, don't you?

Jo remembered what she'd said, too, suggesting the friend had been both drunk and spooked by the cave. Lucy hadn't exactly reacted, but she also hadn't said, "I'm sure you're right." Instead, she'd sounded troubled.

Except he wasn't that drunk. He was totally freaked out.

In retrospect, Jo realized that Lucy had been pushing back. Saying, *Jesse isn't like that.*

Yes, but Lucy had also admitted she had no desire herself to go wandering on her own off the beaten track in the cave. Hosting the party would have been different; she could be the knowledgeable one, the hostess who could offer something that would awe her friends. She wouldn't have been *alone.*

Midafternoon, Jo's own phone vibrated in her pocket, startling her. She was behind the cash register, but between customers, so she took it out. The number wasn't familiar, the area code one she didn't remember seeing before.

"Hello?" she said cautiously.

"Jo? This is Alan Burke."

She turned her head, seeing nobody within earshot and grateful for the momentary isolation. "Hi. Did everything go okay yesterday?"

"Yes, but we had to raise the second car this morning. No bodies," he said, as if reading her mind.

"Oh." Jo tried to think of something brilliant to say.

In that gritty voice, Alan said, "It's too late today, but… I wondered if you could get away to meet me for lunch tomorrow."

Warmth blossomed in her chest. "I…yes. I forgot to do an errand the other day, so I need to get into town anyway."

"Café again? Or do you have another suggestion?"

"I hardly ever eat out when I'm home, so no. The café is fine."

They agreed on a time, and he disconnected. It was probably just as well that she didn't have a chance to squeal like a teenage girl or start second-guessing her agreement given that her stay in the area—and, from what she'd heard, very likely his as well—was limited. A crowd descended on the cash register, everyone eager to express their amazement and ask questions and spend money.

By closing time, Jo was back to focusing on her sister. Lucy was quiet at dinner, but not in a sulky way. Brody insisted on pushing his idea for a "wild cave" tour while they were eating.

"Two guys asked me today." He ignored the scowl on his father's face. "They thought we'd get a lot of people who are interesting in caving but want to try it out in a completely safe environment."

"Who said it would be completely safe?"

"It would be if we made the run over and over until we're confident," Brody argued.

"I said no. I meant no."

Brody's mouth opened as he prepared to push, but his gaze intersected Jo's. His jaw snapped shut and after a moment he bent his head to his meal.

Nobody had much to say after that. Another fun Summerlin family dinner. Playing peacekeeper had never been Jo's ambition in life. She hated conflict…but of course she felt compelled to shield her siblings from their father's irritable stubbornness.

As Lucy rinsed plates and loaded the dishwasher, she said, "I wish Dad would go out. I can't even turn the TV on without him complaining it's too loud."

"He loans you his car, doesn't he, if you want to go hang out with friends?"

"I practically have to *beg*. And the last time I asked, he said, 'Remember what happened to Amy when *she* was driving around by herself.'"

Well, Rod did have a point, even if the way he treated Brody versus Jo and Lucy had always been noticeably different.

Lucy continued in a tone of discontent, "Anyway, Jaelin and Autumn are both working most evenings. Jaelin at the diner, and Autumn at Domino's Pizza. They're my two best friends."

That was particularly inconvenient. At Lucy's age, Jo had had a couple of friends who'd been lifesavers for her.

Wrinkling her nose as she scraped leftovers into a plastic bowl, she said, "I'd rather have your summer job than theirs."

"You *do* have the same summer job as me."

They both laughed.

"I can finish up if you want," Jo offered.

"Really? Thanks." Lucy vanished with haste that amused Jo, leaving her to wipe down counters and dry pans.

Oh, well. Brody had been doing his share. It wasn't as if Jo was eager to get to anything in particular.

She thought she heard Rod going out, but not the sound of a car engine, so Brody was probably still home. Once done, she debated turning on the TV herself—she could surely find something on the one streaming service Rod subscribed to—but decided she liked the quiet. She'd start a new book instead.

After closing the last cupboard, she headed for the stairs and started up just in time to see Rod walking down the hall up above. He wouldn't be going to bed yet, would he?

She was halfway upstairs when he opened his bedroom door. His bellow made her cringe.

"What the hell are you doing in my room, young lady?"

Oh, Lord—Jo had a bad feeling she knew exactly what Lucy was doing in her dad's bedroom.

When an all-out fight erupted, Jo hovered where she was, afraid she couldn't get to her own room unobserved but not wanting to be part of this, either. Lucy must have known the consequences if she got caught.

"I wouldn't have to sneak around if you didn't treat me like a baby—!" Lucy yelled.

"I can't trust you for a minute."

Rod was mad, and understandably so, Jo thought, cringing because *she* had committed the same sin just days ago. Still, Lucy hadn't exactly been demonstrating maturity lately, and he ought to be able to trust both his kids not to dig through his drawers and closet.

Jo crossed her fingers and prayed that her little sister didn't scream back that Jo had already found the hidden keys, so why didn't he go yell at her, too?

Maybe her having done that wasn't smart. Except she truly had believed Lucy needed some reassurance, and that Rod would have said no. Hell, no.

The yelling went on. Brody's door briefly opened then closed. Not blaming him for his cowardice, Jo tiptoed to her own bedroom and sneaked inside, apparently unseen. Not that she couldn't still hear every word, solid wood doors or not. Lucy did not, as far as she could tell, betray Jo. But when the shouting went on and on, Jo finally stuck her head out in the hall just in time to hear Rod yelling, "Two weeks restriction!"

Jo cut in before Lucy could open her mouth again. "Enough already."

Rod turned his glare on her. "Butt out."

She raised her eyebrows. "Who called whom for help?"

He ground his teeth before leveling a stare at Lucy, already quivering in outrage.

"Forget two weeks! You're on restriction until you leave for college! Do you hear me?"

All Jo had wanted was peace and quiet so she could read the fantasy novel she'd picked out. The murder mysteries she usually enjoyed didn't have the usual appeal, not after these past few days.

Lucy screamed something unintelligible and ran into her room, slamming her bedroom door so hard the framed picture hanging in Jo's bedroom shook and ended up crooked despite the solidity of the walls in this old house. Rod stomped down the stairs almost loud enough to shake the house some more.

Jo couldn't call the ensuing quiet any more peaceful than were her thoughts.

ALAN LURCHED TO a sitting position as he emerged from a familiar but newly twisted nightmare, his shout still ringing in the room. God damn. He gave his head a hard shake. What was that about? Was his subconscious trying to tell him that a SEAL teammate had betrayed him? No. No. He'd never believe that. But somewhere in his head, a voice whispered, *How can you be so sure? After losing hostages because his fellow police officers either didn't follow orders or were unwilling to risk getting shot themselves, how can you believe in the* absolute *integrity of* anyone?

Swearing under his breath as he dug his fingers into his sweaty hair, Alan argued with himself. He had trusted his SEAL teammates. That's why it was so hard to know he might never find that kind of tight relationship again.

Chapter Nine

Alan bent to slam his tailgate to secure his latest purchase
of a load of lumber, plumbing supplies and miscellany like
new electrical outlet boxes, nodded his thanks to the gawky
kid working for the lumberyard, then hopped down from
the loading dock. He hoped this was a summer job for a
boy in high school. Otherwise, his age radar must be seriously out of whack.

Shaking his head, he opened the door to jump in, but
cocked his head when he heard an angry shout. It was followed by others. Curiosity led him to the alley, where he
saw the small crowd partway down. Four men surrounding one, who was rotating slowly in place to keep an eye
on all his potential assailants.

Didn't look like a fair fight to Alan.

He jogged that way.

"You moved here just before Christy was snatched,"
one of the guys yelled. "We don't get that many new-
comers."

"I hadn't even heard the name until this week," protested the target.

Different voice. "*I* hear you asked her out. What happened, she say no?"

Oh, hell. Alan increased his pace to a run.

"What's going on here?" he asked as he reached the group.

All four spun to face him. His eyes briefly met those of the guy in the center, who appeared on edge but not in a panic. Good.

"None of your damn business," one of the would-be vigilantes snarled. "We just got things to say to Ryan here."

Ryan held himself tall, weight balanced on the balls of his feet, hands fisted. He wouldn't take what was coming lying down. And, damn it, Alan knew he'd seen him before. The picture formed in his head. Wearing a uniform. The youngest sheriff's department deputy, that's who he was.

Alan said calmly, "You have any real reason to think Deputy—" It came to him, because he'd known someone well with the same last name. "—Meehan ever knew Christy Dodswell?"

"He moved here not a month before she was grabbed," one of the bellicose twenty-something thugs snapped. "Gotta think what changed around here. And here it is. Meehan showed up."

"So you know everyone who moved into not only Mayville, but the surrounding counties? Victims have come from at least three counties, haven't they? Including Christy."

They all stared at him.

"What did you plan? To beat the snot out of Ryan because he happened to be new in these parts when the first victim we know of—" Alan leaned heavily on that part "—disappeared?"

"What d'ye mean, *know of*?"

"I suppose you've all heard my name."

A few sullen bobs of the head.

"Why should we believe you were a SEAL?" one of them asked with a belligerent tilt to his chin.

Alan let his eyebrows climb. "Don't care what you believe. What's important here is that I was a police detective in a good-sized city for several years. This investigation isn't mine, but I have the experience to tell you the chances are good there are more victims than have been named. How hard would it be to grab a young woman who was just passing through town, maybe got a flat tire?"

"There were only two cars," mumbled the bulky guy Alan had begun to see as the ringleader.

"There are a lot of bodies of water around here, you know."

He saw on their faces that they knew.

"Runaways, hitchhikers, young women everyone assumes took off on their own. The four victims we believe are linked? They're probably the tip of the iceberg."

The four thugs were visibly thinking. That was something.

Alan added softly, "You do realize how much trouble you'd be in if you laid a hand on Deputy Meehan, don't you? Assaulting a law enforcement officer is a serious crime."

"We got a right to get answers."

Yep. Ringleader.

"You think of going to the police station and asking to talk to the primary investigator? Or Deputy Frazier, who led the searches?"

Some feet shuffled. Two of the men were looking at the ground now.

"If you have information that would point this investigation at anyone in particular—" Alan let his gaze rest on the young deputy "—either Detective Jantz or Deputy Frazier would be glad to hear it." He let his voice harden.

"On the other hand, if all you have is a list of men in the area who might have moved here in a time range your limited knowledge tells you is suggestive, I'm thinking you'd be smart to go home and pretend this never happened."

Still in an ugly tone, the ringleader began, "We don't have to let—" Seeing that his compatriots were fleeing, he said, "We'll take this up another time."

"That had better be hot air," Alan called after him.

The jerk flipped him off behind his back.

Alan grunted.

Ryan Meehan, sweating only a little, grinned at him. "Thank you for your timely intervention."

Alan smiled and held out a hand. "Something tells me their plans wouldn't have gone well once they tried to take you on."

They shook. Meehan said, "Oh, they'd have made me sorry, but they would have been, too. I know them all. I've ticketed two of them and arrested a third one for assault in a brawl down at the Roundup."

"I'm not surprised. You on your way into work?"

Looking rueful, the young deputy said, "I dodged down the alley to avoid them. I was actually aiming for the lumberyard."

"Where I'm parked."

They walked the short distance together, continuing to talk. Meehan was relatively new in Mayville, but had grown up in Carthage, only a few counties away, so he wasn't exactly a stranger to these parts.

He grinned once more. "This job keeps me close enough I can get home for an occasional Sunday dinner, far enough away nobody in the family expects me to drop everything and run over when they need a handyman or hear a bump in the night."

Alan laughed, understanding on one level even though

he'd never experienced that kind of family. "You plan to report this?" he asked, opening his truck door again.

Meehan went grim. "Damn straight. I might not bother, except… I can't be the only newcomer in the right time frame."

"No." Alan waved away more thanks and hopped in to drive the three blocks to the café.

JO BEAT ALAN to the diner, which surprised her. She suspected he always liked to be there to set up, whatever the situation. She did ask for the booth in back again, although took the side facing the front door. When she saw him walk in a couple of minutes later and their eyes met, she slid out and into the side that meant her back was to the door. Then she drank in the intensity in his unwavering stare and the sight of his tall, powerful body.

"You didn't have to do that," he said, when he sat down.

"No?"

"But thank you. I like to see what's coming."

"Surely nothing that alarming when there's probably not a man in town who would have the nerve to come after you."

"Call it habit." He reached for the menu but didn't start perusing it. "Anyway, you're presupposing anyone who came after me has any brains."

Jo chuckled. "You're right. How silly of me."

He flashed the grin that altered his face so drastically, deepening lines between his nose and mouth, making his eyes glint.

"I just came from a little standoff," he told her. "A few of the local geniuses had decided a guy who moved to town just before Christy Dodswell disappeared had to be the killer. It was four to one."

Hiding a spurt of worry, Jo studied him anew. "You don't look as if you've so much as bruised your knuckles."

"Nope. I talked some sense into them, although God knows how long that'll stick." He smiled past her, even before she realized their waitress was approaching.

Both ordered. He never had glanced at the menu, which meant he'd eaten here more than the once when she'd seen him.

"That's your pickup loaded with lumber out there?" she asked, even though she knew it was. Who else had Virginia plates on a shiny black Ford F-150?

"Yeah, I'm going to tear down the detached garage and build a new one. Seems like a good time to do it. I'll need to have the trusses and what have you delivered, but I can start with the framing. At least around here I don't have to worry about rain."

"Bank says it's eighty degrees right now," she said. "You have more chance of getting burned to a crisp."

"Not me, but you would." He studied her. "I don't suppose you tan easily."

"Or at all." She wrinkled her nose. "I'm tempted to buy stock in a few suntan lotion companies."

That rusty laugh seemed to come more easily than it had the first time she'd heard it. And she was too pleased, given that there was no chance of starting anything with this man. In fact—their last two meetings had ended with him being a jerk.

She frowned. "So what's the deal with this? Are you planning to issue some bad news? A few warnings to mind my own business?"

His mouth tilted slightly. "Neither."

"Then…"

"I wanted to see you."

The few words spoken in a soft, gravelly voice hit her hard.

"I…"

He seemed to don a mask, in that way he had. "If I misled you, you don't have to stay."

That might be real indifference—but Jo didn't believe it. He was as attracted to her as she was to him, even though she couldn't imagine why.

A swallow unstuck her throat. "No. I wanted to see you, too."

Without any obvious movement, he relaxed in a way she couldn't miss. He nodded and said, "How's it going out there?"

Jo blinked. "Home? The cavern?"

"Both."

"Oh…home is tense. Did I tell you I'm here for the summer because of my teenage sister's rebellious behavior?" Well, of course she hadn't, although he seemed to know more about Brody than she'd expect.

"Someone mentioned you have both a sister and brother."

She made a face. "Lucy is sixteen and acting like she's thirteen. She and her dad are going at it, teeth and claws. I'm supposed to figure out why she's so worked up and fix her."

"*Her* dad?"

"My stepfather," she said uncomfortably. "I mostly call him by his name. Rod."

"You're not close?"

Their meals arrived, giving her a moment to realize she didn't know Alan Burke nearly well enough to be completely honest.

"Rod and I have an okay relationship," she said as she spread the napkin on her lap. "He's been good to me."

Alan hadn't moved, and his gaze seemed to see right through her surface explanation. "That sounds less than wholehearted."

"As Lucy would say, Rod is all about the cavern. He started me working in the gift shop when I was twelve, and I was giving tours not that much later. Growing up, I felt like an employee more than a daughter." Strange. She'd never acknowledged that to herself before. She shrugged carelessly, as much for her benefit as for his. "He's sexist besides. *Brody* will inherit the great Summerlin Cavern, not Lucy. That's always been clear."

Alan had started in on his burger, but now he paused. "And not Jo," he said slowly.

"That was never a question." She picked up her own sandwich. "I wouldn't want it, anyway. As Lucy and I agreed the other day, there are worse part-time and summer jobs, though."

Alan smiled, as she'd hoped, but he didn't let the subject of her sister drop. "Have you had any breakthroughs with Lucy yet?"

Jo laughed. "Anyone who can ever claim to have broken through with a teenager is either a certifiable miracle worker or delusional."

His chuckle was more of a rumble. If she was able to rest her hand on his chest, she would feel the vibration. And even the thought was enough to make her cheeks warm.

The corners of his eyes crinkled, letting her know he'd seen the direction of her thinking, but all he said was, "What about Brody? How does he feel about being the anointed heir?"

"He's all about the cavern, too. I talked him into going away to college, but he just let me know he thinks it was a waste of his time. Since his future is running the family business, he can learn more here than he can in any classroom."

"Where'd he go?"

She stiffened but told him.

"Springfield." Alan sounded thoughtful. "Not so far from home."

"Why are you so determined to suspect him?"

He wiped his fingers on the napkin and reached for a fry. "I'm not. I don't know him, but I think he's too young."

Relief filled her. "Of course he is. But you implied—"

"That Detective Jantz might want to talk to him? He probably will, if only because Brody knew the most recent victim well. If he has no ties to any of the other missing women—"

"I'm sure he doesn't." Okay, that had sounded too hasty. "He sticks close to home," she added.

"It's not that far a drive between the homes of any of the missing women," Alan pointed out.

"No, but—" But what? She shut her mouth, then opened it again. "Why are we talking about *my* family?"

"Because I don't have one."

"You told me that. I'm sorry. I'm…just being prickly."

That keen gaze made her feel as impenetrable as tissue paper. "Protective," he corrected her, sounding gentle. "I like that in a woman."

Oh, she understood that, more than she'd admit to anyone. Her mother had cast her off without a second thought. Alan's mother couldn't have been any prize, but at least she'd cared enough to remove him from his abusive home. No wonder he'd rank that quality high on his list.

Jo nodded, and they ate in silence for a few minutes.

When that began to feel awkward, she asked, "Are you planning to stay around here?"

He didn't jump to answer, but finally said, "I don't think so."

Jo eyed him. "Not so sure?"

His mouth twisted. "In the short term, my goal is to get the house and property in shape to sell. And no, probably not to your stepfather. His pressure has begun to irritate me. Beyond that... I don't know."

She wanted to ask what had happened to leave him at such loose ends, but knew that was getting too personal. Two casual lunches did not add up to a deep relationship. Maybe part of the attraction on both their sides was the fact that they were outsiders even if they had roots here in southern Missouri. Were his feelings as disturbed as hers?

An idea struck her that she hated, but it was a good one. She could settle at least part of her recent uneasiness.

"I was thinking," she said.

He leaned back in the booth and waited. Jo bet he was good at interrogation, patient enough to outwait just about anyone.

"This sounds weird, but part of Rod and my sister's recent dispute is because he's refusing to let her or Brody back in any of the cavern offshoots. The two passages off the tourist route are gated and locked."

Alan nodded, his eyes not leaving her face. "Wouldn't want those tourists wandering away."

"No. There was a time we all did a little exploring, usually with Rod. I think what happened was that Brody and Lucy both violated his trust this year by having parties for their friends back in a room in a closed-off passage."

"That would do it."

"Yes, but—" Tell him, or not? He had been a cop, and she didn't want to awaken those instincts. Still, she remembered the day she'd slipped through that gate and wished he was with her. Jo took a deep breath. "One of my sister's friends wandered away from the group and swears he saw a human skull."

"What?"

"You heard me. This wasn't that long ago. Like a month? Anyway, Rod was mad at Lucy and Brody both once he found out about the parties, but I think he actually hoped *he'd* find the skull, too. A mystery would go over well with tourists. That's if the skull really exists, I mean."

Oh, she had Alan's attention now, and wasn't sure she hadn't made a big mistake.

"Rod went back to try to find it, even though he was sure the friend was drunk and imagining things."

"That does seem the likeliest explanation," Alan commented. "Is your stepfather the only one who has looked?"

"No, he took a deputy with him, mostly to reassure Lucy, I think. Deputy Hudson, the one who led one group of searchers."

Alan nodded.

"Of course they didn't find a thing. After that, Rod started hiding the keys so Brody and Lucy couldn't get back in there at all." She hesitated, but once again Alan waited her out. "Lucy was still so upset about it, claiming her friend wasn't that drunk and was really freaked by what he'd seen, that I...well, I found the keys and went looking, too."

"Good God."

To her astonishment, he reached across the table and closed his big warm hand around her much smaller one, probably because she'd been fidgeting.

"I couldn't find anything, either, but I had a tight window for my search. I sneaked in while a tour was going on." She took a deep breath. "Last night, Rod caught Lucy in his bedroom trying to find those blasted keys. He threw a fit."

"Did you rush to the rescue?" Was that a flicker of humor in his eyes?

She wrinkled her nose. "I hid in my bedroom. I think Brody did, too."

Alan chuckled again. "Smart."

"Yes, but—I realized there's a way I could get back in and take my time searching. Just to be sure."

"Why aren't you sure?" The question was so sharp, it felt like a knife slipping between her ribs.

The question scared her because she didn't like the real answer: How could it be coincidental that a human skull had been found during the same time span as a serial killer abducted women so nearby?

What she *said* was, "Because Rusty—our dog, remember?—was apparently with that boy when he claims to have seen the skull. He wandered away from the group because he heard Rusty barking and wondered why. So it's possible…"

"That the dog carried the skull away." Alan was thinking.

"Yes."

"So what's your great plan?"

She squared her shoulders and tipped up her chin. "I want your permission to enter the cavern from your property."

"You want to blunder in, try to navigate through a maze that covers as much as a couple of miles, in search of what might be a drunken kid's imaginary skull."

"I don't blunder," she said stiffly. "I do have experience, you know."

"You could have been knocked out the other day. My answer is no." He let go of her hand and lifted his to signal the waitress. "Are you finished?"

"You're being unreasonable… But yes. I lost my appetite."

"You're willing to take a substantial risk in an attempt to appease a teenager who might have let her imagination get the best of her." Any hint of warmth or understanding had evaporated. All she saw was the impassive man she'd first met. "No."

He took the bill from the waitress Jo had once again failed to hear approaching, scanned it and pulled out his wallet.

He tossed some cash down and slid out of the booth, waiting while she did the same.

"Why won't—"

"Drop it." Out on the sidewalk, he gave a last curt nod and walked away, leaving her steaming behind him, but also failing to understand why he was both adamant and mad.

Chapter Ten

Alan thumped his forehead against the steering wheel in his truck. He'd screwed that one up, hadn't he? Usually, he was pretty good at talking people out of bad ideas—like, say, beating a sheriff's deputy.

After a minute, he pulled himself together enough to start the truck and pulled out onto the main street in town.

Not until, fifteen minutes later, he had turned into his own rough driveway did he identify the reason Jo's request was a trip wire for him. He'd believed she'd agreed to have lunch with him to get to know him. Because she felt this same, powerful draw. Had she thought she had to soften him up before she asked? Finding out she'd accepted his invitation because she wanted something from him, that offended him.

No, that hurt his feelings. So of course he'd lashed out at her, in his ice-cold version of a temper.

He backed up to his garage to make unloading easier, set the brake and turned off the engine, but continued to sit there, staring at the woods that climbed the slope. He'd barely known he *had* feelings that could be hurt, it had been so long since he had even tiptoed close to loving any one person. He might have been sensitized by learning that the people in his former police department he'd come to trust so readily let down the citizens they were hired to protect. Sure, it had been only a few officers, but the unnecessary deaths of innocents rankled until he found himself doubting anyone he was partnered with. The after-the-fact excuses told him those particular officers would be no more reliable on the next high-risk operation, because they were unwilling to accept responsibility and learn from mistakes.

Hell, maybe he'd just been naive, in a way. As a SEAL, he had never once questioned whether he could depend on his teammates or officers. A man got spoiled. In signing on with a police department, he'd thought he would find the same sense of honor and camaraderie.

Truth was, he'd been feeling unrooted ever since he walked away from the Richmond PD. Had he latched onto this attraction to Jo Summerlin out of sheer loneliness?

Maybe.

Irritated at himself, he hopped out and started unloading. As he dropped a bag of nails onto the concrete floor of the garage, a faint smile touched his mouth. He could be wrong about Jo's reasons for having lunch with him, but he felt very sure that he hadn't heard the last of her determination to burrow into the earth from his property. If that wasn't a mulish woman, he'd never met one.

Pausing in the act of heaving a pile of two-by-fours to his shoulder, he wondered if she *would* bother asking again. After all, she'd tell herself, what was he going to do? Have her thrown into jail if he found out after the fact that she'd sneaked into the cavern opening despite his refusal?

If he were being pushed the same way, wasn't shrugging and going ahead despite obstacles exactly what he'd do?

This smile was crooked.

It died slowly when he started to wonder exactly why she was so determined. She was afraid for someone in her family—or was she afraid of what one of them might have done?

And why would that have even crossed her mind?

Jo CROUCHED AT the edge of the woods, dismayed at how much open ground lay between her and the much smaller half-moon opening to the cavern that she remembered from the time Rod had brought her and Brody to explore, back after Alan's father had died and the property was deserted. It appeared Alan had cleared a large swath of land that had been overgrown then. What was left was too stubbly to qualify as lawn, but he'd certainly be able to see anyone crossing his property if he happened to be looking.

This early in the morning, it appeared he hadn't yet come out to start work on the garage. He'd already knocked down part of the original structure, but still had a way to go before he could build anew on the concrete pad. His pickup was parked in front of the half-destroyed garage; a pile of lumber lay to one side. She didn't see any movement behind the windows in the house. He wouldn't still be asleep, would he? If only she could be that lucky.

She hesitated and did some more reconnoitering. She could skirt around a stretch of the open land while staying in the cover of the woods, but not very far. Since the cavern entrance was on the opposite side of Alan's house from the garage, if he did happen to pop out to start work, the house might hide her during her quick dash.

Unless she was going to turn around and go back, she had zero choice—and she didn't want to do that. The tension in the Summerlin house last evening had been awful. Lucy had come down to dinner, but her eyes had barely been visible behind red swelling. Jo didn't consider her chastened, though; if the set of a mouth could be considered mutinous, Lucy's was. Hardly anyone said a word.

Rod glowered, snarled and shoveled in his food. Brody kept his head down and did likewise. Lucy stirred the food around on her plate. Jo had picked at hers.

After dinner, Brody had cornered her in the kitchen. "Just so you know," he said in a low voice after a cautious glance toward the living room, "Dad caught Lucy in his truck, digging in the glove compartment and under the seats."

Jo had moaned. "Did she find the keys?"

"I don't think so, but… What is she *thinking*?"

Jo truly didn't know. There had to be more to this than teenage resentment because her own father didn't believe her. Jo worried at being in the dark about her sister's real fear.

Now, stumbling over a broken branch, Jo grimaced because that might be a lie. *She* wasn't going to all this effort to prove that there was a two-hundred-year-old skeleton tucked back there somewhere in the Summerlin Cavern. If that was true, Rod would have found it. He had every motivation in the world.

What she couldn't get away from was the timing of all this. The juxtaposition of Lucy's friend finding something like that and the disappearance of all those women. Jo didn't want to believe there was any connection between those murders and her family…but a sense of creeping uneasiness stayed with her. The horrible thing was, if a killer was using the cavern, there were only a few possible suspects: Brody; Austin, who constantly hit on women and maybe didn't accept a no as well as she'd thought he did; and Rod, who looked on women with disrespect, possibly including his own daughter and his stepdaughter.

Rod, who returned to the cavern nearly every evening and stayed for hours.

How could anyone else have secretly slipped into the cavern for years?

She could forget all about this awful suspicion if only she could successfully sneak in by this back route, navigate her way to recognizable passages, and be absolutely sure nothing as nasty as she was imagining could have taken place there. Right this minute, she kicked herself for not extending her search the day she'd gone looking. People would have wondered at her absence, but she could have lingered through the cycle until another tour had just set out.

Anyone could have been using this end of the cave to stash victims all these years, given that the property had been deserted. Alan's father had used it to hide his meth lab, from what she'd heard. Other criminals had taken advantage of the state's extensive cave system over the years. But if that were the case...how could a skull have showed up so far away from this opening? What had upset Rusty so much the night Amy disappeared?

Jo moaned. Her mind had been spinning in circles all night. A headache was only one result.

She stopped, clutching a leafy branch in front of her while she scanned again for any movement, then took a deep breath and sidled into the open. When nothing happened, she broke into a run, her small pack bouncing on her back.

Jo went all out. She was fast if she didn't have to run too far. No shout interrupted her race for the dark maw of the cave. Her breath came hard. Almost there. Almost there. Only yards from her goal...

A man stooped to avoid hitting his head and stepped out of the cave opening right in front of her, planted his feet and crossed his arms.

Alan had been waiting for her. His expression was implacable.

Furious and embarrassed, Jo came to a stop.

"How did you know?" were the first words out of her mouth.

Alan couldn't decide if he was most annoyed or gratified that he'd read her right.

"Wasn't hard to tell no wasn't the answer you wanted," he said.

Puffing from the all-out dash, she glared at him. "Why would you care if I do this? I've been through all the way to our end before."

He didn't move. "And how long ago was that?"

"It was…" She opened and closed her mouth a few times. "Ten—no, maybe eleven or twelve years ago?"

Alan shook his head. "You did it by yourself?"

Her cheeks were already red, but he thought she also blushed. "No. Rod and Brody and I did."

"Your father wasn't setting a very good example for you, was he?"

"Stepfather," Jo said sharply.

She really didn't want to own Rod Summerlin, Alan noted. More had to be going on there than she'd let him see.

"This is a bad idea," he told her. "What kind of equipment did you bring?"

Chin jutted, she said, "A helmet. A couple of lights. Pads to protect my knees and arms. Water, snacks. Markers."

"A rope?"

"No, we're on the same level."

He shook his head. "Last time, you trailed behind an expert. Today, you're inadequately equipped for anything to go wrong. Did you even tell a soul what you had in mind, in case you got lost or injured?"

She glared at him.

"Didn't think so. Would you recommend anyone else head in there alone? Without having left word of where they were going?" He jerked his head toward the dark, cool opening behind him.

Did she sag? "You know I wouldn't," she mumbled.

He discovered that he hated the look of near desperation in Jo's eyes. This was no mere impulse, he realized. And yeah, she'd volunteered to accompany him into that cave they'd found during their search, but he hadn't seen any indication that she was exhilarated by the potential challenge. Excitement was the last thing she was feeling now. She thought she *had* to do this.

"Jo, you need to tell me what this is about."

"I did! Lucy's friend found—"

Alan shook his head. "There's more to it." If he sounded harsh, he couldn't help himself. Whatever this was had to connect to those missing women. He couldn't think of anything else that would explain her anxiety. Especially given that Jo's family had the best access to the cavern.

Except maybe for any long-term employees, he amended. He needed to look into that.

She still had her lips pressed together, and he still hated the darkness in her eyes.

He couldn't stop himself from taking a step closer to her and lightly squeezing her upper arms. "You're scared," he said, gentle now. "Why?"

"Why should I tell you?"

Alan hadn't even realized he'd made the decision, but he answered right away. "Because if you do and I agree that this needs doing, I'll consider going with you."

Hope filled her eyes along with a sheen of tears.

"Damn it," he growled, and kissed her.

Shocked at himself, he started to lift his head. But Jo had made a tiny whimpering sound and pushed up on her toes to resume the kiss. He nipped her lower lip sharply and took advantage of her gasp to slide his tongue into her mouth.

God, she tasted good. When he pulled her up tight to his body, she felt even better—slim, supple, feminine. Her fingers bit into his neck as she held on and kissed him back. His thinking blurred and he might have surrendered to the sheer pleasure if his arm wrapping her hadn't bumped into the backpack.

He groaned and tore his mouth away from hers. Voice rough, he asked, "Are you trying to sway me into letting you go ahead?"

She stared at him dazedly, as if it took her a few seconds to parse his words. Then she whispered, "Can I?"

His hands tightened on her. "Probably."

She breathed out an "o-oh." The sound was almost as sexy as her earlier whimper.

"Damn." Alan made himself release her. "You need to be honest with me."

Deep reluctance showed on her fine-boned face, but then she took a deep breath. "I...it's just that I'm probably crazy even to be thinking what I have been. It's nothing but little things added up. Nothing solid."

"I can guess some of it." He backed up enough to keep himself from touching her again. He didn't like thinking that she'd responded to his kiss with such passion for exactly the reason he'd suspected. "Is this an emergency?"

"No! I mean, not that I know. It's one more place to look, that's all."

Hadn't it occurred to her that the man who had been abducting these women might not be killing them right away? That he might hold them for awhile to enjoy them? That Amy Kendall might still be alive?

He almost shook his head. What were the odds of that? She'd disappeared—what?—nine or ten days ago? From the perspective of the killer, it was bad enough that the cops and general public hadn't bought the "she must have taken off on her own" explanation, that they'd mounted searches. Even if she'd still been alive, the news that her car had been found had probably signed her death warrant. That had to have shaken the killer.

And really, the idea that victims had been held in the Summerlin Cavern, one of the state of Missouri's best-known show caves, one toured by hundreds of people every single day at this time of year, many thousands a year, stretched credulity. He wanted to know why Jo thought it was a realistic possibility.

"Talk to me," he said.

A spark of defiance resurfaced. "If you decide I am out of my mind, are you going to keep saying no?"

Deciding, Alan shook his head. "You need to do this. We'll do it together, but not until tomorrow morning. I need time to put together the equipment we should carry, and Drew Frazier and a couple of his friends are due here in about an hour to help me finish taking down the garage and starting to frame the new building."

She nodded and they walked back to his house. No, she didn't want a drink, so they sat on the porch steps in the sunlight that hadn't yet become blistering, and she talked.

Jo KNEW SHE really hadn't used her head. Thank goodness Alan had stopped her! If nothing else, taking off without giving Rod a chance to find a substitute for her had been a crummy thing to do.

Plus, instead of telling anyone where she was going, she'd relied on Alan guessing what she'd done if he heard she was missing. Not smart. What if he'd taken off somewhere for a few days? Worked on his place and didn't hear for ages that she was missing?

Jo had never thought of herself as reckless, but that's what her plan had been.

As it was, Alan had walked her back to her car, stashed in a leafy turnout half a mile toward town from his driveway. After giving it a sardonic look, he'd bent his head and kissed her, quick and hard, before saying, "Make it as early as you can slip away."

Thanks to him, to his promise to accompany her on her quixotic quest, not to mention his kisses, enough of her tension had diminished to leave her feeling she could act normal for the rest of the day.

Despite that kiss, she couldn't help wondering if she'd damaged whatever was developing between them by her defiance of his direct refusal to let her access the cavern from his property. Or was the second kiss meant as reassurance? Jo couldn't tell. She did know he'd already been mad because she'd asked his permission when they met for lunch, although she had no idea why and hadn't wanted to ask.

She wouldn't tell him how hazy her memory was of how she, Rod and Brody had made it from the Burke end of the cave to the familiar passages on Summerlin land. She did remember dark, yawning alternative tunnels and cracks that might lead who knew where. Rod had seemed certain of the route, which in retrospect made her realize he'd taken it before. Maybe from the other end? Possibly repeatedly over the years. His frustration at not owning the whole thing had never dropped below a simmer, that was for sure, which made no sense to her. It had to be ego, because Rod already owned additional sections of the cavern that were show quality, if he wanted to expand.

Once Jo parked at the house, leaving her backpack in the trunk, she ran to the cavern and found Rod organizing a group of tourists. He stepped aside and snapped, "Where the hell have you been?"

"I'm so sorry. A good friend from college called. She's—her fiancé was killed in a car accident yesterday. I was going to let you know I needed a couple of days to attend their wedding in July."

Rod's expression changed. He was buying this, which induced an attack of guilt. He *had* been good to her. These suspicions made her feel like a horrible human being.

Even so, she had to do this. She *had* to.

"She lives in Kansas City," Jo hurried on. "I promised I'd drive up there tomorrow, and…well, probably spend the night. Can you find someone to fill in for me? I'll leave first thing in the morning, and if she seems all right, come home as soon as possible."

"Yeah, I can do that."

It had to be her guilt at lying that made her think he was studying her with more care than usual.

"Tomorrow shouldn't be one of our busiest days," she offered.

Tuesdays were typically the slowest of the week.

"Yeah, yeah. You're here now. Can you take this group?" He jerked his head toward the cluster of people.

She forced a smile. "You bet."

In his usual way, he walked away without another word.

She made it through the rest of the day without anyone appearing to suspect that she was hiding any turmoil. At a slow moment, Austin and she talked for longer than usual, him actually asking what the deal was with Lucy and Rod.

Surprised he'd noticed, Jo made a face. "They've gone to war. That's really why I came home for the summer, you know. To step in as peacekeeper."

"Did something happen?" he asked, his puzzlement appearing genuine.

"Between them? If something incited all this, neither has told me," Jo lied. "You're always around. Haven't things been tense for a while?"

He wouldn't like knowing how his frown deepened wrinkles, adding years to his usually boyish face. "Not so's I noticed, but when she's in school, we don't see that much of her. You know."

"Weekends..."

He shrugged. "I don't pay that much attention. It's just lately—"

Yes, indeed. Who wouldn't notice Lucy's incinerating glares every time her and her father's paths crossed?

Of course, at the end of the day, Austin threw out a hopeful, "I don't suppose you'd like to get away from your family for a few hours?"

He took her polite refusal well. She thought.

Lucy refused to come down to dinner. The two men ate with their usual single-minded dedication. Jo wondered if she herself was losing weight, as little interest as she'd had lately in her meals. Without sharing his destination, Brody took off immediately in his noisy truck. What were the odds Lucy would bound down the stairs to cheerfully help clean the kitchen? Rod growled, "I have to get some work done," and went out the front door.

Jo felt as if she ought to check on Lucy, but her own stress level was plenty high without her sister dumping any more on her. A couple of hours later, voices drifted to her, making her aware that Lucy and Rod were going at it again, but since they were downstairs, she couldn't make out what they were actually saying.

Feet stamped up the stairs. Eventually, Jo heard Brody on his way up at what her bleary eyes told her was almost two in the morning. Rod wouldn't be happy if Brody was hungover tomorrow.

She'd set her phone alarm for 5:00 a.m. The house was quiet when she dressed wearing several layers and grabbed her toiletries from the bathroom to support her pretense of a trip to Kansas City.

All three other bedroom doors were firmly closed. Ugh—she ought to peek in at Lucy before she left. Yet more guilt, because she really should have tried to talk to her last night?

Rather than knocking and waking everyone up, she eased the door open and quietly stepped in. Enough dawn light penetrated the blinds to allow her to see that her sister's bed was empty. Not just empty—clearly un-slept in.

Oh, God. Had this latest fight been the last straw? Had Lucy taken off once everyone else had gone to bed? And... had she taken her dad's truck?

Jo sighed, knowing how furious that would make him. Better to hope Lucy had called a friend to come out and get her. Figuring out where she'd gone would have to wait until tonight. Jo had met several of Lucy's friends now, but probably not all. She didn't know most of their last names, and without Lucy's phone, didn't have num-bers where she could contact them. Anyway, it wasn't as if she wanted to wake Rod and say, "Oh, by the way, your daughter took off last night without telling anyone, but she's okay and will be home when she feels like it."

She'd just hope Lucy came home or called her dad this morning. Jo did take a moment to text her sister, hoping for a response before she and Alan plunged into the cav-ern and lost phone reception. She'd be happier to know where Lucy was.

Slipping out into the hall, she gently closed her sister's

bedroom door to put off for as long as possible Rod noticing her absence.

Then she tiptoed down the stairs to make her own getaway.

With the garage at Alan's place only a skeleton, Jo had no place to park her car where it wouldn't be seen by anyone coming up the driveway.

He'd emerged from the house and was waiting when she got out. "Something wrong?" he asked.

He had managed to look even more daunting than usual this morning, which was saying something. She hadn't expected him to be wearing a one-piece coverall of thin but tough nylon. He'd obviously done enough caving to have the kind of clothing that stood up best to conditions. Well-worn boots with impressive tread. She guessed he'd held on to his equipment from his days as a SEAL. Then, if he'd gone into a cave, he'd have wanted to pass unseen—thus the black coverall and black Wellington boots.

Jo wished she was anywhere near as well equipped. No wonder he'd looked askance at her yesterday.

Remembering his question, she said, "Oh, I was wishing my car was out of sight, but that's silly. There's no reason anyone would come looking for me here."

"Where do they think you went?"

She told him her cover story, and Alan nodded without comment. He looked…not grim, exactly, but purposeful. Without asking, he took her pack from her and rooted through it, then eyed her boots.

"We'll likely be doing some wading. I went to town yesterday and picked up a shell layer that should fit you. We can tape it over your boots to keep you mostly dry." He nodded at her feet. "Don't suppose you have neoprene booties under there?"

Chagrined, she said, "A couple of layers of wool socks. I don't remember having to get wet when we made this trip."

"What time of year was that?"

She tried to recall, but had no idea.

"Probably fall. Right now, we'll be wading some streams. Your socks should be fine, as long as we get boots and pants sealed. At least you brought an extra pair of socks."

Gee, she'd done something right. But she kept her mouth shut, because she was realizing what deep trouble she'd have been in if she had succeeded in setting out on her own yesterday.

She followed Alan to the house. The front porch, including roof, was obviously new, but the interior remained shabby. It looked like he was essentially camping in here, not trying to make the place homey.

She accepted the oversuit from him—yellow, probably all he could find—and said, "I'll pay you back for this."

He grunted. "Go put it on."

Both of them put on their helmets and strapped on knee pads before they left the porch. Her helmet was an old-time, battered one, probably manufactured for a miner, which didn't mean it wasn't perfectly fine. His, of course, she recognized as an ultralight one with a fancy lighting system. Way to make her feel inadequate, she thought wryly.

Ten minutes later, he led the way to the cave opening. Jo rustled in the extremely unflattering, loose-fitting suit she'd managed to get on over her jeans and layered shirts.

Not that it mattered what she looked like, she lectured herself. A fleecy balaclava now circled her neck, uncomfortably warm given the time of year, but she knew it would help her maintain her body temperature once they were deep in the cavern, especially if she got wet. She'd be grateful to be able to pull it up.

She eyed the pack Alan had hefted so effortlessly and wondered what he was carrying. Getting the pack through any narrow places would be more of a squeeze than easing his big body through. The one obvious addition was a coil of rope and some carabiners hanging on the outside. Jo knew they'd stayed on one level during that long-ago adventure, but Alan was prepared if they couldn't for some reason, which was both alarming and reassuring.

He stopped in the opening and assessed her one more time. "You set?"

She nodded, striving for confidence. "Let's do it."

What she was really thinking was a fatalistic, *Let's get this over with.*

ALAN HAD VENTURED into the cavern only once since returning to Missouri a few months back. Then he hadn't had to go far, and had had a specific purpose. Today, he didn't need to hesitate when the passage split fifteen minutes or so on their way. Deciding he'd rubbed in his point well enough, he refrained from stopping and asking, *So, which way?* He respected Jo's determination and didn't want to embarrass her.

He gestured for her to walk ahead, mostly so he could more easily keep an eye on her. Their previous experience had given him some faith in her ability to make smart decisions rather than foolish mistakes, but call him a skeptic: this was a more challenging trip, and he intended to lead when the going got tougher.

If they'd been doing this for fun, he would have taken her the other way, where eventually the remnants of a number of different enterprises could be seen. If he stayed around here long enough, he might clean it up; none of it was picturesque, just gave a sense of local history. Someone had tried some mining in here, God knows what for, and left wooden shoring, oil cans, even blasting cord. At a small pool, what had probably been a summer house for keeping food cool still stood. And last but most offensive was equipment left from his father's manufacturing of methamphetamine. Cleaning that junk out had been the first task he'd set himself after moving into the house. He'd been relieved not to find any actual meth, although this was a big cavern with a lot of nooks and crannies, and plenty could be hiding from him. Still, he thought it likely that other people, including some of his dad's customers, had gone exploring in here after finding out about his death. If there'd been any product left, Alan believed it was long gone.

Initially the way he and Jo needed to take was open, the roof slanting down here and there but typically remaining high enough he didn't have to bend his head. Walls, ceiling and floor were rough. More debris was strewn on the floor than he recalled, but no more than you'd expect from natural changes. Caves were living, breathing entities in a way most people didn't understand. Change was slow and subtle, one drip of water at a time, but never-ending. Cave-ins, or the fall of a large stalactite to shatter below, happened, but given the miles of passages in this cavern alone, were a tiny part of the ongoing story.

He could have moved faster than Jo went, but liked that she stepped carefully. He didn't see her trip once in the first forty-five minutes or so. She stopped only one time, when the ceiling rose high above and the walls opened into

a vast space bigger than any in the Summerlin Cavern that
he'd seen. Drapery formations along one wall added to the
drama. Jo let the beam of her light play across the spectacular folds that might have been heavy stage curtains
hung from the ceiling. They shone a deep gold in the light.

"I remember this." It was the first thing she'd said since
they set out. "Rod talked about what he could do with it."
Wryness in her voice, she added, "It was going to waste,
he said."

"Yeah? What would he do with it? Hold parties?"

Without turning his helmet light directly onto her face,
he couldn't be sure of her expression, but thought she grimaced.

"Probably hoard it," she mumbled. "Am I right in thinking we go that way?" She pointed.

Impressed, Alan inclined his head. She was right on,
maybe a better navigator than he would have guessed.

Twenty minutes or so later, the narrowed passage
opened again, this time into a space where there was no
pretense of a flat floor. Limestone had worn smooth into
slopes tilting this way and that. Fortunately, the one they
had to ascend wasn't difficult to scramble up. From here,
magnificent stalactites and stalagmites, some joined in
vast columns, created the illusion of an ancient ruin carved
out of the native rock like Petra in Jordan. Even the color
wasn't dissimilar, although the sandstone in that part of
the world was nearly a true rose color, while much of the
cavern varied from pale gold to a vivid orange. Once, he'd
been able to visit Petra when he'd been in that part of the
world. Even then, he'd made mental comparisons with
Missouri's magnificent underworld.

From here, a caver could have chosen any of eight or
ten exits, although Alan knew from experience that some
were dead ends. They varied from a crack like an ice cre-

vasse to a large arched opening that could be reached only by rock climbing. Alan led Jo to a giant rift between slanting rock walls that in places had a walkable floor; other brief stretches required they use the technique of a rock climber maneuvering up a chimney, but here they inched along sideways. He had to take his pack off his back for the first time. He attached it to his belt with a stretchy cord and hauled it along behind him like an ungainly overweight pet.

When the crack was at its narrowest, he saw deep unhappiness on Jo's face. Not fear, exactly, but she wasn't having a good time. She was plenty strong enough to move confidently, bracing herself between the wall behind her and the wall in front of her, but he suspected she wouldn't have chosen to go on if she hadn't known the way soon opened into a more conventional cave passage.

"Ugh," she mumbled, when she dropped out of the rift next to him. Her knees momentarily buckled, and he put a hand around her elbow.

"You okay?"

"Sure," she said sturdily.

"Let's take a break," he suggested. "I could use a drink." Maybe, he realized, because for the first time he *heard* running water.

He found a place to sit where he could rest his back against a rock. Jo settled right beside him.

Both rummaged in their packs and came up with water bottles. He took out a packet of almonds, too, and offered some to her. Then he said, "Let's save on our lights," and turned his off. A moment later, she did the same. He blinked momentarily against afterimages, before he was left to stare blindly at the complete darkness.

Something skittered off to his right. Jo jumped.

"Probably a salamander," he said. "I saw one earlier."

She let out an audible breath. "I really don't mind the darkness. It just…"

"Triggers something primal in us," he suggested. "Hear that? It's probably a small waterfall."

"Oh! I hadn't noticed."

He liked her voice. He'd long since become aware of how much voices revealed in the absence of other sensory input. Hers was midrange, imbued with warmth that made him feel as if he'd just spread his hands over a campfire, stroked a purring cat, been wrapped in a woman's arms.

Where she was concerned, her arms wrapped tightly around him sounded good.

Some crunching ensued. After a minute, he asked, "Did you see any of your family this morning before you left?"

"I…no."

Alan zeroed in on that tiny break. The feeling something besides where to park had bothered her earlier.

"What?" he asked, then reached for her hand so he could pour some more almonds into her palm.

"Thanks." She went quiet for a minute. "My sister wasn't in her bed this morning. She either ran away or— No, probably just took off to spend the night with a friend. Rod will be mad, although I may be wrong in thinking she didn't tell him last night."

"She still determined to get back in the cavern?"

"More than ever." Worry vibrated in Jo's voice. "Brody says she looked for the keys in Rod's truck yesterday. Of course, he caught her. She doesn't have the making of a successful undercover agent."

No, the kid didn't, which worried him, too. Lucy's dramatics and blundering around wouldn't amount to much if Alan and Jo's foray today turned into a wild goose chase. But if there was anything real to Lucy's fears—and Jo's— that was another story. The girl could be endangering herself in a way she was too young—and too trusting of her family—to foresee.

His silence hadn't soothed Jo, who said suddenly, "Do you think she's all right?"

"You know she's most likely at a friend's, receiving the sympathy nobody gives her at home."

"*I* give her sympathy."

He didn't hear the indignant sniff, but one was there, and it made him smile, even though... Alan frowned. This expedition wasn't all for Jo's sake anymore. He'd developed his own case of disquiet. An itch—and he'd learned over the years to pay attention to those.

"Ready to move on?" he asked abruptly.

"Of course."

Jo HOPED ALAN couldn't tell how much she hated the one truly tight "choke" they had to get through, a crack narrow enough she had to squirm, shifting one shoulder at a time, releasing all her air at the critical moment, feeling her breasts getting squished and scraped. She didn't remember it being anywhere near this bad, but of course she'd been a lot younger. Slight. She hadn't developed much until she was...oh, fourteen or fifteen, and then slowly.

How Alan would get through, given his greater size, she couldn't imagine. Once she was safely on the other side, he shoved her pack through, then opened his own and handed bulkier items through one at a time. The coil of rope came on its own, as did something squishy that she identified as a sleeping bag. Apparently he believed in taking all the precautions. Then the pack, which he was able to flatten now with only the smaller items still in it. Finally, she all but held her breath as he wedged himself into a space where a large man with his muscle mass couldn't possibly fit.

Somehow he did, easing inch by inch with a grace that told her he'd had plenty of practice in similar tight spots.

Once he was through, he shook himself. "That was easier when I was a kid."

Jo made a face. "I was thinking the same thing."

"I don't suppose you brought a key to the gate, so once we get there we can just let ourselves out instead of taking this trip in reverse."

"Don't I wish."

She sighed, pushed her arms through the straps of her pack and waited until Alan had repacked his and swung it to his back. Then they started out again, Alan having to stoop a little, her able to walk upright.

"Do you know how much longer this will take?" she asked after a minute. Why hadn't she asked him at the beginning?

He must be pondering, because he took his time before saying, "I'm guessing a couple more hours."

Oh, boy. Jo wished she'd brought more food. Seeing the big pack in front of her, though, she suspected Alan had plenty for both of them.

"Do you have a deadline?" he asked.

"No."

He was right about the wading. The next short waterfall they encountered tumbled into a stream that filled the entire passage. It wasn't deep, she saw, when he stepped into it with confidence, but the water was shin deep on him, almost knee-deep with her shorter stature.

"Grab my belt," he instructed her. "If you fall, you'll get soaked. Yell if I'm going too fast."

At least the current wasn't strong.

They stayed in the stream for what seemed forever, but realistically was probably no more than fifteen minutes. Jo didn't bother checking the time.

Another half hour or so along, she began to suspect that she would have gotten lost in here, sooner if not later. She'd planned to mark places when she had to choose one direction or another, so she'd eventually have been able to find her way back out, but the chances of her making it to the Summerlin Cavern end?

Zero, at least without taking all day. And think how much fun spending the night all by herself deep in the cavern would have been?

She stumbled to a stop when Alan did, and let his firm grip on her arm guide her a few steps. He gently eased her to sit on a flat-topped rock, swung his pack off and lowered himself beside her.

"We need to eat and take a rest."

Jo hoped he hadn't noticed that her legs had been shaking.

"Your feet dry?" he asked.

She wriggled her toes. "I think so."

"Good. I brought a couple of ham sandwiches. Does that sound okay?"

"Yes!" Her fervency embarrassed her. Another handful of nuts wouldn't cut it.

His low chuckle warmed her. Again, he turned out his light after he found what he wanted in his pack, and once he dug out his bottle of water, Jo did the same. She accepted a sandwich from him, the handover only slightly fumbled.

They ate in silence for a minute.

"You holding up all right?" he asked finally.

"You don't think I am?" Jo asked in alarm.

"Didn't say that. You're doing fine."

"Oh." She relaxed. "This is a lot longer trip than I remembered."

He made a humming sound.

"You must have done some caving when you were a SEAL."

The pause was brief. "I did. Several parts of the world. I conducted a few training sessions here and there, too. Not everyone had had the chance to go underground, depending on what part of the country they were from."

"No, that's true. Although there are caves in quite a few states."

The big shoulder touching hers moved in what she took as agreement.

When he made no attempt to keep talking, she decided to be bold. "Will you tell me why you quit your job to come home to Mayville?"

If he told her it was none of her business, she wouldn't be surprised. Or, really, offended, because…it wasn't. But he'd been open about his childhood, his father's abuse and mother's determination to get him away. So—

This silence had gone on long enough that she was surprised when he said, "Once I was out of the navy, I signed on as a cop. Did patrol for about a year, but my specialized skills got me promoted fast. I…liked being a detective. Said no thanks to SWAT."

"Would you have been able to do that if your injury kept you out of remaining as a SEAL?"

"Not a hundred percent sure. Didn't want to find out."

She felt his shrug. That contact, shoulders and upper arms and thighs, anchored her. More, it made her very aware of his body in a more visceral way than when she watched him move.

He'd quit talking, and Jo didn't quite have the nerve to demand he spit it out. For some reason, she felt sure whatever had ended his career as a detective was a lot more dramatic than *just thought I'd take some time off.* The story was his to share, or not.

"I mostly liked and trusted the men I worked with." Even in the dark, Jo could tell he'd turned his head as if to look at her. "There were women in the department, just none in my unit."

Jo nodded, however meaningless that was when he couldn't see her.

"Two guys robbed a bank, shot and killed a loan officer and made it out with three hostages. A couple of customers and a teller. I happened to be nearby. By the time I got there, they'd fled into a ramshackle riverfront warehouse. Lots of possible exits. I didn't see that we dared wait half an hour or more for a SWAT team to arrive. They'd have been long gone. This...wasn't an unfamiliar exercise for me."

From his years as a SEAL, he meant.

Tension vibrated through him. Jo felt compelled to grope until she found his hand. He latched onto hers.

"My biggest fear was that they'd kill the hostages once they got to their escape vehicle. Why not, when they'd already killed? I grabbed another detective and two uniforms. They argued, but I made the mistake of thinking once we made a plan, I could depend on them to follow it." He shook his head. "It was a debacle."

"Oh, no," Jo whispered.

"The detective...never made it into position at all. One of the uniformed officers got excited and started firing, giving away his position and, oh yeah, killing a hostage. I took down the robbers, but by then they'd shot a second hostage. In the aftermath, my brass wasn't all that supportive even though while I was cuffing one of the robbers, two of us heard him talking about how much pleasure he'd have taken in throwing the hostages' bodies at us."

"They thought you should have waited?"

"Yeah. I keep asking myself the same question. I still

think all three women would have been dead. What's more,
it should have been a straightforward operation, four of us
against two who were already panicking. As it was, nobody even pinned the detective down on where he'd vanished to. The one who started shooting prematurely..."
Alan shifted. "I imagine he'll be torturing himself for a
good long while, too."

"I'm sorry."

His fingers tightened on hers. "I lost a level of trust and
finally made the decision to quit. Don't know what kind
of recommendation I'll get if I try to get hired with any
other department. Don't know if I want to."

Hearing the desolation in his voice along with the
deep anger, Jo swiveled as far as she could and clumsily
wrapped her arms around Alan. In close to a lunge, he
hauled her into a tight clinch.

If the position and the rough rock beneath her butt
hadn't been so uncomfortable, she'd have been happy to
stay where she was forever.

Especially once his mouth found hers.

Chapter Twelve

An hour later, Alan decided to call another halt. He'd been pressing on hard. Not like Jo wasn't fit, but not many people worked out as seriously as he did. She had to be beat, but she didn't say a word. Just stuck with him, did what she had to do, a quality he admired.

Why had he said so much to her? he asked himself.

Had he been testing Jo? he wondered. Wondering how far *she* trusted him and his judgment? Given how short a time they'd known each other, he shouldn't have put that kind of pressure on her. The way she'd reached for him, though, expressed a whole hell of a lot.

What he really shouldn't have done was kiss her even if he had hungered to do just that since the first time he'd succumbed to temptation where she was concerned. It wouldn't be so bad if this one had been just a kiss, but he'd call it a revelation instead. She'd fit perfectly in his arms, despite their awkward position. He loved her taste, the strength of her fingers digging into his neck and stroking his hair. And, damn, he'd have given just about anything to strip her and make love to her, then and there.

Sure, that would have been romantic.

He grimaced. Had she spoken a single word since he'd reluctantly released her? Why would she, when all he'd done was growl something like, "Bad time and place for this," which could be taken a lot of different ways.

It would help if he weren't so conflicted about this attraction, about whether he could imagine having a relationship with a sweet elementary school teacher. And, no, that wasn't fair. Her family was obviously screwed up in their own way, if not quite on the grand scale of his own.

Unless her stepfather or brother turned out to be a killer, of course.

Behind him, she suddenly stumbled and grabbed at his shoulders to avoid going down painfully onto her knees.

Alan reached back for her hand, steadied her and said, "Break time."

"It hasn't been that long since we, um, had sandwiches."

Kissed, too. And she'd listened to his confidences.

He looked to one side so his headlamp didn't blind her. "We should be stopping at least hourly." Which was true. "This is as good a place as any."

Better than most, he realized, seeing the slope of water-washed stone to one side. The picture that flickered in his mind of stripping her after all and laying her back on that nice, smooth surface stirred the beginnings of arousal. Trying to squelch the whole idea, he decided it would be too gritty. And what made him think she would even consider taking a break for wild sex in the middle of this really fun outing?

Glad she couldn't see him very well, he lowered his pack and eased hers off before they both sat down and stretched out their legs.

"I have some candy bars," she offered.

"Sounds better than my energy bars."

"I've been eating way too much candy this summer." That had to be a smile in her voice. She couldn't be too mad at him. "We sell them in the gift shop. There's this big rack, right by the cash register..."

"That you operate."

"Yes!"

Alan chuckled.

She gave him an Almond Joy, a favorite from when he was a kid. He tore open the wrapping and devoured it, hearing her doing the same—although he bet she ate hers more daintily than his three giant bites.

Something he'd been thinking about as they walked, part of his effort to distract himself from that kiss, and he decided to ask. She'd been curious about his past, so how could she be offended if he was equally nosy?

"You don't talk about your mother," he said.

Jo went still. No more rustling of a wrapper, no chewing. Had she quit breathing?

"She left us," she finally said in a small, dry voice.

He frowned. "How old were you?"

"Thirteen."

Her tone was tighter than any choke in this cave. Did those few, spare words rub her throat raw?

"Your brother and sister couldn't have been very old."

"No. Brody was six, Lucy only two. It was...really awful."

He didn't get it. Why had the kids stayed with the father who sounded like something of a jackass? What mother walked out on a toddler?

"Were they fighting?"

This sigh, he heard.

"Yes. Rod is...really controlling. And a sexist jerk, too. One time when he was going off on how women just didn't have the right stuff, I tried to protest." She went quiet for a moment. "It was only a year or two after the divorce.

He said, 'Look at your mother. Can't think of a better example. Going got rough, she took off.'"

Alan swore. "What a—" He reined in the word that had come to mind and substituted, "creep."

"*I* thought so."

"Did they fight over custody?"

The air shifted, making Alan realized she'd shaken her head.

"No. She just…took off."

"She didn't talk to you first?"

Another faint stir. "She left a note. Promised to be in touch, but all that came were a scattering of Christmas and birthday cards, and only for a few years. Those years were really hard. I had to try to be a mom to Lucy especially, but Brody, too, and go to school. I hated what she did to us."

"That was a lot for a girl that age to shoulder." His hand found hers, too chilled.

"I tried so hard. I did my best. Only then I abandoned Lucy and Brody when I left for college. I've always felt guilty, but I was desperate. I thought they understood, but Lucy threw that at me when I first came home this summer. She felt deserted, and I don't blame her. For her, it was twice over."

Pity squeezed his heart. "You know that's wrong, don't you? *You* were a kid. Where was Rod?"

"Running the business." She paused. "That's not fair. He had to step up, too. Pay for child care during the hours I was in school, do the driving and grocery shopping. You know. Everything I couldn't take over."

Alan wanted to say something really foul. It was all he could do to refrain. Jo's stepfather had expected a devastated thirteen-year-old girl to become a fill-in mother-housekeeper to keep the household running so his life wasn't impacted any more than necessary? Maybe he was misreading this, but he didn't think so.

He was also hit with the crashing understanding that Jo was a thousand miles away from being the sunny, uncomplicated woman he'd tried to convince himself she was, even though he'd seen the shadows in her eyes from the beginning. She bore as many scars as he did, just a different kind.

Then he got struck by a sickening thought. Keep it to himself? No.

"Sounds like your mother could be said to have disappeared, too."

The words just hung there.

Jo made a ragged sound before she whispered, "Oh, dear God. I never thought—"

He had to put an arm around her. She stayed stiff, quivering with shock, doubt, pain.

"She did send cards." Not hard to guess she hadn't been comforted by those cards. Or even convinced by them? Had she thought Rod might be responsible for them, trying to make his kids feel better?

"You recognized her handwriting?" Alan asked.

"Oh, dear God," Jo said again. "I never understood. Her going that way."

"You didn't believe, deep down, your mom would do anything like that."

"No. We were close! She loved us all. I knew she was unhappy with Rod. I came in on her once crying right after she found out she was pregnant with Lucy. I think maybe she'd been considering leaving Rod, but after that she felt trapped. Two children and pregnant? What could she do for a living?"

"I suppose he had her working in the cavern."

"When she wasn't keeping house and taking care of us

kids. She did some of the bookkeeping, too. Of course, he wouldn't have paid her. Unless she stripped joint bank accounts, where would she have gotten money to run?"

Alan wrapped an arm around her. She turned into him and took a handful of his coverall, her hand shaking.

"You didn't say about the handwriting."

"I don't know. I only saw the note she left once. The writing was...ragged, but I thought that meant she was emotional." A swallow. "I was so sure she'd come back for us. I waited and waited. I told myself how lucky I was that Rod never said a word about me not being his child."

Angry, Alan was blunter than he had to be. "Why would he, when you were so useful?"

But she only said, "You're right. I've felt so guilty for letting Brody and Lucy and Rod down later, and now—"

"We don't know," he reminded her. "We may be building..." Not castles in the sky.

Her laugh hurt to hear. "Crypts under the Summerlin Cavern?"

Jo COULDN'T BELIEVE she hadn't ever wondered.

She'd *known*, soul deep, that Mom wouldn't do that to her or Brody and Lucy. And yet she'd bought Rod's story.

If it was a story. How well could a thirteen-year-old girl claim to really know any adult, especially a parent? Kids wanted to believe in their parents. They clung to that faith with fingernails that could penetrate granite.

"Mom wasn't anything like the girls that have disappeared," she argued after a minute. "If that's what you're thinking."

"No, she wasn't." Alan sounded kind, even tender. He must know how hard he'd slammed her. "Maybe the two things don't have anything to do with each other. But you've described a man to me who is controlling to the nth degree and has some contempt for women. He's possessive. Mostly of his land and his cavern, but would he be willing to let his wife go if she took his children with her?"

Really shaking now, Jo held on to a man whose solidity she trusted. "He...he might have offered to let her go, or even Lucy, but never Brody."

"But how could she leave children that young with him?"

Jo was both in shock, and stunned at how thoroughly she'd practiced denial. How could she not have seen this possibility? "If she told him she wanted a divorce, he'd have been enraged."

"I'm sorry," he murmured, his mouth close enough to her ear to ruffle her hair. "Maybe this was a bad time to say anything."

"Because that skull—" Jo couldn't finish. She just couldn't. But a part of her mind was working coldly, clearly. "Even if he did kill Mom, that's not to say he has anything to do with all the women who have gone missing. Only...what if he discovered he enjoyed having ultimate control? Denying her any freedom at all?" Seeing her terror and despair. "Hurting her?"

And wasn't that the worst euphemism ever.

"So eventually he had to replicate the experience," Alan said softly.

She nodded and pressed her face against his chest, wanting a closeness that their multiple layers of clothes denied her. *I don't want to be alone*, she thought with shattering clarity. She always had been, until her eyes had met Alan Burke's. Until they'd exchanged messages she couldn't even decipher.

"I'll feel like a horrible human being if we find out we're wrong," she mumbled.

His chest vibrated with a choked-off laugh.

"I'm so sorry," he said again.

"About?" She raised her head. "Tearing off my blinders?"

"No. About being blind where you were concerned. I tried to convince myself you were a clueless young woman who teaches little kids and doesn't see the real world around her. I'm...scarred, inside and out, and I couldn't see us connecting."

Was he saying...? Despite the anger she felt at her own self-deception and the grief that speared her heart, Jo felt a powerful surge of hope.

"You were here when I needed you," she said. "And, honestly, why would you notice all this stuff I've been hiding even from myself? I tried to tell myself it wasn't healthy to give in to so much anger or the guilt because I didn't totally sacrifice myself for my little brother and sister. I thought maybe if I pretended long enough, pretense would become reality."

"You didn't talk to friends?"

"My friends...aren't that close. They're too nice to understand."

"You might be wrong about that," he said, gentle again.

"Maybe they're all pretending, too." Jo closed her eyes, not that she could see much anyway with only one backup lamp on, and savored the strength she sensed Alan was doing his best to share with her. Then she carefully started to separate herself.

"I'll bet you're also sorry you set yourself up for me to weep all over you." Good try at lightness, she congratulated herself.

"Don't do that," he said. "Did you not hear what I was telling you?"

"I...no." Which wasn't totally honest, but—

"Jo... C'mere." Displaying physical power she'd only

suspected, Alan snatched her up and set her across his lap. Then he bent his head and claimed her mouth in a kiss that felt starved, angry, desperate. A kiss that was exactly what she needed.

She flung her arms around his neck and kissed him back with such fervor, he had to step up a gear to match all the emotions and hunger she was throwing at him.

Once he said something like, "I swore I wasn't going to do this," but she paid no attention to it because he'd somehow stripped off her oversuit and the fleece quarter zip she'd worn beneath it and gotten his hand inside her T-shirt. He found his way inside her stretchy sports bra, too, and she arched convulsively at the feel of that big, hot hand engulfing her breast.

She struggled way less effectively to fight her way through his layers of clothing. Not once did she think, *Is this something we should be doing right now?* She *needed* him, couldn't conceive of not becoming one with this man in every possible way. This wasn't simple attraction, maybe never had been, but right now her emotions were a fierce storm.

"Let me," he growled, picked her up again and set her down so he could stand and strip off clothes. The shadow he cast on a wall showed wild hair, disheveled from removing his helmet, a harshly hewn face, broad powerful shoulders.

He spread something behind her—the sleeping bag, she realized, in a distant part of her mind. And now he was struggling with the laces on one of her boots even as his mouth traveled up her bare belly, his whiskers scraping as he went. The boot dropped off, and he peeled down her pants and long underwear, Jo helping, or maybe impeding, she had no idea. He seemed to lose interest once he had one leg free. His mouth had found her breast and he sucked hard over the stretchy cotton of the bra even as his fingers slid between her thighs. Jo wasn't nearly as good at doing two things at once, but she'd found the zipper that kept her from getting her hand inside his jeans.

It didn't want to cooperate, though, not given the solid ridge beneath. She persevered in the brief intervals when she could concentrate at all, but finally he growled something and took over for that, too. Jo immediately wrapped her hand around him, made even more desperate by the sheer size and power of this man.

"Are you on birth control?"

She bit the hard muscle in his upper arm, all she could reach at that moment.

He was groping in his pack.

Jo's flesh chilled while she waited.

"Man, I'm glad I threw these in," he muttered. He tore the packet and donned the condom.

And then he was kissing her again, his fingers deftly working magic, and she spread her legs even as she tried to pull him closer.

"I want you so damn much," he said roughly, just as he pushed himself slowly inside her.

"Don't stop," she whispered.

He pulled out, drove hard and fast, so deep, she'd never experienced anything like this. All she could do was react: grab him, try to take him even deeper, if that was possible. And she was talking, too, without the slightest idea what she was saying. Pleading, crying out, making incoherent sounds.

She came around him so powerfully, she didn't give him any choice but to join her. The sound wrenched from his chest could have been from the movement of two slabs of rock breaking, being reshaped by an earthquake. Shaken by pleasure that had been both explosive and glorious beyond anything she'd ever known, Jo knew *she'd* been reshaped.

She was terribly afraid she was in love with this complex, damaged, courageous man who might not feel anything even remotely similar for her.

Chapter Thirteen

Grateful they didn't have much chance to talk beyond the practicalities—"Watch your head"—Alan continued to lead the way. It began to eat at him that he'd said so little, but in truth he wasn't sure what would have been kind to her and right for him. He had to do some thinking.

Now wasn't the time for that. He couldn't afford another serious distraction. As it was, he found himself glad several times when passages split to recognize human-made scratches on the limestone walls. They were distinctive enough, he recognized his own style. Only twice did he see ones he thought Drew might have been responsible for. Alan suspected he'd been determined even then to take care of essentials himself. Lucky those scratches had survived. He'd have found the way without help from the kid he'd been, but it would have taken longer, and his sense of urgency kept mounting.

He guessed from Jo's silence and determination that she felt something similar. Either that, or she was able to block out weariness by brooding about a past that might not have been anything like she'd wanted to believe it was. Alan half hoped they'd learn that he'd been wrong—but once he'd suggested her mother was the first woman to disappear, the pieces of the entire puzzle had dropped too damn neatly into place.

Because of that, he had begun to feel some deep fore-boding. He should be here with real backup, not a vulner-able woman who was confident in this environment, sure, but didn't carry a gun and wouldn't know how to respond to violence.

In theory, with his experience he could handle Rod Summerlin, but Rod had the advantage of knowing this part of the cavern far better than Alan did. If Alan went down, could Jo find her way out of here? Could she move fast enough if her stepfather was on her heels?

Alan gritted his teeth. Would she be willing to stay be-hind and wait for him? He knew that answer.

Knee-deep in a stream, recognizing the low-slung ceil-ing ahead, he paused.

"You okay?" he asked quietly.

"Fine."

How many times had she said that?

"We're getting close." He kept his voice low. "I don't hear anything, but we're no more than a quarter of a mile from the party hall you described."

"Oh. I told you I went a little way past that, but—"

Not far enough, he suspected. And maybe that was just as well, since she'd been alone that day. She hadn't said where her stepfather had been when she sneaked in here. If she'd dawdled and he'd gone looking for her, Alan had a bad feeling she would have disappeared, too.

"Once we're out of the stream, we'll have to crawl for a short stretch ahead," he told her. "After that, our voices will carry, so let's keep it down."

Her head bobbed. The strain showed on her face in this eerie mix of shadow and light playing off the walls and odd planes that formed the ceiling, but anger and that de-termination were there, too. She didn't ask if he thought they'd find anything. She had to know they might not, but they'd keep looking as long as it took, Alan vowed. As long as they could do so uninterrupted, he amended. They didn't have to make it all the way back out to his property; they could spend the night whenever he sensed her energy flagged. He still had nuts and energy bars in his pack.

He also carried a Glock handgun in a side pocket of his pack. Next stop, he'd pull it out and tuck it where it would be more accessible.

He tried not to splash any more than necessary, and realized when he stepped out of the water that Jo had fallen behind, partly because she, too, was trying to move quietly. He waited and gave her a hand scrambling out.

"Where's your stepfather this time of day?"

She blinked a few times. "Uh… It's still morning, isn't it?"

He pulled back his glove to reveal a standard wrist-watch. "Almost eleven."

"He should be at work. Either leading tours, helping in the gift shop or manning the cash register. Even if he found someone to replace me for the day, he never slows down."

"Good."

"He go out at night?"

She nodded. "Mostly, he takes his truck. I thought he might have a girlfriend. Sometimes he walks back to the gift shop where his office is."

In other words, the SOB had plenty of leisure time in the evenings to pursue his victims.

Unclenching his jaw, Alan said, "Okay. This should be ideal timing for us to poke around then. This might be a good place for us to leave our packs. We don't want to be slowed down."

He could come back if they needed the first aid supplies, but silence and speed had to come first right now.

Jo nodded and set hers down. He did the same, but took

out the handgun and slipped it in a pocket of his cargo pants. He looked up to see her gaping at him.

"You came…armed?" she whispered.

"We wouldn't be here if I hadn't tried to prepare for anything."

She chewed on her lower lip and finally nodded.

"If we happen on something unexpected, you go back. Don't try to be heroic. Stay unseen if you can. You got me?"

That might be a glare, but he didn't give a damn. If they were to find anything unpleasant, he wanted to see it first. And if Rod Summerlin just happened to be back here during a break from his tours—say, he'd claimed to be taking lunch—Alan didn't want him setting eyes on Jo.

He thought for a minute she'd argue, but she clamped her mouth shut and waited while he lowered himself to his knees and forearms, both of which were padded. His mouth twitched at the memory of having to hunt down one of her pads, which he'd apparently tossed quite a way while disrobing her.

Despite the fact that he was pushing himself forward with his face inches from the rocky floor of the compressed passage, his body reacted to the memory. Their kisses hadn't been the only revelation; making love with this woman had seriously rattled him. Maybe knowing what to say wouldn't be as hard as he'd thought. Nonetheless, that conversation wasn't happening until they'd seen whatever there was to see and were well on their way out of this damn cavern.

Momentarily stuck, he grunted, released a breath and lowered his hips, going for a snakelike propulsion.

Not much bothered by claustrophobia, he was still glad when space opened in front of him, the beam of his headlamp finding a small room rimmed with young stalactites

and stalagmites. As he watched, a drop fell from the closest stalactite. Geology in action. A memory surfaced: the
word *stalactite* came from the Greek *stalasso*, or "to drip."

He rose to his feet and helped Jo to rise, too. A sound
came to him, distant and too soft to identify, rising and
falling, rising and falling. Damn it, was he imagining the
occasional hitch?

"Do you hear—?" Jo whispered.

"Yeah," he murmured into her ear, so close his lips
brushed her.

"I think… I think that's what I heard that day."

He could see why she'd assumed it was one of the natural sounds of the cavern, water or wind entering a crack.
Or even that she was imagining it altogether; spend long
enough in a cave, and you started hearing things that
weren't there. Especially if you were unnerved to start
with.

But they hadn't dreamed this up since they were hearing the same thing.

"This room would be a good place to hide things," he
said, still making sure his voice wouldn't carry. "Did you
get this far?"

Jo shook her head. "One of the passages I looked at was
blocked by a cave-in and one just seemed to go on and on.
The last one was narrow but not that bad. I just got nervous about how much time had passed."

"Okay. Let's look around before we go on."

They split up, Alan feeling comfortable because she
wouldn't be far from him at any point. He'd hear anyone
else approaching; few people had the training he did to
move like a ghost. Once he knew she was turned away, he
unsealed the Velcro securing the pocket holding his gun.

The darkness in the crack he investigated first suggested that it opened into one of the dizzying number of

alternative passages. He stood sideways, thrusting his arm as far as he could reach, letting the flashlight illuminate a short distance. Beyond was nothing but more darkness. And, although sound could be hard to trace in the labyrinth down here, he felt confident the faint noise wasn't coming from this fissure.

Anyway, he'd seen a photo of a self-satisfied Rod Summerlin on the cavern website, something he'd looked up only after meeting Jo the day of the search.

Summerlin wouldn't be squeezing through here, Alan felt confident. The guy wasn't heavy—or at least he hadn't been when the photo was taken—but his stocky build wasn't ideal for cave exploration.

For that matter, Alan thought wryly, neither was his, not once he'd added serious muscle to a boy's rangy body.

He backed out and immediately turned to see what Jo was doing.

The beam of light settled on her shapely butt as she bent over to peer into an odd-shaped opening. Satisfied for the moment, he swept his light around the perimeter of the room, looking for anything of interest. Nothing in particular caught his eye, but he moved toward the deep shadows behind an enormous boulder.

A strangled choking sound had him spinning around.

Jo had backed out by the time he crouched beside her.

"Dear God," she whispered hoarsely. She seemed unable to tear her eyes from the darkness beyond her headlamp beam.

Alan grasped her shoulders and turned her. "What?"

Her throat worked, her gaze now fastened desperately on him. "Bones," she finally managed.

"A skeleton?"

Her teeth chattered. "More than one."

"Damn it." He tugged her closer and wrapped her in

a tight embrace. She burrowed in and shook. The tough woman he'd gotten to know, the one determined to face the nightmare from her past, wouldn't let herself cry.

Then he eased her back and said, "Let me look."

He had to crouch but not crawl. Three feet in, his beam found a chamber that might be five by ten feet. And no, she hadn't imagined anything; there was indeed a jumble of bones.

To one side a skull gave the chilling impression that it was staring at him. Damn, there was a second skull. Neither were near the opening, and he didn't see any scratches on either to suggest a dog's teeth had closed on it. So... there might well be a third, somewhere.

Studying the scattered and heaped bones, he shook his head on that thought. What he saw had to come from five or six bodies, at a minimum. His guess that this serial killer had found victims they didn't yet know about was accurate.

Fabric, or the remnants of garments, was tangled with the bones. Bodies had been heaved in here, next to or atop one another. No care taken, probably no posing. Unlike some serial killers, this guy hadn't been interested in the women once they were dead, except to be sure their remains weren't found. The resulting jumble had occurred because of decomposition and the effects of gravity.

Amy Kendall, he couldn't help thinking, wasn't here. She'd disappeared too recently to be down to bones yet.

Alan continued to sweep the small room with his beam. The ceiling was wet, dripping, the walls slick, almost slimy looking. Water seemed to be draining into a crack or hole toward the far-right corner.

Sickened although he'd seen worse in war zones, Alan rolled his shoulders to release tension. With some effort, he located his phone. Resting on his elbows, he tapped on the photo function and began taking pictures. A couple of dozen, recording as completely as he could the hideous gravesite just in case Rod Summerlin had enough warning to clear it out. As an afterthought, he pulled out the Swiss Army knife he carried in a pocket, looked for an obscure place and scratched both his initials and the date low on the wall.

Then Alan backed out. "I'm sorry," he said simply to Jo, whose shock had turned into something worse. She had that thousand-yard stare he recognized.

"I saw some fabric," she whispered. "Pink with flowers."

Oh, damn; he'd seen that. It had to be synthetic to have survived virtually intact.

"My mother wore that blouse all the time."

NO SUSPICIONS HAD prepared her for anything like this. On some level, she'd wanted to think she was suffering from paranoia, that Rod was the man she'd always believed him to be.

Now she knew. Who else would have killed her mother just as she'd asked for a divorce? *My mother's bones are right there, a few feet away. They've been there all these years, so near. That might be her skull with the dark, accusing eye sockets.*

Jo wished she could believe that the darkness where eyes should have been made Rod even the least bit squeamish. But of course not—if he possessed a grain of conscience, he'd have smashed the skull in rage.

Hard reality hit Jo.

Mom hadn't written that note, or any of the later ones. Only Rod could have done that. Likely Mom would have offered to find a job in Mayville, stay close enough for Rod to see his kids often, but that hadn't been good enough. He'd have been humiliated with townspeople knowing his wife had left him. Letting her, Brody, Lucy and even, maybe, Jo slip out of his control had been more than he could countenance.

Jo wondered dully if he'd struck out without intending to kill her mother, if Mom had fallen and hit her head or something like that. Although, neither of the skulls she'd been able to see had a noticeable indentation.

Had Rod shocked himself by his willingness to kill? He'd been strange in the weeks after she'd thought her mother had left, Jo remembered. Then, that had seemed natural. Of course, he was hurt, his whole life turned on end.

You mean, he flipped all their lives on end, she thought grimly.

I hate him.

But what if she was wrong, and someone else had killed Mom? There could have been an employee back then who who'd started his killing spree with Mom, who was readily available, and kept a key all these years to be sure of continuing access to the cavern. There could be someone else—say, Austin, who'd found Mom's bones and been inspired to do something awful he'd only toyed with before. Or to start stashing victims in the caves instead of whatever he'd done with them before.

She *wanted* to believe Rod didn't have anything to do with this, but she wouldn't kid herself, either. Too much pointed to Rod. He'd had reason to kill his wife, to deceive the children into believing she had deserted them. He had the best access to the cavern, had been furious at the very idea of any of them venturing past the show portion of the cavern. And then there was his thinly veiled disdain for women.

"I wish I'd thought to bring bolt cutters," Alan muttered, pulling her back to the moment. "We could walk right out there, to hell with the tours, and have the police here in minutes."

"But you didn't believe me."

"Did you believe yourself?"

Feeling so much she was, paradoxically, almost numb, she said, "No. Now... That sounds an awful lot like a woman is crying."

Fierce eyes met hers. "Yeah. It does."

Jo felt sick. If only she'd gone farther that day, the crying woman wouldn't have suffered for so much longer. "We have to go on."

"I'd be happier if you'd wait here."

Somehow, she'd known he would say that, and had already made up her mind.

"I dragged you here. Not the other way around. I'm not stopping."

She suspected his mumble was profane, but ignored it.

"Okay." He rose to his feet. "You'll stay behind me."

She could do that. If ever she'd met a man able to meet violence with violence, it was Alan Burke, former navy SEAL and police detective. She was fiercely glad of that. After his honesty about his past, after their lovemaking, she knew she could trust him as she never had anyone else since her mother.

"Quiet from here on out." He softened the order by taking her hand in his and squeezing with remarkable gentleness.

Jo only wished their hands had been bare. She tried to smile but knew her attempt for an abysmal failure. He must have recognized that she'd tried, though, because he dipped his head and kissed her, quick but expressing an astonishing amount.

Then he led the way toward the passage from which she, too, thought the ghostly crying came.

Jo was glad she no longer carried her pack. Lighter on her feet, she'd be able to move with more stealth. She hoped.

The ceiling sloped down, but not as low as in the previous passage, thank goodness.

Alan kept his headlamp on, but she left hers off. Her hands brushed the soles of his boots, and she kept her eyes on the dark silhouette of him against the glow. Her breath came faster as the crying gained in volume. No, it still could be a natural phenomenon, she wanted to believe. Surely, *surely*, Rod wouldn't imprison a woman for any length of time so close to the show portions of the cavern.

Except, it was far enough, at most even those in the party room had heard a suggestion of sound. If poor Jesse hadn't been lured by the dog, Jo and Alan wouldn't be here now. They wouldn't have found the grave site that gave answers to the grieving parents of all these young women.

A part of her mind still had trouble accepting what she'd seen. She'd grown up here, had led countless tours proceeding only a short distance away. Never *imagined*—

And why would she? Most of the time, Rod seemed like an okay guy. Hadn't he been genuinely worried about Lucy?

Or was it that he wanted Jo to shut her up?

She'd quit concentrating on stealth. Her knee whacked a rock that rolled, making noise.

Please not a skull, she thought, in the absolute silence that followed. Alan had frozen; the crying had halted.

"Is someone there?" a young female voice called. It was thin, scared, pleading. "Help! Please!"

Jo wanted desperately to answer, but hesitated. Thank God, because the next thing she heard was a roar of rage and the careless scraping of feet rushing toward them, a nimbus of light dancing over the uneven walls.

Alan began to back up, forcing her to do the same, as hard as it was to hurry when scrabbling backward. She hurt by the time she reached the larger room and leaped up.

"Quickly," Alan growled.

Her mouth opened to protest, but instead she obeyed, dropping into the next crawl.

Gunfire erupted behind her, terrifyingly loud.

Alan grunted and fell forward as something solid clattered on rock. He hadn't been the one firing his gun, she knew in horror. He'd been shot!

Chapter Fourteen

Once an operation stumbled into chaos, there was no re-setting the clock.

Alan knew he couldn't rely on his right arm, and the Glock had dropped from his hand.

Rolling, groping for his gun with his left hand, he kept thinking with cold clarity. It was worth trying to convince Rod this had all been a big misunderstanding.

Unless and until he could line up a shot of his own.

"What the *hell*?" he yelled. Fortunately, he'd never spoken before to this man, who wouldn't recognize his voice. "We're cavers! We're not doing anything!"

Another shot rang out and chips of limestone flew.

If only he and Jo had gotten to the girl—or were there two of them?—a minute sooner, he'd have been prepared had anyone arrived to check on his victim. As it was, Alan didn't have to turn on a light to know his shirt and coverall were soaked with blood and if he stood up, his arm would dangle uselessly at his side. He was a decent shot with his left hand, but not as good as with his right. If he took the offensive and failed, Jo would be left vulnerable—and in the past few hours, *she* had become his priority.

"Go," he growled at her. "We have to hide."

What they had to do was get out of the caves to find help, and do it fast enough to keep the madman behind them from killing again and then cleaning house. Even if Alan had believed he and Jo could retreat the way they'd come, the trip would take too long.

Time for Plan B.

She grabbed his hand. "You're bloody!"

Quiet anguish. All he could say was, "Shot. Let's move."

He had to shove his gun into a pocket to free his good hand to grab the pack. What did he do then in this damn darkness but stumble over hers?

No time to stop. He doubted she had anything essential in it. He pushed her ahead of him, glad she seemed to know where she was going. Drop low, crawl, squirm through the tightest stretch while dragging his pack. His right shoulder hurt like a— He didn't even let himself think the rest. No time to dwell. He'd been injured before and continued to function.

A hint of light glowed behind them. The gunman wasn't going to let them go. Either he was insane, or he had somehow guessed these intruders weren't innocent adventurers.

With a resounding *crack*, another shot skimmed the side of the passage. A chip of rock stung Alan's cheek. Jo made a whimpering sound but never stopped, scrambling as fast as he would have been able to go, anyway.

A scrape, a gasp and a splash of water came from ahead. Jo had emerged and tumbled into the stream.

"Left," he gasped. He'd never hoped more that his memory was solid.

"But we came—"

"Do what I say." Under fire his men followed his orders without argument. Until the one time they didn't. Apologize to Jo later.

Without light, he ended up on his hand and knees in the water. Trying to get to his feet, he almost lost the pack.

Can't afford to, he told himself coldly. Not given where they were going.

Jo wasn't moving very fast anymore. How could she with no light? His recollection of this route was too vague for them to stumble entirely in the dark. The danger of them blundering into a deadly hazard was greater than that of them getting shot.

"Turn your light on," he said, voice scraping in his throat. "Get a quick look ahead."

She did. He blinked, needing his eyes to readjust. "Out of the water."

Another shot, this one going God knew where, but it served as a warning. Jo plunged them back into darkness without waiting for his command. She kept going, too, although he could hear the whistle of her breathing. Not lack of conditioning, he thought, but rather fear.

"We're going, we're going!" Alan yelled, straining to hear any sounds from behind him.

As they fled, he debated finding a hiding place to set up an ambush. That would have been his first choice, except for two factors: his injury, and the reality that the man chasing them knew these caves better than Alan or Jo did. He'd have explored in every direction before settling on the dumping ground for bodies and the best place to hold his captives. The question was, would he believe that the intruders weren't anybody he needed to worry about, or would he continue to pursue them?

Or, worse possibility, go back to erase everyone and everything that could condemn him?

Having no answer, all Alan could do was push Jo on, ignore the agony in his shoulder and the more frightening numbness in his arm and hand, and keep going. They had to get far enough ahead of this crazy SOB to be able to set up a descent into another level of the cavern.

Yeah, and hope Jo wouldn't balk at sliding down a rope into impenetrable darkness.

ALL JO COULD do was grope her way forward in a passage too wide for her to touch each side at the same time. She wished Alan was leading, but knew why he hung back.

How badly was he hurt? That grunt had told her he was injured even before he said, *Shot*. If he'd dropped his gun, had he been able to find it? She'd give a lot to be able to *see* him, if only for a moment, to evaluate his condition with her own eyes.

Her flattened hand her only guide, she took care with every step. She could so easily walk right into a stalagmite rising from the floor or fall over a loose rock or intrusion. If she were injured enough to slow them down even more, Rod would kill them. Jo had no doubt about it.

She didn't let herself question where Alan was taking them. Even more, she couldn't think about that terrified voice.

Is someone there? Help! A whimpered, *Please?*

No! She'd become paralyzed if she let herself focus on anything but fleeing.

The rough wall suddenly wasn't there. Jo stopped, then, without consulting Alan, switched on her headlamp. The passage curved, that's all, and angled downward. Water entered from a crevice up above and ran down the sides, making the cave floor ahead glisten.

Turning off the light, she told herself, *Careful, careful*, and hurried forward.

Twice she slipped, once staggering into the wet wall where she was able to right herself. The second time, she thought she was going down on her butt, but a strong arm caught her and set her back on her feet.

"Are you all right?" she whispered.

"Fine. Keep going."

O-kay.

Once she turned her head and thought she saw a very faint glow behind them, enough for Alan to rear as a tall, dark silhouette. She prayed she was imagining it just because she knew he was there, that there really *wasn't* any light.

The air felt close, her every step louder than it should have been. Alan…no, she could hear him, too, and the incessant trickle of water. This flight couldn't have lasted more than minutes—ten? fifteen?—but felt interminable. She had no idea how long they'd been underway. Was Rod really chasing them?

How could he let them go? she thought hopelessly. Even if they were some weekend cavers who'd stumbled into the Summerlin Cavern, if they found their way out, they'd report someone shooting at them. Wouldn't they? That would bring the police to Rod. He didn't dare risk any interest from law enforcement.

Her thighs burned. She wasn't sure she could feel the fingers she grazed on the wall, although how could they be cold when she wore gloves?

Behind, Alan said suddenly, "Grab onto me anywhere you can. I need to go ahead. We should be coming on a shaft."

A shaft? As in, a *hole*? Did it go up, or— No, of course not. They wouldn't be able to climb. So where did it descend *to*? Did he know? And even if he and his friend had explored this far when they were boys, how could Alan trust in the accuracy of his memories?

Not like this was any moment to question him. Stepping to one side, she let him by and grabbed for the pack he'd slung over his left shoulder. Her fingers closed on the coil of rope strapped to the outside.

He was already moving, and she had to jog a couple of steps to keep up.

This was why he carried the rope, she realized queasily. Not expecting to need it but prepared for anything. She'd vaguely known the cavern was multilevel. It almost had to be, right? The tour entrance gaped about halfway up the ridge. She'd always known water trickled downward from above. That's how these caves were *formed*. And no, water didn't just trickle; depending on the season, it tumbled. And where had she thought all that water was going? Some of it might escape to cascade down the steep exposed hillside into the river, but it made more sense that there was at least one level below the cavern she'd thought she knew, possibly more.

Had the sinkhole once been part of this cave complex?

She stumbled and wrenched her mind back to what she was doing. Every footstep, every uneasy glance over her shoulder. No hint of light. If Rod was back there, he couldn't move any faster than they were able to in the dark, because even a small flashlight would pinpoint his location. He might risk that if he didn't suspect these two people—or did he think there was only one?—had been investigating the sound of crying and the skull a boy had claimed to see.

A splashing sound beneath her feet pulled her back to the here and now. She was having more and more trouble holding onto clarity. Water wasn't just slick now, it had to be an inch or two deep. In winter and early spring, this stream would probably be a flood, possibly impassible. Given the complete darkness and only a sense of resistance against her feet, she couldn't tell for sure how deep the water had become now, and did it matter anyway? Except, the sound of splashing might keep her from hearing someone drawing closer to them from behind.

Alan paused and turned on his headlamp. She had to squeeze her eyes shut against the shocking brightness. He muttered to himself and changed course. The light vanished. She stumbled after him, blinking against the after-flash.

HE CAME ON the pit so suddenly he was damn lucky not to walk right off the edge of it. Alan doubted Jo's grip was strong enough to pull him back if he'd teetered.

While he shut down that surge of adrenalin, he had no choice but to turn his light on again and search the rough edges of the giant hole for a formation of rock strong enough and shaped right to sling the rope around. He hated what he was going to force Jo to do, the risks he was taking for both of them, but this still seemed to be the best option. He and Drew had done this, albeit long ago. The drop hadn't been so great as to leave them dangling with no choice but to somehow climb back up or release the rope and fall an unknown distance.

Pain wasn't helping the clarity of his memories, though. Was this the place he thought it was?

Tuck Jo somewhere safe, lie in wait for her stepfather. Maybe that would still be the better option.

His gut said no. They needed backup.

The beam of his light stopped on the broken bottom of a column that made him think of a giant tooth. Moving as fast as he could, he uncoiled the rope, turned on his headlamp and struggled to form an Italian hitch. With his right hand refusing to cooperate, he had to ask Jo for help. Either she knew her knots, or she understood what he was trying to do, and if her fingers moved slower than he liked, they got it done. He clipped on a carabiner, and then straightened. When he dropped his pack over the edge, Jo cried out, but he said, "There's nothing breakable in it." Then he said, "You have to go now."

She whispered, "I didn't hear the pack hit bottom."

"We don't have any choice, Jo. I've descended this shaft before. You won't kill yourself letting go when you get to the end of the rope."

He saw her terror and gave her a single, hard kiss. "Turn on your lamp as soon as you're over the lip."

She'd had enough training to know how to wrap the ropes around her body to allow her to rappel. All he could see was her face, the fear and yet the resolution. If she'd been frozen with terror...hell. They'd have been screwed.

He had her turn off his headlamp before she went, and she had the guts to back off the edge into the dark abyss with no benefit of light.

Any caver knew that what they were doing was by default foolish, maybe even suicidal. Normally, he'd have set up anchors, have carried more ropes. What he'd fashioned—all he'd had time for—was called a pull-through. The descent could be made by abseil, and at the bottom the caver could retrieve his rope by pulling. Simple—but what this kind of descent didn't allow was retreat. There was no way back up. The caver could only go on. In this case, "on" wasn't a complete mystery, but it was damned hazy in his memory.

He followed her descent by the circle of light that accompanied her. When she called up, "I'm at the end," he could tell from her voice that she couldn't see the bottom of this hole.

When she said, "I'm letting go," he closed his eyes and prayed like he hadn't ever in his life.

A thud was followed by an involuntarily cry. And then a shaken voice saying, "I'm okay. Hurry."

Thank God.

He followed, bracing his feet against the rough wall of the shaft, and let the rope slide between his gloved hands—yeah, he'd managed to bend his elbow and manually place the fingers of his right hand where they needed to be, whether they'd be any use or not—and tighten painfully on his thigh.

He let himself drop with foolish haste into the dark abyss.

To BE OUT of the way, Jo retreated a few feet into what appeared to be a passage and waited. They'd be okay once he got down here, wouldn't they? Rod would have no reason to have been carrying rope of his own, and he wouldn't be able to stop Alan from yanking on one end and whipping the rope through the carabiner and loose.

Hugging herself, she tipped her head up to give him some light. She only knew he was on his way down because of the way the pack swung. Alan himself was still in darkness when a light appeared at the top.

She wanted to scream out his name, but he wasn't blind. Rod—if this was Rod—was crouching, she could tell that much. If he started shooting methodically—

The pack and the rope and Alan all plummeted at the same time. Their pursuer had cut the rope, she realized, starting forward. Alan had been too high. How could he survive?

Heavier than the pack, he hit at almost the same moment, the rope whipping to lash him. Belatedly, Jo turned off her lamp. She heard a deep groan, movement—she thought—and then gunfire, so much she clapped her hands over her ears.

The fusillade was followed by silence and darkness.

And she couldn't move, couldn't make a sound, or give away that she, at least, had lived.

She had to have waited two or three minutes when she dared hope the monster had gone away.

Terribly afraid she was whimpering, Jo stumbled forward. "Alan? Alan?"

"Yeah." That was his voice, oh, thank God, but it was a pained rasp.

"Are you…?"

"Don't…know."

Those words hurt to hear.

She turned on her headlamp. She had to *see* him.

He'd either bounced or rolled six or eight feet away from the pack and the pile of rope. Holes pocked the pack. Alan was bleeding, but maybe no more than he already had been? Jo didn't know.

She fell to her knees beside him. "Where are you hurt?"

"We can't stay out here." He sounded stronger. "Let's get out of sight from up above."

"Let me help."

"I'll roll. Grab the pack. We might need it."

She rose to her feet and scurried forward, her skin crawling at the possibility they were being watched from above. He could have snapped a new magazine in the handgun she hadn't known he owned. But she seized the pack by a strap and a handful of the rope and retreated as fast as she could.

Alan had somehow moved a few yards into the passage and levered himself into a sitting position, back against a rough wall.

When she reached him, he lifted a hand and tried to poke a gloved finger into one of the holes in the pack. "I think it's dead."

"You're joking about it," she said in disbelief.

He grimaced. "Why not?"

She'd been wrong; his face was bloody, but only as if

it had been scraped. The helmet had to have protected his head when he hit the rock floor, but she could see that his headlamp was smashed. Jo wanted to laugh. She wanted to cry. What she did was reach out and grab his good hand.

He squeezed hers so hard, it hurt, but she never wanted to let go.

GETTING TO HIS feet was bad enough. Digging deep through the cotton in his head for his memory of that single, long-ago trip through this lower level of the great Summerlin Cavern was harder.

It all got worse when Jo said suddenly, "I think that was Lucy."

He'd decided not to discard anything from his pack. If they got lost, they'd need it all. Then Jo's words sank in. "What?"

"I'm pretty sure that was Lucy calling for help." Jo's misery was clear. "I told you she wasn't in her bed this morning. I think…she was refusing to give up. He was getting madder and madder, and… I think I said before. If she did find the key last night, and Rod caught her in the cavern, how could he let her go?"

Yeah, Alan bet that's what happened. If Lucy had gotten far enough to discover Amy, or even bloody handcuffs… Or, hell, bones."

"Anyway, Brody is important to him. I doubt Lucy ever really was."

"We can't be a hundred percent sure the killer isn't someone else who caught Lucy back here," Alan reminded her. "Rod brought you home—" he broke off.

"I guess he thought I'd reason with her, and all would be well. He could go on his usual way."

She believed it was Rod after them, and Alan thought the same. Realistically, could an armed stranger stroll into the cavern, then back out again, certain he'd been unseen? *This* visit hadn't been in the middle of the night.

Jo wasn't crying, but he heard the equivalent of a deep, painful bruise in her voice. If it turned out they were wrong, Alan could only imagine the relief she'd feel.

"All we can do is hurry," he said, knowing how completely that failed as reassurance, but it was true. They had no time to waste.

After a moment, she asked, "Can you go on?"

"I've functioned when I was in worse shape."

"Is there anything I can do?"

"Maybe take a look at my shoulder. Might be able to wrap it." The sharp stab in his hip, the wrenching pain in his neck that he suspected was the equivalent of whiplash, at least kept him from feeling the more generalized hurt that would undoubtedly manifest in bruises up and down his body.

"I don't know what I was thinking!" She scrambled to her feet. "Oh, God. Your arm is soaked with blood. What if you're—"

"Bleeding out?" he said dryly. "If I were, I'd be dead by now." As she tugged at his oversuit, he cooperated until she had his arm and shoulder freed. Then he stopped her when she reached for the buttons on his flannel shirt. "No, that might not go back on over a heavy bandage. Let's just try to stabilize it and get going."

He'd brought first aid supplies, including heavy gauze pads and vet wrap, which she used to wrap his shoulder with reasonable expertise. Maybe everyone who worked at the cavern took first aid classes. As she sank back on her haunches, she looked doubtful. "I don't know if that will do any good. A sling would be a good idea, but—"

He'd need to use the arm to the extent it was capable. Yeah.

He insisted they take a drink from the one water bottle that hadn't been punctured by bullet holes and to each eat a handful of nuts. Unfortunately, neither gave him a magical boost in energy. He also swallowed several painkillers, but if they were going to help, it would take time.

Then he reached for his pack.

"No!" Jo snatched it from him. "I'll carry it."

He'd like to have argued but couldn't. He coiled the two pieces of rope and used the Velcro tab to hang them from the pack.

He was just forcing himself to his feet when Jo asked straight-out, "Is there a way out? Can you find it?"

Given their extreme stress and danger, a lie might be the best thing he could do for her right now.

Chapter Fifteen

Whether Alan had been completely honest about their chances of making it out—or out in time to have even a remote chance of saving Lucy—Jo had no idea. All she could do was trust him. He'd gotten her this far. Her fear was that they couldn't move fast enough. Why leave Lucy alive?

Alan had claimed there was an opening to this cave less than half an hour away. Unfortunately, it would bring them out on a steep side hill much like the one where the bobcat had startled her. However, he remembered a dirt road directly beneath, one used by fishermen following the river.

"Drew and I had a hell of a hike home," he'd added wryly. "No fisherman around that day."

And he hadn't dared call his own father for a lift, she assumed.

Right now, she was awed at the strength that allowed a man who'd been shot and had lost more blood than she wanted to think about and who'd plummeted so far to a rocky landing that should have killed him to still move fast enough to avoid the bullets that would have finished him off. Somehow, he was already on his feet holding a light in his hand and leading her with rare hesitations through a maze of cave passages that were wetter than those above.

She gave a shuddery thought to the increased heaviness of earth above them before dismissing it.

A couple of places where Alan made a choice of which direction to go he stopped for long moments first, rubbing his gloved hand over the shiny wet limestone until he seemingly found...something.

Glancing back at her once, he said, "Drew or I marked turns when we were kids."

Twice, he stopped and said, "This isn't right," and they turned back to the previous intersection.

A few times they crossed large spaces, one a spectacular showroom displaying rippling flowstones like the grandest of stage curtains and enormous columns as awe-inspiring as those supporting Greek temples. Another time, she might have taken pictures, but right now, all she could think about was Lucy. What was happening? How much time had passed?

And then she stopped at a sudden realization. "My phone was in my pack."

Alan swung both the light and his head toward her, momentarily blinding her. "We might be able to find it later."

Later.

"Unless *he* picks up my pack."

"Is there anything in it that would identify you?"

Throat tight, she shook her head. "Except my phone, but he wouldn't be able to open it. You have yours, don't you?"

"Yeah." He patted a pocket. "Lucky, since I have Drew's number."

Jo nodded and followed him when he started out again.

He must be in agony, unless he'd passed through that to a merciful numbness. Until she had that thought, Jo hadn't acknowledged, or really even noticed, that *she* hurt, too, from the hours and hours they'd hiked through the rough terrain, the stretches of crawling or creeping, the rope descent, the fear.

None of which mattered compared to her fear for her sister.

When he stopped, she walked right into him. They'd come to…a waterfall? No, she saw, a tumultuous stream was a better description. And there didn't seem to be any way to go but into the water.

He turned around. "We're close to the end, Jo, I promise. This is the tough stretch, though. We have to lie on our backs and let the stream take us. We might be completely underwater for fifteen or twenty seconds at a time. Most of the time, there'll be some air at the top of the passage."

Most of the time.

She replayed what he'd said and didn't like it any better this time.

"If you don't think you can do it, you can wait here. I'll come for you. I'll leave you with lights and my pack. There's food in there, warm clothes—"

Jo shook her head even though she didn't think she'd ever been so scared. "No. I'm not staying behind."

She was enough shorter, her light cast strange shadows on his face again, but she saw intensity and a struggle on his face.

Then he said huskily, "You're an amazing woman."

She tipped forward and wrapped her arms around him. The need for speed kept either from savoring the closeness for any length of time, but it helped.

"I'll have to leave my pack," he said, squatting and setting it down. "Let me find—"

What he had to find, apparently, were waterproof bags. She understood why when he deposited his phone and then his big gun in different ones. As a seeming afterthought, he took off his wristwatch and dropped it in one, too, before stowing both in pockets in his cargo pants.

"Okay," he said, still in that rough voice, "I think you should go first."

Because she was smaller, less likely to get stuck. So she could go on if he couldn't make it, and get help for Lucy.

As fast as the water seemed to be running, would he be able to retreat if he got stuck?

He knows what he's doing, she told herself. This was a different kind of trust. So she only nodded.

NOSE BARELY ABOVE WATER, Alan reached ahead to feel the cave ceiling dropping. Jo had gone through; at least, she wasn't thrashing right ahead, desperate for air.

Alan took a deep breath and propelled himself forward using his feet against the walls of the shrinking passage and his hand on the ceiling.

Maybe he'd tell Deputy Ed Madsen that he'd lost interest in cave diving, he thought with near humor.

The distraction worked long enough for him to find the next pocket of air. *If there was a hell*, he thought, *this might be it*. Or not. He'd seen plenty of forms of hell during operations around the world.

His shoulders wedged him to a stop in an especially narrow spot, although one that, thank God, allowed him to keep his mouth and nose above water. Wriggling to break the logjam wasn't as easy when the one shoulder and arm were laggardly about obeying commands, but he managed and let the water carry him on.

He saw Jo's face again, starkly lit, her determination to do anything to save the sister she loved so clear. If she could love him like that—

It might be too soon to think that way, but Alan knew that if she died in this cave, he wouldn't be getting over these feelings. He'd do anything to kill the bastard that had stolen her mother from her and destroyed and damaged so many other lives.

Another deep breath, another stretch to let the water carry him.

The next time he lifted his mouth for air, he not only found plenty to suck in, he saw that the stream was widening and the ceiling raised. He was seeing because daylight penetrated the cave. At first it was diffuse, almost an illusion, then brighter and brighter. Rolling in the water, knees bumping rocks, he crashed into a larger obstacle, and a hand reached for him.

"What *took* you so long?"

Pushing himself to his knees and taking in Jo's anguished expression, Alan said, "I'm bigger than you. I was more like a cork that kept getting stuck than a piece of sediment that flowed out with the wine."

A sound escaped her that might have been either a laugh or a sob, and she shook her head. "Look! It's beautiful!"

Getting to his feet, he did look, and she was right. Water tumbled over sharp gray rocks in a glittering cascade toward the winding river that cut through the valley below. The typical mix of deciduous trees in the Missouri woods were in bright green leaf. The sky arched above, a pure blue. And there was a dirt track along the river, just as he'd remembered.

Prettiest of all was the soaking wet, battered and exhausted woman beside him.

Alan gave her a jubilant hug, a brief, passionate kiss, then ripped off his glove with his teeth and reached in the pocket with the phone. Jo took the bag from him and opened it. He went to his most recent calls and touched Drew's name.

His friend—yeah, he thought they were friends again, or still—answered on the second ring.

Jo HAD TO help Alan more than the other way around to descend the steep, rocky hillside. He muttered a few curses at his shoulder and the arm that he claimed was starting to come to life, but too damn slowly. He didn't hesitate to let her take some of his weight when that made sense.

Drew Frazier waited at the bottom for them, leaning against a department SUV. He had a second cop with him, not Deputy Hudson, thank goodness. Jo's instinctive distrust of Hudson was probably unfair, but his inclusion now would have made her uncomfortable.

"My place," Alan said as soon as Frazier reached out to clap him on his back. "We'll talk on the way. I've got to clean up a little."

He and she climbed in the back, dripping all over the seats and floor. Alan did most of the talking with Jo only chiming in as needed, mostly to explain the backstory of why she'd been so determined to explore the section of the cavern that her stepfather had made forbidden.

Drew called to have the road into the caverns blocked, then said, "I'll request a warrant while I'm waiting for you."

Naturally, Alan made light of his injuries, but she kept her mouth shut about those.

Ten minutes later, the SUV rocketed up Alan's dirt driveway and slammed to a stop in front of his house. He hustled her inside, said, "Only one bathroom. Once I'm out, it's all yours. I'll find some clothes that will do for you."

"Okay. I'll hurry."

And that's when he broke it to her that she was going to be left behind. It didn't matter what role she'd played thus far, how capable she was, she wasn't a cop, and wouldn't be allowed along on a police raid.

"*You're* not a lawman anymore!" burst out of her.

"Drew's trying to deputize me. Somebody has to lead them in."

"I could do that," she argued, "and I'm not the one who should be in the ER."

"Sorry." Voice and expression were adamant. Why had she bothered to waste her breath?

Furious, she was just as glad Alan and the other men were gone by the time she got out of the shower. If Lucy was alive, she'd need her sister, not a bunch of *cops*.

ALAN DIDN'T BLAME Jo for being royally ticked at being patted on the back and told she couldn't accompany them even as far as the cavern entrance. It wasn't fair, not after the courage she'd shown today, not when he knew she'd have followed orders. Maybe it was just as well that he was no longer in charge, though since the last thing he wanted was her in the line of fire again.

It was true that Drew needed one of them to lead them to the captured woman or women and to the bones. Reading Jo's glare, Alan appreciated her not having spoken up about how disabled he might be. Not finishing what he started wasn't in his genes.

He winced away from the thought that maybe Jo felt the same. She didn't have the same kind of background he did. He hated knowing how badly he'd screwed up, getting caught off guard like he had. The question of whether he'd made the wrong decision to run was going to eat at him forever if the killer had turned right around, because he had plenty of time, and killed another woman and maybe even his own daughter.

When Alan emerged from the house dressed in dry tactical boots, cargo pants and long-sleeve T-shirt, his gun on his hip, Drew waved at the back seat.

He drove as fast down the driveway as he had going the other way. Over his shoulder, he said, "Sheriff Robarts has officially deputized you."

In case Alan had to take an active role—say, in the event of a violent exchange with an unsub who could be a dangerous serial killer. He nodded his thanks.

A squad car was parked to block the turnoff to the cavern, while a second one hovered in wait for them. Alan appreciated the precaution. If any cops had driven in prematurely, there was the chance the sight would have panicked the killer if he hadn't already made a getaway. What if he grabbed a kid? He had nothing to lose at this point.

And that was based on the assumption that he either believed the cavers he'd pursued were strangers who had nothing to do with the investigation—or that there was no outlet from that lower level of the cavern. Or, hell, maybe he thought he'd taken care of them with that last spray of bullets.

The backup deputies peeled off toward the house.

When Alan, Drew and a deputy named Blake Norman walked into the gift shop, nobody who looked like Rod was in sight. A stranger manned the cash register and a long-haired guy who may have been a student was gathering a group for another tour.

Alan walked right to him. "Where's Rod Summerlin?"

Wide-eyed, the kid said, "I don't know. What's this about?"

"He's not leading a tour?"

"No, Brody has the one that's due back in—" he glanced toward a wall clock "—ten minutes."

"All right." Alan lowered his voice. "None of these folks will be going on a tour. Refund their money. We're halting operations for the rest of the day. Warn them they'll have to sit in their cars for a little while, too."

"But Rod has to make that decision—" He read Alan's hard stare just right and nodded.

Hands on the butts of their guns, Drew and one of the other deputies had disappeared down a short hall toward what were presumably offices and restrooms. They reappeared only moments later, shaking their heads.

Alan hadn't seen Rod Summerlin's truck in the parking lot. His tension ratcheted up. Was it possible they hadn't locked the barn door soon enough?

The guy at the register was issuing refunds to people who seemed more curious than mad. "I don't know what this is about," he kept saying.

Somewhere in there, the two other deputies walked in to let them know no one was answering the door at the house, a dog was barking frantically inside and no vehicles were parked there, either in the garage or next to it. Drew instructed one of the two to search the parking lot for Rod's truck, and he trotted out.

As tense as he'd ever been before any operation, Alan could *feel* each second ticking past. He understood why they were holding back; they couldn't let a bunch of tourists get caught up in a risk of being shot or grabbed. But he didn't like having to wait.

He heard the returning group before he saw them. Brody appeared first, caught his eye right away and hustled up to him. "Why are there a bunch of cops here?"

"Your operation is shut down for the day. You need to tell your group that the gift shop is closed, and they should return to their cars."

He expected an argument that didn't come. Brody made his announcement along with an apology. And explained how everyone on the staff needed to help with an active police investigation. They'd be free to leave as soon as possible.

Once he locked the front door behind the last family of tourists, Brody whirled. "Does this have to do with Lucy?"

"What do you know?" Drew asked.

"She's gone." He sounded the next thing to frantic. "Dad was really furious this morning. Jo isn't here, either, but she let us know she'd be visiting a friend today. I wondered, though—" He broke off.

"Wondered?" Alan prodded.

"If she wasn't lying. It's like she knew something she wasn't saying. Things have been…really tense around here lately."

"You were right. Jo is responsible for gathering the information that got us a warrant for this raid," Alan said right out. "She wanted to be here, but we couldn't allow that. She's safe, though."

"Lucy?" The boy's eyes searched Alan's.

The best he could do was say, "We don't know."

At the request for a key to the lock on the gate, Brody shook his head. "I don't know where Dad's been keeping it."

Alan bet there were a couple of copies, one on Dad's keychain. In fact…what if Lucy had taken her father's keys? He'd have noticed they were missing immediately.

"Do you know where your father is?"

"No. He's been…strange today." He frowned. "Mostly in his office, I think."

"His truck doesn't appear to be here. Did you see him leave?"

"No. Maybe somebody else did?"

But it turned out none of the employees had seen their boss in hours, which wasn't a surprise. There weren't enough of them to notice Rod's truck passing from the house unless someone had happened to glance out a window at the right time. Drew left two deputies behind with Brody and the other employees. Their instructions were to keep a sharp lookout for Rod returning in his truck.

Where the hell was that truck? The question stuck like a burr in Alan's mind. Jo's stepfather sure hadn't driven it into the cavern. Was there any chance at all they could have been wrong about who had chased them through the darkness?

He couldn't see it, though.

Summerlin could be on the run. Knowing his obsession with the family name and this damned cavern, Alan had trouble believing that, either. Rod had to know how hard it was to disappear, and that he'd be leaving everything he cared about behind. Still, they needed to check his bank accounts.

Watching Drew and Deputy Norman apply the bolt cutters to get the padlock off the gate, Alan pushed back at worry that would distract him from the moment. Once the gate swung open, the others stepped aside to allow him to take the lead. The silence felt ominous, even though he hadn't expected to hear any crying from here. Still—Rod had had time to kill Amy and—or—Lucy.

Not far in, Alan murmured to Drew, "Pretty sure from Jo's description that this is where the Summerlin kids held their parties." Drew turned his head to examine the room with the lamp attached to his borrowed helmet. Water shimmered in the light.

Only minutes later, Alan heard a whimper. He stiffened, as he was sure the other two men did. All three drew their weapons before Alan led the way, bent over—into a tight passage.

DESPITE HAVING BECOME aware that her entire body ached, Jo didn't think she could bear to just sit here. Alan's house was bare. A recliner sat in front of a TV, but what was she going to do, watch talk shows? Find something to read on the cinder block shelves she'd been surprised to see in his bedroom? Since her phone had been left behind, Alan couldn't even call her with news.

She rolled up the too-large borrowed sweatpants a bunch of times and still had to clutch the waist to be sure they didn't fall down as she paced. Her route led her to the front window in the stark living room. She could just see the corner of the new garage, which was when she was struck by the reminder that the one thing she *did* have was her car. She'd left the keys beneath the mat.

What would it hurt to drive over to the cavern entrance and wait for the men to reemerge? Surely Brody was there, even if the employees had been sent home. She was desperate to know what was happening, to *be* there if Lucy was led out alive. What Lucy needed should come first, even if Jo would be betraying Alan's trust that she'd do as he asked—or, in this case, ordered.

Damn it, either Lucy was alive, or she wasn't. Jo knew Alan would come back for her as quickly as he could.

Groaning, she went to explore those bookshelves after all, even though she couldn't imagine any story, however riveting, distracting her from this agony of waiting. But she chose a book and sat down at the kitchen table. She tried to read. She did. She even poured herself a glass of lemonade and sipped at it. The whole while, she waited tensely for the sound of a vehicle coming up to the house.

The stupid clock on the stove wasn't working, and it looked like the one on the microwave hadn't been set. She could measure the passage of time, though. Fifteen minutes. Half an hour. An hour. And she'd thought time crawled during their journey through the cavern.

Glass shattered at the front of the house. On a lightning bolt of adrenaline, she jumped to her feet. Someone was breaking in!

She raced for the back door and bounded off the porch. Grabbing again to hold up the sweatpants, she ran for all she was worth. If she could get to the car—

The man coming from the front of the house was cutting her off. Automatically measuring distances, Jo knew she wouldn't be fast enough. Then a gun shot tore up lawn right in front of her feet, breaking her stride, stealing precious seconds from her.

He plowed into her as if he were a linebacker, and she crashed down onto her face, his greater weight pinning her. Jo still thrashed and fought wildly, until something jammed into her neck.

The barrel of a gun.

Pretend to be surprised. Innocent, just as Alan had.

"Who are you? What are you doing?" she cried.

"You know who I am," her stepfather said, voice guttural. His chest heaved up and down. "And what I'm *doing* is figuring out the most satisfying way to kill you."

Rage took over. "You killed my mother!"

"Yes, I did. It's too bad I didn't take care of you then, too, but you were too handy. Now you've ruined everything."

It was Alan's hard face she saw when she closed her eyes and thought, *I'm dead.*

Chapter Sixteen

The men moved quietly. They hadn't really needed Alan's lead; it wasn't hard to follow the sound of hopeless crying. Ironic that it filled Alan with exhilaration. They were in time. Something good would come out of this. The knowledge was sweet, after his last police operation.

He was able to straighten at an intersection that wasn't quite a room. Turning left, he had to duck again. He moved now with his Glock held in firing position, his right hand barely supporting the left. A stench reached his nostrils, stronger than the whiffs he realized he'd been smelling for a couple of minutes.

In mere steps, he reached a much larger open space, sweeping it at gunpoint before allowing himself to focus on the two women staring at him. No, girls. Both were manacled to bolts driven into the wall. One was naked, bruised and emaciated, sitting in as close to a fetal position as she could get. The other wore jeans and a sweatshirt. One side of her face was discolored and swollen, the eye barely a slit.

"Lucy?" he asked.

She burst into tears. "You found us! We thought…earlier…"

"That was your sister and me," he said as gently as possible. "Was it your father who was here?"

Her face crumpled as she nodded.

The poor kid. "Bad luck he happened to be here. We had to circle around to get out of the cave so we could make a call."

He tipped his head toward Drew. "Lucy Summerlin."

"You're Deputy Frazier," she mumbled.

Shock not entirely hidden, Drew nodded kindly. "I can't tell you how glad I am to see you two girls." He'd lowered the small pack he carried and now took out a space blanket that he wrapped around the other young woman, who had fallen mute. "Amy Kendall?" he asked, voice soft, even though he, like Alan, had to recognize her from the photo plastered all over town.

Tears ran down her cheeks.

"Your family is going to be really glad to see you," Drew said.

Lucy watched, something fierce on her face that Alan recognized from her sister. She'd have done anything to protect Amy. In a way, that's what she'd done, he thought.

She ignored Deputy Norman, who appeared horrified but was bringing out the bolt cutters. "Where is my father?"

Alan squatted in front of her. "That was going to be my next question. When did you last see him?"

"He chased after you," she said. "We heard gunshots. When he came back, I thought he was going to kill us. He kept saying he was." A shudder rattled her. "He got mad at me a lot, but—"

Seeing her bewilderment, he gripped her knee. "He's your father."

"Except..." Lucy raised her gaze, filled with tumult, to his. "He said he killed my mother."

"Yeah. He did." There'd be time to talk, but this wasn't it. "What happened after he came back?"

Her lashes fluttered. "He said...he said maybe everything would be all right. He thought he'd taken care of some cavers who stumbled in here. He was going to go find out."

"Could you tell which way he went?"

She nodded. "His light was on. You know? He went right out of here."

"Back toward the entrance."

Leaving these traumatized girls in complete darkness. Alan had never hated anyone more. Still, he managed to sound calm. "Okay." He stood and turned to Drew. "You heard?"

"I heard. Howard? You go back and call for medics. Ask for a BOLO on Summerlin's truck, and more uniforms to surround this place. You can find your way out, can't you?"

Consumed by urgency and fear that he shouldn't have left Jo not only alone but unarmed, Alan suggested, "Why don't I go instead? I need to be sure Jo is okay."

Alarm transformed his friend's face as he understood immediately. They should have planned for all the eventualities if Rod wasn't here.

"Go. No, wait. Here's my keys. Call as soon as you get a signal."

"Will do." Alan caught the tossed set of keys and started for the arched opening. "I'll tell Brody Summerlin to wait to lead the other responders in."

Lucy's voice followed him. "Dad—he kept talking about Jo. Saying this was her fault. If he found her—"

A lump in Alan's throat kept him from answering. He only nodded before leaving, moving faster than was safe in passages that hadn't been cleared for the benefit of tourists.

The certainty that Jo needed him made him crazy.

"WHERE'S BURKE?" ROD PUSHED the gun barrel harder into her neck. "Was that the two of you in there?"

What was to be gained by not telling him the truth now? Jo thought. At least she could scare him, damage his God delusion.

"Yes. We called 9-1-1 as soon as we got out. He's gone with several deputies to free Lucy."

Rod wrenched her onto her back. "Maybe she's dead," he snarled.

"You'd kill your own daughter?" That was the hardest part to understand.

"I didn't want to."

Grief swept Jo. That sounded as if he'd already done it. "You're a monster."

"None of this would have happened if your mother hadn't tried to leave me."

"Oh, there's an excuse." She made no effort to hide her contempt.

He backhanded her, and her head rocked sideways, pain exploding over her cheekbone.

"If I'd been married, I'd never have gone out looking."

Dear God, how could he justify his evil, even to the point of being willing to kill his own child? But this time, Jo kept her mouth shut.

His eyes narrowed. "How'd you get out of the cavern? I've explored that level. There's no way."

"Obviously, there is. Alan explored all the local caves as a boy. He has a good memory, too. He led us straight out."

"That's not possible." His voice had risen.

"It is, if you're willing to trust yourself to the water and hold your breath for long stretches." In a bitter way, she almost enjoyed saying that. Rod had claimed to be the great cave explorer, but he couldn't swim. He'd have never considered sump diving, or even the far more tame way they'd floated out of the cave.

He swore viciously. "How long ago did he leave?"

"Like I'd tell you," she spat.

Jo desperately calculated. Would it occur to Alan, once Rod's absence became apparent, that he might come *here*?

Please, she begged silently. *Please let him be on his way back right now.*

AS HE EMERGED from the cavern, Alan paused only long enough to grip Brody's arm. "Your sister is alive. She's going to need you." When the boy started to turn, Alan shook his head. "Medics are on their way. They'll need you to lead them in. Can you do that?"

"Where—?"

"Not that far past the party cave. Take the middle passage. You'll smell waste and hear voices."

The young face hardened, and Brody nodded.

Then Alan dialed dispatch, passing on all the necessary information even as he ran to Drew's department vehicle, threw himself in, and put the car in gear. Ignoring the crackle of voices on the police radio, he accelerated with dangerous speed from the parking lot and along a road with virtually no shoulder separating his lane from a several hundred-foot plunge to the river.

Almost to his driveway, he saw the hood of what he recognized as Rod's old pickup truck barely visible in the single turnoff on this stretch of winding road above the river. He wouldn't have missed seeing it on their way to the cavern if it had been there. Right now, Alan didn't care where Rod had been in the interim, only what he'd find when he reached home. Should he drive in with siren screaming? Call for backup now that he knew Rod was here? Park and sneak in?

Making a decision, he drove a short distance up the driveway, then pulled to the side and parked. He called dispatch again and explained that the man they were hunting was here, at his house, and likely holding Jo Summerlin hostage.

"I'm sneaking in for a look. If I get a chance to take him down, I'll do it," he said bluntly. "But I want backup as soon as possible. Have them come in quietly, spread out around the yard. Sirens and the sound of an engine might trigger him to kill her."

"Yes, sir," the dispatcher said. "It's…really Rod Summerlin?"

"It is."

He ended the call while she was asking another question. Alan took the Remington rifle from the rack in the department vehicle, grabbed a box of ammunition, then set off up the driveway at a jog. Before the tree line, he veered to the left, thinking he might be able to approach using the cover of his pickup and Jo's car as well as the skeleton of the garage and the piles of lumber. The trees grew closer to the house from this direction, too.

An angry voice drifted to him.

God. Jo had to still be alive. Who else would that bastard be berating? They had to be outside, too, which might be bad news, depending on where they were. He could have sneaked into the house—

Then he saw them, the stocky man pinning Jo down right in the middle of the lawn. He had a gun in his hand, the barrel pressed against her neck. Scared to death, Alan realized the SOB would see or hear any approach.

Handguns weren't accurate from any great distance.

Despite the firestorm of emotion building in his chest, Alan remained capable of the detachment to calculate in an entirely familiar way. Unless something changed in the near future—Rod drew Jo to her feet and shoved her toward the house, cavern entrance or head of the driveway—it wouldn't be possible to cuff and arrest him. Alan's best option was to set up with the rifle.

Which would be doable only if his arm would stretch out in front of him…and if he had enough nerve and muscle control to squeeze the trigger gently with the index finger of a hand he could hardly feel.

He'd practiced with the Glock in his left hand plenty of times, but never with a sniper rifle. He had respectable skills with the rifle, but he'd always worked with a team that included one or two exceptional sharpshooters.

Who weren't here.

Okay. Where was the closest he could set up without drawing Rod's attention?

Alan scanned the familiar yard with the eye of a navy SEAL moving on his target.

STAGGERING, FALLING TO her knees again, Jo kept talking. This was her only possible tactic for delay. "Why did you ask me to come back for the summer?" If only she could get him to lower the gun…

Renewed rage lit on her stepfather's square-jawed face. "Because I thought you might be able to make Lucy see sense, of course! Some damn fantasy, and she won't hear about anything else!"

"Was it a fantasy?"

His laugh was even more unnerving than his visible anger. "The crying?"

"And the skull."

"I dragged that stupid deputy as far into the cavern as his nerve would let him go, and we didn't find a thing. Why would my own daughter think I'm lying?"

Because you were?

"Because there was a skull," she ventured to say. "Rusty must have found it."

He stared at her. "The dog? What was he doing in there?" Rod showed his teeth. "Don't tell me they were that stupid!"

Then she wouldn't.

He let loose of a long string of expletives.

"Where is the skull?"

His shoulders moved. "Tossed it in with the others."

The same place her body would go if he had his way— but in this, he didn't. Had he yet grasped that he'd reached the end?

Of course he had. The look in his eyes was answer enough. He intended to savor killing her, the stepdaughter he had never wanted who he now believed had bulldozed the construction of his twisted life.

But she also saw his uneasiness when he scanned their surroundings, not liking how exposed they were.

"Move it!" he snapped, yanking her to her feet and shoving her forward, his body almost pressed to her back so he could keep the gun in position.

Were they heading for the house? The cavern he believed should be his? Once in there, she'd have no hope of rescue.

Better to die quickly than let this monster possibly rape her before he put a bullet in her head, and then his own.

She stumbled, crying out. "You're hurting me."

A hideous expression on his face, he ground the barrel of the gun harder into her cheek until she whimpered involuntarily.

"You want to die *now*? Is that it?"

No, she didn't want to die, but even less did she want to give him any satisfaction whatsoever. He'd killed her mother and very likely her sister, stolen her family from her. Jo summoned all her rage and hate so as to be ready for the smallest mistake on his part that would let her take him off balance.

ALAN HAD TO wait until they disappeared into the house before he ran, staying inside the edge of the woods until he reached the back. The door stood open; he bet Jo had fled out that way when she heard Summerlin coming in the front.

Seeing no movement in the back windows, he took a chance and sprinted for the back porch, where he pressed himself to one side of the door. He carefully leaned the rifle against the wall; it would be no use to him in close quarters.

A voice came to him. Jo's.

"If you just hadn't grabbed Amy, none of this would have happened. I mean, Lucy was already up in arms, I was home... What were you thinking?"

Alan clenched his jaw. Was she baiting this bastard because she thought she could keep him talking, or because it gave her courage? Maybe even satisfaction?

Don't let it backfire.

Her stepfather did say something in return, his rumble harder to make out. Alan could tell they weren't in the kitchen, though, so he gripped his Glock in his left hand, braced it with his barely responsive right, and slipped into the house.

He'd learned which floorboards squeaked, so he was able to move swiftly and silently across the room. The pained sound Jo let out allowed Alan to pinpoint their location. Living room.

Two more steps, peering around the corner, he saw them.

Summerlin mostly had his back to Alan. The side of Jo's face he could see was swollen. She wouldn't see him.

What would the SOB do if Alan challenged him? Whirl to shoot at him? Or shoot Jo?

Alan waited. He'd been known for his patience, once upon a time, but when Jo was the one in danger…

Moving with shocking speed, she grabbed her stepfather's arm and shoved it up until the gun almost pointed at the ceiling. Alan took his chance even as she seemed to be trying to knee Summerlin in the groin at the same time.

"Police!" He stepped into the room. "Hands in the air!"

With a snarl, Summerlin tore free from her grip and turned the barrel of his gun downward. Toward her. Alan pulled the trigger.

One shot was all it took.

AT THE CRACK of a gunshot, Jo could only struggle to understand why there was no pain. The next instant, Rod's body fell into hers, blood everywhere.

Screaming, she shoved at him, rolled out from under the weight, freezing when she could see his ruined head.

"Jo!" Roaring her name, Alan gave an extra push to free her from Rod.

"Alan?"

He dropped to his knees next to her, paying no attention to her stepfather's body only a foot or two away. She had never even dreamed of seeing a look on his face so frantic, as if losing her would have been unendurable.

She reached for his hand. "You shot him."

"I did. *God.*" He seemed to want both hands to tear open her shirt, then his fingers to thread through her blood-soaked hair. "You're hurt. Where are you hurt?"

"I'm not." Aches and bruises didn't count. "I'm not. He was going to kill me, but I think he wanted to—"

He could tell she didn't want to say the words, and finally did grip her hand. Hard. "I guessed. That's probably the only thing that kept you alive long enough for me to get here."

Jo made herself sit up. "Did you find them?" Her throat tried to clog. "The bodies?"

"We didn't get as far as the bones. I came back as soon as we found your sister and Amy Kendall, Jo. They're alive."

"He told me he'd killed them."

Alan shook his head. "Amy isn't in good shape, but she's young. Given a lot of help, she'll make it back." Something almost like a smile lifted one corner of his mouth. "I think Lucy is mostly furious." He grimaced then. "In shock. Her dad told her he'd murdered her mother. That he had to kill her because she wouldn't let up. That's…all going to hit her sooner or later."

At a thunder of footsteps on the porch, she started, then realized a uniformed man had entered with a handgun held in firing position. Even as he lowered it, a sound from the back porch suggested a second officer would be on them any second. A siren came from the road, but continued on toward town.

"That's probably the ambulance." Alan sank onto his butt, looking exhausted.

And why wouldn't he be? For a moment, their day flashed through her mind: him intercepting her right in front of the cavern entrance, the long, confusing trip through the dark labyrinth, the bones, the confrontation with Rod, the gunshots and plummet into the hole. The eventual escape, and everything that had happened since.

"You need to go to the hospital," she said, aware of the two cops staring down at her dead stepfather.

"Yeah. I kind of guess there'll be a few questions, too." His eyes, still desperate, met hers. "Will you come with me?"

"This time, you couldn't stop me."

Epilogue

The first person Jo saw in the hospital waiting room was her brother, who met her with outstretched arms. His face showed the remnants of tears he didn't seem to have noticed. "You're okay," he mumbled near her ear. "Dad didn't find you?"

Her own eyes burning, she pulled back. "He did. He's dead, Brody. Do you know what he did?"

Her brother nodded, his throat working. "I'm glad he's dead. I'd have killed him myself if I could."

The three of them sat down and Jo told him about the things Rod had said, and that Alan had shot him to save her.

Brody held out a hand to Alan. "You saved both of them."

Alan smiled crookedly. "I think your stubborn sister saved Lucy, at least." Then he grinned. "Both your sisters seem to be stubborn, come to think of it."

Brody laughed, a little out of control, then let his head fall forward and gripped his hair, pulling it hard. "I can't believe all this."

"Where's Lucy?" Jo asked. "And...and Amy?"

"They're both back there. The nurses kicked me out, but I'll bet they'll let you go in," he told Jo. "Amy's parents are here."

Jo was momentarily distracted when an older uniformed police officer walked in, looking around. His face was familiar. She must have seen a photo. He came straight to Alan. "Can I have a word?"

"Sheriff." Despite Jo's hand darting out to stop him, Alan stood. He and the sheriff walked a distance away and talked for a few minutes, Jo watching him in alarm.

When she saw that blood had soaked through his shirt, she jumped up and went to him. "Excuse me. Alan was *shot* today. They'd better have three doctors working back there."

The sheriff looked startled by her militant tone, but nodded, his gaze lingering on Jo's face. She paid no attention, marching Alan up to the counter, then accompanying him as if it was her right when a nurse immediately escorted him back to an ER stall. But once they sat him on a bed in a cubicle, he said, "Go see your sister. She should come first."

"I'm…" Heaven help her, she was crying. Why now?

Alan smiled with tenderness that squeezed her heart. He held out his good hand to her. "They're going to need you, you know. Brody and Lucy."

They would. Jo had already realized that. She had a chance to make up for the years she'd stayed away. Tomorrow, she'd give her notice to the school district in Illinois and try to find a job locally. She didn't even have to ask to see that Alan understood. What scared her was wondering what he'd do.

"I'm not going anywhere," he said, as if reading her mind. "I need you, too."

She flung herself against him, held him while they exchanged strength and comfort, exactly as they'd done so many other times during this nightmare of a day, and wiped her tears and probably some snot on his already filthy shirt.

When she lifted her head, he studied her wet, blotchy, swollen face as if he didn't even notice the nurse or doctor who'd just pushed back the curtain to enter.

Voice husky, he said, "The sheriff hinted that I might replace the useless detective who was nearing retirement anyway. Even if that doesn't happen, we can make this work." Muscles flickered in his jaw. "You and me. Assuming…"

She didn't need him to finish the sentence. "There's nothing I want more." Ignoring the audience, she kissed him. Not very well, or for very long, but he looked satisfied, and she felt buoyed by hope when she rushed out to find her sister.

* * * * *

SECRET ALASKAN HIDEAWAY

KAREN WHIDDON

Chapter One

Rainy season in August hadn't been an understatement, Dr. McKenzie Taylor muttered to herself as she gripped the steering wheel. She kept her focus on the taillights of the car in front of her. Alaska might be beautiful, but since it had been overcast and pouring rain ever since she'd landed in Anchorage, she couldn't actually tell. Now the downpour made it difficult to even see the road. Though only late afternoon, she had her headlights on, praying she'd make it to her destination before what light remaining in the sky vanished.

Worse, her phone GPS had stopped working half an hour ago due to lack of reception. She had no idea where she actually was, other than on the correct road. Hopefully. She thought she might be getting close to the tiny Alaskan village of Blake, which would be her home for the next two years, even though she'd yet to see a sign announcing the distance.

Without a working GPS, she'd need to pull over and look at the folded paper map the gas station attendant several miles back had insisted she take. Now she understood why. If not for her luck in having a car in front of her, she'd have given in to extreme worry by now.

Having someone to follow helped keep her calm and grounded. And she still had a screenshot of the email they'd sent her with directions to her cabin.

Wind-lashed rain buffeted her Jeep and her wipers could hardly keep her windshield clear enough for her to see. She would have preferred to creep along at a much slower speed, but she had to keep up with the vehicle in front of her or she'd lose her guide. For whatever reason, that driver felt comfortable going at a normal rate of speed despite the limited visibility.

The sound of the pavement under her tires changed. The metal and wood railings that appeared on both sides of the road meant she was on some sort of a bridge, though she could barely make out the river flowing below due to the rain.

Inexplicably, the car in front of her picked up speed. As she nervously pressed the gas pedal to increase hers, the other vehicle swerved hard left, crossing into the opposite lane before careening back and hitting the railing hard. Kenzie stepped on her brake, sending her Jeep fishtailing on the slick road. Heart pounding, she watched, horrified, as the other car went airborne, up and sideways, rolling as if in slow motion before disappearing as it plunged into the rain swollen water below.

Damn, damn, damn. Since there wasn't a shoulder, she kept going, praying the bridge would end soon. It did and as soon as she could safely pull over, she parked and turned on her hazard lights. Out of habit, she grabbed her phone since she knew she should call 911, but she still didn't have a signal. Rescue, if possible, would be entirely up to her.

Taking a deep breath, she opened her door, regretting that she hadn't thought to buy an umbrella as cold rain slammed into her. Heart pounding, she began the steep descent, slipping and sliding on the muddy earth, grabbing hold of branches and rocks. Soaked and chilled instantly, she hurried as much as she could, aware she had to be careful not to fall and injure herself.

Finally, she reached the bottom, drenched, her hands muddy and bleeding. The roar of the river mingled with the sounds of the driving rain. A few feet from the edge, she could see the car, still only partially submerged, water swirling around it and the rocks it was wedged between. Had the driver made it out? If not, she'd need to swim out there and try to help before the car traveled too much farther downstream.

Just as she was bracing herself to jump into the no doubt icy water, she spotted a person breaking the surface and trying to swim. Head bobbing, splashing against the current, moving slowly in an attempt to reach the shore.

From where she stood, shivering, it appeared to be a losing battle. But then, miraculously, the swimmer somehow made it out of the middle of the fast-moving water, into what appeared to be a shallower area. Here, the water hit chest-high.

A man, she thought, though she couldn't yet be certain.

"Hey!" she called out, not sure if her voice would carry over the sounds of the rain and the river. "Over here!"

Somehow, he heard her and managed to fight against the current long enough to come ashore fifty yards downstream from where she stood. As he emerged from

the water, she saw her initial assessment had been correct. This was a male, a very large one at that. For the
first time, she realized she might have placed herself in
danger. One of her first purchases in Anchorage after
her Jeep had been a pistol, but it was still inside the box
in her back seat. Not much help to her there.

Still, she'd had no choice. She couldn't have simply
driven on after watching the car plunge off the bridge.

As he made his way toward her, she turned and
began up the embankment, trusting he would follow.
Unless… The thought occurred to her when she'd gotten
halfway toward the top. Unless he was injured. Which
wouldn't surprise her, considering how far his car had
fallen.

Grabbing hold of a sturdy bush, she turned to look
back over her shoulder. He'd made good progress, she
thought, pushing sodden hair out of her face. "Can you
make it up to the road?" she shouted, the wind attempting to carry her words away.

"I think so," he hollered back. "I have to."

Glad he understood the situation, she resumed her
climb. So cold her hands were numb, she clenched her
teeth to keep them from clattering.

Finally, she reached the road. Her Jeep's blinking
hazard lights were a welcoming beacon. She hurried
over to climb back into the driver's seat, turning the
heat on full blast. Chilled to the bone, from her soaked
clothes and icy skin, she needed warmth. *Now what?*
she wondered, as she waited for the man to join her. The
nearest hospital would be back in Anchorage, which
was over a two-hour drive. If he needed medical attention, she'd have to render aid herself. If he was too

badly hurt, once she reached Blake she had the option of calling for a plane to get the patient to the hospital. Apparently, even a village as small as Blake had its own landing strip.

Finally, after what seemed like an eternity, the man climbed up onto the roadway and headed straight for her vehicle.

When he got in, the first thing she noticed was that he was shivering as violently as she. The second, as he turned to face her, was that despite his rain-plastered hair and the bruises that purpled his face, he had really good looks. Rugged features, including a strong jaw and high cheekbones, and light blue eyes. He struggled to fit into the passenger seat, making her realize she hadn't imagined his size. He appeared to be well over six feet tall, with broad shoulders, large hands and long fingers.

"I'm a doctor," she told him, her voice as brisk as she could make it. "Let me take a look at you, as best as I can in this space. Do you hurt anywhere?"

He turned, his blank stare giving her cause for concern.

"I don't know who I am," he said, his voice horrified. "Or where I live. I don't know anything."

"You must have hit your head in the crash." Attempting to reassure him, she lightly touched his shoulder. He flinched away. Undeterred, even though she kept her hands in her lap, she continued, "The memory loss is likely only temporary."

Some of the panic left his gaze. "Do you think so?"

"I do." Another thought occurred to her. "One question. Do you remember if there was anyone else in the car with you?"

"I don't know." He rubbed his temples. "I don't

think so, but I can't be certain." Expression dubious, he glanced at the window and the rain still pounding them. "I'm thinking I'm not going back out there to check."

Even if he did, he'd be too late. By now the car would have either gone under or traveled farther downstream. If someone were still trapped inside, she doubted they'd have a chance.

Keeping those thoughts to herself, she nodded. "Going back would be too risky. Buckle in and we'll get going. I'm hoping to make it to my destination before dark. Though I've read it doesn't get dark until after nine thirty around here at this time of the year."

Silently, he did as she requested, clicking the seat belt into place. "Where are we?" he asked, swallowing hard.

"Alaska," she answered. "A few hours northwest of Anchorage."

When he didn't respond, she put the shifter into drive, windshield wipers on high, and carefully pulled out onto the road. Without another vehicle to follow, she found herself creeping along, terrified she'd accidentally drive off the road or the edge of some cliff.

Even with the car heater on full blast, she couldn't stop shivering, no doubt due to her sodden clothes. She glanced over at her still-silent passenger, who sat hunched in the front seat, arms crossed in front of him.

"Are you okay?" she asked. "After a wreck like that, if we were anywhere else, I'd be taking you straight to the nearest hospital."

"I'm fine," he responded, his voice a deep rumble. "Cold, a bit sore, but as far as I can tell, nothing is broken."

Eyeing the darkening bruises on his face, she sighed. "I suspect you're going to hurt like hell tomorrow."

"Maybe so." His shrug indicated the prospect didn't bother him. "I just need my memory to come back."

Though still raining, the intensity of the storm seemed to be letting up. She could actually see more than twenty feet in front of her. Relieved, she allowed herself to drive a little bit faster.

A sign came into view. *Blake—twenty miles.*

"We're almost there," she said, more relieved than she cared to admit.

He swung his head around to stare at her. "Is Blake the name of the town where you live?"

"It will be, yes. They call it a village instead of a town though. I've actually never been there. I'm from Texas. I'm a new doctor and I signed a contract to provide medical care in Blake for the next two years. In exchange, they'll take care of my not-insignificant medical school debt."

"That's a thing?" he asked.

"It is." She smiled. "I couldn't pass up such a generous offer, even if it means I'll be living and working in the middle of nowhere."

"What are you going to do with me once we get there?" he asked, his voice as tight as his expression. "I have no idea who I am or where I belong. You can't just dump me off somewhere."

He had a point. "I wasn't planning on it," she told him. "If you're from around here, maybe someone in Blake will recognize you."

"I can't do that." His flat tone and closed-off expression concerned her. "Not yet. Please. I need at least a day to try and figure things out."

Considering, she kept her gaze on the road. She might

be crazy, but she had a gut feeling about this. It would be all right. How could she not help this man, who'd managed to survive the not survivable?

"You can stay with me," she softly replied. The raw gratitude on his handsome face made her heart hurt. "For now, we're in this together. Hopefully, the rest will sort itself out."

Expression once again shuttered, he nodded. "I appreciate it."

"I'm McKenzie Taylor," she said. "Kenzie for short."

"Dr. Taylor."

Pleased, she nodded. "Yes. I'd ask your name, but you said you don't know it."

He thought for a moment, then shook his head. "It's not there. Yet. I'm hoping you're right and that it'll soon come to me."

"It will. Here." Reaching into the console, she pulled out her phone and handed it to him. "Open up my photos. I've got a screenshot in there with directions to the cabin where I'll be living. Can you take a look at it and read it out loud to me?"

As his large hand closed over her phone, she shivered. To cover, she made a quick remark about getting out of these wet clothes, which only made things worse. Cheeks flaming, she shook her head, wondering what on earth had gotten into her.

If he noticed, he gave no sign. Instead, he turned her phone over in his hands as if he wasn't sure what to do with it. But then, he appeared to figure things out, touching the photos icon on the screen and pulling up her albums.

"It should be the first picture," she said, suddenly

and absurdly nervous about him scrolling through her personal pics.

"I've got it." He glanced at her, his blue eyes glazed. "We need to check the next mile marker. It says there's no street sign on the turnoff road."

Sure enough, they were almost there. She turned off on the dirt—now mud—road, glad she'd gotten a vehicle with four-wheel drive. Still, she couldn't help but worry she'd get stuck.

Luckily, she didn't.

"There." He pointed. Set in a clearing surrounded by trees, the small wooden cabin looked more primitive than she'd been led to believe.

Maybe the rain made it look worse than the photo they'd sent her. She pulled up near the covered front porch and eyed her companion. "Ready to make a run for it?"

He grinned. "I am."

The change in his expression completely lit up his face. Boyish charm combined with rugged good looks could be a dangerous combination.

"Do you have a key?" he asked.

Somehow, she found her voice. "They said they left one under the doormat."

"Do you have luggage?"

"Yes." She turned and pointed to her three suitcases in the back. Dry clothes would be heavenly. "I'll get them. You go on inside. I'll be right there."

Instead of doing what she'd asked, he came around and grabbed her largest bag, hefting it up like it weighed nothing. Once he had that, he grabbed another, leaving the third for her to bring in. He trudged up the steps, setting the suitcases down on the covered porch, and rummaged under the doormat until he found the key. Right behind him, she waited while he unlocked the front door, his sheer size making her feel absolutely tiny.

As they entered, she flipped the switch just inside, immediately flooding the room with light. "I'm glad they had the power turned on."

"Me too," he rumbled. "Though it's still cold. But look." He pointed, still shivering violently. "You have a fireplace. With dry kindling stacked on the hearth. Let me see if I can get a fire started."

While he worked on that, she took a look around. The small cabin appeared tidy, with well-used furniture. She had a couch, one armchair and a square end table with a lamp. At one end of the room, she spotted a small kitchen and a two-person dining table. A doorway led to a tiny bedroom with attached bath. *Not bad*, she thought. Rent free, all utilities paid, this would be her home for the next two years.

"I got a fire going," her unexpected houseguest said, pushing to his feet. By dint of his sheer size, he made the entire cabin seem smaller.

Then, before she could respond, his expression went slack and he fell, crumpling in a boneless heap, clearly unconscious.

Luckily, the couch sat right there and caught him, keeping him from any further injury. In full physician mode, despite her own discomfort, she hurried over. Seeing the way he still shivered with cold, she knew the first thing she needed to do was get him out of his wet clothes. The fire he'd started had become a small blaze, putting out some decent heat.

In a small linen closet, she located a few plush towels and grabbed two, carrying them over to where he lay, still out.

She started with removing his soaked work boots and socks. From there, she was able to tug his jeans and undershorts off, using a towel to cover his private area. Once she'd done that, she managed to get his legs up onto the couch so he wasn't hanging half off. Inside his jeans pocket, she discovered a cell phone, but the water had destroyed it.

Removing his sodden shirt was more difficult. Once unbuttoned, she tried to lift him up to get the shirt out from under him, but couldn't. Instead, she shimmied it little by little, then gave it a few hard tugs.

Once she'd removed his wet clothing, she dried him with the other towel. His muscular body, she noted, trying for a clinical detachment, appeared fit, as though he spent a fair amount of time working out. A perfect male physical specimen.

Without X-rays, she couldn't tell for sure if he had any broken bones or internal injuries. Since he had a lot of purpling bruises, she didn't think he'd emerged from the accident as unscathed as he'd hoped.

Still, he'd been moving fine and hadn't complained of any pain. All those were good things.

His only major symptom appeared to be memory loss, which she felt quite sure would be only temporary.

Pushing to her feet, she grabbed a blanket from the bed and covered him. She'd try waking him in an hour just in case he had a concussion, but right now she wanted nothing more than a hot shower and a change of clothes.

WARM. FOR THE first time in what felt like forever, he was warm. He stirred, struggling to open his eyes. Where was he? *Who* was he? Heart pounding, he sat up, realizing he was completely naked underneath a blanket.

Rain pounded on a metal roof and he remembered. Some of it. There'd been some sort of accident and he'd ended up in a fast-moving river. A woman had helped him. A pretty doctor named McKenzie. This was her cabin.

"There you are," a soft feminine voice said. Her. He blinked, trying to focus, belatedly realizing he hurt like hell all over.

"I just finished heating up some soup," she continued. "Plus, I made a couple of grilled cheese sandwiches for us. I think you might feel better once you get some food into you."

He nodded to show his agreement, wincing as the movement sent sharp pain lancing through his head.

"I need to examine you again," she told him, clearly noticing his discomfort. "After we eat."

About to stand, he remembered his clothes were gone. "I'm naked," he said. "Did you undress me?"

Though twin spots of color bloomed high on her cheekbones, she held his gaze and nodded. "I had to. Your clothes were—are—soaked. After I got you out of them, I dried you off."

"Thank you." He couldn't imagine how difficult that must have been. After all, he'd guess he outweighed her by over a hundred pounds.

"No problem." She gestured toward his blanket. "Go ahead and wrap that around yourself while we eat. This cabin came not only fully stocked with food, but with a washer and dryer. I went ahead and washed what we both were wearing. I just put everything in the dryer, so your clothes won't be ready yet."

Following her into the kitchen, he saw she'd placed their meal on the table. Two bowls of steaming tomato soup, including two perfectly toasted grilled cheese sandwiches, along with two tall glasses of water.

"I couldn't believe they'd gotten me all that food," she said, pulling out her chair. Judging by her jerky movements and the way her gaze kept darting toward him and then away, he made her nervous. He supposed he couldn't really blame her. She was a woman alone in a remote cabin with a man she didn't know. He wanted to tell her that he wouldn't hurt her, but suspected that hearing him say such a thing might have the opposite effect.

"You're too kind," he said instead, pulling out the opposite chair and slowly sitting. "I feel like I've been run over by a truck."

"You've got a lot of bruises," she agreed. "Though without access to my X-ray machine in my new clinic, I have no way to tell if you've broken anything. I'm not due to start work until Monday, but I imagine we can stop by my clinic before then if necessary."

Picking up his spoon, he sampled the soup. Warmth flowed down his throat, for which he was grateful. "I don't think anything is broken," he told her. "That's a different kind of hurt. I'm just banged up."

Though she nodded, her expression seemed doubtful. But she took her cue from him and for the next several minutes it got quiet while they both concentrated on their food.

He finished before her, making him realize he'd been shoveling food into his mouth as if he hadn't eaten for days. Who knows, maybe he hadn't.

"Would you like another sandwich?" she asked, putting her half-eaten one down.

"No thanks. I'm good." Hating this awkward sort of politeness that had come over them, he tried to come up with a way of getting them at least back to the way they'd been in the car. She'd been fierce and fearless, determined to save a man she didn't even know. "I owe you a world of thanks," he said. "For what you did back there. I don't know how I'll ever be able to repay you."

She waved off his words with one graceful movement of her hand. He noted her nails, though cut short, were painted a bright pink.

"Has anything come back to you? Like your name? Or what happened to make you drive over the side of that bridge?" she asked.

He gave her question the careful consideration it deserved, squashing a flare of panic when he realized he still drew a blank slate. "No. Not yet."

"Once this rain lets up, I think we should drive into Blake and ask around. If you're from here, people will recognize you. That might help jog your memory."

This time, the panic made his throat close. He didn't know why, but he felt positive going into town would be a horrible idea. "I can't," he managed. Then, aware of the way she watched him, he took a deep breath. "I'm going to be honest with you. I have no idea who I am or what happened, but something tells me I'm in some sort of danger."

Without saying anything, she continued to watch him.

"I'm serious." He spread his hands. "I know you don't owe me anything and you've certainly done more than enough, but could you let me stay here a few days? I can sleep on the couch. I just need some time to figure things out, which I can't do until my memory comes back."

She tilted her head, which caused a section of her long auburn hair to fall in a curtain over her face. As she brushed it away with her long, graceful fingers, he realized she was more than merely pretty. She was beautiful. She was also a woman alone with a strange man she didn't actually know. He couldn't blame her if she refused. Yet with everything inside of him, he hoped she wouldn't.

"You can stay," she finally replied, unsmiling. "But you should know that I do have a pistol and I know how to use it if necessary to protect myself. You seem like a nice enough person, but I feel it's only fair I should warn you. This little village of Blake and the surrounding area is counting on me to provide medical services for the next twenty-four months, and I don't want to let them down. Are we clear?"

Though he found her speech endearing, he knew enough to hide his smile. "I'm glad you have a gun. I honestly believe that kind of protection is necessary for a woman living on her own in such a remote place." He took a deep breath. "It's not much but I promise while I'm here, I'll also protect you if you need me to."

Her brown eyes searched his face. Then, almost as if she understood he felt the need to repay her in any way he could, she nodded. "Thank you," she finally said.

"One more thing." While he hated to ask, his gut instinct told him he had to. "Would you hold off on mentioning my accident and the fact that my car ended up in the river? This is a remote enough area that I think it will be a while before anyone notices."

Judging by the tightening of her mouth, she didn't particularly like that request. "Why? You're acting like you have something to hide. Do you?"

He spread his hands in what he hoped was an appeasing gesture. "I don't know. And I won't until my memory comes back. But for whatever reason, I can't shake the feeling that I'm in some sort of danger. That's why I want to lay low until I can figure things out."

"Danger." A frown creasing her forehead, she eyed him. "What kind of danger and from whom?"

"I wish I knew. Right now, I have no idea."

Still holding his gaze, she finally shrugged. "Well, I'm guessing no one who wishes you harm will find you here. We'll do the best we can. You're welcome to use the shower if you want to get cleaned up. Your clothes should be dry by the time you finish. Now if you'll excuse me, I need to get unpacked and then make a few phone calls to let people know that I've arrived." With that, she disappeared into the bedroom.

Now that she'd mentioned it, a shower sounded like heaven. Moving slowly, since any movement at all made him realize he got sorer by the moment, he made his way toward the small bathroom located off the bedroom.

Kenzie had placed her suitcases on top of the bed and had gotten busy unloading them. She glanced up when he entered and smiled. "I put a clean towel and washcloth out for you. Enjoy your shower."

Struck dumb by the sheer beauty of her smile, he

managed a nod before slipping into the bathroom and closing the door. Heart pounding, he took a moment to collect himself. Along with not knowing his name, he also had no idea of his character or what kind of man he might be. The image of Kenzie smiling at him next to a bed had sent a bolt of pure lust through him, even though her smile told him she had no idea of her effect on him.

Shaking his head at himself, he dropped the towel, his arousal unsurprising. Kenzie definitely was easy on the eyes. He worried about her, though. He might not know his own name or where he belonged, but he knew enough about life to understand how dangerous things could be for a woman like her alone. She trusted too easily, making him want to caution her against being too careless. He would too, eventually, just not today. Instead, for as long as he was around her, he figured he'd do his best to protect her as repayment for her kindness. Even if that meant protecting her from himself.

Chapter Two

Kenzie hadn't been aware she'd been holding her breath
until she heard the sound of the shower starting and she
exhaled. Her guest seemed like a gentle giant, but she
more than anyone knew how deceptive initial appearances could be.

Rummaging around in her bag, she located the box
containing her brand-new SIG Sauer P320. She'd chosen a compact version and 9mm so she wouldn't have
as much kickback when firing. Though she'd taken numerous classes and spent hours at the firing range in
order to get her Texas concealed handgun permit, this
was the first pistol she'd ever owned.

She'd felt a bit of trepidation when purchasing the
gun, but having it made her feel more secure. While
she considered this entire Alaskan move an adventure,
she hadn't planned on having a very large, very disoriented houseguest. Right now, he didn't seem dangerous, but who knew whether that might change once his
memory returned.

In fact, letting people know she'd arrived would be
wise. She pulled out her phone, relieved to see she now
had reception, even if only one bar showed. She'd pro-

grammed Jane Norman's number into her contact list since the mayor had been her point of contact throughout the entire process.

Jane picked up on the second ring. "Dr. Taylor! I take it you've arrived at your cabin safely?"

"I have," Kenzie responded. "Despite the rain. Thank you so much for stocking the place with food. I appreciate that more than you know."

"Delighted to do it. Would you like to meet up for lunch tomorrow? I'd love to show you around the village." She chuckled. "Such as it is. Blake is really a one streetlight kind of place."

"Lunch sounds wonderful. Noon?"

"Perfect," Jane responded. "I'll text you the directions to City Hall. You can't miss the sign. Our local watering hole is called Mikki's and we can lunch there."

The shower cut off just as Kenzie ended the call. Remembering all he had was a towel, she all but ran for the dryer. His clothing seemed dry enough, so she carried it back and tapped on the bathroom door. "I'll leave your clothes outside the door," she said. "Everything is warm and dry." And then, because her bedroom really was small, she retreated to the kitchen to give him a little privacy.

Weird how she suddenly found herself with a roommate, even if the situation was only temporary. Though she had no idea if harboring this man was a good idea, she knew she couldn't simply turn him out into the Alaskan wilderness with nothing but the clothes on his back. Hopefully, once his memory returned, he'd have family or friends he could contact to help him.

His notion that he might be in danger slightly concerned her, but she guessed certain paranoid tendencies could surface accompanying loss of memory. In medical school, amnesia or amnestic syndrome had been treated as if it were unimportant and unlikely. Not much was known about the condition, and there was no specific treatment. Brain trauma could definitely be a cause, and considering the type of accident her John Doe had been involved in, that was highly likely.

When he emerged a few minutes later, hair damp but fully clothed, he looked as if he felt better. Despite the scattered yellow and purpling bruises on his face and arms, she found him ruggedly attractive. The shower had clearly refreshed him.

"That felt amazing," he said, his smile crinkling the corners of his light blue eyes. She couldn't pull her gaze away.

Clearly oblivious to his effect on her, he stretched, wincing. "Ouch."

At that, her physician instincts took over. "I wonder if you might have bruised a couple of ribs. We'll get you into my clinic as soon as possible so I can take a few X-rays."

He waved her comment away. "Not necessary. I'm sure I'll heal up pretty quickly." Yawning, he covered his mouth with one large hand. "I hope you don't mind, but I'm going to lie down on the couch and try and get some shut-eye. I'm exhausted."

"Let me see if I can find another pillow and get you a couple of blankets," she said. Outside, the rain continued to drum on the metal roof.

She found what she needed in a small linen closet in her bedroom and hurried back to the couch. Her guest had already stretched out, awkwardly trying to fit his large frame onto the too-small sofa. Though she felt a twinge of pity for him, she wasn't about to offer him her bed. If she were to have any privacy at all, she'd need to hold on to her own separate bedroom.

When he saw her carrying the blankets and a spare pillow, he got to his feet and took them from her. "I really appreciate this," he said, his gaze direct. "Honestly, if there's some way I can repay you once I'm back to normal, I promise you that I will."

Ignoring the tug of attraction she felt when his bright blue eyes met hers, she smiled. "No repayment necessary," she replied. "I hope you have a good night's rest."

With that, she retreated to her bedroom, wishing she had a door to close. Since she didn't, she went into her bathroom to change and brush her teeth. Then she hurried to her bed, slipping beneath the covers before turning out her light.

The sounds of someone moving about in the other room woke her. Disoriented, she sat up in bed and dragged her hand through her hair, not sure for a moment exactly where she was. When she remembered, she realized the sounds she heard were her unnamed houseguest, no doubt making a cup of coffee in the kitchen.

Again, she felt a quick flash of panic. What had she done, letting a strange man stay alone with her in an isolated cabin? Shaking her head at herself, she pushed back the covers and swung her legs over the side. She decided to take another hot shower, and brought fresh clothing along with her pistol into the bathroom with her. She also locked the door.

Thirty minutes later, clean, hair blow-dried and a little makeup applied, she felt like a different person. Still, she strapped her holster on, because she'd rather be safe than sorry.

The tantalizing smell of bacon hit her the moment she opened the door.

"I made breakfast," he said, smiling. For a moment, her stomach did a funny little dip at the sight of him in the tiny kitchen. He might be a big man, but he seemed affable and even a bit goofy, though comfortable in his own skin.

Her jumpiness wasn't like her. But she had gone someplace as far away from Texas as she could get. She felt like a fish out of water already, and taking in a stranger—a *large male* stranger—further complicated things.

He made them both plates and carried them over to the table.

"You still don't trust me." Dropping into the other chair, he dug into his heaping plate. "I guess I don't blame you. There's no telling what kind of person I actually am."

Something about his choice of phrasing reminded her of home. Though he didn't have the Texan drawl she was accustomed to, she suspected under other circumstances the two of them would have hit it off quite well. Even if she wasn't looking for any kind of relationship right now.

She had a plan and she would be sticking to it. Two years working here and then, with her mountain of medical school debt paid off, she'd return to Texas and open her own general practice.

"I'm not sure how to respond," she replied, taking a small bite of her own scrambled eggs. "I'm trying to help you out, but…"

When she didn't finish, he pushed to his feet. "Do you want me to go? Because I will. I hate that I'm making you feel uncomfortable."

"Go where? You don't even know who you are." Then, hopeful, she looked up at him. "Unless you're trying to tell me that your memory has returned."

"It hasn't." He sat back down, pushing his hand through his short hair. "And you're right. I don't have anywhere to go. I don't even have a car. It's in that river." He sighed. "Still, if you want me out of here, I'll leave. I'll figure something out."

"You don't have to go anywhere," she said, meeting his bright blue gaze so he'd know she meant it. "In fact, I have an idea. Let's take a trip into Blake. I've talked to the mayor and she wants to meet me for lunch and show me around. I'm eager to see where I'm going to be working for the next twenty-four months. Seriously, I think something like this might do you some good. Maybe help jog your memory."

"I can't." He looked back at her with the haunted eyes of a trapped animal. "I don't know why, but something is telling me that for now, it's important I stay hidden. Please. I know how this sounds. But could you humor me? Just for a few days, until my memory comes back?"

She stared at him hard, unable to help but wonder if she might be harboring some sort of criminal. The weight of her holster felt only slightly reassuring. "Don't you think it'd be better to try and see if someone might know you?"

"No." Shaking his head, he swallowed. "I can't explain it, but I can't shake the feeling that I'm in some sort of danger. I need to keep my head down until my memory comes back and I understand what is what."

Not for the first time, she wondered if he might have a TBI, traumatic brain injury. She knew she didn't have the necessary imaging equipment to make that sort of diagnosis, but if necessary, she could make arrangements to get him to the hospital in Anchorage for an MRI and CT scan. Assuming, that is, that he allowed such a thing.

"I won't pretend to understand your reticence," she told him. "But I get that, sometimes, gut instincts are all we have to go on. I'll respect yours, for now."

He smiled, clearly relieved. "Thank you."

After they'd eaten, he insisted on cleaning up. She went back to her bedroom to finish unpacking, and then stepped outside to check out the weather. On the front porch, she stopped, awestruck. Sunlight lit up a verdant forest, lush greens and browns, the lingering raindrops lending everything an almost magical sparkle.

"Wow," she marveled out loud.

The screen door squeaked as he joined her. "Amazing." He turned slowly, his expression captivated, as if seeing all of this for the first time.

Watching him, his eyes bright with wonder, she felt a profound sense of kinship, like they'd both come to this beautiful landscape together. "I wasn't expecting it to be this beautiful."

He nodded. "The winters are harsh, but even then, this place is spectacular. Each season brings its own kind of beauty."

Her heart skipped a beat. Before she could comment, he shook his head. "Does that count as a memory? I guess it does. It might not be much, but I know that Alaska is my home."

Fighting the urge to hug him—and where had *that* come from?—she smiled up at him instead. "It's a start. I'm confident you'll remember more and more, even if it does come in bits and pieces."

Checking her watch, she realized she needed to get going. While she had written directions to get to Blake, she wasn't sure how long the drive would actually take. Plus, if she arrived a little early, she could always take a stroll down Main Street and check things out for herself.

"Be careful," he said, as she grabbed her car keys and a cross-body purse. "I'm not sure what condition the road will be in, but please don't try and drive through water."

This made her smile. "We have rain in Texas too," she pointed out. "The saying goes *don't drown, turn around.*"

With a jaunty wave, she climbed into her Jeep and drove off.

It wasn't until she'd gone a good way down the winding road that she realized she hadn't seen a single house yet. How isolated was her cabin? Just as she had begun to worry she'd somehow gone the wrong way, she spotted another cabin, set back off the road.

After that, she had periodic sightings of other homesteads, perched high on hillsides or hidden in lush enclaves of trees. Though she'd been told her lodgings were only ten miles outside of the village, the drive definitely seemed much longer. She had to wonder how she'd make it to work once the snows came. Coming from Houston, she'd definitely never driven in snow before.

Finally, she came to a small sign that read Welcome to Blake, Population 1068. Eagerly, she continued on, excited for her first glimpse of her new home.

Small had definitely been an understatement, she thought as she completed one final curve and Blake came into view. When the mayor had mentioned Main Street, Kenzie had envisioned a cute, touristy type place, like some of the small towns she'd visited while on vacation in Colorado.

Instead, Blake clearly existed only to serve its residents and those who lived nearby. As she approached the mostly deserted downtown area, she saw that most of the businesses served double or triple duty. Cruising slowly past, she saw a general store, a combination restaurant/doughnut shop/bar named Mikki's, and what appeared to be a drugstore, clothing store and shoe store combo. While there were a few empty storefronts with boarded up windows, at the end of the street she saw a real estate office that also served as a tourism bureau and fishing outfitter.

But the building that interested her the most was the brick one with the large sign that read Medical Clinic in bright red letters. Her workplace for the next two years.

Since she was early, she went ahead and pulled into the empty parking lot. No doubt the building was locked and she wouldn't be able to go inside until the mayor gave her the key, but she wanted to check it out anyway. The structure looked serviceable and sturdy, if a bit dull. The faded red brick seemed to blend with the landscape and the lack of windows made her wonder if it was equally dark and dreary inside.

After getting out, she strode up to the front door. Just in case, she tried it. To her shock, it wasn't locked. Opening it, she stepped inside. The lights were on, which she found strange, but welcome. As she moved through the waiting area, with a nicely decorated reception desk, a woman came around the corner, with a pistol pointed directly at Kenzie.

ONCE HIS HOST had left the cabin, he felt even more like an interloper. Losing his memory frustrated him, infuriated him and worried the hell out of him. What if it didn't come back? What if he was doomed to spend the remainder of his days on Earth, wandering around in a fog with no past, no present and no name?

Unacceptable. He needed to try to figure out a way to help his mind remember everything he'd forgotten. But how?

He decided to start with what he did know. He'd been driving a car that had—for whatever reason—gone off a bridge into a river. Did he know for certain he'd been driving? No. Had he been alone? Again, he wasn't sure, though the idea that someone might have been with him made him sick to his stomach. Because while he'd made it out, no one else had.

For now, he had to believe he'd been alone and the driver. What had made him swerve and go over the side of the bridge? He closed his eyes, tried *hard* to think, but instead he got a fierce headache. Blank. All blank. All that he remembered of yesterday was emerging from the cold river in the pouring rain to find a woman waiting. Nothing at all before that moment.

He'd obviously been heading in the same direction as Kenzie. While he knew with a visceral certainty that Alaska was where he belonged, he didn't know specifically where. Was Blake, Alaska, his hometown? Did he have a history here, a family and friends, maybe even a job? For that matter, what did he actually do for a living? Eyeing his large hands, the lack of callouses on his fingers, he reckoned it hadn't been physical labor. Then what? But no matter how hard he tried to concentrate, his mind stubbornly remained blank.

Furious, he considered going for a walk to burn of some energy. But immediately, his seemingly irrational fear of being seen asserted itself and he knew he'd be staying put. At least for now, until he figured some things out.

He might not remember much but he suspected patience had never been one of his virtues.

Shaking his head, he knew he needed to focus again on what little he *did* know. Another thing he'd realized while looking at himself in the mirror was his excellent physical condition. Clearly, he worked out. Was he a personal trainer or a gym owner?

Again, he drew a blank. None of these thoughts brought the slightest jolt of recognition. And none of them even came close to answering the most important question he had. What kind of man was he? A good one or bad?

While he naturally hadn't wanted to admit as much to Kenzie, his nagging internal insistence that he couldn't allow himself to be seen concerned him. A lot. Because what reason could he possibly have for feeling as if he were in danger if not for some sort of shady dealings? He really hoped that wasn't the case. He didn't like to think of himself as a less than honorable person. But with nothing else to go on, he had no choice but to explore the possibility, as sickening as he found it to be.

He'd had a cell phone with him, though the water had ruined it, but no wallet, or keys, or any sort of identifying information. No doubt the car would have had a license plate and registration info, but with it at the bottom of a river, those would be damn near impossible to get without notifying the police.

And he wasn't even sure it had been his car. Why he would think this, he had no idea.

He hated this blankness. The not knowing what had happened was bad enough, but far worse was having no idea who he was or anything at all about his past and hell, even his present, felt like a special kind of torture.

His physical body might be bruised and battered, but his inner self had taken the worse beating by far. He could only hope Kenzie was right and all of that would return to him soon.

If only there were something he could do to speed the process along. He stepped outside onto the front porch, appreciating the beauty of the remote location. At least with such a long drive, no one would spot him just by passing by. Anyone would have to make a special trip and since Kenzie was so new to these parts, he doubted she'd have any visitors yet.

Safe. Right now, at this very moment in time, he felt safe. While he wasn't sure why that was such a huge issue, deep inside he knew it was. And he owed all that to Kenzie. Someday, he hoped he'd be able to repay her.

Deciding if a vehicle came by that he could easily hide behind a tree, he decided to take a walk. Later, when Kenzie returned, he thought he might ask her to drive him back to the river, hoping the sight of the crash area might do something to jog his memory. Right now, he was willing to try anything, as long as he could do so without any outsiders spotting him.

Exploring the forested area around the little cabin, he felt some of his tension ease. Though the house sat on a hill, the land behind it gradually rose even higher. He located a footpath of sorts and climbed all the way to the top. Here, even with all the evergreens, he had a view of not only the cabin but the long driveway and even part of the road beyond.

As he stood on a large boulder, surveying the primitive area below, he flashed back to…something. A memory? Gunshots, people screaming, running until more gunfire cut them down. Blood, so much blood.

And then, as he tried to process the horror he was witnessing, everything disappeared.

Blinking, he forced himself to relive what he'd just seen. Location? No idea. If he'd seen the shooter's face, he couldn't recall what it had looked like. Unless… A horrifying thought occurred to him. What if he had been the one doing the shooting?

Immediately, he shied away from such an awful thought. Yet, as distasteful as he found the idea, he couldn't entirely discount it. Truly, he had no idea if the dark blood of a murderer ran in his veins.

He could only hope this vision, if reality, had been

of someone else gunning down innocent people in cold blood, and not him. Jaw set, he decided that until he had proof otherwise, this would be what he'd believe.

Instead of returning to the cabin, he carried on hiking through the woods. He continued climbing, enjoying both the exercise and the clean pine-scented air. When he reached another area with good views, he stopped to catch his breath. In the distance, he could see the ribbon of water that had to be the river he'd driven the car into.

Turning slowly, the magnitude of earth and sky, mountains and valleys, made him realize one thing. Whatever else he didn't know, this state was his home, where he belonged.

Because he didn't wear a watch and had no phone, he had no idea how long he'd been hiking. He'd completely lost track of time. For all he knew, he might have been outside for hours.

Making his way back took longer than he remembered. But when he finally caught sight of the cabin again, Kenzie's Jeep was still gone. Which meant he hadn't stayed out in the mountains as long as he'd thought.

Relief flooded him. Once he'd picked his way carefully down the steep hillside and made his way to the porch, he took a seat in one of the wooden rocking chairs.

The vision. It had played out like a movie inside his mind. Had it actually been reality? Or some sort of weird dream? Though he supposed such a thing would count as some sort of breakthrough, how could he possibly tell Kenzie about it? They were virtually strangers and she definitely wouldn't feel comfortable with a man who might have been part of a mass shooting.

For now, he decided he would keep what he'd remembered to himself. Once he knew more, maybe had some answers, then he'd know how what he'd seen related to him. In the meantime, he'd concentrate on being the best damn houseguest he could be and work on regaining his full memory.

Speaking of being a houseguest… He decided to go inside, fix himself a sandwich for lunch and see what he could do about cleaning up around the place. Later, he'd check out the contents of the refrigerator and pantry, and figure out what he could pull together for an evening meal.

Cooking. He enjoyed cooking. And he actually had quite a talent for it. The certainty of this knowledge filled him. This time, there'd been no vision, no movie, just a simple statement of fact inside his mind that rang true.

Finally, something good he could share. He got busy making himself a sandwich, figuring he'd plan a really great meal for later, to show Kenzie how much he appreciated her help.

Chapter Three

"Can I help you?" the gun-toting, hard-faced woman demanded, her tone hostile. Though Kenzie had immediately put her hands up to indicate she wasn't a threat, the other woman made no move to lower her weapon.

"I'm Dr. Taylor," Kenzie said, keeping her voice steady despite her pounding heart. "What are you doing in my clinic?"

Staring hard, the other woman studied her, as if trying to judge the validity of Kenzie's response. Then finally, she shook her head and slowly re-holstered her pistol, her steely gaze on Kenzie the entire time.

"I'm sorry," she finally said. "You don't look like a doctor, so I'm going to need to see some ID."

With her adrenaline still pumping, Kenzie decided she'd had enough. "You first. I need to know who you are and what you're doing here."

"If you really are Dr. Taylor, you'd know who I am," the other woman huffed, her narrow gaze locked on Kenzie's face.

"Humor me," Kenzie drawled.

"Fine. I'm Annette Gladly. I work here."

Kenzie took another deep breath. "You work here doing what?" she asked.

"Everything." Annette lifted her head and gestured at the waiting room in general. "I'm the receptionist, medical assistant and file clerk. I do whatever needs to be done to help the doctor. Old Doc Clarke often said he didn't know what he'd do without me." Pride rang in her voice. "If you really are the new doctor, you'll quickly learn that I'm invaluable."

"I see." Already, Kenzie suspected Annette wouldn't be easy to work with. Especially if she continually questioned Kenzie's authority. "I assume you've received some kind of medical training?"

Gasping as if Kenzie had just said something horribly offensive, Annette turned away, completely ignoring the question. She reached for the phone that sat on the reception desk and punched in some numbers. "I need to speak to the mayor," she said. "This is Annette Gladly from down at the medical clinic."

Kenzie crossed her arms, waiting. "She and I are meeting for lunch in about twenty minutes," she said.

"She?" One brow rose. "She who?"

"The mayor. Jane Norman," Kenzie replied. "I stopped by here on my way to meet her."

This response made Annette snort. "Shows how much you know. Jane isn't the mayor, though she likes to act like she is."

Again, Kenzie had to squash an intense feeling of dislike. "You know, if you hope to continue working here, you might tone down the rudeness a little bit," she drawled.

Annette rolled her eyes. "Please. As if you could

begin to run this clinic without me." She returned her attention to the phone. "Hey, Greg. Some woman walked in here claiming to be the new doctor. Says she's meeting Jane for lunch in a little bit. Can you verify any of that?"

Kenzie had never had much of a temper, but this Annette person surely was a trial on her patience. She also wasn't sure why Jane Norman had led her to believe she was the mayor, but figured that could be easily sorted out over lunch. Kenzie preferred things to be straightforward and simple. After putting in all those years in medical school and then her grueling stint in residency, she just wanted to be a doctor without drama or whatever else Annette was trying to drum up.

While Annette carried on her phone conversation, Kenzie decided to explore the rest of the clinic. Though she had every right to do so, she couldn't help but hope Annette wouldn't decide to shoot her in the back.

Going through the door that separated the waiting area from the rest of the clinic, Kenzie discovered a small reception area on the other side of the sliding glass window. Beyond that, a short hallway led to two exam rooms, a large well-stocked supply closet and a room with what appeared to be an antiquated X-ray machine.

She took her time checking out everything, slightly surprised that the overbearing Annette hadn't come charging back to check on her.

When she returned to the waiting room, she realized Annette had concluded her phone call. Maybe the mayor—or whoever Jane actually was—had set her straight.

"My apologies," Annette said, her voice as stiff as

her posture. "I was only trying to protect the clinic. I've been working here, getting ready for your arrival."

Kenzie simply nodded, not trusting herself to speak. She strode to the front door and let herself out without saying another word.

Then chastised herself for not being more firm, she drove to the end of Main Street and took a right on First Avenue. A sign proclaimed she'd arrived at her destination—City Hall. The building appeared to have once been residential and who knew, perhaps the mayor still lived in part of the two-story Victorian-era house. It had been painted a cheery pale yellow and seemed well-maintained.

Once she'd parked, she sat in her Jeep a moment and practiced calm breathing. Annette and her attitude had unnerved her. This, combined with the fact that she had a strange man who claimed to have no memory staying in her cabin, along with the way Jane had misrepresented herself, and she had the beginnings of a massive headache.

Things would get better, she told herself, getting out of the Jeep. They had to. She was a good doctor and had worked hard to become one. Now she'd finally be putting all her knowledge to use. Ever since accepting the position here in Blake, she'd been trying to look at all of this as one big adventure. So far, she hadn't been wrong.

The moment she stepped up on the wide covered porch, the front door opened. A slender silver-haired woman wearing jean capris, hiking boots and a flannel shirt with the sleeves cut off came out to meet her.

"You must be Dr. Taylor!" she exclaimed, grabbing

hold of Kenzie's hand, shaking it vigorously. "I'm Jane Norman. It's so good to meet you after all those phone conversations."

"I agree." Once Jane had released her hand, Kenzie looked around. "I'm sorry, but I was under the impression that you were the mayor. I met a woman named Annette at the clinic and she said you weren't."

Jane laughed, a grin-inducing guffaw of a sound. "She's right. I'm not the mayor. My husband, Greg, is. I just do all the work!" She laughed again, her sparkling gaze inviting Kenzie to join her.

"That's right," a booming voice said. A large man came through the doorway, his immense belly preceding the rest of him. With his full white beard, white hair and rosy cheeks, he was a dead ringer for Santa Claus.

"I see you staring," he said, grinning at Kenzie. "And yes, I play Santa Claus every year for the kiddos. I tell Jane it's my calling in life."

"It is," Jane chimed in. "And he frequently ropes me in to play Mrs. Claus. I don't mind because the children love it."

Kenzie could feel the tension easing out of her. She liked these two already. "I'm sorry I made an unscheduled stop at the clinic. I couldn't wait to see it."

Greg and Jane exchanged a glance. "Not a problem," Jane said. "It is going to be your workplace for the next two years. I hope Annette wasn't too…off-putting. She is a tough person to get to know, but once you do, she's very loyal and hardworking."

"That's nice." Nodding, Kenzie decided to keep her opinion to herself. After all, she'd have ample time to see if Annette could make her change her mind. "I can't wait to have you show me around Blake. What I've seen so far is beautiful."

Her comment had Greg beaming again. "Our little village might not seem like much to someone from the outside, but we love it. And you will too! Come on." He gestured toward the door. "Let's get out and explore."

"How about we eat lunch first?" Jane interjected. "I'm starving."

"We can do that," Greg agreed, taking his wife's arm. He glanced at Kenzie. "I hope you don't mind walking. I thought we take the Main Street tour on foot. We can stop at Mikki's and grab lunch."

"That place looks amazing." She nodded at their pleased smiles. "I noticed it on the way in."

"Best restaurant in Blake," Greg quipped. He and Jane exchanged glances before they both spoke at the same time. "It's actually the *only* restaurant in Blake."

Jane grabbed Kenzie's arms and led her outside, with Greg following behind. "How are you liking the cabin? I made sure to stock it with food and toiletries. I had to have a bit of work done. When old Doc Clarke went to live with his daughter, the place fell into a bit of disrepair."

"That cabin belonged to the former doctor?" Kenzie asked.

"No," Greg chimed in. "It belongs to the village. It's allocated to be lodging for whatever doctor we have living here at the time."

Before Kenzie could think of a response, Jane squeezed her arm. "Did you happen to do any reading on the history of our village?" Jane asked. "It's not your usual used-to-be-a-mining-camp-in-Alaska story."

"I did not," Kenzie admitted. "Between getting everything ready for the move, I barely had time to think."

"That's okay," Greg chimed in. "Janes loves to tell the story."

Jane grinned. "I do. But I'll wait until we've snagged a booth inside Mikki's."

Once they reached Main Street, Mikki's was on the same block. Walking inside with the older couple, Kenzie felt as if she were stepping back into the past. Wooden floors that creaked as they walked across. Matching walls and ceiling, all made from what Kenzie thought was cedar. A huge ceiling fan hung down from where it was mounted way up high in the middle of the room, circulating air that smelled like a combination of cigarette smoke, coffee, doughnuts and whiskey. The entire room had been decorated in artwork that could best be described as modern mystical with a dash of psychedelic thrown in.

Noticing Kenzie looking, Jane elbowed her in the side. "Unique, isn't it?"

"It is," Kenzie agreed, tearing her gaze away from a particularly strange painting.

There were only five or six other customers inside the main dining room and half of them sat at the bar.

"We'll have a booth please," Jane told the hostess, a young heavily tattooed woman with choppy purple hair.

Kenzie slid in across from Jane and Greg. She smiled at the way they held hands like a couple of newlyweds. "How long have you two been married?" she asked.

"Forty-two years," Greg said, grinning. When the hostess returned with menus, he slid his away unopened. "I always order the same thing."

Jane nodded. "He does. He's a creature of habit, thank goodness. I'm pretty sure that's the only reason why we're still together."

Her comment had Greg rolling his eyes and snorting. "As if," he said. Then, leaning across the table to look Kenzie in the eye, he stabbed his finger at her menu. "Order the cheeseburger," he said. "It's really good."

"I was thinking about the salmon," Kenzie said. For whatever reason, her choice appeared to amuse both the Normans.

"Salmon is plentiful around here," Jane pointed out. "Really, really plentiful."

"I see." Kenzie looked from one to the other, not understanding. "Then I take it to mean the salmon is fresh."

"It is," Greg began.

Jane cut him off with a hard squeeze of his arm. "Let her have her fish. She's new. She'll get tired of it soon enough."

They both laughed again. They were still chuckling when the hostess stomped over to take their orders.

"The special of the day is—" she began.

"Salmon," both Jane and Greg chorused, giggling. "How's he fixing it this time?"

The tiniest of smiles appeared on the young woman's face. "Some kind of cream sauce over pasta. It actually smells really good."

"I'll have that," Kenzie said. "Along with a glass of iced tea."

"Hamburgers here," Greg ordered. "And fries. The usual."

"Beer too?"

"Of course," Jane replied.

Once the waitress left, the older couple settled down.

"You were going to tell me about Blake," Kenzie prompted. "How it didn't start out as a mining town like so many others in Alaska."

Jane's faded blue eyes lit up. "Yes! Well, parts of it did start as a mining camp, before it became Blake. Our village is named after its founder, Blake Rousseau." She paused for effect.

Wracking her brain to see if she recognized the name, Kenzie finally admitted defeat. "I'm sorry. I have no idea who he is."

Greg snorted. "No one does. That's the beauty of the story."

"Shh." Holding up one hand, Jane continued, "Anyway, Mr. Rousseau fancied himself an artist. He dabbled in both painting and sculpture. He was a trust fund baby out of Sacramento with a lot of money and time and decided to visit Alaska for inspiration."

"After he got here, he didn't want to leave," Greg picked up the story. "He ended up buying a couple hundred acres and building his artists' colony in the middle of an old mining area. Some of the houses, like ours, have been here since the late 1800s."

"Where?" Kenzie asked, thinking that might be a fun place to visit.

"Right here." Jane gestured at the interior of Mikki's. "This was the main building, where everyone could go to paint. Most of the artwork you see hanging on the wall is from those days."

Involuntarily, Kenzie winced. "Did all this happen in the late sixties, early seventies perhaps?"

"You nailed it," Greg crowed. "And I'll tell you what. Looking at them might give you a stomachache right now, but they grow on you."

The food arrived. Two huge burgers with fries for the Normans and a beautiful piece of salmon arranged over pasta for Kenzie. It looked absolutely amazing.

Digging in, Kenzie realized appearances hadn't been deceptive. "This is amazing."

"Mikki's a pretty good cook," Jane said, taking a huge bite of her burger.

"Fortunately for us," Greg added.

Silence fell while they all devoured their meal.

Plate clean, Kenzie leaned back in her chair and took a long drink of her iced tea. "What happened to the artists' colony?" she asked. "I mean, obviously it's no longer here."

"A lot of the participants were only in it for the drugs and sex," Jane said. "For a while, I think it was kind of like a cult. Then Blake died. He left all of his money—and the colony—to his sister back in California. Without funding and someone to pay the bills, all the other artists drifted away one by one. Some stayed nearby, but most returned to the lower forty-eight."

"The village sat abandoned for a few years," Greg said. "Until Blake's sister, Nancy, put the entire thing up for sale. And not as one lump chunk. She parceled it out, allowing individuals to purchase their own little pieces of property. That's how we got our house."

"Yep." Blotting at the corners of her mouth with her napkin, Jane took a swig of her beer. "And we formed our village. Nancy's only request was that we name the place after her brother. That's how we got the name Blake."

"Like the paintings, the name kind of grows on you after a while," Greg added, grinning.

Kenzie nodded, realizing she really liked these people. They reminded her of her favorite aunt and uncle who lived in deep east Texas, minus the thick Southern accents. She so badly wanted to ask them if anyone had reported a man missing, but couldn't figure out a way to do so without arousing suspicion.

WITH THE HORRIBLE vision replaying over and over in his mind, the man with no name tried to focus on the second, and better, things he'd realized. He now knew that he liked to cook. While that was something, he understood it was actually more than that. He was a *skilled* cook, maybe even a chef. While he wasn't sure if preparing food was a hobby or a vocation, the notion made him happy. Something good, unlike the scene of mayhem and blood and death.

Still, he'd give much to be able to remember his name.

After he finished eating his sandwich, he rummaged through the refrigerator and pantry to see what ingredients they had on hand. Whoever had stocked the cabin for Kenzie had done a really good job. She had a variety of proteins—beef, pork, chicken and fish, most of which was salmon. In fact, salmon occupied at least half her freezer, which meant the healthy fish was plentiful in these parts.

Of course it was. This was Alaska after all. He peered back into the freezer, looking for Alaskan king crab and finding none. Shaking his head at himself, he grabbed some beef tips and decided to try his hand at making beef bourguignon. From…memory. The idea made him feel giddy. Inexplicably, he could see the list of ingredients in his mind. The only item he couldn't manage to find was cognac, understandably.

Humming under his breath, he got busy. He'd just put everything into the oven when he heard a vehicle pull up outside.

For an instant, he froze, pure panic threatening to engulf him. Moving quickly, he went to the window, exhaling as he saw Kenzie's Jeep. What had he expected? Chastising himself, he located a bottle of Merlot and a corkscrew.

"Hey!" She came through the door like a whirlwind, her smile lighting up the room. "It smells good in here."

Collecting himself, he smiled back. "Thanks. I discovered I know how to cook. I just put dinner in the oven. It won't be ready for a couple of hours, but I have a feeling it'll be good. Maybe even great."

"Wow." Her restless energy palpable, she moved around the cabin, not exactly avoiding him, but not getting too close to him either. "I had a tour of the village, what there is of it, and learned about its history. We stopped at a local restaurant for lunch and I had one of the best salmon meals I've ever eaten."

Salmon. He knew so many ways to prepare it and told her so.

"That sounds promising," she said, still smiling as she turned to face him, two stemless wine glasses in her hand. "Have you remembered anything else?"

The gory scene flashed into his mind. Just as quickly, he pushed it away. "Only that I'm pretty sure that Alaska is my home. I feel a definite kinship with the scenery here."

She nodded. "Still no name?"

"No. I'm trying not to be impatient." Taking the glasses from her, he set them down. Then he opened the bottle of wine and poured them both a glass. "Do you want to sit outside on the front porch with these?"

"Sure," she replied, after a moment's hesitation. "I can tell you about what I saw and learned today. Maybe something will help jog your memory."

They carried their drinks outside. Once they were settled in the big wooden rocking chairs, she turned to him. "Until you remember your name, I've got to call you something. Do you have any preferences?"

Taking a sip of his wine, he thought for a moment. "Not really. Nothing comes to mind. I wish it did."

"John Doe," she announced, glancing sideways at him. "It's easiest since that's the most common. It'll do until your real name comes to you."

This made him shrug. "I hope it's soon."

"I honestly think it will be." Sipping her wine, she leaned back in the chair and closed her eyes. "I think I'll fit in well here. I'm a good doctor and this place needs me. Now I've just got to figure out what to do about the woman who apparently comes with the clinic."

He listened as she told him about some woman named Annette who'd pulled a gun on her. His first instinct—to protect Kenzie, go down there and confront this Annette—he pushed away. As Kenzie continued, he realized she could take care of herself.

She told him about the village, from the history to all the different shops and people she'd met. She really seemed to like the mayor and his wife, Greg and Jane Norman. She even paused when saying their names, as if she hoped him hearing them might jog his memory.

Hell, he hoped so too. But nothing came to mind, so after a brief pause and another drink of wine, Kenzie continued talking.

Realizing they'd both finished their wine, he got up to refill their glasses and to check on dinner.

While inside the cabin, he took a deep breath, aware he needed to gain some perspective. While he'd only met this woman yesterday, he felt a bond with her, in addition to the tug of physical attraction. Some of that had to be due to the fact that he currently was adrift, an empty vessel, reaching out for something or someone to latch on to. While he knew that would all resolve as soon as he had his memory back, he didn't like the way he felt in the meantime.

The meal appeared to be cooking just fine, so he refilled their glasses and rejoined Kenzie outside.

"It's so beautiful here," she mused. "Now that it actually stopped raining. In Houston, where I come from, August is the hottest month."

"August is the rainy season here," he said, surprising himself. "And you being from Texas explains your Southern drawl."

She turned to look at him. "I did my residency at the Mayo Clinic in Minnesota. I worked hard to make my accent more neutral. From what you're saying, that didn't happen?"

Damn it. Now he'd stepped in it. "I meant that as a compliment," he told her. "I think your accent is charming."

Some of the tension seemed to leave her shoulders. "Thanks. Some of my fellow residents gave me hell over it. I don't know why that bothered me so much, but it did."

She shrugged and took a sip of wine. "They'd also heard that Texans didn't like the cold. While that might be true of most Texans, I learned to truly enjoy Minnesota. It turned out I had a real knack for winter sports. I loved ice skating and snowmobiling and ice fishing. I even learned how to use snowshoes. I brought mine with me."

"All of that will come in handy here," he replied. "I enjoy snowmobiling myself. Wow. Another puzzle piece."

This made her grin. "That's great. It sounds like even more of your memory might be returning."

"I hope so. I can't adequately express how frustrating it is, not to know my own name. Or other basic things, like where I live and what I do for a living."

"Or if you have a family," she added, her voice soft. "A spouse, maybe kids, who might be missing you."

"I'm not married." His response came automatically, surprising him. "No kids either."

She nodded. "What about your parents? Are they still alive?"

This time he drew a blank. "I don't know," he replied, rubbing his left temple with the same hand. He allowed some of his frustration to come through in his voice. "I just don't know."

"Hey, it's going to be okay." She touched his arm with her small hand. "It hasn't been that long since your accident. You've already remembered a few things. I'm sure more will come to you."

"I hope so," he replied, taking a drink of his wine to cover how badly he suddenly wanted to kiss her. He wasn't sure why, or how much of this intense attraction might be due to the fact that he currently was a bit of a blank slate, but everything about her mesmerized him. Honestly, he hoped this would be a temporary thing, vanishing once he came back to his true self.

He owed her a debt of gratitude, for sure, something he might never be able to repay. But unwarranted desire had to be the last thing he or she needed right now. He didn't want to give Kenzie even the slightest reason to kick him out. So, he'd take care to keep things platonic. Help her as much as he could.

"Are you all right?" she asked. "You kind of went away there for a moment."

Blinking, he refocused. "Sorry. I got lost in thought." He pushed himself up from the chair. "I need to go check on dinner."

Once inside the cabin, away from her, he took a deep breath. The entire house smelled wonderful. He could only hope the meal tasted as great as it smelled. In retrospect, the wine had been a mistake. Loosening inhibitions was the last thing he should do.

He grabbed a couple of pot holders and opened the oven. Perfect timing. Removing the pan, he set it on the stove top to cool and realized he should have made a loaf of French bread to go with it.

Lifting out the bakeware, he set it on top of the stove. He'd just released it when another flash of memory slammed into him.

A platter of food had been in his hands when the gunshots started. He'd heard the first shot and had begun turning when the others broke out. The platter hit the floor right before he had. Again, the entire bloody scene played out, just like a movie. Except he knew this was real.

"Stop," he shouted, hands fisted, perspiration beading his brow. "Just stop."

Kenzie rushed into the cabin. "What is it? What's wrong?"

Shaking, he couldn't answer. His vision had glazed over and he honestly thought he might fall.

Apparently, Kenzie reached the same conclusion. She grabbed his arm and steered him over to the kitchen table, shoving him into a chair. "Sit," she ordered. Once he'd done that, she checked his pulse. "Breathe," she said softly. And then, as he did, she crouched down on the floor next to him. "Can you tell me what's wrong?"

This was no longer something he wished to hide. Whatever had happened had been horrific, and he knew he'd been an innocent bystander rather than an instigator.

"I saw a shooting," he said. And then proceeded to share every gory detail he could remember. "I'm not sure where or when, but I was there." He shuddered, shaking his head. "It was really bad."

She squeezed his shoulder. "Hang in there. It's all going to be okay. You're safe now."

"Am I?" He met her gaze, his voice as bleak as he felt inside. "I still don't know what happened, or why I was there. But this has something to do with that feeling that I'm in danger. I think whoever shot all those people wants to finish the job."

Chapter Four

Watching her John Doe lost in the horror of a memory out of context, Kenzie offered comfort the only way she could. She wrapped her arms around him, enveloping him in a hug. The poor man couldn't stop shaking. Clearly, to him the memory felt immediate and real.

At first, lost inside himself, he didn't react to her embrace. Determined, she hung on, realizing he smelled good, a masculine combination of soap and outdoors. Because he was so large, she had to stretch to get all of him in her embrace, but she managed, even though this meant full body contact.

Gradually, his tremors began to subside. And his breathing slowed. When he raised his head and met her gaze, the horrified blankness had left his expression.

"I'm sorry," he said, holding himself perfectly still. "I didn't mean—"

"It's okay." Realizing she still clutched him close, she loosened her hold, just a little, strangely reluctant to completely let him go.

She wasn't sure who moved first, but as her lips found his, her entire body ignited. Open-mouthed, deep, wet and arousing, kissing this man felt akin to baring her soul. She couldn't get enough, didn't want to stop, though she managed to drag her common sense from wherever it had gone to hide and take a step back. Their gazes locked. They were both breathing hard.

Because all she wanted with every fiber of her being was to kiss him again, she took another step back. Should she say something? Would he? The one thing she didn't want to hear would be for him to claim the kiss had been a huge mistake.

To prevent that, she spun around and made her way toward her bathroom. Maybe taking a quick shower would help her regain her common sense. And if she felt a little bit as if she were fleeing, so be it. Because in a way, she was.

For the rest of the evening, Kenzie devoted herself to pretending the kiss had never happened. Thankfully, he did the same. She knew she'd likely lie awake in her bed later—alone—and relive that moment, but for now she neither wanted to discuss it or redo it.

Finally, they bid each other a cordial good night and Kenzie retreated to her room. She'd existed in a semi-aroused state all night, aching to find herself locked in his arms again, and to take such an enthralling kiss just a bit further. Somehow, she'd managed to get a grip on her desire, though just barely.

When she went to bed, she couldn't help but imagine him joining her for a night of earth-shattering passion. Even though she knew he wouldn't do so without an invitation, she allowed herself to fantasize, finally seeking her own release before she fell asleep.

The next morning, once again Kenzie woke to the sound of John Doe rattling around in the kitchen.

They'd begun to fall into a temporary routine, which she supposed might give him comfort since right now he had no roots. She wasn't sure how exactly she felt about that, but then where this man was concerned, she wasn't certain of anything. Especially that kiss.

Then she smelled bacon frying and her stomach actually growled. She had lots of favorite scents, like her mother's garden in Houston after a midafternoon rain, gardenias and a cake baking in the oven. But above all, the smell of bacon frying ranked right up there as an all-time favorite.

Grabbing her clothes, she rushed into her bathroom to wash up, brush her teeth and throw on a bra and T-shirt over her pajama bottoms. Though she wanted to rush into the kitchen, she forced herself to saunter out as if she weren't dying for a plate of bacon.

"Good morning." His smile lit up his blue eyes. Again, she realized what an attractive man he was, made even more so by the fact that he stood at the stove cooking breakfast.

"Mornin'," she replied, heading in the direction of the full pot of coffee. She poured herself a cup, adding milk and a teaspoon of sugar before turning back toward him. "That smells like heaven. When I was a kid growing up, I'd spend summers with my grandmother down in Galveston, and I loved waking up to the smell of bacon and eggs."

"Well, that's good because I've made bacon and eggs for breakfast. Toast too."

She took a small drink of coffee, feeling an odd combination of gratitude and unease. "You don't have to cook for me all the time, you know," she pointed out. "I mean, I appreciate it for sure, but don't feel like it's required."

His steady gaze made her feel foolish.

"What else have I got to do?" he asked. "I know I love to cook and that I'm good at it. You've been kind enough to allow me to crash at your home. At least this way, I can make an attempt to repay you. It's not much, I'm aware, but right now it's all I have."

"Okay." Dropping into a chair, she took a larger drink of her coffee. "Since you put it that way, can I have a slice or two of bacon?"

This made him laugh, a deep masculine sound that she felt all the way to her core. "Coming right up."

He brought her a plate of food that would have looked at home in any restaurant. Two perfectly cooked eggs, sunny-side up, hash browns, toast and three pieces of bacon, crisped exactly the way she liked them. Along with this, he poured her a small glass of orange juice. Getting a similar plate for himself, he sat across from her and smiled. "Dig in," he said.

Needing no urging, she did. Everything tasted as good—or better—than it looked. Though a simple breakfast meal, she couldn't help but be impressed. "Where'd you learn to cook like this?" she asked, half-way through cleaning her plate.

"I don't know." He shrugged. "No surprise there. Making food must be really important to me since it's been one of the first memories to return."

"Must be," she agreed, pushing away her clean plate. "Thank you for breakfast. That was excellent."

"You're welcome." He eyed her over his coffee cup. "What's on your agenda for today?"

"I don't really have anything planned," she admitted. "Is there something you'd like to do? Maybe that might help jog your memory?"

"Well, I considered revisiting the bridge where my car went off the road. I have to believe the guardrail was damaged, so eventually someone has got to notice it, right?"

"You'd think so," she agreed. "But maybe not for a while in such a remote area. If you think it might help you, I'm game."

Though he kept his expression impassive, she swore she saw a flash of fear go across his face. "I think I'll pass for now," he said. "Maybe that's something we can do later."

She decided to be direct. "What are you afraid of? And don't tell me you're not, because I'm pretty good at reading emotions."

"You're right about the fear." He spread his hands. "But I don't know. It's just there. I have an overwhelming sense that I'm in some sort of danger. From who or why, I have no idea."

Not sure how to respond to this, she settled on reassurance. "You're safe here," she said firmly. "So please, try not to worry too much. Look how much has already come back to you and it's only been a few days."

"True." Unfolding his large body from the small chair, he grabbed both their plates and carried them to the sink. "I went hiking yesterday. The physical activity and the solitude helped me think. I'll probably do that again today."

Watching him, she felt a rush of affection. Which, if she stopped to analyze it, was strange. Maybe. Because in the short time she'd known him, she thought they'd formed a sort of friendship. The kind two people living in close quarters might be apt to do. And if she found herself occasionally wondering how it would feel to have those strong, muscular arms wrapped around her, or how his kiss would affect her, she put it down to a young single woman's normal libido. He was a perfect masculine specimen after all.

And the mystery of not knowing what had happened to him only made him more appealing. Go figure.

"I think I'll go into town again today," she said. "I really enjoyed talking to the mayor and his wife. And I'd really like to make a second stop at the clinic, hopefully without Annette shooting my head off."

This had him shaking his head. "Just be careful. From what you've told me, that woman sounds unhinged."

"I'm trying to keep an open mind. I think maybe I just took her by surprise." While she wasn't entirely sure she believed her own statement, she really hoped it was correct.

After a quick shower, Kenzie dressed. "It's all yours," she told her houseguest. "I'll be back later. I'll probably have lunch in town. I'd really like to start getting to know the locals."

As he gazed at her, for a moment he looked so forlorn, so lost, that she wanted to hug him. And then he blinked, summoned up a smile, and the moment passed. "Please don't ask any questions, but if you hear anything about a missing man, let me know."

"I will," she promised softly. She managed a jaunty wave on the way out.

Driving into town, she wondered again about how the man with no name already felt like a friend. As if she'd known him for years. And, if she were being perfectly honest with herself, if they'd met under other circumstances, she would have been attracted to him. Now, even if he didn't have a dark cloud hanging over him, was not the time to be thinking about relationships. She had a new practice to establish, patients to see and trust to build. She'd need to devote all of her spare time to that and only that.

Feeling settled, she drove to Main Street and parked. She figured she'd stop in to see Jane and Greg, but she hated to do so unannounced, so she texted. Jane responded immediately by calling her.

"What's up, Doc?" Jane chuckled as she spoke, clearly amusing herself.

Kenzie explained she was in town and wondered if it would be all right for her to pay them a visit.

"Of course, you can," Jane replied. "And no need to ask in the future. We keep an open-door policy around here. People are always coming and going and that's how we like it."

"I'll walk over then," Kenzie said, ending the call. Life in North Houston had been fast-paced, impersonal and hectic. She'd done her undergraduate work in Austin, then had gone to medical school at Baylor in Waco, Texas, which was the smallest city of them all. But compared to Blake, Alaska, Waco had been huge. She'd never lived in a really small place like this.

Jane met her on the front porch, pulling her into a hug as if they hadn't seen each other for months. "Greg and I were just talking about you," she said.

"Good, I hope?" Kenzie asked, smiling.

"Yes, of course. We were discussing you taking over the clinic."

The door squeaked as Greg joined them. "*She* was discussing you taking over the clinic," he clarified. "As usual most times, I just listen."

"True, true." Clearly undeterred, Jane shook her head, sending her dangly earrings flying.

Though she figured she probably shouldn't ask, Kenzie knew she'd find out eventually. "What about me and the clinic?"

"I think you should have a grand opening," Jane declared, her eyes sparkling. "It would be a chance for everyone in the village to meet you and maybe let Annette start scheduling appointments."

Kenzie couldn't keep herself from grimacing. She still wasn't sure she planned to allow Annette to continue working at the clinic, but decided to keep that to herself for now. She wanted to give the other woman a fair chance.

If Jane noticed Kenzie's reaction, she didn't comment. Instead, she continued to enthusiastically make plans for what she now referred to as the social event of the season.

What season? Kenzie wanted to ask. *The rainy season?* Instead, she nodded and listened, finally agreeing to do whatever Jane wanted to set up. The older woman was a force of nature and obviously used to getting her way.

"We'll do it during the daytime though," she said, nixing Jane's plans for a cocktail hour. "I want it to be a meet-the-doctor kind of thing. Friendly but professional. I won't see patients without an appointment, unless it's an emergency."

"No cocktails?" Janes shook her head, her bright smile dimming. "Pooh, there goes all the fun."

"You can have a separate happy hour if you want," Kenzie offered. "But I'd prefer the two events be completely separate, maybe even different days."

"Fine," Jane agreed. "I'm thinking we can do something this Friday. Four days is more than enough notice."

"That'll work for me." Kenzie nodded. "Especially since I'd planned to start seeing patients on Monday." Which would be exactly as her contract stated. Arriving on Saturday, she'd been given a little more than a week to settle in.

"Great!" Jane clapped her hands together. "I'll get started planning it. Do you want me to call Annette or would you prefer to do it?"

"You go right ahead," Kenzie replied. While she'd need to look over her contract again, she didn't remember seeing anything stating she had to keep on any previous clinic employees. On the one hand, Annette could prove herself invaluable, with her years of experience and the fact that she clearly knew everyone in Blake.

But if she didn't lose her attitude, Annette would make Kenzie's life a living hell.

"What time should we start on Friday?" Jane wanted to know.

"I guess normal clinic hours," Kenzie replied. "8:00 a.m."

"Perfect." Now completely involved in her planning,

Jane had begun furiously scribbling notes on a yellow legal pad. "I'll make sure we have food too."

"Not a buffet," Greg cautioned, walking into the room. Clearly, he'd overheard the entire conversation. "Just snack-type things."

"I agree," Kenzie chimed in. "Cookies, brownies, things like that. Nothing that has to be refrigerated or heated up."

With Jane busy, Kenzie turned to Greg, trying for casual.

"By the way," she asked, hoping it sounded like an afterthought. "Does Blake have a police department or something like that?"

"No." Greg immediately answered. "Lots of Alaskan villages have VPSOs—Village Public Safety Officers. They're often hired by tribal councils. Since there's not a lot of crime in the smaller villages, these guys spend a lot of time fishing and socializing. Some stay, others move on. Here in Blake, we decided to put our money into hiring a doctor instead."

Which would be her. And maybe the old doctor who had devoted most of his life to taking care of the people of Blake. "I see," Kenzie replied. There went her plan on discreetly having law enforcement check to see if there had been any men reported missing. "What do you do if you turn out to need a police officer?"

"We call for a state trooper." Greg sounded unconcerned. "But nothing like that ever happens around here."

Only Jane, who apparently could multitask with the best of them, picked up on the possible reason behind

Kenzie's question. "Why, dear?" she asked. "What specifically is concerning you?"

"Nothing," Kenzie lied, thinking about her male houseguest. She had to assume that eventually John Doe's vehicle would wash ashore somewhere. It couldn't stay submerged forever, not in such fast-moving water. "I was just curious. Life is sure a lot different here than I'm used to."

"It's better," Jane and Greg chimed in together.

"I'm sure it is," Kenzie agreed, smiling. "I'll let you two get to planning. Let me know if I need to do anything other than show up."

"You don't." Jane's emphatic response made Greg laugh out loud. "This is going to be so much fun."

After leaving the mayor and his wife, Kenzie made a quick stop at the general store. While the cabin seemed homey, she had the urge to purchase a few household items to make it feel more like her own place. What she wanted to buy exactly, she didn't know.

Stepping inside, once again she had the odd feeling of going backward in time. Wooden floors, shelves stocked with livestock feed, birdseed and pet food on one side, and human grocery items on the other. There was even an area with inexpensive clothing items for sale. Hoping whoever worked here wasn't the type to gossip, she grabbed a couple of men's shirts, some sweat pants, jeans, underwear and socks, and even a pair of sneakers. She'd taken a look at her John Doe's single pair of boots to get the size there. She supposed, if pressed, she could claim these items were all for her, though the huge size versus her petite frame wouldn't lend credence to her lie. She also grabbed a couple of rain ponchos and a spare umbrella.

That done, she decided to walk around the rest of the store and aisle shop.

One entire corner had been stocked with wall art and crocheted blankets, with a small sign noting that said everything in this area had been handmade by various residents of Blake.

Delighted, Kenzie grabbed a small metal basket and made a beeline for that corner. She chose a hand-made lavender-scented candle, a crocheted lap blanket in greens and blues, a jar of apple butter and another of pickled beets. She took her time looking over the various pieces of art. While she wanted something to hang in her cabin, and maybe another piece for her clinic, she'd always been particular about this sort of thing. She couldn't articulate what she liked, not exactly, only that she knew it when she saw it.

An entire wall had been turned into a casual art gallery. All mediums were displayed, from photographs to pencil drawings to acrylics and oils. Large and small, mostly scenery and wildlife. Many were quite good, but none of them called to her.

"You must be the new lady doctor," a deep male voice rumbled from behind her.

She turned to see a portly older man, wearing overalls over a T-shirt, eyeing her kindly. "I am," she answered. "Dr. Taylor."

He stuck out a beefy hand, engulfing hers as they shook. "I'm Kip Roberts. I own this joint."

"Nice to meet you." Gesturing toward the wall, she smiled. "You have quite the display here."

"People love being able to show off their talents," he said. "I don't get too many sales, because we're off the beaten path for most tourists. The locals tend to buy more of the homemade soaps and jellies. Are you looking for anything in particular?"

"Not really," she admitted. "I'm actually just enjoying the art." She held up her basket. "And I've already decided to make a few purchases of my own."

"Excellent." He nodded. "Take your time. Just holler for me when you're ready to check out."

"I will," she promised. After he walked away, she went back to perusing the display.

Halfway down the wall, a medium-sized pencil sketch caught her eye. Somehow, the artist had managed to capture the very essence of a herd of deer grazing in a meadow. Continuing to look, she soon found more by the same person. All were of wildlife—a bear, an eagle and a fox—and a beautiful salmon leaping from the water.

They were each marked twenty-five dollars, which seemed ridiculously inexpensive. She knew she had to have them all. And if she was lucky, she hoped to one day meet the artist who had such a close bond with animals and the skill to bring them all to life.

"There you are." Kip grinned good-naturedly at her, nodding when she carefully handed over her small stack of art. "I'm glad you found something you like."

"They're beautiful," she told him. "I hope to one day meet whoever drew these. He or she is very talented."

Laughing while he rang up her purchases, he began individually wrapping each piece. "Oh, I imagine you'll be meeting her very soon. She'll be working for you in the medical clinic. Her name is Annette Gladly."

Kenzie almost dropped her wallet. "She sketched all these?" she asked, barely able to contain her disbelief.

"She did." Busy wrapping everything, Kip didn't appear to notice her shock. "She also dabbles in watercolor, though she hasn't brought any in for the wall since her last lot sold."

To her relief, he didn't remark on the men's clothing at all, simply ringing everything up before folding it and dropping it into a bag.

When he gave her the total, she handed over her credit card, struggling to process the fact that she'd just purchased over a hundred dollars of artwork created by the sour-faced woman at the clinic.

Once everything had been bagged up, she thanked Kip and accepted his offer to help carry everything out to her Jeep. Once the bags had been loaded, he stepped back and thanked her, asking her to come again.

"Definitely," she replied. Climbing in, she gave him a jaunty wave and put the shifter into Reverse. Perhaps she'd misjudged Annette based on a bad first impression. Anyone who could sketch like that couldn't be all bad.

The drive back to the cabin, while beautiful, reminded her exactly how isolated she was. She couldn't help but wonder why the old doctor had chosen to live so far away from the village, but she guessed he might have welcomed the peace. For the first time, she found herself wondering about Dr. Clarke. Had he signed the same kind of contract as she? If so, how many years ago had that been? She'd had the impression he'd been elderly when he retired, moving away to live with his daughter in the lower forty-eight out of necessity due to his health.

No doubt, Annette could fill her in. That is, if they could manage to get on the right side of each other long enough to have a conversation.

Pulling up at the cabin, she wondered if her houseguest had managed to recall anything else. Amnesia wasn't something they'd spent a lot of time on back in medical school. The general consensus seemed to be that it was mostly temporary and some physicians even seemed inclined to disbelieve the condition even existed. As far as she could tell, aside of a lot of bruises, her John Doe appeared healthy. Therefore, his lack of memory should soon correct itself.

As for the kiss... She pushed it to the back of her mind. While kissing him had honestly rocked her world, she'd make sure nothing like that ever happened again.

HEARING KENZIE'S JEEP pull up out front, he wasn't surprised when his heart rate skyrocketed. Ever since his arrival here, she'd treated him with kindness. Dealing with memory loss, he'd been successful with keeping his desire for her on a back burner.

Until she'd kissed him.

He'd make sure she never learned how close he'd come to completely losing control.

Though that morning they'd both played off the kiss with humor, treating it as if it had been some crazy, unfortunate accident, he hadn't been able to stop thinking about it. While Kenzie had been gone, he'd taken another long hike, hoping the physical activity might help jog another memory, but so far nothing had happened.

He'd returned to the cabin after a couple of hours and done some cleaning and meal-prep work, marveling at how with food, he simply seemed to know what to do instinctively. Was this skill born of a hobby? Or was cooking somehow tied in with his occupation? He hated not knowing.

"Hey there!" She walked inside, juggling multiple plastic shopping bags. "I have more in the Jeep. Would you mind grabbing them?"

"Not at all." Glad to have something to do so he wouldn't stare at her, he hurried outside and retrieved the rest of her purchases. "Looks like you bought out the store," he teased, setting them down on the couch.

His comment made her grin. Damned if she wasn't even more beautiful when she smiled.

"I got you some clothes," she said. "By now, that one pair of jeans and that T-shirt are getting way overused."

"True," he admitted. "But what explanation did you give for buying men's clothing?"

She looked up from sorting through the bags. "I didn't. No one asked. For all they know, maybe I like to wear it sometimes."

Even though the size would be far too large. He tamped down a niggling worry, telling himself not to be so paranoid.

"Here you go," she said, handing him two bags stuffed full of clothing. "I bought mostly the basics. It's not a lot, but it should tide you over for now."

Accepting the gifts, he felt so moved his throat closed up. She'd already been good to him, done more than most people would have. The fact that she would do this, spend her hard-earned money buying clothing for a man she barely knew, humbled him.

"Are you all right?" she finally asked, eyeing him.

He nodded, glancing down at the stuffed shopping bags. "Thank you," he managed. "And I know I keep saying this, but I promise I'll repay you someday."

She waved away his words, smiling again. "Look what else I bought. A few things to make this cabin feel more like my home."

The lap blanket looked cozy, and suited her somehow. He could imagine her curled up on the sofa, reading, with a fire roaring in the fireplace and the blanket tucked over her legs.

"I got some artwork too," she said, holding some wrapped frames and frowning. "I'd like to get your honest opinion of it."

Since her frown would seem to indicate she wasn't pleased, he had to wonder why she'd purchased the artwork in the first place. "Let me see."

Slowly, she unwrapped the first piece, setting it down on the coffee table. There were four others, all exceptionally done pencil sketches of wildlife.

He picked up one depicting a salmon leaping from the water to examine it more closely. "This is amazing," he said, watching her face. "They all are. Why are you ambivalent about them?"

With a grimace, she pointed. "I wasn't. At first. I fell in love with them the instant I saw them. I didn't learn who the artist was until after I'd paid." She shook her head. "I can hardly believe it. The man who runs the general store told me Annette Gladley did them."

"The woman who pointed a gun at you in the medical clinic?"

"The very same." With a sigh, she picked up the sketch of a herd of deer and examined it. "I've been trying to reconcile my first—and admittedly awful—impression of her with the sheer beauty of these."

"You don't really know her," he pointed out. "Maybe it'll just be one of those things that takes time." Aching to touch her, he settled for reaching out and briefly squeezing her arm. "Meanwhile, don't let that one awful incident with her affect how you feel about this amazing art."

"It's hard not to," she admitted. "But I'm definitely going to try. Especially since I'll be seeing her again real soon."

She told him about Jane's plans for an open house. "On Friday, so that gives her a few days to get everything in place. I got the impression she was hoping to turn it into a huge party, but I've asked her to keep it professional. I'm going to be these people's physician after all."

"I wish there was something I could do to help," he said, aware he'd made a mistake the minute the words left his mouth.

"Oh, but there is." Brightening immediately, she smiled. "Until you figure things out, I thought you could help me in the clinic. I could use an assistant. Someone other than Annette, that is."

The thought of letting others see him had dread coiling low in his gut. He might not know much about what had happened to him, but he knew without a doubt that his best chance of safety would be to stay hidden. The memory of the gunshots, even though he had no idea what had happened or why he hadn't been hit, were proof enough of that for him.

"I thought that's what Annette did," he replied, keeping his tone light. "I'm thinking you should give her a chance before you bring in outside help."

His words made her grimace, but if she caught on to his underlying reason of wanting to stay hidden, she didn't comment.

"You're right," she finally said. "I guess I'll just have to wait and see how it goes on Friday."

Though he hadn't known her very long, more than anything he wished he could do something to help her. Something that didn't involve him revealing himself to the people of Blake, Alaska. Until he knew exactly what the threat might be and where it came from, that was the one thing he couldn't yet do.

Chapter Five

Kenzie could tell her houseguest had become restless. She guessed she couldn't blame him. Though less than a week had passed since his car had gone into the river, having no memory for more than a few days had to be incredibly difficult and frustrating. That, coupled with his irrational feeling that he was in some sort of danger, made helping him a challenge. But help him she would. She was a physician and helping people with medical problems was in her DNA.

Though she knew very little about him, she enjoyed his company. Most likely because neither had any expectations. They weren't trying to forge a relationship or anything serious like that. Therefore, she found being around him freeing, like the kind of casual friendship where she felt completely comfortable being herself. Which was the best kind.

A lot of that had to do with him being a blank slate, she knew. But no matter how little of his past he might remember, certain personality traits would remain unchanged. She could tell he was a kind man, a thoughtful one, and she found herself looking forward to what each new memory he discovered might bring.

Since Friday and the open house was still a few days away, she decided to take the next couple of days to finish unpacking and explore the area around her cabin. John Doe had mentioned hiking, so she thought she'd do that. With him, of course. Since only a few perplexing memories of his had returned, she was interested to see what she might do to help him jog them.

Returning to the river, to the area where his vehicle had gone off the road, might help. While she didn't want to traumatize him, she knew he needed and wanted answers. He appeared to hate living in this limbo of blankness and she couldn't blame him.

She didn't want to push too hard, but could tell he'd need a little encouragement. Accompanying her on a hike might just help with that. And she was excited at the prospect of getting a little exercise. She'd even purchased a pair of high-end hiking boots before she'd left Houston.

While she wanted to relax before jumping into her new life, she also felt compelled to keep busy. She wasn't sure she remembered how to cope with downtime, since she'd had so little of that these past few years. And while she had some experience of being alone, she'd always known her friends and family were only a short drive away. One of her biggest worries about accepting the contract here in Blake, Alaska, had been wondering how she'd cope without a backup system of people she knew she could rely on. After meeting Jane and Greg, that particular fear had lessened somewhat, but she had to admit, having John Doe around had made her first few days 100 percent better. Even though she knew he wouldn't be with her for long, since once his memory returned he'd go back to wherever he came from, she enjoyed his company. With time, she thought they could become friends.

Friends. Truth be told, she couldn't stop thinking about the kiss. She'd dated a bit during med school and residency, though the grueling hours had made committing to any sort of real relationship impossible. There were kisses, and then there were *kisses*.

Worst possible timing. Ever. Pushing away any thoughts of attraction, she knew she had to keep herself focused on simply helping him figure out who he was and what had happened.

After showering and blow-drying her hair, she put it into a ponytail and dressed in jeans and her new hiking boots. She knew she should have broken them in before actually using them for hiking, but she hadn't had the chance.

Walking into the kitchen, following her nose to the mouthwatering scent of homemade baked goods, she wished John Doe a good morning and headed to the coffee maker.

"Would you like a piece of coffee cake?" he asked. "It just came out of the oven a few minutes ago."

"Yes, please," she replied. Dang, she could get used to this. After making her brew, she sat down. He joined her, bringing two plates of his confection.

"Caffeine." Smiling, she took another deep drink. "I wouldn't make it without it."

"Me neither," he said. "You're all dressed up. What's on your agenda for today?"

"We're going hiking," she announced, then took a bite of the really spectacular coffee cake with butter spread on top. "This is amazing. Cinnamon and apples, right?"

Her compliment made him smile, lighting up his eyes. "Among other things. I'm glad you like it."

"I do." Enthusiastically, she ate more, washing it down with her coffee. "You're an amazing cook."

"Thank you." He ate too. "What do you mean we're going hiking?"

Pushing away her now empty plate, she drank more coffee before replying. "It's time I got some exercise. Plus, I want to explore this immediate area, since I'm going to be living here a while. I thought you could take me to all the places you've hiked to before."

Intent on forking up the last of his own cake, he didn't even acknowledge her. She watched him chew, appearing deep in thought about something.

"Earth to John Doe," she said. "Did you hear me?"

"My name isn't John. It's Brett," he replied automatically. Then, rearing back slightly, he gave her an incredulous stare, his blue eyes bright. "Wow. How about that? I actually know my real name."

It suited him, she thought, nodding. "Perfect, Brett. How about a last name?"

His smile dimmed. "I... I don't know."

Her heart sank. With a last name, they could have done some internet digging and figured out where he'd come from and where he belonged. Assuming, she realized with a start, she even had internet here. Since there wasn't much cell phone reception, she rather doubted that. She only hoped they had something like satellite in town.

"I hate this," Brett said, crestfallen. "What good is

remembering only part of my name? I don't understand how this works."

"I'm sure the rest of your name will come to you," she told him. "In the meantime, how about we get some exercise? I need to work off all of your fantastic cooking."

This comment had him smiling again. "Let me go change and we'll head out," he said.

While he got ready, she packed a small backpack with bottled water and protein bars. While she hadn't done any actual hiking, she had read up on it and knew it was better to be prepared. Since they were in Alaska's rainy season, she added the couple of lightweight rain ponchos she'd bought earlier.

Less than five minutes later, he returned. "Let's do this," he said, smiling.

Handsome, she thought, her entire body clenching. In the past, she'd always gravitated toward tall slender men. But something about Brett's large frame appealed to her. When she was with him, she felt protected. Maybe even safe.

Outside, they walked side by side toward a steep hill on the back side of the cabin. "There's a small path here," he said. "And then you get to the top of this hill, there's another trail that leads even higher. I climbed all the way up, and the view is incredible."

The damp earth and foliage had a woodsy scent, and the cloudless sky reminded her of home. Mood buoyed, she let him lead the way, climbing up right behind him, and wishing she'd thought to purchase a walking stick. When she said as much to Brett, he turned and grinned at her, a lopsided smile that made her pulse race.

"We can make those," he said. "We'll grab a few good pieces of wood on the way back down."

The simplicity of the hike brought her a simple kind of peace and comfort. For the first time since she'd arrived, she thought she might actually like it here, at least if she survived the winter. In Houston, any temperature less than fifty degrees was considered cold. And she'd only seen actual snow twice in her life.

When they finally reached the summit that he'd mentioned, Brett spread his arms. "See?" he exclaimed. "You can see everywhere."

Glad to be able to stop and catch her breath, she turned, allowing herself to take it all in. "So many trees," she mused. "And mountains. It's like some kind of wilderness paradise."

"Yes." Clearly delighted, he motioned at the valley below. "Paradise indeed."

Once she'd drank her fill of the view, plus recovered from the uphill trek, they began making their way back down. She liked that Brett didn't feel the need to engage in small talk. His silence allowed her to enjoy the experience far more.

Once they were back at the cabin, he looked at her, his eyes twinkling. "What's next?" he asked.

"I thought we'd go for a drive," she said. And then she told him where she wanted to go and why.

Reluctantly, he agreed to get in her Jeep and take the drive back to the river. Since they'd already been hiking earlier, she just figured they'd drive out there and park, maybe even take a short hike upstream, just to see if his vehicle might have become visible.

Instead, as she rounded the curve in the road that

led to the bridge, she saw several other vehicles parked in the overlook area. One of them was marked Alaska State Troopers.

Glancing at Brett to try to gauge his reaction, she realized he sat frozen in his seat, jaw clenched.

"I'll keep driving," she said.

"Thanks." Once they'd gone past, he turned to look at her. "I'm not a fugitive."

Considering that very thought had crossed her mind, she wondered how to respond. She settled on a neutral comment. "I didn't say you were."

He'd already turned to look back at the bridge. "What do you think they're doing there?"

"Well, it's possible that someone may have spotted your car." She kept her tone as light as she possibly could.

"Damn it. I'm not ready."

Slightly alarmed and well aware she couldn't show it, she sighed. "Not ready for what?"

Jaw still tight, he glanced at her, his expression hard. For the first time since she'd met him, she felt a frisson of fear. "Brett?" she asked. "Are you okay?"

Though he opened his mouth to speak, nothing came out.

"You're scaring me," she said.

He blinked and then heaved a deep sigh. "I'm sorry. I'm not sure what just happened. I felt locked up, in a dark place. Worse, I have no idea why."

Accepting his explanation, mainly because right now she had no choice, she pulled over onto a dirt side road. "We're going to turn around and go back home. To do that, we'll have to go over that bridge again."

Slowly, he nodded. "I understand."

"Good. We're not going to stop, I promise. And to-morrow, I'll go into town and see if I can find out what's going on."

"Thank you." He touched her shoulder, which made her jump a little. "I'm sorry I frightened you."

"It's all good," she lied. "We really need to figure out what happened to you though."

"I agree."

Did he? Keeping her concerns to herself, she managed to smile and nod. "Then let's do this."

They made it back over the bridge without incident. Whatever was going on below near the water, she couldn't tell from up on the road. Though Brett's face took on a bit of a deer-in-the-headlights expression, and he held himself rigid, he didn't comment again. He also didn't relax until they'd turned back onto the driveway leading to her cabin.

She parked and killed the ignition. Turning to face him, she took a deep breath. "What are you so afraid of?" she asked, wondering if she'd come to regret her question. She hated that she now doubted him. Truly hated it.

"I don't know." His reply came automatically, the same response he'd been using all along.

"I think you do," she pressed. "I've been trying not to push you, but the way you reacted earlier wasn't good, to say the least. I'm actually concerned now."

He swallowed hard. "Would you like me to leave?"

"Of course not," she reassured him, even though putting him out had been one of the options she'd briefly considered. "I hope I don't regret this, but I truly want to know the truth. As I'm sure you do."

"Correct." Looking away from her, he opened the door and got out of the Jeep. Still moving stiffly, he went on into the cabin without a backward glance.

Kenzie remained where she was, her stomach churning and her chest tight. She hadn't opened her laptop since arriving, and maybe now might be a good time to see if she had internet. She could start by doing a search with the name Brett and shooting, and see if anything came up.

She got out and went inside.

The instant she set foot in the living room, Brett approached her. "I wouldn't blame you if you asked me to go," he said. "I'm confused and though I feel pretty certain I'm not a bad person, I don't really know. If our positions were reversed, I wouldn't feel comfortable being around me right now either."

His words made her feel slightly better. "You don't have to leave. I just think we need to try harder to get your memory back. The sooner we can figure out the truth, the better for both of us."

His smile lit up his blue eyes. "Thank you. And yes, I agree. I hate not knowing. In the meantime, let me see what I can rustle up for dinner."

Watching him putter around in the kitchen, whistling tunelessly, she put her newfound trepidation to the back of her mind. Anyone who could cook like Brett did couldn't be all bad, right?

Still, she went into her bedroom and retrieved her laptop. Before opening it, she did a quick search of the cabin, looking for anything that might resemble a router. She found nothing.

Just in case she'd somehow missed it, she sent Jane a quick text, asking. Jane replied immediately, apologizing but letting Kenzie know the only place she'd have internet would be in town.

"Good thing I didn't plan on streaming movies or anything," Kenzie muttered, putting the computer back inside her backpack. "When they said this cabin was remote, they weren't kidding."

"No Wi-Fi?" Brett guessed.

"Nope. I'm beginning to wonder if we'll even be able to pick up any local channels on the TV."

"You should be able to just fine," he replied. "There's a heavy-duty external antenna outside. Since you're going to be here so long, you might look into seeing if satellite television and Wi-Fi is available out here."

"Thanks," she said, glad he seemed back to normal. Of course, he always seemed happiest when puttering in the kitchen. "I'll ask Jane when I see her at the open house on Friday."

BRETT DIDN'T LIKE the fact that Kenzie now clearly had doubts about him. He couldn't blame her. He doubted himself too.

He had no idea why the thought of talking to the police about his car plunging off the bridge into the river terrified him, but it did. Maybe because he knew they'd want details about what had happened and he didn't have them. But also because he suspected there was more than what appeared on the surface.

Had someone else been in the vehicle with him? If

so, had that person been a friend or a foe? He tried like hell to remember. Something. Anything. But no matter how hard he tried, his recollection of that day began with him walking out of the river in the pouring rain to find a beautiful woman waiting for him.

Yearning for the truth had now taken on an entirely new dimension. He couldn't bear to have Kenzie look at him with even the slightest bit of fear in her beautiful brown eyes.

So he did what little he could. He cooked—his sole creative outlet and something he suspected had always brought him solace. He hoped in some small aspect his food could do the same for Kenzie.

For their evening meal, he made braised chicken thighs in a white wine sauce, couscous and blanched green beans. He somehow knew how to make all sorts of recipes from memory, yet couldn't come up with his last name.

"This is amazing," Kenzie enthused after her first bite. "You should really consider doing this professionally."

Though he smiled, he didn't try to hide his frustration. "For all we know, maybe I do. I could be a chef somewhere. Both times when I had the memory or vision of the gunshots, I was holding a platter of food."

"Like you worked in a restaurant," she agreed. "Once I get to town and can access Wi-Fi, I'm going to do a search for shootings inside restaurants within the last few months. I know this kind of thing happens a lot in the lower forty-eight states, but I'm going to make my search specific to Alaska. That should help narrow it down. If I get a hit or two, maybe that will help us figure out who you are."

Though he nodded, he didn't have a lot of confidence that her idea would work. For one thing, he didn't know if he'd been one of the victims, or an employee, or even a customer. Still, maybe seeing photographs of a few restaurants where shootings had happened might jog his stubborn memory.

That night, he had his first vivid dream. The kind where, upon wakening, he found it difficult to distinguish between reality and the dream world. He'd stood on a piece of land, alone, surrounded by snow-capped mountains. Alaska—his heart sang with the joy of knowing he stood where he belonged. On his land, one with nature. He planned to build a home here someday, he knew. Whether a vacation home or permanent residence, that had yet to be determined. There were too many factors in play for him to reach a decision at this time.

Factors. Like what? Did he have a wife, a family? Or even someone special in his life? Parents or siblings, good friends and coworkers? How had it come to be that no one appeared to be looking for him, or at least that he knew of, ever since he'd gone off the bridge?

His subconscious mind remained closed off, even while in the throes of sleep. He knew his first name, which meant something. He could only hope the rest would come soon.

An analogy had come to him in the dream. He saw himself as a fractured man, comprised of various puzzle pieces. Some, like this land and his cooking ability, fit easily into place. Others were missing, and try as he might in the dream, he couldn't seem to locate them.

Frustrated, he sat up in his makeshift bed on the couch. While not completely uncomfortable, it wasn't wide enough or long enough and he had to admit he'd considered more than once making a bed on the floor. Only the thought of Kenzie's reaction to this stopped him. She'd been kind enough to allow him to stay and he didn't want her to think he had complaints about her hospitality.

Though early, he went ahead and got up and made himself a cup of coffee. Craving simplicity, he made a pot of steel-cut oatmeal and ate a solitary breakfast, leaving some on the stove for Kenzie to eat later.

She wandered in just as he'd started his second cup of coffee, her hair tousled as if she'd just rolled out of bed. Clearly unaware of how she affected him, she flashed a quick smile before going to get her own cup of coffee.

Even with her back to him, she looked sexy as hell in her oversize T-shirt and flip-flops. Eyeing her, his mouth went dry. He told her about the oatmeal and she nodded. "I need coffee first," she said.

He tried not to stare at her while she made it. He might not remember much about himself, but he knew when a woman appealed to him. And Kenzie most definitely did. He'd been trying not to think of the kiss, but he'd never seen a woman with a more kissable mouth.

Groaning when she took her first sip of coffee, Kenzie closed her eyes and took a second. Even that he found sensual as hell.

Damn he had it bad. He needed to get a grip on himself, starting now.

"Are you okay?" Kenzie asked, watching him over the rim of her mug. "You seem lost in thought."

Blinking, he nodded. "I'm fine. Are you ready for that oatmeal?"

"Maybe later. First, I want to try something," Kenzie said, her brown eyes sparkling. He had to admit, his thoughts immediately jumped to places they shouldn't go and his body stirred.

"Try what?" he asked, well aware he needed to get his libido under control.

"I want to ask you some questions, rapid fire. And I want you to just say the first thing that comes to mind. Don't even think about it. Just say whatever it is. Even if you don't think it makes sense."

Slowly, he nodded. "I see where you're going with this. Sure, we can try."

Her radiant grin made it all worth it. His breath caught in his throat. Damn, she was beautiful. Even stranger, she didn't appear to have even the faintest clue how she affected him. He'd need to make sure it stayed that way.

"Great." Still beaming, she gestured toward the couch. "Why don't you sit down, close your eyes and we'll get started?"

Once he'd done as she asked, he watched as she dropped into the armchair across from him. She had a pad of paper and a pen poised to take notes.

"Close your eyes," she prompted.

"I think better with them open," he replied, well aware how easy it would be to drift off into fantasies about her with them closed.

"Okay." She shrugged. "As long as you can say

the first thing that comes to mind without stopping
to think."

"I can. Hit me with your best shot."

His choice of phrasing made her smile.

"Home."

"Alaska."

"Car."

"Gone," he replied, wincing a little at the banality
of his answer.

Undeterred, she continued. "Job."

"Work."

She shook her head. "This isn't how it's supposed
to go."

"I get that. But you told me to say the first thing that
came to mind, so that's what I'm doing. If I stop and
try to think about my answer, I might be able to elaborate." He shrugged. "And it's also entirely possible I'll
draw a big blank."

"I agree," she said. "Which is why I want you to
say whatever immediately pops into your mind. Let's
continue."

"Pet?"

"Dog," he replied. The image of a black-and-white
longhaired dog filled his mind. "Peppa."

Excitement made her eyes sparkle. "Is that a dog's
name? Do you have a dog?"

As soon as he tried to concentrate, the image faded.
"I don't know," he said haltingly. "I know that name,
and in my mind I saw a beautiful black-and-white border collie. What I don't know is if she's mine, or someone else's. Or even if she's alive, or from the past. I

kind of feel like she might have been a childhood pet, but can't be sure."

Kenzie made a face. "Frustrating."

"Tell me about it." He rubbed his temples. "My head is starting to ache."

"Don't get discouraged," she said. "Let's keep going. Who knows what else you might remember."

Now he had a full-blown headache throbbing behind his eyes. "If it's okay with you, let's take a break. We can try again later."

Eyes narrowed, she studied him. "What's wrong? Does your head hurt?"

Though he felt foolish, he slowly nodded. "I'm not sure if it's a reaction to all of this, or what."

"Most likely it is," she said. "We'll stop for now. Let me get you a cup of black coffee. Sometimes that helps."

She made them both coffee and sat down with him to drink it. "I'm both dreading and looking forward to the open house," she said. "I'll be glad to get to know some of my patients, but I'm still worried about dealing with Annette. I can't very well call her out in front of anyone, yet I can't let her treat me the way she did last time."

"I agree." Whether because of the coffee or the fact that they'd stopped trying to force his memory into action, his headache had already begun to subside. "I'm sorry I can't go with you to the open house," he said, genuinely contrite. She'd done so much to help him and he wished he could repay her with more than just cooking meals. "I've been trying like hell to figure out a way, but I can't. I even considered—and I know this is going to sound strange—wearing a disguise."

Instead of laughing at him outright as he'd expected, she cocked her head and considered. "What kind of a disguise? You have to be careful with something like that as it could make you stand out even more than if you just went as yourself."

"I know." He eyed her, willing her to understand how badly his wanting to help conflicted with the need to stay hidden. "Do you think there will be children there? Maybe I could be a clown who you can say you hired to entertain the kids." He kept his tone light.

Expression skeptical, nonetheless she didn't immediately shoot down his half-hearted suggestion. "You know what? That's so over the top it might actually work."

His heart sunk. Though he did really want to help her, the sense of danger felt too real and too strong. He hadn't expected her to take him seriously.

"Except they'll likely want to know where you found me," he said, aware he should have clarified that he was only kidding. "In a village this small, everyone knows everyone else, even the ones who live far on the outskirts. Which means I would have had to come from farther away, like Anchorage."

"Or…" she said, clearly thinking out loud. "I could say I brought you with me from Texas."

Stunned, he stared at her. Did she really want him there that badly? "They'll think we're a couple," he informed her. "I'm not sure you want to start your relationship with these people with a lie. Plus, what if someone were to recognize me? For all we know, I could be from around here."

She met his gaze. "Would that really be such a bad

thing?" she asked softly. "It might be just what you need to figure things out."

"Except for the whole I-think-I'm-in-danger thing," he reminded her.

She crossed her arms. "I know, and I get it. But you really don't have anything to base that on. Irrational fear could simply be a residual effect from your car going off the bridge."

Swallowing, he shook his head. "What about the shooting? It's possible they were after me."

"It is," she agreed. "But you don't know that for sure. You might have only been an innocent bystander."

"Or a witness." He didn't speak out loud his real fear—that he might have somehow, as inconceivable as it seemed now, been involved in the shooting itself. "Either way," he continued, "I'd rather stay hidden until I figure out what's going on."

Watching him closely, she finally nodded. "I can respect that. I honestly don't know what I'd do if our situations were reversed."

Her cell phone rang. Glancing at the screen, her face lit up. "It's Jane," she said, and then answered. "Jane! What's up?"

He walked out on the front porch to give her some privacy. Dropping into one of the rockers, he struggled with a feeling of despair. What the hell was wrong with him that he couldn't remember? Had he hit his head when the car went off the bridge? Or was his amnesia more insidious, a deliberate effort by his subconscious to forget?

The thing he hadn't wanted to point out to Kenzie, what seemed obvious, was that if he truly was in some sort of danger, by her very proximity to him, he'd placed her in danger too. She didn't deserve that. All she'd done was help a complete stranger.

The cabin door opened and Kenzie walked out onto the front porch, her phone still in her hand. She tried to speak; her lips moved, but nothing came out. Her complexion had gone pale, as if all her blood had leached from her face.

"What is it?" he asked, pushing to his feet. "What's wrong?"

When she looked at him, he could have sworn he saw a quick flash of fear in her gaze.

"That was Jane," she finally replied, her voice shaky. "She called to tell me the news. A man's body was found floating in the river near the bridge. That must be why the police were out there yesterday."

Chapter Six

Kenzie didn't want to suspect Brett of anything, but this latest development put a different twist on things. "Do you think this man might have been with you in your car?"

Brett stared at her, clearly shocked. "I don't know," he answered automatically. "I hope not." He dropped back into the chair, as if his legs had given out on him.

She sat down in the chair next to him. "This is important. The body is being sent to Anchorage for an autopsy. I'm thinking they're going to be looking for the car next."

"Damn." When he met her gaze, his tortured expression made her chest ache. "I don't know what to think."

Reaching over, she touched his arm. "I have a hundred questions." She sighed. "Unfortunately, I know you won't have any answers. Yet."

That came out sounding more like a threat than she'd intended.

"I confess, I'm fighting the urge to run," he told her. "Why would I want to flee unless I've done something wrong?"

Why indeed? She wasn't sure what to tell him, or even

what to tell herself. In the end, she settled on a platitude of sorts. Because she didn't know what else to say. "All we can do is hope for the best. Your memory *will* come back, I promise. Until then, just do the best you can to remember."

"Right." Voice bleak, he stared off into the distance. "Bad enough that I don't know what happened to make that car go off the bridge. Or that I have no idea if there was someone else inside. What's worse than that is the idea that I might have somehow deliberately caused harm to another person. From a shooting or this accident."

She only meant to comfort him, but somehow she found herself straddling him, his rugged face between her hands as she gazed into his eyes. "Stop it," she ordered. "Right now. You can't worry about something you don't know is real."

And then without conscious intention, her mouth was on his. They kissed—that *kiss, again!* It sent heat blazing instantly between them, searing her nerve endings. All rational thought and doubt disappeared. There was only him, and the feel of his hard muscular body beneath her.

Savage desire pulsed through her. She couldn't think, couldn't breathe. All encompassing, the feel of his hand stroking her skin, cupping her breast. The swell of his arousal, pressing against her own damp and ready body. Material separated them and she wanted it gone. Needed it gone.

She pushed up off him, her gaze still locked on his, and stripped off her clothes, all of them. Naked, her desire plain in every curve of her body, she waited impatiently for him to do the same.

Desire turned his blue eyes so dark they almost looked black. He made short work of ridding himself of his own clothing, reaching for her the instant everything hit the floor.

While she sensed he thought he should take control, it wasn't what she wanted right now. "Sit," she ordered, giving him a small shove with the intention of putting him back into the chair.

Grinning, he allowed this, the strength of his arousal beckoning, a tempting invitation she couldn't resist. Again, she straddled him, this time without any barrier between them. Rising up over him, she sank slowly down, letting the hard length of him impale her. He filled her, somehow completing her. She held herself absolutely still, her gaze locked on his before she kissed him. A deep wet kiss, all tongue and desire and need. The kind that sent shivers through her soul. Her body clenched around him, already so far gone she knew she'd shatter in an instant if she moved.

"I can't..." he gasped, bucking his body up, into her, making her hang on like riding a bucking bronco. Though she'd wanted to maintain control, it felt so damn good, so she went along with his strokes. Building, building, mouth upon mouth, bodies intertwined, so close she could hardly tell where she ended and he began.

Wild. Unbridled lust, more sex than lovemaking. Exactly what she'd needed, without even realizing it.

She'd never felt anything like it. She couldn't help but wonder if she ever would again.

After, sated and warm, she lay in his arms and tried to summon up an iota of regret. Since she couldn't, she allowed herself to relax and enjoy the feeling.

"Thank you for that," he murmured. "That was something. You made me feel human again. Seen. Felt."

"Oh, I definitely felt you," she responded wryly. "I want you to promise me something. When you remember who you are and where you belong, promise me you won't let yourself feel guilty over this."

Expression surprised, he raised himself up on one elbow and looked at her. "Guilty? I'd think it'd be more like wondering how we can arrange to do it again."

This made her laugh, which he'd no doubt intended. "You're something else, Brett with no last name. I'm really glad we managed to cross paths."

"You sound as if you expect things to change soon." Voice troubled, he brushed a strand of her hair away from her face. "Even if my entire memory were to return tomorrow, I think I'd still want to figure out a way to continue to get to know you."

That was just it. He'd hit the nail on the head. She didn't know him, not really. He wasn't entirely himself, a man with only partial memories. Not wanting to get into anything too deep and spoil the moment, she sighed. "I guess we'll just have to wait and see."

That night, as if by tacit agreement, she retired alone to her room and he slept on his makeshift bed on the couch. Tomorrow was the open house at her clinic and she definitely wanted to be well rested. Spending the night making love, while enjoyable, wouldn't guarantee that she'd get much sleep.

In the morning, she woke early, cheerful and full of

nervous energy. She showered, wrapped her hair in a towel and headed into the kitchen for coffee. Surprisingly, Brett was nowhere to be found.

He'd left a note on the kitchen counter, letting her know he'd gone for an early morning walk. If today hadn't been so important, she might have gone out looking for him. Instead, she made her coffee and carried it back into her bedroom so she could drink it while she dried her hair and applied her makeup.

She heard the front door open and close as Brett returned. He went straight into the kitchen and judging from the clanging of pots and pans, started cooking something.

A thought struck her. That would be another thing she'd miss when he went home to where he belonged. His amazing cooking.

Shaking her head at her own foolishness, she reminded herself not to get too attached. They'd only known each other less than a week, but she truly liked him. And the sex… Well, that had been amazing too. She truly couldn't wait for his memory to come back so she could learn who he really was and what had actually happened when his car had gone into the river. Despite the other body, she couldn't bring herself to believe that Brett had done anything criminal or evil. She didn't think he had it in him.

Of course, she could be wrong. All she could do now was wait and see.

A light tapping on her bedroom door had her poking her head out of the bathroom.

"Are you hungry?" Brett asked. "I made breakfast. Nothing fancy, just scrambled eggs and toast."

"Yes, thank you," she said, smiling. "That's perfect for settling my nervous stomach."

"Then come eat." To his credit, he didn't mention the open house while they ate. Instead, he talked very little, appearing withdrawn and contemplative. This too, she could understand. They were both trying to navigate their changing relationship or whatever it might be. Right now, she'd definitely prefer keeping it light.

After the meal, when she got up to do the dishes, he waved her away. "I've got this," he said. "You've got a big day today."

"I appreciate you," she replied, meaning it. Sometimes, she secretly felt amazed that her best friend in Alaska was a man with no memory whom she'd rescued from a river. She smiled at him. "And you're right. It is going to be a big day."

With that, she headed into her bedroom and closed the door.

Confidence warred with nervousness as she got ready. While she knew she was a good, well-trained doctor, she also hoped to fit in and become part of this town. She wanted to look capable and professional, yet also warm and approachable. She went with minimal makeup and pulled her hair up into a neat bun. Two seconds later, deciding that hairstyle made her appear too severe, she turned it into a messy bun. A little less constrained, but still up. She'd already decided in advance that she'd wear one of her white physical coats with her name stenciled on it. Underneath, she settled on a pair of black slacks, comfy flats and a magenta silk blouse. Small diamond ear studs and her favorite silver necklace in the shape of a lotus flower completed her look.

Finally satisfied with her appearance, she left her small bedroom and went out to tell Brett goodbye. As usual, she found him in the kitchen, though instead of stirring something on the stove, he had a pad of paper and a pen, and appeared to be making notes.

"What are you doing?" she asked.

When he looked up, his eyes widened. "Wow. You look amazing." Then, remembering that she'd asked him a question, he gestured with the pen. "I seem to just *know* recipes. Like I can look at a couple of ingredients and then just realize what I need to put together with them to make something. I thought I'd start jotting them down."

"Good idea. Maybe you can publish a cookbook someday."

"Maybe." He shrugged. "Though I have no way of knowing if these are my recipes or someone else's. It just feels good to write them down as they come to me. Like an exercise working on my memory."

"Sounds great." Scooping up her Jeep keys, she fought the impulse to go to him and kiss him goodbye. "Well, I've got an open house to attend. Are you absolutely sure you don't want to go?"

Somber now, he nodded. "I'm sure. Have a good time. I'm sure you'll wow them."

"Thanks." With a quick wave, she started toward the door.

"Wait."

Turning, she eyed him. "What's up?"

"While you're there, will you see if you can find out anything about that body they found? I need more information so I can figure out how I am or am not involved."

"Of course," she replied, and then took off. Only

when she sat in the driver's seat and started the engine did she realize how fast her heart raced. He'd effectively managed to remind her of the fact that she truly knew nothing about him.

And yet...she felt as if she did. She shook her head at her own lack of logic. They'd not only kissed, but they'd made love. Or had sex, clinically speaking.

Sometimes, she wondered what kind of person she'd become here, in the wilds of Alaska. Maybe because she'd come here without knowing a single soul, or because she'd finally finished her residency and could call herself a doctor, but she felt freer than she had in years. Strong, proud and confident. And along with all that, came Brett. A handsome, sexy man who could cook. Plus, she liked him. No matter the reason, he had a strong effect on her. Which was a distraction she simply didn't need but craved anyway.

Putting him from her head, she pulled away from the cabin, down the long drive and then onto the now-familiar road. Today, the drive into the village seemed to be shorter. By the time she pulled up to the clinic, she felt calmer, more in control.

Today, in the bright sunshine, the building didn't appear so dismal. Just a solid brick structure built to withstand any bad weather.

Kenzie parked in the spot marked Reserved for the Doctor, smiling slightly at the fact that she had her own spot. One or two other vehicles occupied the small parking lot, which meant a few people had clearly arrived early. Guessing one of them would be Annette Gladley, she steeled herself and walked in the door.

Again, the brightly lit reception area took her by

surprise. There had been a few welcoming additions since her last visit. A huge vase full of colorful silk flowers sat on a side table, and several magazines had been placed on another. A multicolored area rug opened up the small room, making it appear warm rather than clinical.

And several beautiful watercolor paintings had been hung on the walls. Kenzie moved closer, knowing before she even got close enough to see the signature that they were Annette's work.

Once more, she marveled at their beauty.

From one of the rooms in the back, she heard voices and then Jane's loud bark of laughter. Relieved that Jane and Greg were here to help with her second meeting with Annette, she hurried down the hallway toward the break room.

Jane saw her first. "Dr. Taylor," she exclaimed, coming forward with her hand outstretched. When Kenzie reached her, Jane pulled her in for a bone-crunching hug instead. Over Jane's shoulder, Kenzie saw Greg grinning. Annette, meanwhile, shifted her weight from foot to foot, appearing both uncomfortable and resigned. She'd dressed up for the occasion, wearing a colorful maxi dress and strappy sandals.

The instant Jane released her, Kenzie turned to Annette, determined to try to start off on the right foot. "Hi, Annette. You look amazing."

Annette reacted by narrowing her eyes, as if she thought Kenzie's compliment might be a trap.

"She does, doesn't she?" Jane interjected, clearly trying to smooth things over. "Look at her earrings. She made them herself."

Kenzie checked out the intricate beads and silver teardrops dangling from Annette's ears. "I love them," she said. "If you ever make some and put them for sale in the general store, I'll buy a pair."

"Thanks," Annette managed, her face pink. "I haven't gotten around to doing that, but I'll let you know if I do."

"Perfect." Kenzie beamed. Turning back to Jane, she sniffed the air. "What is that delicious smell?"

"Appetizers," Greg answered. "I made spinach-artichoke dip, crab dip, some pizza rolls and sausage queso. We have all kinds of chips, sparkling water and cookies for dessert. I'm setting everything up here in the break room for people to enjoy."

"I think we should put everything in the reception area," Annette chimed in. "We're not giving tours of the clinic. Most everyone has been here before. This is more about meeting the new lady doctor."

"I agree," Kenzie said, earning a surprised half smile from Annette. "Let's move everything up there. And whoever did the decorating, I love it."

"That would be me," Annette replied, face pink again. "The old Doc took all his hunting trophies with him, so I did a little redecorating. I'm glad you like it."

How about that? A civil conversation. Maybe this working relationship could be salvaged after all.

AFTER KENZIE LEFT, the tiny cabin felt far too quiet. Brett prowled around, aching inside for no discernible reason. He had the strangest sense that time was closing in on him. Why or how or even what that meant, he had no idea.

There'd been a body pulled from the river. The very same one where he'd almost lost his life. Coincidence? He doubted that. Had the other man been in the car with him? Had he been a friend or foe? These were all the sort of things he really needed to remember.

He decided to hike down to the river. By now, the crowd would have dispersed and law enforcement would have moved on. Though it hadn't helped before, he'd also been with Kenzie. For some reason, he realized he needed to go alone.

Figuring he had plenty of time before Kenzie returned, he grabbed a couple bottles of water and a protein bar and stuck them in Kenzie's old backpack. He figured she wouldn't mind him borrowing it.

Setting out, he realized he felt happy. As weird as it sounded, he liked his life, living solely in the moment and sharing it with her. Of course, he understood he couldn't go on forever like this, a man with no past, but that didn't mean he couldn't appreciate the simplicity that came with having no baggage.

All he could do was hope it didn't all blow up in his face once he knew the truth.

Since he'd hiked all over the area near the cabin, he knew he could get to the river quicker if he went through the woods, rather than try to follow the road.

The hike still brought him peace, despite knowing he intended to try to reclaim his memory of a turbulent moment in his past.

Up he went, carefully climbing the hill. At the top, he stopped again to savor the view. His spirits lifted as he gazed out over the rugged landscape, following the flight of a bald eagle wheeling and dipping above.

Clouds dotted the blue sky, though they didn't appear to be the kind that carried rain.

In the distance, the river shimmered like a bright ribbon. It appeared farther away than he remembered, but still reachable, though the hike might take a bit longer than he'd planned.

Determined now, he pushed forward, keeping a careful eye out for bears since he figured they'd be closer to water.

Finally, he got close enough to hear the roar of the rapids as the water tumbled over rocks. One more hill to climb and then he'd make the descent, coming out on the opposite shore from the road and the bridge where he'd plunged into the water.

Once he reached the summit, he paused to catch his breath. He'd been pushing himself, hiking at a pace much faster than he usually did. He needed to be careful to conserve enough energy for the long hike back to the cabin.

But he'd made it. The steep slope down to the river appeared treacherous. He'd have to be extremely careful and take the descent slowly and cautiously, going from tree to tree and using them as anchors. The last thing he needed would be to lose his footing and tumble into the rapidly moving river. No one would even know how or where to find him.

Slow and easy, he told himself, beginning to make his way down. He paused often, mapping out his route ahead of time. Every step would be planned.

Finally, he reached the bottom. Here, the land flattened out a bit more. Winded, he sat down on a boulder a few feet away from the fast water. Glancing up and across, he could see the twisted metal guardrail where his vehicle had hit it, and realized the police would surely have been looking for the vehicle. He wondered if they'd found it and if so, would there be anything to tie him to it?

The sound of the water soothed him. Above, a huge bald eagle wheeled and drifted, riding the wind currents. Alone, the anxiety that had plagued him at first ebbed slowly away.

He didn't know how long he sat there, but he must have dozed off, because the next thing he knew he was inside the car again, in the back seat, working on untying his hands, which were bound behind his back.

The rain beat down, obscuring the driver's vision, making him curse. Brett realized he didn't know the man at all, and also understood his own life was in grave danger.

Somehow, he managed to loosen the knot, freeing his hands enough to restore circulation. He took care not to alert the man driving, who continually glanced at Brett in the rearview mirror. Something about the flatness of his gaze left no doubt he didn't plan to let Brett escape the car alive.

Which meant Brett would have to save himself. He continued to work his hands free. When he finally succeeded, he made his move, wrapping the rope around the driver's throat from behind. Well aware they would crash, Brett knew that was a chance he would have to take.

Unfortunately, he didn't see they were on a bridge crossing over a river.

Startled, furious, the driver fought back, all the while

trying to maintain control of the car. Brett tightened the noose, wincing as the other man gasped for breath, hoping he'd simply lose consciousness instead of his life.

And then they were airborne. Brett's head slammed into the roof of the car, so hard he saw stars. He also lost his grip on the rope, which didn't actually matter as they plunged into icy cold water that was thankfully deep.

Rocks and rain. Water swirled around them, coming inside, filling the car. Realizing if he wanted to live, he had to get out now. But the electric windows had short-circuited and wouldn't open. He'd have to break one. Just in case, he tried the door, but the water pressure kept it from opening.

There. In the front seat. A crowbar. Most likely meant to beat Brett to death later. He grabbed it and swung it hard, shattering the window, bringing an onslaught of more water.

Somehow, Brett found himself outside the rapidly sinking vehicle, his head hurting so badly he thought he might have fractured his skull. For a moment, he lost consciousness, and when he came back to himself, he could no longer even see the car. He swam hard against the current, swallowing water, trying to figure out how he'd gotten here, what had happened. Other than the excruciating pain in his head, all he knew was he had to stay alive.

Then he saw her. A woman, drenched in the pouring rain, standing at the edge of the water, shouting for him to swim to her.

Kenzie.

Stunned, Brett opened his eyes, breathing hard, feeling sick to his stomach. Now he finally knew what had happened, though not why or all the details.

What he did know was that he hadn't been in the car willingly. Judging from the fact that his hands had been bound, he'd been taken prisoner. The driver, who'd likely drowned and was the body that'd washed up earlier, had not been anyone he knew.

What Brett didn't know was how all this tied together. Somehow, he knew that the man who had kidnapped him had done so because of the shooting. Though he now felt quite confident the rest of the mystery would come to him in time, he no longer had the patience to wait. Once Kenzie returned from her open house, he wanted to ask her if they could go back to her clinic and use the Wi-Fi, assuming she even had it there. An internet search might definitely go a long way toward getting him answers much more quickly.

Energized with a sense of renewed purposed, he hiked back to the cabin and settled in to wait. Since cooking always helped calm him, he started working on a complicated tiramisu dessert to go with the homemade lasagna he'd planned for dinner.

Whistling while he worked, once again he felt grateful that cooking brought him so much happiness.

Finished, he straightened up around the cabin and waited for Kenzie to return.

When she pulled up in front of the cabin, he went outside to greet her. Climbing out of her Jeep, with such a bright and joyful smile that she practically glowed, she looked so beautiful that he stopped short, momentarily struck dumb.

"Hey there," she said, not noticing. "The open house

turned out to be quite a success! I met a bunch of people from town and most everyone seemed welcoming."

"Most everyone?" he asked, unable to do anything else but smile back at her.

"Well, there were a few people who expressed their disappointment that I wasn't a man." Grinning, she climbed up onto the porch and plopped down into one of the rocking chairs. "But they'll get over that soon enough."

When he made no move to join her, she tilted her head. "Are you in the middle of something?" Without waiting for an answer, she continued, "If not, please sit. I have so much I want to tell you."

Without hesitation, he sat. Chest aching, wanting her, needing her, and all too aware he had to keep his distance and let her have her moment, he listened. She told him all about the open house, from the various townspeople who'd made an appearance to the food. And finally, she described a much-changed Annette. "I actually think we might be able to work together," she said.

Finally, she paused for breath. "What about you?" she asked. "How did your day go?"

"I hiked," he replied. "Are you hungry? I made a lasagna and it'll take about an hour to cook. I can put it in the oven now, or wait until later."

"Let's wait. I snacked quite a bit at the open house. Are you okay with having a late dinner?"

"Definitely." He took a moment, trying to formulate how to explain what he'd realized earlier. In the end, he simply told her what he'd remembered, and how.

When he'd finished, he met her gaze, seeing only acceptance. "The man that drowned was a bad man then."

"I think so, yes. I believe all of this is tied into the other memory, the shooting at the restaurant. If you're up to it, I'd like us to run into town and see if your clinic has Wi-Fi. It'd be helpful if we could run an internet search. Surely, something will come up."

"Of course." She jumped to her feet, her brown eyes sparkling. "I forgot to check while I was there earlier, but it would make sense for a medical office to have it. Let's go and see."

"Everyone would be gone by now?" he asked, hating that he still felt the need to hide. "Like Annette?"

"Definitely. I was the last to leave," she replied. "And I'm the one who locked the clinic up."

"Let me grab your laptop." After going inside, he located her computer and brought it outside.

On the drive to the clinic, Kenzie regaled him with more stories about some of the more eccentric townspeople she'd met. "There's a man who has a pet deer," she said. "He raised her from a fawn. She sleeps inside his house just like a pet."

Her vibrant happiness had him smiling along with her, despite the turmoil swirling inside. Maybe today he'd finally have the answers he'd been seeking. To think a quick internet search might reveal who he was and what had happened to him. The idea felt overwhelming.

Once inside the clinic, she turned on the lights and then went to look for any kind of router while he booted up the computer. Waiting, he looked around. "This is really nice."

"I know," she called back. "Annette did a little redecorating. She has good taste."

A moment later, she returned. "I'm not finding anything to indicate this place has Wi-Fi or DSL or any kind of internet."

"The laptop is searching," he told her. "So far, it's not finding anything at all. Not even from any neighbors." Though since they were downtown, he doubted most of the shops would bother with internet. Maybe it was considered a luxury and for home use only.

"Let me check with Jane and Greg," Kenzie said. Punching the button for speaker phone, she called the mayor. Jane answered.

"I'm wondering about internet," Kenzie asked. "As in, is there any here in town?"

"Am I on speaker?" Jane asked, sounding curious.

"Yes. I wanted to have my hands free," Kenzie explained. "Do you know if there's any kind of internet?"

"Well, we can't afford satellite," Jane said. "And from what I hear, the connectivity is spotty at best. A bunch of us here in Blake ended up going with DSL and fixed wireless. Most times, it works. But sometimes it's spotty. In the winter, it often goes out for days."

Brett shook his head. Good information to have, but clearly Kenzie needed to be more specific.

"Does the clinic have it?" Kenzie asked. "Internet, I mean."

"No," Jane replied. "Old Doc Clarke wasn't a big fan of modern technology. He was old school. He only barely used a computer so the lab could email test results, and that was only after they refused to keep sending them to him by fax. He had them sent to the mayor's office and would go pick them up there."

"Okay. Then I'll need to get it installed, both here and at my cabin. Can you text me the info on who to contact?"

"Sure," Jane said. "But be aware it'll be a bit of a wait. It seems like supply can't keep up with demand. I've been hearing it can take close to a month before they can make it out for installation."

"A month?" Shaking her head, Kenzie clearly tried not to sound too incredulous. "I'll have to see if they can fast-track the medical clinic. Surely, they'll prioritize health care providers."

"Maybe so." Jane sighed. "In the meantime, you're welcome to come over anytime and use our DSL. It's not the fastest in the world, but it gets the job done."

Kenzie and Brett exchanged a look. "I just might take you up on that," Kenzie said. "Thank you."

"No problem. Give me a minute and I'll shoot you a text with the names and numbers of the top three internet providers."

Ending the call, Kenzie slid her phone into her back pocket. "Well, there goes that idea."

"You'll have to go to the mayor's house, use their DSL and do a search for me," he told her. "On your personal laptop, of course, so they can't see your search history. I can write down a few of the things I remember, if that would help."

"Sure." She eyed him. "This might sound weird, but sometimes I'm afraid of what I might find."

Surprised, he couldn't help but shake his head, hoping his internal despair didn't show on his face. "Believe me, I get it. I worry about that all the time. It's hard not to."

He took a deep breath, searching for something re-assuring to say. "All we can do is hope in this case that the truth is what we want to hear."

Chapter Seven

The next morning, even though it was a Saturday, Kenzie got to work trying to secure internet. After making contact with two different internet providers, she chose the one who could get out the soonest. She consoled herself with the fact that two weeks was definitely a lot sooner than the one-month time period Jane had predicted.

Brett had made them pancakes for breakfast. Kenzie swore they were the best she'd ever tasted, which made Brett laugh. After cleaning up, Brett went off to take a shower while Kenzie called Jane to see if she could stop by and use her internet.

"I can't talk long," Jane said, almost whispering. "There's been big doings going on."

"Already?" Kenzie checked the time. It was only 10:35 a.m.

"Yes, already," Jane replied. "Turns out a car washed up yesterday afternoon on the McClendons' place. Part of their land borders the river. Greg thinks it has to have been the one the dead guy was driving when he went off the bridge."

Kenzie's heart skipped a beat. Remembering what

Brett had told her he remembered about the accident, she wanted to hear more. "Have the police been out yet?"

"No. But they're on their way. And there's more." Pausing for effect, Jane raised her voice just a little. "Two strangers, both men, have been roaming around town looking for a missing friend. Or so they say. They got here yesterday too. And this morning, as soon as they found out about the dead body and the car turning up, they got really agitated. They insisted someone take them to look at the vehicle."

Fascinated, Kenzie listened. Around here, people apparently started early, even on a Saturday.

"We were eating our usual Saturday breakfast at Mikki's, along with half the town," Jane continued. "Those two guys came in and started asking questions. When they learned Greg had already contacted the state troopers, one of them threatened him! With a knife? Can you believe that?" Jane asked, her tone incredulous.

"Threatened him? At Mikki's?" Kenzie asked.

"Yes! I was shocked speechless. All because the guy wanted Greg to call off the police. When Greg refused, that's when the guy pulled a knife." Jane chuckled. "Greg took care of that. A pistol trumps a blade, every time."

Still trying to process everything, Kenzie said the first thing that came to mind. "Wow. Alaska really is like the wild frontier."

Her comment cracked Jane up. "I guess you could say that," Jane finally said, once she'd finished laughing. "I assume you know how to handle yourself with a weapon?"

"I do," Kenzie admitted. "I took lessons and got certified to carry before I came here. Since I flew, I purchased a pistol and ammo in Anchorage, right after I took delivery of my Jeep."

"Smart woman," Jane said, her voice approving. "I'm just glad you didn't run into those two fellas though. Whatever they were up to, it wasn't good. We heard they spent all afternoon yesterday asking around town, while we were busy with the open house."

"Wow." Heart still racing, Kenzie tried to speak calmly. "I'm just glad they didn't decide to show up at the clinic."

"Me too," Jane responded. "Everyone at Mikki's had just been talking about how they got a bad feeling about them when they showed up, demanding to speak to the mayor." Heaving a big sigh, Jane appeared to be enjoying the sheer drama of her story. "Luckily, we'd finished eating before the confrontation, but it was unsettling for sure."

"I'll say. I can't even imagine. I'm just glad they're gone," Kenzie said.

"Oh, me too. Good riddance. They were shifty fellows, and believe me, we've had more than a few of them drift through Blake before."

Shifty fellows. Immediately, Kenzie thought of Brett. If June knew his story, would she consider him shifty? Kenzie suspected she might.

"Anyway, enough about all this. What can I do for you today?" Jane asked.

"Well, I was planning to stop by and see about using your internet," Kenzie said. "But clearly this is not a good time."

"I'm sorry," Jane apologized. "It is a bad time. Maybe tomorrow would be better. Sundays always are quieter. Though honestly, it just depends on how long it takes for the state troopers to get back to us."

Since she started work at the clinic on Monday, Kenzie hoped she could do this tomorrow. "What about Mikki's?" she asked, the thought just occurring to her. "Do they offer Wi-Fi for their customers?"

The question made Jane chuckle. "Doc, you're thinking too big city. Out here, people aren't as connected as they might be in somewhere like Anchorage or Seattle."

"I take it that's a no then?" Kenzie asked, her tone dry.

"Sorry," Jane apologized. "Sometimes I keep forgetting you're new to this part of the country."

"It's all good," Kenzie said. "I'll check back in with you tomorrow." Then she ended the call.

"Wow," she muttered to herself, going for another cup of coffee even though she'd already had two. While the sounds of the shower had cut off, Brett had not yet emerged from the bathroom.

Sitting down to wait, she tried to curb her impatience. This entire scenario was already strange enough. Now, after what Jane had told her, it had gone into the realm of downright frightening. She really wanted to see Brett's reaction.

Something must have shown in her face because when he walked into the kitchen, his easy smile faded. "What's happened?" he asked. "Do I need to sit down?"

"You might want to. I just got off the phone with Jane. I'm still trying to process what she told me."

Pulling out a chair, he sat facing her. "I'm listening."

She told him everything that Jane had said, beginning with the car washing up and ending with the two men threatening Greg at knifepoint.

When she'd finished, Brett sat quietly, apparently contemplating what he'd heard. "You say the state troopers are on their way?" he finally asked.

"Yes, though Jane isn't sure how long it will take for them to get here."

He nodded. "I'm pretty sure the car wasn't mine, but the guy's who'd for whatever reason captured me. If those two men were friends of his, it's likely they were also looking for me."

"I guessed that," she admitted. "But I wanted to hear your thoughts. Does hearing this jog any more memories?"

Again, he considered. "No. At least, not yet. I really wish we could search the internet."

"Me too," she admitted. "I'm going to try tomorrow, if Jane isn't busy. I've tried to use my phone to access it several times, but there's hardly any reception out here. I'm lucky I can even make phone calls."

This last comment made him smile, though it was a mere shadow of his earlier, more carefree one. "One day at a time," he said. "That's all I can do. After all, it's not like I have much of a choice."

Heaven help her, but she ached to kiss him again. More than that, she wanted to wrap herself up in his arms and forget everything but the taste and feel of him.

Something must have shown on her face. He made a sound, a wordless cry of desire that matched the fierce need swirling inside her.

This time, he took the lead and she let him. He kissed

her, and then moved his mouth to her neck, the hollow of her throat. He tugged on her T-shirt and she obligingly helped him tug it over her head, leaving her in the bright red bra she was glad she'd put on earlier.

Expertly, he removed it, cupping her breasts in his hands before bending his head to take one nipple in his mouth.

A bolt of lust shot through her at the sensation of the rough texture of his tongue. She moaned, communicating her desire. She reached for him, feeling the hard bulge of his arousal pressing against his jeans. While she fumbled with his belt, trying to free him, he continued to worship her breasts before helping her free him. She circled the swollen length of him with her hand, laughing as he inhaled sharply.

By then she was ready, hot and wet. She wanted more and she wanted it now. Moving away from him, she kept her gaze locked on his face as she shimmied out of her jeans while he did the same.

Now that they were both naked, she moved toward him. But when she tried to push him back and climb on top of him, he shook his head. "Not this time, Kenzie," he said. "First, I need a condom." Grabbing his jeans, he extracted one from his pocket and began putting it on, far too slowly for her taste.

Still, watching him was a turn on. She resisted the urge to help him, mouth dry, trembling with need.

"Come here," he finally said, reaching for her.

Bemused and aching, she reluctantly tried to leash her rising passion. She had to admit, she was curious to see what he had planned. "I want fast and rough," she told him helpfully. "And I want it now."

This made him chuckle. "Too bad. This time, we're going to take this slow."

She tried to groan with disappointment, but when he gently pressed her back onto the couch, she held it back. Maybe now, he'd climb on top of her. She needed him inside her, all of him, so badly she thought she might scream in frustration.

He slid his hands over her, exploring her body while he once again captured her mouth with his. Again, she tried to tug him down onto her, but he resisted. Instead, he nudged her legs apart with one hand. *Finally*, she thought, arching her back in preparation for the hard length of him.

Instead, he kissed her there. The press of his mouth, the swirl of his tongue, and she almost lost every shred of control. "Brett!" she gasped his name, her hands coming up to hold onto his hair. He continued to make love to her with his mouth. Every stroke of his tongue sent waves of pure pleasure radiating through her. As she felt the beginnings of her climax, she bucked, hoping he didn't stop, praying he would continue.

When her release took her, she called out his name. Her body pulsed, over and over, until she finally came back down to earth and the convulsions quieted.

Only then did he enter her, so hard and swollen he filled her, even as slick as she was. Gaze locked on hers, he began to move, slow and deliberate, as if he feared she might be tender after her climax.

Instead, her passion quickly reignited. She tried to use her body, her hands, her mouth to urge him to move faster, but he only shook his head and grinned.

Though frustrated, she found his lopsided smile so

damn sexy her entire body convulsed. When he felt this, he only grinned wider. "We're going to take our time," he managed, somehow still restraining himself when she arched her back and pressed her body up against him.

"I don't want to go slow," she told him, letting her impatience show. "I need you fast and deep and hard."

"Two out of three ain't bad," he drawled, continuing his deliberate movement as he lowered his mouth to hers for a deep wet kiss.

Her climax hit her all at once, like a freight train. She cried out, spasms rocking her as she clenched him. She knew the moment when he lost control, his grin replaced by a look of such fierce intensity that her entire body clenched again.

Finally, he did what she'd been wanting. Pounding into her as if he couldn't get enough. She welcomed this, encouraged it, and then, to her disbelief, she felt a climax building yet again.

They found release together, something she'd always thought impossible. She hung onto him while they both shuddered and even after the trembling quieted and their heartbeats slowed.

This man, she thought, *this extraordinary and beautiful man*. He'd come into her life in a rainstorm, and while she knew she'd helped him by allowing him to stay with her, he'd helped her more. Coming alone to Alaska, a place she'd never seen, had been one of the most difficult things she'd ever done. Brett, by his presence, had made her feel less alone, less vulnerable. In fact, being with him made her feel...happy.

The realization shook her. She barely knew this man.

In fact, he didn't even remember much about himself. Maybe that's why she felt such a fierce attraction to him. Without knowing his background, he'd become a man of her own creation.

Shutting down the self-analyzing, she told herself to enjoy him, *this*, and try to live in the here and now. Snuggling in next to him, she closed her eyes and did exactly that.

HOLDING KENZIE IN his arms, Brett felt a crazy mix of satisfaction and a deep longing to be whole. She deserved a normal man, one who knew who he was, what he wanted and where he was going. Not some charity case she'd taken on because she had such a big heart. He wanted to be more for her, because he'd come to realize what a unique and special woman Kenzie was.

Once again, he went over what he knew, as if by forming a mental list of each bit of information, he might somehow form a coherent whole. He'd been involved in a shooting, at a restaurant somewhere. After that, he had no idea what had happened to him, but he guessed maybe he'd gone into hiding. Made sense. While he still didn't know for a fact whether he'd been on the side of right or wrong, he had to believe he was a good guy. Most people would feel the same way, he imagined.

Kenzie stirred, stretching lazily in his arms, her body still snuggled up against him. He took a deep breath, loving the light fruity scent of her shampoo, the silky smoothness of her skin and the way her curves fit perfectly to him.

Something tickled the back of his memory, lurking

just out of reach. He couldn't help but feel if he tried hard enough, he could grasp it and pull it into view.

"Are you okay?" Kenzie asked softly, raising up on one elbow to look at him.

He couldn't help but smile at her. "I am," he replied. "How about you?"

"Better than fine." She snuggled back against him. "I could stay like this forever."

Forever. He kind of liked the sound of that. Except he couldn't. How could he even begin to think about forever when he didn't even know what that meant?

But then she stiffened, as if she suddenly realized what she'd said. "I didn't mean that like it sounded," she said, easing away from him. "I'm sorry. This is all very…confusing."

He felt the loss of her body's warmth intensely. "I agree," he replied. "But I think we should take things one day at a time, let ourselves enjoy each other's company."

"You're right," she agreed, though she still kept her back to him. He couldn't help but admire the swell of her naked behind. "I'm sorry. There's no need to complicate things."

Though that had been exactly what he'd been trying to say, for some reason hearing her speak the words hit him wrong, damn it. He wanted to complicate things, he realized, a little bit shocked. In fact, he wanted things messy and involved and…

Stop. There could be none of this, not even an attempt at beginning a relationship, until he figured out the truth about who he was and what had happened to him.

Though he suspected it would kill him, he'd do his damnedest to keep things casual.

"Did you ask Jane to tell you if there was any new word on the car that was found or the guy who washed up dead?" he asked, completely changing the subject.

Kenzie, who'd begun gathering up her clothing to carry to the bathroom with her, paused. "You know, I didn't ask. But knowing Jane, I figure she'll call me right away if anything else came up."

"You have a point," he admitted. "And in case I haven't said so, damn you look hot."

His compliment had her grinning. "Right back at you," she said before hurrying off to the bathroom.

Chest tight, he watched her go with a strong combination of affection and longing. How could he even begin to understand or make sense of his feelings for her, when he wasn't even sure he had any right to have them? Of course, the lack of a wedding band made him feel pretty sure he didn't have a wife and kids waiting for him to return home.

Beyond that, he didn't know much. Dr. Kenzie Taylor was a special woman, unique and kind, well-educated and smart. It would take a special man to earn her love. He didn't remember enough about himself to decide if he deserved someone like her. No, he shook his head at his own thoughts. Not someone like her. But her. He was rapidly developing a thing for Kenzie. He'd need to slow it down until he knew more.

As he always did when he found himself with too much time on his hands, Brett went into the kitchen and began looking through the fridge and pantry to see what ingredients he could put together to make something delicious for later.

Happily working away, he grabbed this and that, rummaging for certain seasonings, his brain on autopilot. He wasn't even sure what the end result would be. He just moved by instinct, somehow *knowing* what to use to make the tastiest combination.

He got so involved in his meal preparation that he didn't even notice when Kenzie emerged and walked into the kitchen to watch him.

"What are you making?" she asked, startling him.

"I'm not sure yet," he answered, glancing back at her with a smile. "I haven't decided on the protein. It'll either be beef or pork. I'll decide when it all comes together."

She walked over to stand beside him, looking at all the varied ingredients he'd assembled. "I don't know how you do it."

The light fruity scent of her shampoo distracted him. Giving in to impulse, he put his arm around her shoulder and hugged her quickly, immediately releasing her and going back to his task.

"I don't know how I do this either," he said. "Maybe once I know everything, I'll understand it. For now, I'm simply allowing myself to enjoy."

"And me too." She flashed him a grin. "I have to say, your cooking is out of this world."

Pleased, he ducked his head. "Thanks."

"There's still hot water left if you want to shower," she said.

"Thanks." He glanced back at what he'd assembled

so far. "I just need a few more minutes and then I'll do that."

"Sounds good." Making herself a cup of coffee, she went outside to sit on the front porch while he finished up. He wanted to go with her, but he didn't. Just because he'd begun to crave her company as if she were sunshine, didn't mean he should give in to the longing.

After deciding to go with pork as the protein, he was able to hone the exact ingredients and spices he'd need, as well as choose what he wanted to make for side dishes. Only then did he take himself off to the shower.

When he emerged, hair still slightly damp, he grabbed his own coffee and joined her outside. Though still comfortably warm, the overcast sky and slight breeze hinted at more rainstorms to come in the near future.

"Hey," he said, dropping into the chair next to her. "You've got a big day tomorrow. Are you ready?"

She looked up and then slowly nodded, her brown eyes contemplative. "I am. But I've got the first-day-of-work-at-a-new-job jitters too."

"That's understandable. At least you've met a few people since you had that open house. I imagine that helps." He made himself smile. "I'll make you something awesome for lunch."

"How about we just have sandwiches?" she asked. "Since you are making something complicated for dinner."

If she wanted sandwiches, then he'd make her the best damn sandwich on the planet. "Sounds good," he said, just as her cell phone rang.

She stood, setting her coffee mug on the porch floor.

Pulling her phone from her back pocket, she frowned. "Unknown Caller. And I don't have much of a signal." Still, she answered anyway. "Hello?"

Since he couldn't hear the other end of the conversation, he watched her. Her frown told him she didn't like whatever the caller had to say. When she hung up without saying a word, her eyes were shiny with tears.

Immediately, he got up and went to her, gently gathering her in his arms. "Who was it?" he asked.

She held onto him for a moment before stepping back and meeting his gaze. "I don't know," she replied. "But whoever it was had a lot to say about how dare I think I could be the doctor Blake, Alaska, needed and that he wished I'd go back to wherever I came from."

He could see how badly this had hurt her. But then, as he ached to find the right words to comfort her, she lifted her chin and shrugged. "They can't all be fans, right?"

Startled, he laughed. "True."

"I'm a damn good doctor," she said. "And I'll do a great job here for my two-year contract. I get that some of the old-timers might have trouble with the idea of a female physician, but they'll simply need to get over that."

"I agree. It might take a little bit, but I'm thinking they'll come around after they see you in action."

"Thanks for that." She hip-bumped him. "I just hope that man who called doesn't ever need medical help. Because short of making the two-plus hour drive to Anchorage, I'm all he's got."

"They'll be lucky to have you," he said, grabbing his half-full cup and dropping back in his chair. He almost added that *he* felt lucky to have her, but stopped himself in time. Right now, they were enjoying each other's company. She'd opened her home to him—and maybe a tiny bit of her heart—and he'd forever be grateful. He hoped to someday repay her for all she'd done.

Right now, he'd do the best he could as her friend and sometimes lover. No matter what he learned about himself when his memory finally came back, he could only hope that didn't change. Then and there, he vowed not to let it.

Chapter Eight

On Monday, Kenzie arrived at the clinic an hour before opening time, driving carefully and slowly in another downpour, glad she'd gotten to know the road. The rain had started shortly before midnight and showed no sign of letting up anytime soon. To her surprise, when she pulled into the clinic parking lot, she saw another vehicle parked in the staff parking area. Which meant Annette had gotten here before her. Great. Just great.

Disappointed, yet aware she'd need to conceal that, Kenzie parked, grabbed her umbrella and made a mad dash for the back door. Once she reached it, she turned the handle and found it locked. She debated whether to knock, but instead she dug in her pocket for the key.

Door unlocked, she stepped inside and closed her umbrella, dripping water onto the linoleum floor. She'd hoped to have a little quiet time before Annette arrived, but she definitely couldn't fault an overly punctual employee.

"Good morning," she called out, not wanting to surprise Annette and end up facing a pistol again.

"Doctor Taylor!" Annette hurried around the corner, a mug of coffee in her hand. "I didn't expect to see you this early. I wanted to make sure everything was ready for you."

"I appreciate that." Kenzie smiled. "I thought I'd grab a cup of coffee and then go over today's appointments."

"Appointments?" Annette gave her a blank stare. "We don't take appointments. People just come in when they need to."

Stunned, Kenzie said the first thing that came to mind. "That doesn't sound very efficient."

Annette frowned. "Maybe not, but it's the way we've always done things."

"You mean the way Dr. Clarke did things," Kenzie pointed out gently. "I'm going to change that. And I'll need your help getting out the word. Of course, we'll still see someone on an emergency basis, but I'd prefer all routine medical care be scheduled."

Annette opened her mouth and then closed it. "Yes, ma'am," she finally said. Then, before Kenzie could say anything else, Annette spun on her heel and left the room, her spine ramrod stiff.

Clearly, Kenzie had managed to offend the other woman. But what had Annette expected? Naturally, any new doctor would make changes to the way things were run. And Kenzie was well within her rights to do so.

Deep breath, she told herself. She made a cup of coffee and carried it into her small office. She really had intended pulling the files of that day's patients and reading through them, but since she now had no idea who they would be, that idea was useless. Which meant she'd be operating on the fly. She didn't mind for emergencies, but for routine care she preferred to be prepared.

Without files to review, she had a bit of time to kill.

A little disconcerted, she took a seat behind her rustic metal desk. Digging in her bag for the plaque she'd had made back in Texas, she pulled it out and placed it on her desk. *Kenzie Taylor, M.D.* She got up, walked around to the front of the office and studied it, smiling with pride. She'd worked hard to get to this place, and she intended to work hard while she was here.

Grabbing her coffee, she took a sip and decided to make another quick tour of the clinic. Both of the exam rooms were spotless, as was the single restroom. In the reception area, Annette sat at her desk doodling or drawing on a sketch pad.

Bracing herself, Kenzie walked up to the other woman. "I meant to ask you this earlier, but I understand you're also a licensed nurse."

Annette's head snapped up, her look briefly hostile before she smoothed out her expression. "I am a Registered Nurse," she said. "Or was. I let my license expire. I worked for about ten years in an ER in Anchorage before moving back home to Blake. Dr. Clarke's former assistant had retired and he specifically contacted me and asked me to come work for him."

"Wonderful," Kenzie replied, realizing her question had somehow managed to offend the other woman. "I'm glad to have someone with your experience here to help me."

Some of the hardness in Annette's gaze softened. "I'll do my best. I should tell you that some of the people here aren't happy with the idea of a female doctor. They were used to Doc Clarke and are set in their ways."

Kenzie nodded. "I expected that. It'll just take time.

Once they get to know me, I feel confident they'll come around."

Though Annette nodded, judging by her expression, she didn't agree.

"Let's get through today and then we'll talk about setting up appointments going forward from now on," Kenzie continued.

"Are you planning on turning people away?" Annette wanted to know. "If they show up here, asking for medical help and don't have an appointment?"

"Of course not," Kenzie reassured her. "Though please don't share that with anyone, okay? Unless there's a medical emergency, I'd like to encourage everyone to make appointments."

Muttering under her breath, Annette shook her head and walked away.

Kenzie stared after her, not sure how to react. The one thing they didn't teach in medical school was how to deal with employees. She guessed that particular kind of expertise would be a skill she'd develop over time.

At exactly 9:00 a.m., Annette reappeared and unlocked the front door. Ignoring Kenzie, she went to her desk, took a seat and picked up her sketch pad and began working on something. Again, Kenzie debated trying to initiate conversation, but decided to let it go for now. Some people didn't take well to change. Clearly, Annette would need time to adjust.

The first patient, an older man, arrived shortly after 9:15 a.m. He shuffled inside, moving as if he found walking painful. Kenzie watched from her office doorway as Annette greeted him by name and handed him a clipboard with paperwork for him to fill out. Annette seemed friendly, efficient and professional, which was a good thing.

Finally, the patient was shown into one of the exam rooms. Annette, being the nurse, took the initial information, had him undress and put on a paper gown before coming to get Kenzie.

"Here you are," Annette said, thrusting the clipboard and paperwork at Kenzie. "That's Tommy Boyd. He's got a boil he wants lanced."

"Did you take a look at it?" Kenzie asked, beginning to flip through the papers.

"No."

This made Kenzie look up. "That's part of your job. I'll need you to look at it, clean it up and prep it for me. Please gather all the instruments I'll need and have them in the room waiting for me."

Annette stared at her as if she'd started speaking a foreign language. Since everything Kenzie had requested was standard operating procedure in every medical clinic she knew of, Kenzie stared back.

"Is there a problem?"

Slowly, Annette shook her head. "No." Then she leaned in and whispered in Kenzie's ear, revealing the location of the boil.

"I see. Those are actually fairly common on people's rear ends. Please get everything ready and let me know when you're done."

"Yes, Doctor." Annette bustled off, to Kenzie's relief. For a moment there, she'd wondered whether she was going to have to battle her nurse over every small issue.

After that patient left, things got quiet. Annette sat at her desk reading a magazine and Kenzie got a pen and a pad and made notes of things she wanted to buy to personalize her office. Despite the previous doctor taking all his personal belongings with him when he'd left, the small room for some reason still had a masculine feel to it. The dark paneling on the bottom half of the walls might be one of the reasons why. A can of paint would do wonders to brighten things up. Maybe an artificial plant, some framed photographs, and books for the built-in bookshelves.

Lunchtime came and went. Kenzie had brought the lunch that Brett had prepared. Since he'd refused to tell her what it was, it would be a surprise.

Opening the bag carefully, she smiled when she saw the plastic storage containers he'd tucked inside. One contained a beautiful colorful salad, the other grilled chicken and the third salad dressing with a note to let her know he'd made it himself.

Smiling like a fool, she put everything together and began eating.

Annette wandered in and did a double take when she saw the salad. "That looks good," she said.

"It is," Kenzie replied, wishing she could tell the other woman that right now she had her own personal chef. "Healthy too," she said instead.

When Annette didn't leave, Kenzie put down her fork. "Is there something I can help you with?" she asked, hoping to go back to eating her lunch in peace.

"Not really. I just wanted to say I'm sorry your first day has been so slow." Though her voice sounded properly sympathetic, Kenzie swore she saw a gleam of joy in Annette's eyes.

Or maybe she was just projecting. After all, why

wouldn't Annette want the new doctor to be happy? She had to know Kenzie wasn't going anywhere anytime soon. She'd signed a two-year contract after all.

Kenzie managed to summon up a smile. She tried not to think about the hateful man who'd called her. "It's all good. Slow means everyone is healthy, right?"

"Right," Annette responded. "I mean, Blake *is* a really small village. Even before, this clinic never was really super busy, except maybe during flu season."

Grateful for the small olive branch, Kenzie nodded. "Good to know," she said.

"And that's why requiring appointments doesn't make sense," Annette continued. "The foot traffic is so small anyway. It's rare you even have more than one patient here at a time."

"That's interesting," Kenzie said. "I appreciate your insight and help."

Annette smiled, just a tiny bit smugly. "You're welcome."

"However," Kenzie continued, aware she needed to clear the air, "I will expect you to support me once I make a decision, even if you disagree with it."

After a brief pause, Annette nodded. "I will. As long as you don't mind me giving you my opinion first, we're good."

Relieved, Kenzie stood and held out her hand. "Agreed."

They shook.

"I think we might get along just fine," Annette mused. "Once we work out the rough edges."

This made Kenzie laugh. "I agree," she said. Annette

laughed too, turning and walking away. Kenzie went back to eating her salad.

Once she'd finished, she got up and walked out to the front of the clinic, crossed the still-empty waiting room and looked out the front window. Rain still came down in sheets, making little rivers run down the side of the paved road.

"Imagine if all that was snow," Annette said from her desk. "Because it will be soon enough. I hope you like the cold."

"Not particularly," Kenzie answered honestly. "I grew up in Houston and am much more accustomed to the heat."

Though Annette's eyes widened, she didn't make a snide comment like Kenzie half expected. Instead, she reached into a desk drawer and pulled out a glossy catalog. "I'm guessing you don't have proper winter clothing then. I'd suggest ordering it now, even though it's only late August. You'll need to buy good quality. It's a bit more expensive, but well worth the cost."

Accepting the catalog, Kenzie thanked her. "I've been thinking about doing that, but I wasn't sure where to go or what to buy. Will you help me choose?"

"I will." Annette beamed. "Just let me know when, and we can look at some coats together."

"Since the waiting room is still empty and I doubt anyone is going to venture out in this weather unless they're really sick, why don't we take a look now?" Kenzie grabbed one of the waiting room chairs and brought it around to the side of Annette's desk.

Before half an hour had passed, Kenzie had chosen two coats, one long and one short, some snow pants, a couple of caps, mittens and gloves, and socks as well as snow boots.

"This is going to cost a lot," Annette mused, using her phone calculator to tally up the price. Arching her eyebrows, she showed the total to Kenzie. "At least you'll get free shipping," she said.

"That I will. And I guess I'll have to call in the order, since we don't have decent internet." Which felt positively archaic, but it was what it was.

Kenzie grabbed the catalog and the pad with all her notes and carried it back to her office. A phone call and a few minutes later and she was all set to face her first Alaskan winter.

"Thank you for all your help," she told Annette, handing her back the catalog. "I likely would have bought the wrong things if I'd tried to do that on my own."

"No problem." Beaming now, Annette stood. "I'm always glad to help."

Unable to keep from glancing at the clock, Kenzie sighed. "With no patients and no internet, it's going to be a very slow afternoon."

"I agree." Annette pushed to her feet. "Do you maybe want to take a look at the body? I know you doctors like that kind of stuff."

"Body?" Kenzie asked, confused. "What body?"

"The one that washed up in the river. Since Blake doesn't have an actual funeral home, all dead bodies are stored here until they can be sent to an undertaker in Anchorage. In this case, the medical examiner will travel here to do the autopsy."

Heart rate increasing, Kenzie took a deep breath.

The body of the man who'd been in the car with Brett was here. In her clinic. "What kind of shape is the body in?" she asked. "I imagine if it had been in the water awhile, it's deteriorated."

"I'm not sure." Annette shrugged. "I haven't looked at it. The FBI is supposed to be coming to retrieve it."

"The FBI?" This caught Kenzie's attention. "Why are they involved? I thought the state police were working it."

"No idea." Clearly unconcerned, Annette motioned for Kenzie to follow her. "Come on, I'll show you where the refrigeration storage is."

"That's okay." Kenzie shook her head. "I don't need to see anything like that, at least not right now. I mean that wasn't my patient or anything."

Judging by Annette's skeptical expression, she planned to press more. But luckily, Kenzie's cell phone rang. "It's Jane," she announced. "Excuse me, but I need to take this."

"I'm sorry to bother you at work," Jane began. "But I'm calling everyone and I wanted to make sure to catch you."

"What's wrong?" Kenzie asked.

"There's going to be a town meeting tonight," Jane said, her loud voice full of excitement. "Two FBI agents and a representative of the state police want to talk to us. It'll be at Mikki's at six. We're strongly encouraging everyone who can to attend."

Intrigued, Kenzie agreed to be there. "Is this about the dead guy and the submerged car? Or the two men who came through town and threatened you?"

"I think all of it," Jane replied. "They haven't really

shared a lot of information with Greg. They said this meeting is necessary for the safety of our entire village."

"Interesting."

"Yes. Please tell Annette for me. I'll see you both there. I've got a ton of other people to notify." Jane ended the call.

Kenzie looked up to find Annette eyeing her. Quickly, she filled her in.

"Wow!" Annette excitedly grabbed her own phone. "I hope you don't mind, but I want to make some calls of my own. Once I tell all my friends and family, I'll text Jane so she knows she doesn't have to call them." She winked. "That's kind of how things work around here. Jane knows she can tell several key people, and they'll help her spread the word."

"That sounds oddly efficient," Kenzie murmured. She wished she could call Brett, but since he didn't have a cell phone, she couldn't. She'd have to wait to tell him until she got home.

BRETT WASN'T SURE what time exactly to expect Kenzie, but she'd told him the clinic stayed open until 5:00 p.m., so he figured it would be soon after that. Unless she had an emergency, that is.

The unrelenting sky had continued to dump water all day and as of 4:00 p.m., it showed no signs of letting up. Confined to the cabin and slightly bored, he'd gone to sit outside under the covered front porch and watch the rain come down.

Even this—the gray and gloomy sky, the waters running downhill and onto the drenched trees and earth—he found beautiful. Though the rain hid his view of the mountains and even the road beyond the driveway, here he felt safe and comfortable. Dare he say even happy? He looked forward to Kenzie returning home, to hearing about her day and watching her reaction as she sampled the salmon he planned to make them for dinner.

Around 4:30 p.m., he got up and went back inside. He'd cleaned the place that morning, a task that hadn't taken very long but had still provided some satisfaction. He wanted everything gleaming when Kenzie returned after her first day of work. In fact, he wished he could give her flowers too, but since he had no way to get them, he couldn't. Maybe another time.

This last thought surprised him. Another time. He'd been thinking toward the future. Considering he didn't know the past, that was like taking a giant leap of faith that there even would be a future.

Along with the salmon, he made a delicious pasta salad and prepped asparagus spears. Once he had everything ready, all he needed to do was cook, which he didn't want to do until Kenzie got there. He'd chilled a bottle of Pinot Grigio, amazed at how the cabin had been stocked with an assortment of wine. He got out two glasses and placed them on the table before pouring himself one. Then, at five o'clock sharp, he took his wine and went back out to the front porch to wait.

The rain had let up quite a bit and had become more of a drizzle than anything else. Glad Kenzie didn't have to drive home in the downpour, he settled in to wait.

His damn heart gave a leap of joy—*joy!*—when he caught sight of her Jeep coming up the drive.

When she got out of her vehicle, hurrying toward the porch, she smiled. "Hey there!" she said.

Smiling back, he asked her if she'd like a glass of wine.

"I would," she answered. "We can sit out here and I can unwind."

Domestic much? Or was he overthinking? Mentally shaking his head at himself, he went inside to fetch her wine, setting his own down on the porch next to his chair.

When he returned, she'd taken the seat next to his. He handed her the drink and sat. "How was your first day?" he asked, still smiling.

She took a sip of wine before answering. "Kind of slow. We only had three patients all day. Oh, and Annette told me the body of the guy that was found in the river is stored in a makeshift morgue-type refrigerator at the clinic."

"What?" He did a double take.

"Yeah. Apparently, Blake is too small to have a funeral home, so dead bodies are held at the medical clinic until someone from Anchorage can pick them up for cremation or embalming and burial."

"Wow."

"I know. I was flabbergasted at first. Then, I wondered if I should sneak you in to see it. Who knows, maybe doing that might help jog your memory."

The idea held zero appeal. "I think I'll pass."

His response made her grin. "My sentiments exactly. Annette seemed to think I'd want to take a look at him. I told her no."

He watched her take another sip of wine. "I was thinking salmon for dinner," he said.

"I'd love that, but Jane called. There's a town meeting at six. I'm definitely going, so I've got to head back soon. I thought I'd catch dinner there. I really wish you'd come with me."

Squashing his disappointment, he nodded. "I do too," he admitted. "But until I've recalled more about who I am and what actually happened, I'll be hanging out here. I'm sorry."

Though she nodded, he couldn't help but wonder if she'd begun to grow tired of his excuses. He couldn't blame her if she had.

Reaching out, he lightly touched her arm. "I'm really interested in hearing what they have to say though. You can tell me all about it when you get home." And after he ate the meal he'd planned to share with her by himself.

"Most everyone in Blake and the surrounding area will be there," she said. "The place will be packed. It's doubtful anyone would even notice you."

"Maybe not," he conceded. "But I still can't take the chance. I'm sorry, Kenzie."

To his surprise, she set her wineglass down and got up, going around behind him and giving him a quick kiss on the side of his face. "It's okay. I understand."

Then she let him go, grabbing her wineglass as she headed back into the house. As she grabbed the door to open it, she looked back over her shoulder at him, with a sad little smile. "No matter what happens, or who you turn out to be, I'll always be your friend. Don't you ever forget that."

With that, she disappeared into the cabin.

Friends. With benefits. He took a long swallow of the wine, wondering why her comment stung so much. He knew he should feel the exact same way. He *did* feel that way, plus more. His problem. And maybe something he could deal with once all his other issues were resolved.

He'd just finished his wine when the door opened again and she breezed past him. "I've got to run," she said, smiling. "I'll fill you in on everything once I get back."

She jumped into her Jeep, backed it up and then drove away. He continued to stare after her long after her taillights had disappeared, aching with an out of proportionate sense of loss.

Then he went inside, made the dinner he'd planned for the two of them and ate it by himself. He felt... lonely. Weird, especially since Kenzie had only been in his life a short time.

Yet, he missed her. More than he should have, he supposed, though that didn't make the ache inside feel any less acute.

He'd once again gone outside, breathing in the pure Alaskan air and sitting on the front porch, when she pulled up. The sky had barely begun to darken, even though it was nearly nine o'clock. She parked, jumped out of her Jeep and flashed a huge smile. "You missed the most interesting meeting," she said. "Let me grab a glass of wine and I'll fill you in."

"You sit," he told her. "I'll get us both some."

When he returned with wineglasses in hand, she accepted hers with that same smile still in place. She waited until he'd sat down before she began talking.

"I arrived there thirty minutes early," she said. "I was planning on picking out a seat and getting some dinner and a drink before it all started. Evidently, everyone else had made the same plans, because the line of people waiting outside Mikki's stretched down the sidewalk." She shook her head.

"Since I could tell the small parking area was already full, I ended up parking two blocks down and walking back." Taking a sip of wine, she sighed. "I'm sure glad I didn't wear heels."

"Did you eat?" he asked. "I have some leftovers from dinner if you want me to reheat them for you."

"Thanks." She patted his arm. "But I managed to grab some nachos, which I ate standing up."

"The salmon was better," he quipped, which made her laugh.

"No doubt. Anyway, the meeting started promptly at six. On time, which is unusual, at least in my experience."

Impatient, he nodded, waiting for her to get to the meat.

"There were two FBI agents and a state trooper. After, I had to let him into the clinic to collect the body. Anyway, it turns out the dead man was part of a gang."

Shocked, Brett stared. "A gang in Alaska?"

"That's what the FBI representative said. Apparently, there are a few different ones trying to grab turf in Anchorage. Oh, and the car was a rental, and the person who rented it must have used a fake ID, because they had no leads there. But…" She took a drink of wine. "Here's the interesting part. They kept asking if anyone had seen another man who might have been traveling with the dead guy."

"Me," he said flatly, glad he'd stayed behind. "They were asking about me."

"I have to think so," she agreed. "And while they didn't come out and say so, the inference was that this other person—you—was also part of the same gang."

A gang. "That's ridiculous."

"Is it?" she came back. "You don't actually know. Anything is possible."

"Not this. I'm not in a gang," he insisted, meaning it. And then, suddenly and without warning, he knew everything. Who he was, what had happened. All of it.

Some of his shock must have shown in his expression, because Kenzie froze.

"Brett?" Kenzie asked, her voice gentle. "What's wrong? You look like you've seen a ghost."

The analogy made him laugh. "In a way, I have. I… remembered. Just now."

Brown eyes wide, she stared at him, her lips parted. "Remembered what?"

"Everything. All of it. My full name is Brett Denyon and until recently, I owned a very successful restaurant in Anchorage."

Slowly, she pushed to her feet, the movement graceful. "You seriously remember?"

With his gaze locked on hers, he also rose, carefully placing his wineglass on the floor. "I do." He gave in to impulse, grabbing her around the waist and swinging her around, almost as if they were dancing a celebratory jig. Her long auburn hair swirled around her,

"When?" she breathed, once he'd released her. She smoothed her mussed hair with her hand.

"Just now, when I said I wasn't in a gang. The moment I said that, it all came flooding back."

"Tell me," she demanded, dropping back into her chair and motioning for him to do the same. "Tell me everything."

Once they were seated, he took a deep drink of wine as memories came flooding back. So much info, all at once, but also like it had always been there, just hidden. He knew he'd never take his life for granted after this.

"I'm a native Alaskan. I was born and raised in Anchorage. I'm an only child. My parents moved to Florida as soon as I graduated high school, seeking a warmer climate. They're still there." He took a deep breath and continued, "I've always loved to cook, and even as a teenager, I knew being a chef was my calling, so I went to culinary school."

"That explains why you're such an excellent cook," she said, smiling with her eyes as she sipped her wine.

"Thanks. Once I graduated, I apprenticed under some of the finer chefs in the lower forty-eight states." He gave a rueful smile, wondering how to condense his entire life into a few minutes of talk. "That kept me away from Alaska for longer than I liked, but it was worth it. I learned a lot and saved as much money as I could."

"When did you get back here? Are you from Blake?"

"No." Taking a deep breath, he got ready to tell her the rest of what his newfound memory had revealed. "Anchorage. When I got back, I opened my own restaurant. Whether by luck or whatever, it became an instant success." He flashed a quick smile. "I was named most eligible bachelor of Anchorage last year."

There. He'd figured out a way to let her know he wasn't married. He didn't want to sound like a sappy fool, but now that he knew who he was, his growing feelings for her felt stronger somehow.

Taking a deep breath, he took a drink of his wine and tried to gather his thoughts. She simply sat quietly and watched, him, giving him as much time and space as he needed.

Though he knew she had to be curious as to the rest of it—how he'd ended up in the car with a known gang member and plunged into the river—she didn't prod him, allowing him to continue at his own pace. He appreciated that more than he could express.

Finally, he felt ready to continue. "My restaurant was doing well, rocking and rolling. I had a great group of core employees, numerous loyal customers, and some pretty important people even visited my restaurant."

"What was it called?" she asked. "Your restaurant?"

"Glacier Grill." He grinned, shaking his head at the cheesiness of the name. "When I first started out, I couldn't think of anything, so when one of my friends suggested it, I jumped on it. Now I actually like it."

"I do too," she said softly. "Did you remember what happened in that shooting you kept seeing?"

"I did. Things were going really well. I was living life, loving life and then one night a group of men came in during the evening service and shot up the place." The memory made him blanch. "Several people died, including John Germane, a top congressman who'd been picked to run for president. Many more were hurt, and they set fire to the building."

He didn't tell her he'd been shot, a minor wound, or

that he'd ignored the pain and blood and had gone back into the burning dining area again and again, dragging as many people out to safety as he could before he collapsed from a combination of smoke inhalation and loss of blood.

Thinking about that night made him shudder. Now, finally, those nightmares made sense.

She seemed to sense how difficult reliving the horror of that day was for him. "I'm glad you made it out safely."

Barely. "I did," he agreed. "The firefighters arrived way too late for my restaurant to be saved." He swallowed hard. "The shooters got away. I talked to the police and the fire inspector. Because of John Germane's death, the FBI got involved. Turned out I was the only person who'd gotten a good look at the shooters."

"Let me guess," she finally spoke. "They were part of the same gang that's been canvassing Blake. And the one the dead guy who was in the car with you belonged to."

"Most likely." He swallowed hard, aware she had to be wondering how he'd wound up in a car with one of them. "It turned out the FBI had been trying to get this gang and its leader for a while. Now they finally had something concrete, with me as their star eyewitness. They put me in the witness protection program until the trial. I refused to leave Alaska, so they sent me to a safe house one of the agents owned. On the way there, I got a really bad feeling, so I decided to stop at one of my friend's vacation cabins on the Neacola River."

"Isn't that the same—"

"River you fished me out of? Yes. I don't know how

that guy found me, but he did." Brett shook his head. "He caught me by surprise and knocked me out. When I came to, I was tied up in the back seat of his car. He said he had orders to bring me back alive. We were on the way to wherever he was taking me when I broke free."

"You were struggling with him and that's why the car went off the bridge," she said. "Wasn't it?"

"Exactly. And that's why I couldn't shake the feeling I was in danger, even if I wasn't sure exactly how or why."

"Wow." The light had begun to fade. Still, her hair gleamed in the last bit of daylight, making him ache at her beauty.

Unaware, she continued, "I'm so glad you have your memory back. It must be a huge relief to finally know." One more sip of wine and she'd drained her glass. "So, Brett Denyon. What will you do now?"

That was the million-dollar question. Realistically, he knew he should reach out to the FBI and let them know he was safe. Yet, they hadn't been able to protect him, despite sending him to a remote location mostly off the grid. And the fact that the gang had been actively combing Blake, looking not only for their missing gang member but also for him, didn't do much to help make him feel safe and secure.

"I'm not sure," he replied. "Right now with all this going on, I think it'd be best to continue to lay low. If you're okay with me still staying here, that is?"

To his relief, she immediately nodded. "Yes, I'm fine with that." Her shy smile made his heart skip. "I've actually kind of gotten used to having you around here, if you really want to know the truth."

What could he do after a statement like that but kiss her? Pushing up, he crossed over to her chair, bent down and covered her mouth with his. When they finally broke apart, they were both breathless and grinning like fools.

"Ready to go inside?" he asked, holding his hand out to her in case she wanted help getting up. Smiling, she placed her hand in his and allowed him to pull her into him. With his arm around her, they walked back inside.

He could get used to this.

It dawned on him now that he knew what had happened, his very presence might place Kenzie in danger. He told her so, which caused her to shake her head.

"No one has even the slightest idea you're staying here," she said. "I haven't mentioned you to anyone at all. You're safe, I'm safe and it's all good."

Before he could protest, she pulled his face down to hers for another kiss. He allowed this to quiet the visceral worry now simmering inside him. He knew he'd have to face it eventually and figure out a way to keep her safe. Even if it meant he had to leave her.

Chapter Nine

First thing the next morning, after checking into the clinic and telling Annette to call her if they got any patients, Kenzie drove to Jane's house. She'd brought her laptop, because she fully intended on looking up all the info she could find, not only on Brett Denyon but his restaurant, Glacier Grill.

Jane appeared surprised to see her this early, but graciously led the way into the house. "Let me get the Wi-Fi password," she said. "And you can link to my printer if you'd like, in case you need to print something."

"That would be awesome." Kenzie impulsively hugged her. "I can't tell you how much I appreciate this. I've got someone coming to install Wi-Fi, but it's going to take a bit. There are few things I need to look up before then."

"I understand." Smiling, Jane patted her shoulder. "You doctors always need to stay up to date with the latest medical developments."

Kenzie didn't have the heart to tell the other woman that this wasn't medically related. Instead, she waited while Jane went into the other room, returning with a yellow sticky note. "Here you go," Jane said, handing it over. "It's called Mayor Link."

"Thank you again." Kenzie sat down in one of the overstuffed armchairs and opened her laptop. "I won't be long. I have to get back to the clinic. So please don't pay any attention to me."

"The printer is right there." Jane pointed. "It's a state-of-the-art color laser printer. I just filled it up with paper, so you should be good to go. It's called Mayor Printer."

"I see a pattern here."

Her comment made Jane laugh. "We're not all that original, that's for sure. But having similar names for everything makes it easy to remember."

Busy logging on, Kenzie glanced up, smiled and got right back to it, barely noticing when Jane left the room.

Not surprisingly, she found numerous news stories on the restaurant shooting. There were also quite a few on Brett himself, along with photos. In some of these, Brett was accompanied by women, a different one each time. They each had one thing in common. Whether blonde or brunette, each woman was beautiful enough to be a model. While each gazed adoringly up at Brett, he appeared indifferent, staring straight at the camera with a half smile on his handsome face.

Out of my league, Kenzie thought, grimacing at herself. The down-to-earth Brett she'd come to know seemed nothing like the sophisticated, suave man in the photos.

Since she didn't have a lot of time to sit and read, she printed everything, immediately shoving each piece of paper into a manila folder so Jane wouldn't see it. She'd go over all of it later once she was back at the clinic, and again with Brett when she got home.

Luckily, Jane's printer was fast. Kenzie got everything printed in under twenty minutes. She logged out, closed her laptop and went in search of Jane to thank her.

She found Jane in the kitchen, talking on an old-fashioned wall phone. Kenzie mouthed, "Thank you!" and waved before letting herself out. She drove back to the clinic, surprised to see two pickup trucks in the parking lot. Since Annette hadn't texted her, she'd assumed no patients had come in.

Letting herself in the back door, she froze at the sound of an angry man shouting, followed by Annette's voice asking for a *Jim* to stay calm.

Kenzie steeled herself, took a deep breath and walked down the hallway toward the front. She dropped off her manila folder on her desk as she passed her office. When she reached the reception area, she understood why Annette hadn't texted back. Two men stood facing each other in the small reception area, both of them with guns drawn and pointing at each other. Annette stood behind her desk, pleading with them to calm down and put the weapons away.

With no clue how to handle the situation, Kenzie decided to wing it. "What's going on here?" she demanded as she walked up front.

"Who the hell are you?" the larger of the two men growled, not taking his gun off his nemesis.

"I am Dr. Taylor," she said, her voice like steel. "And I'm asking you gentlemen to put away those guns while you're inside my clinic."

"And if we don't?" the shorter of the two asked, his lip curling.

Maybe because she didn't have a real answer, Kenzie lifted her chin and looked him right in the eye. "You will. Put the pistols away right now."

To her relief (and surprise), the two men looked at each other and did. Legs spread, guns holstered, they crossed their burly arms and continued to glare at each other.

Once they were both unarmed, Kenzie knew better than to let her relief show. "Annette?" she asked, without taking her gaze off the men. "Please show whichever one of these gentlemen got here first into an exam room. Once you've finished getting him ready to be seen, do the same with the other. I'll be there as soon as you let me know they're ready."

With a jerky nod, Annette motioned to the larger man. "Jim, please follow me."

Giving the other man a baleful grimace, Jim stomped off after her.

Once they were gone, Kenzie motioned to the remaining patient. "Please have a seat. My nurse will be with you shortly." Then, without waiting for a response, Kenzie headed to her office.

Only once she'd taken a seat behind her desk, did she look down and realize her hands were shaking. "What the hell?" she murmured under her breath. This really was like the wild frontier.

A few minutes later, Annette appeared. "You did good back there," she said. "Better than I did, for sure."

"Thanks." Kenzie took a deep breath. "Do you have any idea what that was all about?"

"I do. Jim, the big man, got divorced. Bubba, the other one, married her. They used to be best friends, and now they're mortal enemies. Jim came in because he has an ear infection and Bubba won't tell me why he's here. He just says he wants to talk to the doctor."

"Sounds good." Standing, Kenzie shoved her hands in the pockets of her lab coat. "Is Jim ready for me?"

"He sure is," Annette responded, her voice once again professional. "I've laid out all the necessary implements on a tray."

"Thank you." Kenzie headed off to take a look at Jim's ear.

"It's definitely an ear infection," she told him after taking a look. "I'll get you some antibiotics. Take them for ten days and you should be good as knew."

Annette, bless her heart, had left the necessary pills out for Kenzie. Since the town didn't have a pharmacy, the medical clinic kept a supply of basic meds and the doctor would dispense them from there.

Once Jim had been taken care of, Kenzie sent him up front to see Annette while she went to talk to her other patient.

Bubba sat on the edge of the exam table. He looked up when Kenzie entered, his expression grim. "I'd rather see a man doctor," he complained.

"Well, there isn't one," she countered. "Now what can I help you with?"

He leaned closer, whispering something so low she could barely hear him.

When she finally understood, she nodded gravely. "We have a little blue pill that should help with that," she said. "I'll get you some and they should take care of your problem."

"Thanks." Still not meeting her gaze, he nodded. "I'd appreciate if you could keep quiet about this."

"Of course. Doctor-patient confidentiality and all that. Let me go get your meds and I'll be right back." She slipped out of the room and went to the storage area where the medicines were kept. Measuring out enough for thirty days, she typed the instructions into her label generator, printed it, and then affixed the label.

Once both patients had paid and gone separately on their way, Kenzie returned to her office. She figured she'd have time to read all the news stories she'd printed about the shooting at Brett's restaurant.

But before she could even open the manila folder, Annette came in and dropped into one of the chairs across from the desk.

"I know Jim had an ear infection," she said. "But what did Bubba want?"

"It was a personal matter," Kenzie replied smoothly. "He asked me not to discuss it with anyone."

Annette regarded her, clearly puzzled. "I'm not just anyone. I'm your nurse."

"Yes, you are." Kenzie smiled to soften the sting. "However, I'm going to honor Bubba's wishes."

Now Annette frowned. "I can simply read the notes in his file," she pointed out. "So why not tell me?"

She had a point, except for one thing. "You could, if I'd made notes in the file. But since I haven't, there isn't anything to read."

Hands clenched into fists, Annette glared at her. "Let me tell you something," she said, her tone vicious. "I've lived almost my entire life in this town, and you've been here all of what, a week? How dare you act like you're better than me?"

"Better than you?" Kenzie asked. "I'm simply honoring a patient's wishes."

"That's ridiculous." Jaw tight, Annette radiated fury. "If anyone should know what ails people in Blake, it should be me, not you."

"That's enough." Equally sharp, Kenzie stood. "Annette, I need to remind you that you work for me. I'm the doctor here, not you. And as such, I decide what happens. Are we clear?"

"Oh, we're clear." The bitterness on Annette's face repeated in her voice. "And you might be a doctor, but no one here respects you or even wants you here."

When Kenzie started to speak, Annette held up her hand. "Don't bother firing me. I quit. Good luck running the clinic with no help." With that, she spun around and went to the reception area to gather her belongings.

Well aware how much damage a disgruntled former employee could do, Kenzie followed her. Arms crossed, she watched while Annette cleaned out her desk.

"I'll need your keys," Kenzie said, holding out her hand.

Lip curling, Annette dug into her purse, extracted a key ring and removed two metal keys. Instead of placing them in Kenzie's outstretched hand, she tossed them onto the desk, where they landed with a clatter. Then, she marched to the front exit, slamming the door for good measure on her way out.

As soon as she'd gone, Kenzie's knees went weak and she dropped into a chair. To be honest, she'd been expecting something like this to happen sooner or later, just not on her second day of work.

She'd need a new assistant. With that in mind, she got out her cell phone and called Jane.

"She what?" Jane asked, her voice full of disbelief. "Annette has worked at that clinic for almost twenty years. I can't believe she quit. What on earth happened?"

"I'd really rather not go into it," Kenzie replied, smoothing a wayward lock of her hair away from her face.

"You sound exhausted," Jane pointed out. "Was it really that bad?"

"Bad enough, and yes, I am tired. The reason I'm calling is to see if you know of anyone who I can hire to replace Annette."

"We don't exactly have a dearth of registered nurses here in Blake," Jane quipped.

"It doesn't have to be a nurse," Kenzie said, her stomach twisting. "Right now, I just need an able body who can help me out. They'd have to be reliable as well."

"And honest."

"Right." Kenzie's head had begun to throb. She honestly hoped there were no more patients for the day, because all she wanted to do was go home, have a glass of wine and lie down.

"I'll let you know if I think of anyone," Jane promised. "Though to be honest, right now I can't."

Kenzie forced herself to sound cheerful or, failing that, optimistic. "Thank you! I really appreciate that."

After ending the call, she went back to her office and forced herself to begin reading the articles she'd printed. As interesting as they were, she couldn't focus. Instead, she found herself watching the clock, wanting to get home so she could talk to Brett.

As soon as she had the thought, once again she found herself wondering what she would do once Brett returned to Anchorage and his life. Because leave he would. She understood that now. He'd had a good life, a successful life, with his own restaurant and plenty of attractive women to date. Why would he give that up to stay here, in a remote Alaskan village, with a woman he barely knew? Short answer—he wouldn't. And she couldn't blame him.

Who would have ever guessed she'd find it so difficult to say goodbye to a man she barely knew.

Now that everything had come back to him, Brett had a decision to make. He knew he should contact the FBI and let them know he was safe. However, despite their assurances otherwise, he had zero confidence in their ability to protect him. He'd much rather take his chances on his own, either contacting them just before the trial or simply showing up at court unannounced.

Plus, truth be told, he didn't want to leave Kenzie. Even if he could go back to Anchorage, and right now he couldn't, there was nothing waiting for him there. He'd lost the only thing that had mattered to him—his restaurant. The townhouse he rented had never been more than a place to sleep when not at Glacier Grill, so he had no desire to return there with nothing but time on his hands. This small cabin in the middle of nowhere felt more like a home than the place he'd lived for the last several years.

And, of course, Kenzie. He hadn't actually known her very long, but they had a strong connection, the kind he'd never felt before.

Now that he remembered who he was and what had happened to him, he understood he'd had a full and productive life before the shooting. There'd been no shortage of beautiful women to date. But while he'd enjoyed himself, something had always been missing. Something... Or someone. Someone like Kenzie.

Immediately, he shook his head at his thoughts. Over the years, he'd learned to follow his gut instincts. Everything inside him told him Kenzie was unique. Special, a one in a million woman.

The question was what could he do about that?

Trying to get his mind on other things, he began peeling potatoes and doing some other meal prep for the next couple of days' dinners.

When Kenzie pulled into the driveway and parked, Brett heard her all the way in the kitchen. He'd been pulling together ingredients to make a quick and easy meal when the sound of tires on gravel alerted him.

She blew into the cabin as fast as she'd driven into the drive. Some of her hair had escaped the neat bun she'd made and her brown eyes were wild. "What a day!" she said, heading straight for the refrigerator and the open bottle of wine they had corked there. After pouring herself a large glass, she turned to face him.

"Annette quit," she announced, taking a long drink. "And that was after I had to deal with two angry men pointing pistols at each other."

He grabbed a second glass and poured himself some wine. "Come on," he said. "Let's go sit out on the front porch."

Her grateful smile felt like a reward.

Once they were settled side by side in the rockers, she told him how her day had gone. He listened, watching her as she sipped her wine. The sun made her auburn hair appear on fire.

"What are you going to do?" he asked, once she'd wound down.

"That's just it. I don't know." She shook her head. "Jane said there aren't a whole lot of people available to do that kind of job. I've got to have some kind of help."

"I'll do it," he offered, surprised at himself. "Now that I know what's going on, I'll be able to take precautions."

Expression surprised, she looked at him. "I'd really appreciate that. Do you think you'll need some kind of disguise?"

"No." He considered. "I don't know. Maybe. Also, I'll need a decent cover story. Obviously, we can't tell people the truth. And it's not like the FBI will be stopping in to visit."

A smile trembled around the edge of her mouth. "Are you sure?"

He wasn't. "Yes," he replied. "It's the least I can do after all the help you've given me."

Setting down her wineglass, she jumped up and hugged him. Somehow, she ended up in his lap. Which he quickly realized was exactly where he wanted her to be.

Later, with the sky deepening to purple and pink,

they held each other and talked. Not of anything consequential, or even remotely serious. She told him amusing anecdotes from her residency, and he regaled her with tales from culinary school. It was, he thought, one of the most enjoyable evenings he'd ever had.

When they finally headed inside for the night, he wondered if this time she'd ask him to share her bed. He'd relish the chance to simply hold her while she slept, then waking up and making love again. Though such a thing would be next-level intimacy, now that he had himself back, he felt ready for that.

She stood, paused, her brown eyes locked with his. His pulse quickened, no longer slow and steady. He held his breath, mentally willing her to issue the invitation.

But she didn't. Instead, she smiled sweetly and told him good-night. He stood still, waiting until she'd left before dropping back onto his makeshift bed on the couch.

The next morning, he woke up missing her. But as he pushed up off the sofa and stretched, he realized the fear had gone. He'd been living with an undercurrent of it running through his veins ever since he'd emerged from the river, made more terrifying because he'd had no idea of the source.

Now that he knew from where his danger came, he'd lost that blind terror. He could take steps to hide from his enemies, especially since they had no idea he was here in Blake. Since he figured it would be highly unlikely they'd show up at Kenzie's medical clinic, he felt confident he could help her. Actually, the time had come for him to start trying to repay Kenzie for all she'd done.

While Kenzie showered, he whipped up a simple pan of oatmeal for breakfast and chopped up some fresh strawberries.

In a hurry, Kenzie ate hers standing up, thanking him before hurrying back to her room. Slightly amused, he cleaned up the kitchen and sat down to wait.

When she reemerged, her hair in a jaunty ponytail, she smiled at him. "Ready to go?" she asked.

He nodded and followed her out to her Jeep.

Glad when she turned up the radio, singing along to music as she drove, he looked out the window and tried not to overthink anything. He'd be at the clinic to help Kenzie, and surely the news stories and articles about his restaurant and the shooting were old enough that no one would recognize him. It wasn't like he'd been a celebrity anywhere outside of Anchorage after all.

They pulled in to an empty parking lot. Kenzie turned to him and smiled. "Are you ready?" she asked.

He nodded. They got out of the Jeep and went inside, Kenzie turning on lights as she went. "Here we are," she said, smiling brightly. "I really appreciate you helping me today."

She gave him a tour of the place, showing him his desk and where he could find supplies. "Since you're not a nurse, you won't have to get patients set up for me. All I can ask you to do is get people checked in, verify their insurance if they have it and take them to one of the exam rooms."

He nodded, grateful when she finally disappeared inside her small but tidy office. Then he sat down and began scrolling through the scheduling software she'd opened up on his computer.

The first thing he'd noticed was that there were no appointments scheduled. Zero, nada, zilch. But then he remembered Kenzie telling him how she and Annette had argued about that subject and that right now patients were seen on a drop-in basis. He wondered how long it would be before the first patient arrived.

When he'd thought of the medical clinic, he'd assumed it would be a bustling place, full of sick people, similar to one of the urgent-care locations he'd visited in Anchorage. Instead, the place was empty even an hour after Kenzie had unlocked the doors.

Finally, someone walked in. An older silver-haired woman, who carried herself with an air of confidence, breezed through the door. She stopped short when she caught sight of him, and then looked him up and down. "Oh, my," she exclaimed. "Who are you and where did you come from?"

Before he could respond, Kenzie bustled into the reception area. "Jane! What brings you here today?"

Jane barely even glanced at her. "I see you've found someone to help you," she said. "And let me be the first to tell you, I get it."

Kenzie and Brett exchanged a glance. "Get what?" Kenzie asked, slightly frowning.

Finally, Jane tore her gaze away from Brett. "Well, I came to talk to you about Annette. I know you told me she quit, but she's going around spreading all kinds of nonsense around town. She's telling everyone who will listen that you fired her."

Kenzie's brows went up. "That's a bold-faced lie."

Appearing unconcerned, Jane shrugged. "You know

that, and I know as well, but the rest of the townsfolk might very well believe her."

"Why?" Kenzie asked. "Why would she want people to think she got fired?"

"She's trying to make you into everyone's enemy," Jane replied, shaking her silver head.

Brett spoke up. "But generally, when someone gets fired, there's a good reason. Someone like Annette has surely shown her true colors long before now."

Jane turned to look at him. After a moment, she laughed. "You're right about that. Truth is most of us know what Annette is like. The problem is no one really knows Kenzie. And people do like to gossip."

"I'm not here to be popular," Kenzie interjected. "I came to Blake to practice medicine."

"I know that, dear." Jane actually patted Kenzie's shoulder in the way of an indulgent older aunt. "But you also want people to trust you."

Kenzie opened her mouth, as if she intended to argue, and then closed it. She took a deep breath, clearly considering her words before she spoke. "What do you think I should do?"

But Jane wasn't paying any attention to her. Instead, she was studying Brett, a tiny frown in between her brows. "I know you from somewhere," she said.

Immediately, he shook his head. "I don't think we've ever met."

"You look awfully familiar," Jane insisted.

"I get that a lot." Brett told the white lie easily. He could tell that Jane was the kind of woman who, once she latched on to something, would continue to pursue it doggedly until satisfied. Best to head her off before she got too invested.

"Jane!" Kenzie drew the older woman's attention back to herself. "I need your help here. What do you think I need to do in order to counter Annette's mission to make me the most hated woman in Blake, Alaska?"

"I'll have to think about it," Jane answered. "I think you definitely need to eat at Mikki's at least once or twice a week. Maybe you and your…new employee can stop by for drinks after work." She shot another inquiring look Brett's way.

The clinic door opened and a young woman with two small children in tow entered. "I need to see the doctor!" she exclaimed, glancing from Brett to Kenzie and back again. "My daughter is really sick."

Kenzie sprang into action. "Come with me," she said, leading the woman to the first exam room. "Can you tell me a little bit about what's going on with her?"

She closed the exam room door before Brett could hear the woman's answer. He looked at Jane and shrugged. "That part is supposed to be my job, but I'm guessing she didn't want to take the time to train me."

"Understandable." Eyes twinkling, Jane let her gaze roam over him. "Where did you say you two met again?"

"We didn't," he answered, his tone equally easygoing. "Is there anything else I can do for you today, ma'am?"

The *ma'am* made her wince. Still, despite his clear attempt to dismiss her, she parked her hands on her hips and stayed put. "You also didn't tell me your name," she said. "What should I call you?"

Instead of using his given name, he decided to go with his old nickname from his high school days. "Call me Buddy," he replied. "And you're Jane, right?"

"Right." She appeared about to say something more, and then shook her head. "Tell Kenzie I'll talk to her later." And with that, she sailed right on out the door.

Relieved, Brett eyed the closed exam room door and wondered if there might be anything he could do to help. Deciding he might as well ask, he tapped on the door lightly before peeking inside. "Is there anything I—" he began.

"There you are!" the young mother exclaimed the instant she saw him. "I was wondering when the doctor was going to get around to seeing us. No offense, nurse," she said as an aside to Kenzie, who was taking her child's temperature. "But I'd feel better having an actual doctor take a look at my Madison."

Incredulous, Brett froze. "You *are* having an actual doctor examine your daughter," he said. "She's the physician, not me."

With that, he backed on out of the room, closing the door behind him.

Chapter Ten

It took every ounce of control Kenzie had not to laugh out loud as Brett hastily backed away and closed the door behind him. She shouldn't have been surprised that her patient's mother, Heather Onderko, had mistaken him for the doctor. Most people honestly did seem to think all physicians should be male. It rankled sometimes, but she'd gotten used to it. As one of the physicians she'd worked with during her residency had said, it was up to them, the female doctors, to change people's perception. Even if that happened one patient at a time.

"It's all right," Kenzie assured the young woman, whose two small daughters watched, wide-eyed. "I understand the former doctor was male." She checked the thermometer, nodding. "Your daughter does not have a fever. So that's a good thing." She moved her gaze to meet the young girl's, who was four years old. "Now Madison, why don't you tell me what hurts?"

"My tummy," the little girl replied, tearing up. "It hurts really bad."

"Did you eat something you shouldn't have?" Kenzie kept her voice light, hoping the child would feel safe enough to tell her. "It's important that I know."

Slowly, Madison nodded. Stealing a glance at her mother, she swallowed. "I ate Muffin's food."

"Muffin?" Kenzie asked.

"That's our cat," Heather answered. "How much of Muffin's food did you eat, honey?"

Instead of answering, the little girl began to cry. "I don't want to get in twouble," she sobbed. "I'm sorry, Mommy."

"It's okay," Kenzie interjected, after exchanging a quick glance with Heather. "We are just trying to figure out how much you ate so we know what we need to do to help you feel better."

Little Madison raised her head and opened her mouth, as if she intended to speak. Instead, she projectile vomited all over the exam room and Kenzie. Kenzie grabbed a trash can and held it for her patient, figuring there would likely be more.

There was.

"It's okay," Kenzie said. "Get it all out. Once you're done, I bet you'll feel a lot better."

Finally, Madison stopped retching. Moistening a few paper towels, Kenzie cleaned her up as best as she could before doing the same for herself.

"Do you feel better now?" Kenzie asked gently. After Madison shyly nodded, Kenzie turned to Heather. "Instead of a regular dinner tonight, maybe let her have some crackers and ginger ale. Nothing too heavy or fatty. She should feel normal by tomorrow, and in the morning, she can resume her regular diet." Then, lifting Madison's chin with her finger, Kenzie smiled. "Just no more cat food, okay?"

"Okay," Madison agreed.

"I like you," Heather Onderko told Kenzie. "I'll let all my friends know we have a good new doctor here in Blake."

"Thank you," Kenzie replied. "I really appreciate that."

After she sent the Onderko family on their way, Kenzie was glad she'd kept a clean pair of scrubs in the back room. She changed, wadding up her soiled pants and placing them into a plastic bag to take home and wash later. She hadn't brought an alternate pair of shoes, so she settled for cleaning hers up as best as she could. Once she'd finished, she spritzed on some disinfectant to help relieve the smell and walked out into the reception area. There, she found Brett sitting behind the desk, looking so uncomfortable and out of place she stopped short.

When he saw her, his frown only grew deeper.

"What's wrong?" she asked, her heart skipping a beat when his bright blue eyes met hers.

"I just can't stop worrying about that woman, Jane. She kept insisting she recognized me from somewhere." He shook his head. "What if she figures out the truth? She seemed awfully persistent."

"She is," Kenzie agreed, resisting the urge to hug him. "If she does, maybe I should have a private talk with her and ask her to keep everything to herself."

He chuckled at this. "I doubt that will work. From what I could tell, that woman appears to thrive on gossip."

"You might have a point." Kenzie shook her head. "Obviously, I don't know her all that well, but Blake *is* a small town. Everything I've read about small towns anywhere would seem to indicate they tend to be a hot-bed of gossip and rumors."

He muttered a curse under his breath.

Kenzie eyed him. "Let me ask you something. Would it be so terrible if people learned who you are? From what I hear, Alaskans look after each other. Maybe it wouldn't be a bad thing to have an entire town watching your back."

"Except all it takes is one person," he pointed out. "Someone who wants to make an extra buck, or whose cousin is friends with one of the gang members. Before you know it, they'll have the gang back here in town. I can't allow that to happen. Neither you nor anyone else around here deserves to be placed in that kind of danger."

She heard the rest of his thoughts, even though he didn't vocalize them. He'd never be able to live with himself if he were responsible for anyone being harmed on his account. She couldn't say she blamed him.

"For now, all of that is nothing but speculation," she said, keeping her voice brisk. "However, I understand if you decide you don't want to continue assisting me here."

He stared at her, his blue gaze dark. "I'm not going to abandon you, Kenzie. Jane is only one person. If she figures out who I am, no doubt she'll come to you first. If and when she does, maybe she'll listen when we explain why it's so imperative to keep my identity quiet."

Kenzie nodded. "She seems reasonable. And she is the mayor's wife. So hopefully we can get her to understand if she does manage to connect the dots."

"Hopefully so," he agreed. Then, he sniffed. "What is that awful smell?"

Now she had to keep her expression impassive. "That little girl who just left? She threw up all over exam room one. I'll need you to clean that up please."

To his credit, he didn't even blanch. "No problem," he said, unfolding himself from the desk chair.

Bemused, she watched as he headed to the kitchen to fetch cleaning supplies.

Two more patients arrived about an hour apart. Both elderly, their visit seemed to be more of an effort to size up the new doctor than for any medical illness. Kenzie examined them anyway, answered a lot of questions about her training and experience, and when they left, they both seemed happy.

Kenzie and Brett ate the lunch he'd packed. He'd made some thick sandwiches, using homemade bread and thick slices of leftover roast beef topped with shredded provolone cheese.

"These are amazing," she told him, forcing herself to eat slowly rather than devouring her meal.

Her comment made him grin. "Thanks. You're pretty amazing yourself, you know. I think you're going to fit right in here in Blake."

Delighted, she nearly kissed him. "That's the nicest thing you could possibly have said."

"I mean it."

The bell over the front door tinkled, announcing the arrival of another patient and effectively ending their lunch.

The internet service provider company called that afternoon, luckily catching Kenzie in between patients.

They'd had a few cancellations and wanted to know if they could come out and get everything up and running in both the cabin and the medical clinic. She barely managed to restrain herself from jumping with joy as they gave her an appointment the next day. Once she'd ended the call, she couldn't resist a quick victory dance in her office.

"Good news?" Brett asked, leaning on the door frame as he watched her.

"Yes!" Grinning, she excitedly told him. "I'm bringing this clinic into the modern world. We'll have internet."

"That's great. I just wish I could access my bank accounts. I'd like to repay you for everything you've done. Plus, I'd really like to get another cell phone."

Instantly, Kenzie felt awful. "I'm so sorry. I don't know why I didn't think of that. I can see if the general store sells any phones and get you one to use temporarily."

"I'd appreciate that," he said. "Just let me know the cost and I'll add it to the list."

"The list? What list?"

His slow smile started a spark low in her belly. "I'm keeping track of everything you've done for which I need to repay you."

"That's not necessary," she told him. "You helping me out in the clinic is repayment enough, believe me."

He shook his head and didn't reply.

At the end of the day, after locking up, they rode home together. The quiet companionship felt wonderful, especially after work. Though tired, Brett's presence brought a pleasant buzz of energy.

That night, they made love again, though she stopped short of inviting him to share her bed. That was a line she wasn't ready to cross. Not yet. Maybe not ever.

In the morning, she greeted him in the kitchen. He handed her a cup of coffee, the warmth in his gaze heating up her blood. She forced herself to turn away, not wanting to be late.

On the way to the clinic, they made a detour to the general store. Leaving Brett in the Jeep, Kenzie hurried in and asked the teenager behind the counter if they sold any kind of cell phones.

"We have the prepaid kind only," he said with a shrug, pointing toward the far wall. "They don't work really well out here, but I guess they're better than nothing."

"Thanks." She went over and, going on impulse, picked up two. They were only twenty dollars each, including the minutes, so she figured it wouldn't hurt to have a spare.

Once she got back into the Jeep, she handed the bag to Brett. "Here you go. All they had were those cheap prepaid phones, and I'm not sure if you can add more minutes, so I got you two."

"Thanks." He peered into the bag. "I imagine I'm really going to miss my smartphone, but this is better than nothing."

"True. And at least it's untraceable," she joked. "So if you want to call the FBI and let them know you're alive, I don't think they can locate you."

"I probably should do that," he responded, completely without enthusiasm.

Once they arrived at the clinic, she unlocked the

door and they both went inside, turning on the lights as they went.

"I wish this place had an alarm," he said.

"Here in such a small town, I imagine there isn't a need," she replied. "There's really nothing of value here, other than meds. And the narcotics, which are the main thing any thieves might be after, are kept under lock and key."

"Good to know." He frowned. "I'd just installed security cameras in my restaurant before the shooting. They fed to a service off-site, so the film survived the fire. Which was how the police were able to identify the shooters, though they didn't capture who shot the congressman." He swallowed. "I'm the one who actually saw that. The only eyewitness. I wasn't entirely sure I needed the cameras, but after all that, I was definitely glad I had them. They at least gave the police an idea of who to look for."

"I can imagine." She touched his arm. "Nothing like that is going to happen here."

Expression grim, he shook his head. "I certainly hope not. But a lot of that depends on no one finding out I'm here."

"You worry too much." Though she wanted to stand up on tiptoe and kiss his cheek, she headed to the kitchen to get a pot of coffee started instead. "It's all going to be fine. I have a good feeling about all this."

"I hope you're right." Coming up behind her, he nuzzled the side of her neck, sending shivers down her spine. When he moved away, only the fact that they were at work kept her from calling him back.

A moment later, her cell rang. Caller ID showed Jane's number.

"Good morning," Kenzie said. "You're calling bright and early this morning."

"I knew I recognized your new assistant!" Jane crowed, so loud that Kenzie had to move her phone away from her ear. "He's a famous chef from Anchorage."

"Famous?" Kenzie countered. "I don't know about that."

"Regionally famous." And then Jane launched into the story about Glacier Grill and the shooting. "The question is what's he doing here?"

Kenzie tried for a noncommittal sound, but Jane wasn't fooled.

"Fess up," Jane demanded. "How do you know Brett Denyon and what's he doing in Blake?"

"It's a long story," Kenzie replied, looking up to see Brett standing near the doorway, arms folded in front of him. "And if you can swing by the clinic, I can let him tell it to you. But for right now, I need you to give me your word to keep quiet about this. His life could be in danger if anyone learns he's here."

"Seriously?" For whatever reason, Jane sounded skeptical. "How do you know that's even true?"

"I just do. Trust me. Swing by the clinic when you can and at least hear him out."

"I will." Jane hesitated for a moment. "I hate to say this, Kenzie. I know you're an educated woman, a doctor. But you wouldn't be the first one to be taken in by a good-looking charmer. I could see by the way you two look at each other that there's something physical going on."

Not sure how to respond to that, Kenzie cleared her throat. She wanted to tell the older woman that was none of her business, but also didn't want to offend her. Especially not now, when Jane knew Brett's true identity.

Finally, she settled on saying the truth. "I trust him, Jane. He's a good man. Come by and talk to him and decide for yourself."

"I'll do that," Jane replied. "And I'll likely bring Greg. He has a really good BS meter. He'll be able to tell in an instant if your new friend is giving us the truth."

Hearing Kenzie's side of the conversation, Brett fought back the instinct to pack his stuff and run. He didn't know Jane personally, but he recognized her type. The kind of woman who loved a good gossip better than anything. No matter what she promised Kenzie, he'd bet Jane wouldn't be able to resist telling at least one of her friends about him.

One person was all it took.

After Kenzie ended the call, she met his gaze and sighed. "Don't look like that," she implored him, correctly interpreting his expression. "Jane's a sensible woman. I'm confident once we talk to her, she'll keep your existence under her hat."

Instead of sharing his doubts, he settled for a curt nod instead. The bell over the front door announced the arrival of the day's first patient, and Brett hurried out to the reception area to greet them.

A steady stream of patients kept them busy until lunchtime. When Kenzie finally turned the Open sign on the door to Closed so they could have their hour lunch, they both looked at each other and smiled.

"I think this is going to work out!" she exclaimed. "This is exactly how I envisioned practicing medicine here to be."

The rush of pride and affection he felt had him pulling her in for a hug. Unfortunately, at that exact moment, the front door opened, making Kenzie wince. "I forgot to lock it," she said, pulling apart.

Jane stared at them, frowning. A large man crowded into the room behind her, unsmiling. "It's only me and Greg. I hope we weren't interrupting anything."

"Of course not." Kenzie flashed a smile. "We were just about to eat our noon meal."

Greg scratched his chin, appearing slightly uncomfortable. "I hate to interrupt your lunch," he began.

"But we're very interested in hearing how Mr. Denyon came to be here," Jane interjected. She smiled at him, batting her eyelashes. Weirdly, he wondered if she thought she was flirting.

Brett told his story, sticking to the facts as he knew them. To her credit, Jane listened without a single interruption, though her eyes got wide as he described the car going off the bridge and into the river. She shook her head when he told about Kenzie rescuing him and taking him in, despite his memory loss.

Finally, he wound down. Greg appeared thoughtful rather than skeptical, and Jane practically bounced up and down with excitement.

"I have questions!" she exclaimed. "So many questions. Have you notified the FBI or the state police that you're here?"

Brett swallowed. "Not yet. I haven't decided if I should, to be honest. Somehow, the gang members found me, even though I had gone off the grid. The only people who knew my location were the FBI."

"Which means you think they have a leak," Greg said, eyes glinting. "That makes sense."

Through all of this, Kenzie had remained quiet, letting Brett do all the talking while she kept a watchful eye on the mayor and his wife. Until now. "That's why we're asking both of you to keep quiet about Brett. We can't take the risk of those gang members coming after him again."

"I imagine not!" Jane huffed. "Especially since you'd now be right in the middle of all that. You're the town doctor! We can't have you placing yourself at risk."

"I won't be at risk if no one knows Brett's here," Kenzie pointed out sweetly. Her stomach chose that moment to loudly growl. She gave a rueful smile at the sound. "I'm sorry. I'm really hungry."

Jane and Greg took the not-so-subtle cue. "We'll get going and leave you to eat your lunch in peace," Jane said. "Please rest assured that neither of us will breathe a word about any of this."

With that assurance, the two of them breezed out the door. The instant they were gone, Brett exhaled. "Do you think she means it?" he asked Kenzie.

"Who knows?" Despite her light tone, worry lingered in Kenzie's gaze. "All we can do is hope for the best."

Back in the small break room, they wolfed down their lunch. This time, instead of sandwiches, Brett had put together some pita pockets. They'd barely finished when the bell over the door announced another patient's arrival.

Instead of a steady stream of patients, they had four more before closing time. Nothing too serious, though when a young boy came in with a broken arm, Brett watched Kenzie handle taking an X-ray, setting and casting the arm, and sending the boy and his worried parents on their way with the proper medications.

The internet company came and got everything installed, promising to take care of Kenzie's residence tomorrow.

For the first time, Brett realized once he'd gone, Kenzie would be doing all of these things alone. Going to work, dealing with vendors, waking up and making her own coffee, and… living life. This knowledge rankled more than it should have. Especially since he still didn't know if his very presence placed her in danger.

Once they'd closed up for the day, Kenzie flashed him a tired smile and mentioned how much she looked forward to a hot shower. Of course, his mind immediately flashed to images of him joining her, their bodies naked and slick, and the pleasure they could bring each other.

"Brett?" Kenzie asked, cutting into his thoughts. "Are you ready to head back to the cabin?"

More aroused than he should be, he nodded, not trusting himself to speak. He managed to get himself under control and make it out to her Jeep without her noticing anything.

"Would you mind stopping at the general store and picking up a few things?" he asked. "We need to restock some of the groceries. Especially the perishables, like produce, dairy and meat." He produced a list he'd made earlier. "Not a whole lot of stuff, but the basics."

"No problem." Her easy smile made him wonder if this was what it could be like, being in a committed relationship. He'd always heard the day in, day out ordinary times were what wore on people. In the past, he'd taken pains to make sure any relationships he'd had were too brief to ever get to that place.

But now, waking up to see Kenzie's face every morning, driving to and from work with her, having meals together and sharing space didn't feel arduous. Not at all. In fact, he felt comfortable, more at peace than he could ever remember feeling. The only thing he missed was being a chef at his own restaurant.

She parked along Main Street, a few spaces down from the entrance to the general store and held out her hand for his list. "I'll be right back," she said. "I guess you can duck down or something if you want to make sure no one sees you."

Though he felt slightly foolish, he nodded. "I'll do that."

Once she'd disappeared inside, he slouched in his seat, practically laying it down. Though he hadn't spotted any people strolling the sidewalks near the store, he didn't want to take a chance.

A few minutes later, Kenzie returned, carrying three paper bags full of groceries. "That was easy," she announced, stowing them in the back of the Jeep. "It always amazes me how plentiful—and fresh—the seafood is here. I got your crabmeat and more salmon. They practically give that away. The only thing they didn't have was mushrooms. He said there wasn't really much of a demand for them out here."

This made him laugh. "Hey, if they had everything else, I count that as a win." Though he felt foolish, he didn't sit back up until they'd pulled away from downtown. She glanced at him but didn't comment, although he swore he saw a flash of disappointment in her eyes.

On the way out of town, they were both silent, lost in their own thoughts.

While he couldn't help but worry about potential damage the mayor's wife could cause, Brett considered how well he and Kenzie worked together. After his second day, while he'd begun to feel marginally competent in the medical clinic, he couldn't help but wish she could see him in his element, commanding his restaurant kitchen, dealing with staff and customers and managing to keep everyone happy and satisfied. And the food! He'd taken pains to make sure everything he served tasted out of this world.

Life had been good. Pretty damn close to perfect. Except even then he'd known he'd been missing something, even if he couldn't articulate what that something might be.

He suspected he might have found it. Impossibly here, in Blake, Alaska, in Dr. Kenzie Taylor. He just didn't have the slightest idea how to integrate the life he'd hoped to someday rebuild in Anchorage with what she had here.

"We're here," Kenzie said softly, bringing him out his thoughts. "Did you doze off?"

"Maybe so." With a shrug, he hopped out of the Jeep and went around back to get the bags. "You go ahead and take your shower and I'll see what I can pull together for dinner."

"How about we go out to eat at Mikki's instead?" she suggested, tossing him a smile over her shoulder. "That way you don't have to cook after already spending a long day at the clinic."

"Cooking is how I relax," he told her, not sure why he felt so offended at her suggestion. "Plus, remember I'm still keeping a low profile. Other than working with you, I don't plan on making any appearances in town."

She'd already opened the door and stepped inside the cabin. "Suit yourself," she said. "I'm going to shower. And if you change your mind, I can always go pick something up and bring it back."

Mind already assembling the ingredients for the evening meal, he didn't even bother to respond to that.

By the time Kenzie emerged from her shower, her hair still damp and her feet bare, he'd put all the groceries away and had begun what'd he'd come to think of as one of his signature dishes, crab cakes with semolina polenta. He hadn't expected the general store to carry the semolina flour, but to his surprise they had. Along with this, he planned to serve a warm spinach salad.

"That smells amazing," she commented, wandering over to take a look at his prep work.

"Thanks. It's one of my restaurant's most popular dishes," he replied, not bothering to hide his pride. "It can be a trick for some of my newer cooks to get the perfect mixture, but once they do..." He rolled his eyes.

She poured herself a glass of wine and sat down to watch him work. Here, working with food, he allowed himself to slip into the zone, similar to what he'd heard athletes and artists describe. For him, cooking became an intricate dance, using all his senses to create the perfect dish. Even something like this, a meal he'd made a hundred times before, felt new each time he made it.

When he finally plated the food and looked up, he realized Kenzie watched him, her gaze raw. Suppressing the urge to give a theatrical bow, he carried their plates over to the table. "Try it," he ordered. "I want to see your face when you have the first taste."

Her gaze never left his as she lifted her fork. The instant her lips closed over her piece of crab cake, her eyes widened. Chewing, she swallowed and moaned. "Oh, that's good. So, so good."

His body stirred. Quickly, he sat down before she could notice. Though he picked up his own fork, for now all he wanted was to watch her eat the food he'd prepared.

She'd demolished half of her crab cakes before she realized he hadn't touched his. "Aren't you going to eat?" she asked.

Desire pulsing through him, he managed to nod and began shoveling food into his mouth without really even tasting it. He cleaned his plate in record time.

When he met her gaze again, the rawness of his desire must have blazed in his eyes, because she gasped. "Are you… Do you…?"

"I'm so turned on right now," he told her.

"I almost jumped your bones while you were cooking," she admitted. "But I wanted to taste what you made, so I restrained myself."

Pushing up out of her chair, she held out her hand. "Let's go have our own dessert," she said, laughing.

And so they did.

After Kenzie kicked him out of her bed so she could sleep, he cleaned the kitchen and then dropped down onto the couch. He pulled out one of his new cell phones—*a burner phone*, he thought. She'd prepaid for 120 minutes on each, which he appreciated. He'd mainly wanted to have a way to contact her if they were separated. He hadn't really even considered talking to the FBI.

Maybe he should. He could touch base, check in, let them know he was alive without revealing his location. As long as no one knew where he was he—and Kenzie—should be safe.

Not yet, he decided. *Maybe tomorrow.*

Long after Kenzie had likely fallen asleep, Brett tossed and turned on the couch, unable to rest. Finally, he gave up and went to the kitchen to get a drink of water. The full moon outside brought enough light in through the kitchen window that he could see. After he got his water, he considered going to sit outside on the front porch for a bit and breathe in the fresh air. And that's when he heard the sounds.

His first thought was it had to be a bear. They were known to seek out food around remote cabins like this one. Crossing from window to window to try to see, he kept as quiet as possible so he didn't alert the animal to his presence.

A shadowy form moved across the side of the house. Then another. Brett froze. Not a bear. Men. At least two of them.

And from what he'd seen, they were armed.

What the hell? Had the gang somehow learned of his whereabouts?

Moving quickly, he hurried into Kenzie's room. He needed to wake her, but without her making a sound. Kneeling down, he whispered her name into her ear while putting a finger across her lips.

She came awake instantly. "Brett? What's going on? Why are you here in the dark?"

"Intruders," he told her. "Circling the cabin outside." Swallowing hard, he knew he had to be strong. Defend her no matter what. He'd brought this danger to her by his very presence. He'd never forgive himself if she got hurt. "Stay away from the windows, just in case. They're likely armed."

"Oh, hell no." Swinging her legs over the side of her bed, she reached into her nightstand drawer. "I'll use this pistol. I bought a rifle too and it's in the closet. The ammo is on the floor next to it."

Once they were both armed, they moved silently in the dark house over to the front door. "Stay on the back side of it," he whispered. "If they come through, we'll have the element of surprise on our side."

She nodded. "I'm guessing they heard a female lives here alone. Guessing they're thinking I'm unprepared," she whispered. Her smile flashed white in the moonlight. "We'll show them." She reached under the couch and pulled out a baseball bat. "These come in handy sometimes."

If he hadn't known better, he'd have thought she was *enjoying* this.

Chapter Eleven

Another sound, boots on the porch. Then someone tried the knob. Blood pumping, Kenzie listened, gripping her baseball bat.

"It's locked," a man said, low-voiced.

"Can you pick it?" someone else asked. "Quietly. We don't want to wake her."

Her. Which meant these men hadn't come for Brett.

"Give me a sec," the first guy replied. There were a few scraping sounds and then the lock popped. "We're in."

The doorknob turned. Kenzie held her breath. Slowly, the door opened. Gripping the bat, she stayed back, waiting until they were all the way inside. On the other side of the doorway, Brett did the same. She figured the interior darkness worked in their favor.

Two men—good, there weren't more—stepped into the cabin. Before their eyes had time to adjust to the darkness, Brett moved.

He body-slammed the guy closest to him, letting loose with a left hook to the jaw that sent the intruder to the floor. At the same time, Kenzie swung her bat, putting all her strength into it. She hit the man squarely on the back of the head, wincing at the awful sound that it made. Instantly, he dropped, almost on top of his buddy.

Heaving a sigh of relief, Kenzie shakily lowered her bat, though she didn't drop it. "It sounded like they were after me instead of you," she said. "Lowlifes preying on a woman living alone."

Brett turned on the light. Both men were dressed all in black. They appeared to be in their mid-thirties. Neither of them looked familiar, which was a relief. She wasn't sure how she'd react if it turned out one of them had been her patient at the clinic.

"Let's get their guns and then we'll see what we can find to tie them up before they come to," Brett said.

Nodding, she grabbed the pistols and moved them to the kitchen. "I saw some clothesline rope in the cabinet under the sink," Kenzie said him. "Let me grab that."

No surprise, but her hands were still shaking. She located the rope and brought it back to Brett, letting him take care of tying up the intruders.

Once the two unconscious men had been secured, she went ahead and checked them over for serious injuries. "I want to make sure I didn't do any real damage to this guy," she said, indicating the one she'd hit with the bat. "Nothing appears to be broken, but I'll need to keep an eye on the swelling."

"Once a doctor, always a doctor," Brett teased.

"That's very true." Satisfied both men would live, she pulled out her phone. "Still no signal," she said, heart sinking. "I need to call the police or something." But who? Blake didn't have a police force. She'd call Jane, she decided. Jane and Greg would know what to do.

Brett agreed. "You need to get a satellite phone," he

suggested. "Or a landline. Either one would work better than trying to use your cell out here. It's a dead zone."

Aware he was right, she made a face. "I'll have to drive closer to town and make the call. It's weird, because sometimes I can get a signal here. I have no idea how to duplicate that right now though."

"We can try one of my prepaid phones," he suggested, standing up after making sure both men's hands and feet were securely bound. "But first, let's see who these two yahoos are."

"Okay." Digging in the back pocket of the man closest to her, she pulled out a wallet, then an ID. "Raymond Lee. He's from Anchorage," she said, passing over the license to Brett. "Do you recognize the name?"

Studying it, he shook his head. "No. Should I?"

"I don't know." She shrugged. "I just checked in case he was one of the customers at your restaurant or otherwise involved with what happened."

Except they'd been here for her. She'd heard them talking about being careful not to wake the woman up. She grabbed the other man's license too and studied it.

Looking up, she saw Brett watching her. "I'm glad you weren't here alone," he said. "No matter where you go, there's always going to be men who can't wait to take advantage of a helpless woman."

"I'm not helpless," she scoffed. "What I am is prepared. That's why I took all those handgun courses back in Houston and got my concealed carry license for Texas."

"They didn't know that," he pointed out. "But I'm definitely glad we were able to stop them in their tracks."

One of the men stirred, moaning. Kenzie froze, bracing herself in case he tried to come at her again.

"He's not going anywhere," Brett assured her. "I promise."

She tried her phone again. "Still no bars."

"Let's check one of mine." Brett grabbed his cheap phone off the end table and turned it on. "Looks like this will work." He handed it to her.

"How is that possible?" she asked, taking it.

"I don't know," he replied. "Different service provider? Different cell tower? No idea. But go ahead and use it while you still can." He shrugged. "You never know. It might work one minute and not the next."

Since he had a point, she looked up Jane's number and called. Jane answered on the second ring, sounding both half asleep and thoroughly pissed off. "Whoever this is, you'd better have a damn good reason for calling in the middle of the night."

"Jane, it's Kenzie. And I do."

Once she'd outlined what had happened, Jane sounded much more awake. "I need to put in a call to the state police," she said. "Is that going to be all right, with you-know-who being there?"

"Yes, I think so," Kenzie replied. "I mean, it's not like he's wanted by the law or anything."

"Do you think that's who they were after?" Jane pressed. "I swear, I didn't tell a single soul about him."

"I know you didn't," Kenzie hastened to reassure her. "From what I could tell, they'd heard a woman lived alone in a remote cabin, and they thought they could break their way in."

Jane gasped. "That's terrible. Do you know who they are? Are they locals?"

"I don't think so. We pulled ID from their pockets and both of their driver's licenses list Anchorage addresses."

"Then how did they find out about you living alone?" Jane asked. "They couldn't have been just passing through. Maybe they recently moved here. Do you mind giving me their names?"

"Not at all. Hold on a second." Kenzie grabbed the two IDs from the coffee table. "Raymond Lee and Jeffrey Boxer."

Jane went quiet. After a moment, she spoke again. "Neither of those names sounds familiar. But I've jotted them down. Let me notify the state police and then I'll do some digging."

"Okay." Glancing at the intruders, now captives, she sighed. "Any idea how long it might take for the police to send someone out to retrieve them? If it's going to be awhile, is there someplace I can take them? Like a temporary holding cell or something? I'd prefer they not stay here. This cabin is small enough."

"I'll work on that too," Jane promised. "We don't have a jail or anything. Actually, there hasn't ever been a lot of crime here in Blake."

"Thanks, Jane. I appreciate it."

"No problem. And, Kenzie, what number is this that you're calling from? I don't recognize it." Jane asked.

"It's Brett's cell," Kenzie answered. "For some reason, it works here at the cabin when mine won't."

That made Jane chuckle. "Technology," she commented. "I'll call you back as soon as I talk to the state police."

Ending the call, Kenzie handed Brett back his phone. "I don't know what we're going to do with them," she said, waving her hand at the two, still mostly unconscious, men. "I'm hoping law enforcement can make it here and pick them up before too long."

"I'll give you a thousand dollars," one of the men said, Raymond Lee if she remembered right. He raised his head to showcase a purpling black eye. "One thousand in cash, if you'll just let us go. We promise to leave quietly and won't ever come back."

"Not happening, buddy," Brett answered. "You can't just break into a lady's cabin with who knows what plans and expect her to just look the other way."

"Two thousand." Sounding desperate, he upped the offer, this time making eye contact with Kenzie. "Cash money. Come on, this place isn't that fancy. You know you could use it."

Slowly, Kenzie shook her head. "I'm the town doctor," she said. "And somehow I think you might already know that."

Raymond snorted. "I've heard. And a piss poor one at that."

Suddenly, everything made sense. Kenzie exchanged an incredulous look with Brett. "Did someone send you here?" she asked. "Tell you all about the single lady living alone?"

"No." Not sounding the slightest bit convincing, Raymond looked away. "I mean, we heard about you and how pretty you were when we stopped to have a drink in town. But that's it."

Kenzie didn't believe him. And, judging from Brett's expression, neither did he.

"Are you friends with Annette Gladley?" Kenzie crossed her arms and waited, already certain.

Raymond blanched. "No." His denial came out weak. "Not friends."

"Relatives then?" Kenzie pushed, knowing there had to be some connection.

Slowly, Raymond nodded. "She's my second cousin. Matter of fact, me and Jeff are in town visiting her. She's going to be really mad when she finds out we got caught."

"I bet she is," Kenzie agreed. "I'm guessing all this was her idea."

Raymond's silence spoke volumes.

"We need to let the police know about that also," Brett interjected. "That woman needs to be arrested."

Though Kenzie agreed, she couldn't help but feel sad. Annette had gone out of her way to cause discord, even giving up the job she'd held for years. Now she'd apparently orchestrated a personal attack on the town's new doctor, her former employer, who had come here to help serve the town's medical needs. "I just don't understand," she mused out loud. "What kind of twisted person would do something like this?"

"Agreed." Brett's tight jaw matched the fury in his gaze. "While I don't know for sure what you two idiots intended to do, I have a pretty good idea."

"Three thousand," Raymond offered, his voice pitched high with desperation. "I can pay cash, if you'll just untie us and let us drive away."

Both Kenzie and Brett ignored this request.

Jane called back. "I've spoken to dispatch. They'll send a state trooper this way at first light. Is everyone okay?"

"Physically, yes. Mentally, I'm not certain." Kenzie told her what Raymond had said about Annette.

"I'm shocked," Jane said, her voice somber. "I've known that woman since she was a teenager. I can't believe she'd resort to something like this. She's such a talented artist. I can't reconcile the two."

"I know." Kenzie sighed. "I love her work. I purchased several of her pieces to hang on my wall. I don't think I'll be doing that now."

"I'm sorry," Jane replied. "When word gets out, a lot of people are going to be so disappointed." She took a deep breath. "Anyway, expect someone from the state police sometime tomorrow. The exact time depends on where the closest officer is located. If I hear anything else, I'll give you a call."

"Don't forget to look into finding a place where these two intruders can be held. I'd really like to get them out of the cabin."

"I understand. I'll do the best I can," Jane promised and ended the call.

"The police won't be here until tomorrow," Kenzie passed the information along to Brett. "And while Jane is working on finding somewhere else these two can be held, it's likely they'll have to stay here until they can be taken into police custody."

"That's fine." He gestured toward the bedroom. "I'll watch them for now. Why don't you try and get some sleep? Tomorrow is still a work day."

Blinking, she shook her head. "Tomorrow is Saturday. The clinic is closed. Heck of a way to spend a day off though." She'd had plans. Involving a hike and a picnic and Brett. Instead, they'd be spending the day watching over two criminals until law enforcement could come to collect them.

She looked over to find Jeffrey Boxer watching her, his eyes narrow slits in his swollen face. "I'm going to sue you for hitting me with that baseball bat," he said. "I think you might have cracked my skull."

"That's entirely possible," she said cheerfully, though she knew she hadn't. "Hopefully, you won't die while waiting for the police to arrive."

A flash of panic crossed his face. "You're a doctor. Fix me up."

About to say something flippant, she realized she didn't have it in her nature to torment another human being. "You're fine," she told him. "I checked you over while you were out. You'll have a good-size lump on the back of your head, but nothing is broken."

Glaring at her, he muttered an obscenity under his breath before closing his eyes.

Kenzie shook her head and turned to Brett. "You know, when I imagined working in an isolated town in Alaska, I never imagined dealing with something like this."

He pulled her in for a quick hug, kissing her head. "I'm sorry. It can only get better from here."

Which was, she thought, exactly the right thing to say.

AFTER FINALLY CONVINCING Kenzie to go back to bed, Brett settled in on the couch, pistol in hand, to keep an eye on the two men. Fury simmered low inside him. He couldn't help but picture what these fools had planned to do to his Kenzie.

His Kenzie. He let the thought settle, knowing now wasn't the time to try to analyze things.

"Who are you anyway?" Raymond Lee asked, eyeing Brett's gun. His companion had closed his eyes and appeared to have drifted off into a fitful doze.

"None of your business." Glaring, Brett dared the other man to press.

Clearly, Raymond wasn't good at reading signals. "Annette didn't say anything about the lady doctor having a boyfriend," he continued. "We wouldn't have broken in here if we'd known."

As if that excused anything. Instead of responding, Brett glared at the other man, silently urging him to shut the hell up.

Instead, Raymond began blabbering. "We're not bad guys, dude. Seriously. All we were supposed to do was rough her up a little and scare her enough that she'd go back to wherever she came from. That's all. We weren't really going to hurt your lady."

"Really?" Brett allowed some of his rage to show in his expression and in his voice. "You honestly expect me to believe you broke into a sleeping woman's home, with the intent of ambushing her in her bedroom, and you only were going to *scare* her?"

Finally, the scorn in Brett's voice seemed to reach the other man. Blanching, he looked down and mercifully went quiet.

By the time dawn had begun to lighten the sky, both of Brett's prisoners had fallen asleep. Brett had taken to getting himself up and pacing every so often, trying to stay awake. He couldn't take the chance of either of these men escaping.

His cell phone rang shortly after 6:00 a.m. Since the only person who had this number would be the person Kenzie had called, he knew it had to be Jane.

He answered.

"This is Jane, the mayor's wife," she said. "I've been calling Kenzie, but the call isn't going through, so I tried you."

She barely paused for breath before continuing. "A state trooper is on his way and should be there by mid-morning. They asked if Kenzie wanted to press charges. I told them I didn't know, but I felt sure she probably will."

Brett managed to cut in, interrupting her stream of words. "She definitely will," he said. "And I'll definitely let her know the police will be here soon."

"Let me talk to her," Jane demanded. "I've also heard from Annette and she wanted me to convey her apologies."

His instant flare of anger shocked him. "Kenzie is still asleep," he replied. "I'd be happy to have her call you once she gets up."

Jane's silence told him he'd managed to surprise her, though he wasn't sure why. There was no way any man would leave Kenzie alone with the two intruders, even if they were tied up.

"I'll give Kenzie your message," he said and ended the call.

He looked up to see the one named Raymond awake

and watching him. Brett ignored him, heading for the kitchen to make a cup of coffee.

"I need to use the restroom," Raymond called out after him. "Please, man. I've got to go really bad."

"The police will be here soon," Brett responded. "You can tell him all about it."

Kenzie wandered in a few minutes later, rubbing the sleep from her eyes. "Mornin'," she drawled, glancing back toward the two men on the living room floor.

"Jane called. She wanted me to let you know a state trooper is on the way. And asked you to call her when you get a chance. She said she'd heard from Annette."

The mention of her nemesis's name made Kenzie frown. "I don't really care to hear anything Annette has to say. And I don't understand why Jane would think I would."

He shrugged. "I'm not sure. Maybe you should ask her."

"I will, but not right now. I don't feel like dealing with anything else until these two are arrested and hauled away."

Brett planned to make himself scarce once the trooper arrived, but Kenzie immediately vetoed that idea. "You helped me take these guys down." She smiled at him, gratitude shining from her eyes. "You kept me safe. He's going to need to take your statement."

"What if he recognizes me?" Brett asked, sotto voce.

"So what if he does?" she countered. "It's not like you're a wanted criminal or something. It's not his job to worry about where the FBI might have stashed you."

She had a valid point. He couldn't just disappear and leave her to explain how the intruders had been subdued. "I'll stay," he said. "I'm actually getting sick of having to hide."

Flashing him a huge smile, she squeezed his shoulder. "I can only imagine. I'll be glad to see you living your life in the open again."

Her choice of phrasing made him think. In the open, exposed. While she may not completely realize it, until the trial, he was still a target. The only eyewitness to the murder of a United States congressman.

Briefly, he considered pointing that out, just so she knew not to let down her guard. But since he suspected she might be getting tired of hearing about the reasons he needed to keep a low profile, he didn't.

The police officer arrived shortly after ten o'clock and rapped sharply on the front door. After glancing at Brett, Kenzie let him in, pointing to the two bound men now sitting up on the floor. Raymond glared at her, while the second man still seemed dazed and out of it.

"I'm Officer Dade," the burly bearded policeman said.

"Dr. Kenzie Taylor." She held out her hand. "And this is my assistant, Brett."

Brett noticed she didn't use his last name, which he appreciated.

"Those two are Raymond Lee and Jeffrey Boxer," she continued. "They broke into my cabin last night."

"Good job subduing them, ma'am," Officer Dade said, grinning.

"Thanks." She could have pointed out that Brett helped, but Brett suspected she didn't want to draw any attention to him.

After taking Kenzie's statement, the policeman turned to Brett. "I take it you can corroborate all of this?"

"I can." Brett nodded.

"What are you going to do with us?" Raymond spoke up.

"Arrest and book you. After I read you your rights, that is." Which Dade didn't appear to be in any hurry to do.

"I'd like them out of here," Kenzie pointed out.

"I understand. But I also need to go have a talk with someone named…" He checked his notes. "Annette Gladley."

Kenzie perked up at that. "Are you going to arrest her too?"

Before the police officer could answer, Raymond Lee spoke up. "Leave her out of this," he said. "She's a good person. She just wanted us to scare Dr. Taylor. She just didn't know about the boyfriend." He glared at Brett.

Officer Dade shook his head. "I'm taking you two with me," he announced. "When we get there, you can tell Ms. Gladley that yourself."

Quickly, he read them their rights, allowing them each a brief stop in the bathroom. Then, with Brett's helped, he marched them out to the car, shuffling along since their hands and feet were still bound.

As soon as they were safely secured in the back seat, once he'd closed the car door, Officer Dade turned to Brett, one bushy eyebrow raised. "You look familiar," he commented. "Though I can't say from where."

"I get that a lot," Brett replied, hoping the other man would drop it.

Instead, the policeman continued to eye him. "What did you say your last name was again?"

Damn it. For a second, Brett debated lying. But then again, he'd done nothing wrong and had nothing to hide. He thought it extremely unlikely this random cop would connect him to what had happened weeks ago in Anchorage.

"I didn't," he replied. Then, taking a deep breath, he held out his hand. "Denyon. Brett Denyon."

After they shook, Officer Dade inclined his head. "Even your name sounds familiar, though I can't place it. Ah, well." He turned to make his way to the driver's side of his patrol car. "I'm sure it'll come to me. Take care, now."

"You too." Brett watched until the state trooper drove away, refusing to acknowledge his overwhelming sense of relief until the vehicle had completely disappeared from sight. Then and only then did he allow himself to exhale.

Kenzie had followed them outside, though she'd remained on the front porch. She held out her arms and he walked right into them, holding her close. "It's all over now," he told her. "Those men will never bother you again."

"Darn right they won't," she said, raising her face to his for a kiss. "I hope word gets out that the lady doctor is armed and willing to defend herself."

Instead of replying, he kissed her. Long and hard and deep. When they finally broke apart, she swayed, grabbing a hold of him as if she needed his support to stay upright. Thoroughly aroused and ready for her, he waited to see what she would do.

"Later," she promised, smiling softly, the desire in her eyes echoing his own. "Right now, I really need to get away from this place." She swept her arm toward the cabin and beyond. "Not just the cabin, but this town. How about we go for a drive?"

"Sure," he immediately agreed. "I think we could both use a break."

Holding hands, they went back into the cabin to grab a few things. He packed a quick picnic lunch, making simple sandwiches. Since he didn't have time to prepare anything elaborate, he grabbed a bag of potato chips, a couple of dill pickles, some apples and two cans of sparkling water. On impulse, he grabbed a large slice of the chocolate cake he'd baked earlier and wrapped it up. Once he had everything stowed in a small ice chest along with ice, he went looking for Kenzie.

Chapter Twelve

Kenzie wasn't sure why, but instead of getting ready to take a drive with Brett, she dropped down onto her bed and covered her face with her hands. She wanted to cry. More than cry. Howl. The kind of gut-wrenching, curl-up-in-a-ball-and-let-it-all-out kind of weeping.

And she wasn't sure why.

This both surprised and worried her. She'd never been the dramatic type, or given to allowing her emotions to have too much control over her.

In Houston, whenever she'd felt overwhelmed like this, she'd headed for the gym. Thirty minutes of hard pedaling on the bike, or running on the treadmill, and she'd always managed to get any wayward feelings under control.

Here, she didn't have access to a gym. Briefly, she wondered if she should take up jogging or buy a bike. Or, since it would soon be winter, maybe she could learn how to ski. Otherwise, she could just use snowshoes.

"Are you all right?" Brett asked from the doorway, startling her.

Taking a deep shuddering breath, she raised her head and met his gaze. "I'm not sure," she admitted. "This has all been too much. And yet…somehow, I feel like in the end, I emerged stronger."

Brett nodded and she braced herself. She knew men often wanted to fix things, and she got that. As a physician, she often felt that way herself. But right now, she didn't need him to offer solutions. She wanted comfort and then…to pretend her mini-breakdown had never happened.

"You did," Brett agreed. "Kenzie, in my opinion you're the strongest woman I know." With that lopsided grin that never failed to make her heart skip a beat, he gestured toward the front door. "Are you ready to go? I packed a picnic lunch for us. Nothing fancy, but in case we find someplace where we want to hang out."

This man, she thought, knew exactly what she needed. Jumping up from the bed, she nodded. "I'm ready. Let's head on out."

With him carrying the loaded ice chest, they headed out to her Jeep. The sky had gone from partly cloudy to dark and ominous.

"I don't like the look of those clouds," Brett said. "It looks like we're about to get more rain."

"Well, it *is* rainy season," Kenzie joked. "I tried to check my weather app, but I can't get anything to work on my cell, even with our new Wi-Fi."

"Hopefully, it'll hold off until we get back." Brett stowed the ice chest in the back seat. "I'm looking forward to seeing some new scenery."

"Me too."

When they reached the main road, Kenzie turned in the opposite direction of the way into town. "We're going to have to cross that bridge," she told him. "Are you going to be all right with that?"

"Sure," he said, his casual tone matching his relaxed expression. "Now that I know what actually happened, I'm good."

"Okay."

The downpour started before they even made it a mile down the road. Sheets of windblown rain obscured her vision, eerily reminiscent of her first day here. The day she'd watched the car in front of her go off the side of the bridge.

A quick glance at Brett revealed him sitting ramrod straight, a look of determination on his handsome face. Inside, she imagined he must be worried. It would be only human to worry about reliving the horror he'd experienced.

"This isn't going to work," she said, gripping the steering wheel and slowing to a crawl. "I'm going to find a place to turn around. We'll try this again another time."

Relief flashed across his expression, though he quickly tried to hide it. "I think that's a good idea," he said. The rain drumming on the roof just about drowned out his words.

Kenzie finally spotted a driveway and pulled into it, backing out and turning her vehicle around.

As they drove slowly back toward the cabin, Brett's cell phone rang, startling them both. "The only person who has this number is Jane," he said. "And I don't feel like talking to her. Do you want to answer it?"

"Nope."

As soon as the ringing stopped, it started up again. Brett groaned. "She's nothing if not persistent."

"She's probably going to keep calling until you answer," Kenzie pointed out, coasting over to the side of the road. "Let me deal with her."

As soon as Kenzie said hello, Jane launched into a garbled story, talking so quickly that Kenzie could barely make out the gist of it. Meanwhile, the storm continued to rage outside, making Jane cut in and out.

"Slow down," Kenzie finally ordered. "You're breaking up too much. I can't understand what you're trying to tell me."

"Annette disappeared," Jane finally managed, shouting. "I went over there to talk to her before the state trooper came. I think I might have let it slip that you had a male houseguest."

Kenzie's blood froze. "You *think*? Either you did or you didn't. Which is it?"

Jane sighed. "I'm awfully sorry. It just kind of slipped out. She was saying she'd heard you'd already gotten help at the clinic. I've always liked Annette and I wanted her to explain to me exactly what happened to make her leave the job she's done for so many years."

Since Kenzie didn't care about Annette's rationale, she tried to make Jane stick to the point. "I just need to know whether or not you told Annette who Brett actually is."

The ensuing silence, so unlike Jane, seemed answer enough. Thunder chose that moment to boom, followed immediately by a huge flash of lightning.

"Do you have any idea where she's gone?" Kenzie

asked, striving to keep her voice calm, despite her racing heart.

"That's just it," Jane cried. "I don't. But I suspect she feels she's found another way to hurt you." Her voice crackled, fading in and out. "After all, with the state police looking for her, she might feel she has nothing to lose."

More thunder, another flash. Though intellectually, Kenzie knew they were safe inside the car, she'd begun to feel like a sitting duck. "What do you mean *nothing to lose*?" she shouted. "That doesn't sound good at all."

Jane said something completely unintelligible. Kenzie asked her twice to repeat it.

Suddenly, the line stopped crackling and Jane's voice came through, clear as a bell. "Remember when those men came to town, looking for their missing family member? And it turned out he was the guy who drowned after that car went off the bridge into the river?" Clearing her throat, Jane paused expectantly.

The fierce part of the storm appeared to have passed them by. Though it still rained, the furious wind and thunder and lightning seemed to have moved on. But Jane's words made Kenzie's stomach churn. She didn't like where this was heading. "I do remember," she managed. "What about them?"

"Well, I'm thinking Annette went after those men. She knows they were looking for Brett."

"How?" Kenzie demanded, shooting an incredulous glance Brett's way, wishing he could hear this entire conversation. "How on earth would Annette make that connection?"

Jane coughed loudly. "Well, when Annette and I

were talking about him, she pulled him up on the internet. Did you know one of the articles says he went into the federal Witness Protection Program?"

Damn, damn, damn.

"Jane, what have you *done?*" Kenzie cried. "I don't think you completely comprehend how bad this could be."

In the seat next to her, Brett shook his head and grimaced. Kenzie imagined he'd gotten enough info from hearing just her side of the conversation to be equally horrified.

The rainfall slowed to a steady thrum and the dark sky began to lighten up. Now Kenzie could see the road ahead of them. Still, she made no move to put the Jeep back into Drive.

"I'm sorry," Jane rushed to say, squeaking out the words. "But I promise you, I'm trying to make it right. I've got people out trying to find Annette before she causes any more trouble, plus the state police are looking for her. But, Kenzie, I think it's time to call in the FBI."

"I'll need to talk to Brett first," Kenzie responded, feeling sick. "Then I'll get back to you."

If she'd thought things couldn't get any worse, she was wrong.

"Well, the thing is," Jane admitted, "I've already called them."

"What?" Kenzie nearly hung up on her. Instead, she clenched her teeth and struggled not to yell. "Explain. What exactly did you say?"

"You're angry," Jane protested, her voice small. "I don't know how to make this right."

"Tell me what you said," Kenzie demanded.

"I just let them know that Brett Denyon was alive and here in Blake." Jane sounded contrite. "Look, I think what I did was for the best. The FBI can protect him."

"Except they didn't." So furious her hands shook, Kenzie took a deep breath. While she'd known from the get-go that Jane was a meddler, this time she'd gone too far.

"I'm going to let you go," Kenzie told her. "Before I say something I might regret. Please let me know if you or anyone else is able to locate Annette." With that, she ended the call, half expecting Jane to call back immediately. The fact that she didn't told Kenzie Jane might have realized how badly she'd messed up.

A quick glance at Brett showed him watching her, grim-faced. "I got the gist of most of that," he said. "I can't go back to your cabin."

"Of course, you can." Determined, Kenzie considered pulling out onto the road into the light rain and driving them toward home. But she felt too shaky still, so she continued to sit where she was, breathing in and out and trying for calm. "Where else would you go?"

"I'll figure that out," he said. "I refuse to put you at risk."

"Brett." She turned to face him. "Those men who broke into the cabin were there because of me," she pointed out. "And despite you being in considerable danger, you helped defend me. Please don't deny me the chance to do the same for you."

He cupped her face with his hands. "I appreciate that, but this is very different. Those two guys weren't killers. While they definitely had bad intent, if these gang members come, they won't be messing around. They'll shoot first, ask questions later. They'd think nothing of burning the cabin down with us inside."

"I don't care." Trembling with emotion, she leaned forward and pressed her lips against his. "I don't want to lose you."

To her shock, he turned away. "Right back'atcha," he said, his voice already distant. "Which is why I won't be going back to the cabin. Since Jane has so graciously made the FBI aware of my location, I'll contact them. They'll find somewhere to hide me for now."

She wasn't buying that. "That doesn't make sense. You've already told me you don't trust the FBI. You said you felt like there might be a mole."

The man sitting in the passenger seat beside her might as well have been a stranger. "I'll do what I have to do," he said. "Don't worry about me, just take care of yourself. I'll try to contact you when this is all over."

Try. She couldn't help but pick up on his choice of words. Was he trying to tell her that their brief romantic interlude had come to an end? That they were over?

For a second, as her throat closed up and tears stung her eyes, she wanted to argue. To fight for him, for *them*, damn it.

But she wouldn't. Because he clearly didn't want the same thing she did. To him, what they'd share must have been a summer fling. And now, once the trial was over, he'd go back to Anchorage, to his old life. No doubt, he'd open another restaurant.

"Whatever you want," she replied, proud that she managed to keep her tone cool as she put the Jeep in gear and pulled back out onto the road. "Do you want to at least go back to the cabin and collect your things?"

Staring straight ahead, he considered. "I think that'll be safe, so yes. Give me five minutes and I'll be out of your hair."

Under any other circumstances, she would have let a statement like that go. But this was different, he was different, and no matter what did or didn't happen in the future, she considered him a friend. "I'll need to drive you somewhere, won't I?" she asked. "It's still raining."

"I won't melt." He flashed a grim smile. "But thank you for the offer."

"You're welcome," she said, her tone overly bright. "And though you haven't asked, I'll manage. Don't worry about me. At all."

Pulling up in front of the cabin, she slammed the Jeep into Park, jumped out and tore off inside without looking back.

SITTING IN THE passenger seat of Kenzie's Jeep, Brett made no move to follow her. What a freaking mess. He had no idea what to do about the strange, ominous turn events had suddenly taken. While he'd known a gossipy woman like Jane Norman would be trouble, he hadn't expected things to escalate this far.

Enough was enough.

Until now, he'd done a lot of hiding and trying to stay behind the scenes. And, until his memory had returned, he'd had good reason. But that ended now. Time to put an end to the shit show.

He had several options. One, he could seek out the FBI, demand they put him back in WITSEC and do a better job of keeping him safe until the trial. On the surface, that choice made the most sense, but he'd grown weary of hiding.

His second choice, which might work if life were a video game or action-adventure movie, would be to take matters into his own hands and go hunt down the gang members who wanted to eliminate him. But Brett was a chef, not a commando, and he suspected if he tried something like that, all he'd end up doing would be getting himself killed.

Despite his in-the-moment words of a few minutes ago, there was no way he'd be abandoning Kenzie either. While the focus of the gang might be entirely on him, this Annette person seemed determined to bring Kenzie down, no matter what she had to do in order to accomplish that.

Slowly, he got out of the Jeep and headed toward the cabin. The downpour had become a mist, though judging from the gathering storm clouds, a second round was on the way.

He burst inside, unsurprised to see Kenzie had shut herself away in her bedroom. He couldn't blame her.

"I'm an idiot," he said. "Kenzie, please let me in. I need your help."

To his relief, she let him in. Expression wary, she stepped out into the living area. Crossing her arms, she leaned against the doorway to the kitchen, watching him and waiting.

"My being here puts you at risk," he said.

"Annette put us both at risk," she countered. "And yes, Jane too. I might have been wrong, asking you to help me at the clinic, but I honestly didn't think it would go this far. For that, I apologize." Eyes huge in her too-pale face, she appeared both vulnerable and determined, all at once.

Damn, he loved this woman. "Don't take this on yourself," he told her. "The reason or the how doesn't really matter. Neither of us is safe here. You need to leave with me."

She stared at him as if he'd suddenly sprouted two heads. "I can't go anywhere. I have a job, a medical practice. People are counting on me."

He swore under his breath. "You won't be a whole lot of help to them if you end up getting yourself killed."

Chin lifted, she glared at him. "I'm staying put. I don't have a choice."

"There has to be a compromise," he said, thinking out loud.

"Or a solution." Her slow smile told him she might have come up with one. "Let me call Jane again and ask her and Greg if they'll meet with us. I'd like to wait until we're all four together before I discuss my idea."

She made a quick phone call, outlining what she wanted, and then ended the call. "They're in. Let's head over there and see if we can work something out."

Though curious, he decided not to ask. Kenzie had made it clear she wanted this to be an open discussion. While he couldn't say he actually *liked* Jane, especially after what she'd done, he didn't know her well enough to dislike her. He'd simply wait and see.

The rain still held off, making the short drive into town uneventful. Fifteen minutes later, they pulled up in front of a yellow two-story Victorian-style house. A large sign in front read City Hall.

"Here we are," Kenzie said, her bright, cheery voice at odds with her worried expression. "Let's do this." She climbed out of her Jeep and bounded up the sidewalk, only to have to turn and wait as he made his way more slowly.

Once he'd reached her, she rang the doorbell. Immediately, the door opened. "Kenzie!" Jane exclaimed, pulling her in for a quick hug.

Brett noticed that Kenzie appeared to be merely enduring this, offering a quick embrace of her own before stepping back. "Come in, come in." Jane's gaze swept over him as she stepped back, ushering them both inside. A large man who only needed a red suit to play an authentic Santa Claus stepped forward, enveloping Kenzie in another hug before turning to face Brett and holding out his hand.

"Greg Norman," he boomed as they shook. "Do you recognize me?"

Brett grinned. "I do now."

"Sit, sit." Jane indicated chairs around a large dining table. "Can I get you two anything to drink?"

"No, thank you," Kenzie politely declined. She pulled out a chair and sat. Choosing one next to her, Brett did the same, as did Greg.

Jane remained standing. "I'm so glad you decided to come over so we can clear this up," she began. "First, let me tell you—"

"Jane," Greg warned, interrupting her. "Please take a seat and let Kenzie have her say."

Swallowing, Jane pulled out a chair, reluctance clear in every move she made. She sat, crossed and uncrossed her arms, and then jumped back up to get a glass of water.

Kenzie waited until Jane had once again gotten settled. "I came over here because we have a situation and we're going to need some help," she said.

"We?" Jane asked, looking from Kenzie to Brett and back again. Inwardly, Brett bristled, but he held himself still in order to give Kenzie the opportunity to say her piece.

"Yes, we. Brett and I." Kenzie exhaled. "You know the situation, but what you don't know is Brett doesn't trust the FBI to keep him safe. They've already failed at that once. He's considered taking off and hiding on his own, but he doesn't want to leave me here unprotected."

Greg nodded. "We can protect you, if that's what you're asking," he said.

"Thank you for that." Kenzie smiled, a toned-down version of the smile Brett had come to love. "However, I don't want Brett to go either." She nudged him playfully. "I've kind of gotten used to having him around."

Jane frowned.

"Maybe it's my cooking," Brett interjected, trying to lighten the mood. Only Greg laughed. Both Kenzie and Jane simply stared at each other.

"What is it you want to do?" Jane finally asked, apparently giving in.

"I want to call a town meeting," Kenzie announced, looking from Jane, to Greg and finally to Brett. "We are going to need everyone's help. It's going to take a village, as the saying goes. They might not know me all that well yet, but I'm now a part of Blake, and will be for the next two years."

Greg nodded and after a moment Jane did too, though her expression seemed to indicate she wasn't convinced.

"How quickly can we get this done?" Kenzie pressed. "I'd like to have everyone on board before the FBI arrives in town."

Jane shook her head. "That might not be possible. The FBI seemed very excited to learn Brett was alive and here in Blake. I got the impression they were sending agents immediately."

"Make it happen." Kenzie voiced her demand quietly. "You helped cause this mess, Jane. You need to help resolve it."

Since her logic was not arguable, Jane pressed her lips together. "Fine. Let me make a few phone calls and see if I can get something set up for tomorrow."

"Make it tonight." Kenzie's firm insistence made Brett proud. "I need to find out exactly where we stand as quickly as possible."

Once she'd secured a nod from Jane, Kenzie pushed to her feet. "Thank you both," she said. "Call me as soon as you have details."

"I will." Now that she had a task, Jane seemed animated. After lifting her hand in a quick wave, she'd already taken out her phone and appeared to be sending text messages.

Greg walked them to the door. "I want to apologize for Jane," he said, once they were out on the large front porch. "She has a good heart, but she doesn't always think things through."

Kenzie nodded. "Can I count on your help tonight at the meeting?"

"Of course, you can. I'll do whatever you need me to do to help." Greg hugged her once more before turning to Brett. "Nice to spend time with you," he said. "I'm looking forward to getting to know you."

Shaking hands, Brett smiled. "Same."

Greg stood on the porch and watched until they got back into the Jeep. Only when Kenzie started the engine and backed away, did he turn and go inside.

"What's your plan?" Brett asked. "I gathered that you plan to ask the entire town to help out, but how, exactly?"

"I'm not sure," she admitted, surprising him. "But this thing with Annette got me thinking. She tried to divide the town, to turn everyone against me. If she could convince enough people that I'm some kind of monster, patients would be hesitant to come into the clinic. The village's basic medical needs wouldn't be met. If that happened, she could make a case stating I was in violation of my contract."

He stared. "Do you really think Annette did that much long-term planning? It seemed more to me like petty revenge against someone she dislikes."

Kenzie shrugged. "Again, I don't know. What I do know is that I need the people of Blake to support me, to support us. You're an Alaskan native and what happened to you shouldn't have ever occurred. I have to believe if everyone closes ranks around the two of us, they should be able to keep us safe."

"I like that idea," he said, considering. "Assuming you got enough people to agree to help, it might even work."

Her smile lit up her face. "Thanks. Even if Annette does have some supporters, I'm thinking if I simply tell the truth, I might persuade them to think differently."

Maybe she had more faith in humankind than he did, but he believed her. "I'll do whatever you need me to do to help," he said.

Though she kept her attention on the road, she reached over and lightly squeezed his arm. "Thanks. I hope you don't mind getting up in front of everyone and telling your story. They need to hear it directly from you, especially since we're going to ask for their help protecting you."

He nodded. "Makes sense. But Jane's already contacted the FBI. You know they likely already have a couple of agents on the way to retrieve me."

Navigating the twists and turns of the road like a pro, she didn't immediately respond. "We need to brainstorm about that. There's got to be a way we can make that work for us."

They'd just parked in front of the cabin when Kenzie's cell phone rang. "It's Jane," she said, answering and putting the call on speaker.

"Okay, we're on for six tonight," Jane said. "At Mikki's, just like the last meeting."

"Perfect! We'll see you there." Kenzie thanked her and ended the call. She turned and high-fived Brett. "That gives us a little time to prepare."

Inside the cabin, they spent the next hour going over any potential questions and the best way to answer them. Brett couldn't help but admire Kenzie's thoroughness. Once she'd set her mind to something, she did everything possible to make sure she succeeded.

He found her focused and determined self sexy as hell. In fact, watching her pace the living room in front of him, he ached to reach out and pull her onto his lap, and show her how much she turned him on.

Except he didn't want to mess with her frame of mind, so he decided he'd just wait until after the village meeting had ended and then once they'd returned home, he'd take his time making love to her so she had no doubt how she affected him.

"Are you ready to go?" she asked, making him realize she'd likely already posed that question at least once.

"Sorry, I was thinking," he said. "But yes. I'm ready. Let's do this."

Grinning, she grabbed him and pulled him over for a quick kiss, releasing him almost immediately. "Come on!" She grabbed his hand, pulling him with her toward the door.

Her jubilant mood felt infectious and he couldn't help but smile as they climbed into her Jeep. She made him believe anything might be possible, even this, when he still had some serious doubts. If anyone could rally the townspeople, Dr. Kenzie Taylor could.

As she drove, she kept up a steady stream of chatter, which let him know she was nervous, even though she tried to hide it. To distract her, he asked her if she wanted to eat at Mikki's when the meeting was over.

"Sure." Glancing at him, she grinned. "I've been trying to get you to do that with me for a while now."

"I know." He smiled back. "But since I'm about to make my presence known to the entire town in a few minutes, I don't have any more reason not to."

"That's true," she agreed, navigating a turn with ease. Just as she came out onto the straight patch, a pickup truck came racing from the opposite direction, on the wrong side of the road.

Brett barely had time to shout a warning. Kenzie turned the steering wheel hard to the left, hoping to pass the other vehicle in the left-hand lane.

But when the vehicle swerved again to head directly toward her, she overcorrected, sending her Jeep off the edge of the mountain.

The last thing Brett heard was Kenzie scream.

Chapter Thirteen

The other vehicle clipped them on the front passenger side, sending them spinning. Kenzie gripped the steering wheel hard and struggled to maintain control of her Jeep. But there wasn't anything she could do to stop them from rolling over, a sickening half turn on the side, stopped only by the trunk and lower branches of a large evergreen tree.

The airbags deployed, too late, she thought, though they were forceful and pushed her back so hard it felt like one massive shove by a giant hand.

Her seat belt harness kept her in her seat, though her head slammed into the side window, hard enough to make her see stars.

Damn, it hurt. She felt like her skull had cracked open. And Brett—what had happened to Brett? She struggled to turn her head to look, but she couldn't seem to make her body obey. She couldn't see anyway since a film of red completely obscured her vision.

Blood, she realized. There was so much blood. But she knew head wounds tended to bleed a lot, so she tried to twist and grab a towel from her back seat. This feat too proved beyond her. Belatedly, she realized she needed to unclip her seat belt, but her fumbling fingers couldn't seem to make it work.

"Kenzie?"

From what seemed a great distance, she could hear Brett calling her name. She swiped her hand across her eyes, trying to clear her vision enough to look for him. His worried face loomed close. He looked as terrible as she felt, all bruised and battered and bloody. One of his eyes had swollen shut.

"Kenzie, we need to get out of here in case they come back and try to finish the job," he rasped.

Which meant he didn't think this had been an accident.

Feeling weak and dizzy, no doubt from the loss of blood, she swore, trying not to break down in tears. "Damn it. I can't get the seat belt clip to release. Can you help me?"

"Hold on." Reaching around her, he fumbled a bit, but managed to free her, careful to catch her before she fell.

"There's a couple of towels in the back seat," she told him. "I need something to stop this bleeding, or I'm going to pass out."

"Let's get out of this car," he urged, handing her a towel. "Right now, we need to get away from this vehicle."

"Okay." She tried but couldn't manage to open the door. "It's stuck."

"This way." Lifting and tugging her, he helped her across the console and out the passenger side door, coming out on top of the vehicle.

"Careful," he said, steadying her. "We'll need to climb down."

Somehow, they made it to the ground. Her legs gave out the instant her feet touched the earth. She wiped her face with the towel and then pressed it hard against her head, hoping to stem the bleeding.

"Kenzie?" Brett's face loomed close in her limited vision. "We need to get you some medical help?"

This made her laugh, even though it hurt. "I *am* the medical help around here. I'll be fine. We've got a meeting to get to."

"There's no way—" Brett began.

"Give me your phone," Kenzie ordered, holding out her hand. "I need to call Jane and yours works better than mine for whatever reason."

He handed her his phone. Accepting it, she took several deep breaths, willing her strength and equilibrium to return. Meanwhile, Brett kept glancing back up toward the road, as if he expected the person who'd hit them to make an appearance.

Which wouldn't be good.

"Let's move a little ways away," she suggested, pointing. "Maybe behind those boulders, just in case someone comes looking, wanting to finish the job."

Relief flashed across his handsome face. "I agree. Come on, let me help you."

Though she took his arm to help her up, once she was standing, she shook him off. "I'm feeling better," she declared, taking an unsteady step toward the rocky outcropping. Once they'd moved around behind it, she eyed Brett and then used his phone to call Jane.

Jane answered on the first ring. "Where *are* you?"

she hissed, keeping her voice low. "You're thirty minutes late. People are beginning to get restless."

"Someone tried to run us off the road," Kenzie explained, her voice catching. "The Jeep is on its side."

"Oh, my goodness! Are you all right?"

"I think so." Kenzie exhaled. "Nothing broken as far as I can tell. We're both pretty banged up and bloody. And I'm not sure the Jeep is drivable. I need you to come get us."

"What?" Jane gasped. "I'll come, but surely you're not considering going forward with the meeting after all that? We can reschedule."

"No." Kenzie ground out the word. "That's what whoever hit us wants. We're attending that meeting come hell or high water. Can you please either come get us or send someone to pick us up? And let everyone know we're on our way."

"Where are you?" Jane asked. Once Kenzie gave their location, Jane told them to sit tight and she'd be on the way.

"Will you be all right here?" Brett asked. "I'd like to go up to the road and watch for her."

"Go." She waved him away. "Just be careful. Whoever ran into us is still out there."

"I know." Expression grim, he exhaled. "Stay hidden. I'll be back as soon as Jane arrives."

Kenzie tried to nod, but the movement made her head hurt, so she settled for a quick smile.

It didn't seem like any time had passed at all before she heard voices. She got to her knees and, holding on to one of the boulders, peeked around the edge. Sure enough, Brett and Jane were heading down the slope toward her.

"Whoa." Jane recoiled when she caught sight of Kenzie. "I thought Brett looked bad, but you…"

"I'll survive." Kenzie pushed to her feet. "Once I get cleaned up and can take a look at my head wound, I'll be fine."

"Do you want to do that first, before we go the meeting?" Jane asked, her expression hopeful.

"No. I want people to see me the way I am right now. They need to understand what I'm up against with Annette."

Jane looked from Kenzie to Brett and back again. "Do you think Annette was behind this accident?" she asked. "Because that would be a new low, even for her."

"I don't know," Kenzie admitted. "But I can say if it had been someone looking to hurt Brett, they would have come down and made sure to finish the job."

"She's right," Brett agreed, taking her arm to help her navigate up the hill. "So it either was a horrible hit-and-run accident, or someone intended to hurt us."

"What kind of vehicle was it?" Jane asked.

"A white pickup," Kenzie answered. "Unfortunately, it all happened so fast that I didn't get a good look at the driver."

They reached Jane's SUV. Once she'd unlocked the doors, Kenzie took the front passenger side and Brett got in the back.

"I called Joey Bartko," Jane announced, once they were both inside her Explorer. "He's got a tow truck and can get your Jeep out and take it back to his garage for repairs."

"Thank you." Kenzie leaned back in the front passenger seat and closed her eyes. "My head hurts like a mother."

Brett leaned forward from the back and lightly touched her shoulder. "Are you sure you're up for this? People will understand if you need to postpone the meeting."

"We're going." She turned and looked at him, his broken, battered face so dear to her. "I have a point I want to make, and as horrible as this accident was, it helps to make them understand."

As they turned onto Main Street, Jane made a phone call. "Greg, it's me. I've got them. We're about to park, so will you please let everyone know the meeting is about to begin?"

Greg must have answered in the affirmative, because Jane ended the call. She turned into the full parking lot and took an empty spot marked with a sign that read Mayor Only. "One of the perks of your husband holding public office," she quipped.

Kenzie opened her door and stepped outside. Still slightly dizzy, when Brett offered his arm, she took it. "Thanks," she murmured. She wanted to conserve all her strength so she could make an entrance.

Jane opened the front door, motioning for Kenzie and Blake to go ahead of her. Judging from the noise level, the place was packed. Good. The more, the merrier.

Still holding onto Brett with a death grip, Kenzie straightened her spine, inhaled and released him. Head held high, well aware of how terrible she looked, she strode into Mikki's. Behind her, Brett struggled to keep up. One side of his face was pretty banged up and he'd have one hell of a shiner in a few hours, but both of them bore visual testament as to what had just happened to them.

As they made their way to the small platform in the front of the room, several people gasped loudly. Gradually, as heads turned, the room went silent.

Kenzie and Brett finally reached the platform. A small table and two chairs had been set up for them, along with a microphone. Once upon a time, Kenzie had been terrified of public speaking, but the fear had left her halfway through her residency.

Now, as she looked out over the crowded room, filled with residents of Blake—her town, her village—she felt better. Stronger. And centered. That these people had shown up for her meant the world. She spotted a uniformed police officer in the back of the room, flanked by two other men in dark windbreakers who were most likely with the FBI. She wasn't sure if the FBI agents were there to help or something else.

"On the way here, someone tried to run us off the road," Kenzie began. "They came at me on the wrong side of the road. When I took evasive action to avoid them, I rolled my Jeep. This—" she gestured at herself and at Brett "—is the result. We're lucky we weren't hurt worse."

Several in the crowd started talking, mostly among themselves, though someone called out a question to Kenzie. "Did you see who did it?"

"A white pickup," Kenzie answered. "I didn't get a good look at the driver. Either it was a terrible accident, made worse because the other vehicle didn't stop, or it was intentional and meant to scare me."

Now more people began to talk amongst themselves.

Some of the voices sounded angry. Kenzie waited a moment, then cleared her throat, asking for their attention once again.

"I asked for this gathering because I need your help," she said. "*We* need your help. By now, I'm certain some of you have heard awful things about me. Some of you also may have been filled in about my friend Brett here, and what happened to him."

She talked about Brett's situation first, making sure to mention he was an Alaskan native, just like most of them. She told them about the FBI, the failed attempt to keep him safe and the attack by the gang member that had resulted in the car going off the bridge into the river. She could see the stunned reactions of many of the townspeople, and she also noticed how the law enforcement officers straightened, listening with rapt attention.

"Next, a little background on me," she continued. "Some of you met me at the open house at the medical clinic, but if you didn't, let me tell you about my education and what I bring to Blake to take care of you all."

After she'd finished a short listing of her qualifications, she went into a brief summary of what she hoped to accomplish in Blake, the relationships she hoped to build and the care she intended to provide.

Then, she took a deep breath and asked if there were any questions.

Immediately, a large man in a baseball cap stood up. "Why'd you fire Annette Gladley?" he demanded. "She's been our nurse for over twenty years. We like her and trust her."

Now came the tricky part. All she had to go with was the truth. "I didn't fire her," she responded quietly.

"Annette quit. She wasn't a fan of some of the changes I intended to make, so she left."

Instead of accepting her answer and taking a seat again, the man shook his head. "That's not what she said. She's been telling us the truth about you. You can't come in here from the lower forty-eight, all fancy and trying to change things up. We won't stand for it."

Kenzie nodded. "What is it you do for a living, Mr...?"

"Morrison," he said. "And I make furniture and other things out of wood. Been doing that for thirty years now."

"I see. And how would you feel if I came into your shop and proceeded to tell you how to run your business?"

"It's not the same," he started to protest.

She cut him off. "It's exactly the same. I'm a doctor. I went to school for a long time to become one. The medical clinic is my business. If an employee wants to disagree with me privately, well that's their right. But to attack me over it and refuse flat out to even work with me, that's another thing entirely."

"So you *did* fire her," the man crowed. "I knew it."

"I did not," Kenzie snapped back. Returning her attention to the rest of the crowd, she continued, "Some of you might already be aware of this, but Annette sent two men to my cabin to attack me. They've been arrested and I'm pressing charges. Apparently, one was her relative visiting from Anchorage and I guess the other was his friend. She sent them to scare me. How messed up is that?"

Again, the room erupted, everyone talking at once. Jane got up and joined Kenzie at the front of the room, stepping in front of the microphone. "And there's more. Law enforcement has made several attempts to talk to Annette, but it seems she's disappeared. However, we have learned she owns an older model white Ford pickup, the same type of vehicle that just tried to run Kenzie and Blake off the road."

Now the noise level became deafening. Everyone began talking at once and some people shouted to be heard over the others. Kenzie sat down and Brett took her hand. They both watched, bemused. Jane shook her head, said a few choice curse words away from the microphone and marched back to her seat.

The uniformed police officer and the two men wearing the FBI blazers began moving toward them. Next to her, Brett tensed.

The FBI agents reached them first. "Brett Denyon? We'd like a word with you." They glanced at Kenzie. "Privately, if you don't mind."

"I do mind," Brett began.

Kenzie squeezed his hand. "It's okay. You go and talk to them, and I can fill this police officer in on the accident."

BRETT DIDN'T LIKE leaving Kenzie alone, not even for one second, but he went ahead and followed the two FBI agents outside. He already had a pretty good idea of what they'd say, and turned out he wasn't wrong.

The first one, an older man who called himself Mc-Murphy, launched into a reprimand, interspersed with demands. He wanted to know why Brett hadn't made contact, what on earth was he thinking, to disappear for so long, didn't he understand they had a big trial coming up, and that he was their star eyewitness? Their legal team hadn't been sure if the trial would be able to go forward, and the word on the street was that the gang had already claimed victory.

Brett let the agent rant and rave, nodding occasionally and catching the eye of the younger agent, who gave what appeared to be a sympathetic half smile.

Finally, McMurphy wound down. Arms crossed, he glared at Brett. "Well? What do you have to say for yourself?"

"Just one thing," Brett replied. "Maybe two. You guys did a lousy job protecting me. Actually, it was so bad it felt like you set me up on a ledge with a bull's-eye on my chest." He took a deep breath, glaring back at the senior agent. "Where the hell do you get off telling me I should have followed your protocol? I have a sneaking suspicion if I had, I'd be long dead by now."

"The only reason they found you was because you didn't go directly to the safe house," McMurphy argued. "We had people waiting to escort you there, but you never showed."

He hadn't showed for a reason. He'd had a bad feeling all along, and he'd made a snap judgment to take a different path. He could have explained this, but Brett suspected someone like McMurphy put no stock in gut instincts. "I decided against it," he said, crossing his arms and daring the other man to argue. "But in the end, it didn't matter. Someone intercepted me before I could get anywhere. Even if I'd been heading to meet up with your team, they would have grabbed me before I made it to the rendezvous destination."

Now both McMurphy and the younger agent

frowned. "That's not possible." McMurphy's voice sounded flat. "No one but our agents knew your location."

"Boom. That likely means you have a mole," Brett pointed out. "Another reason why I'm none too happy Jane notified you of my whereabouts. I've done a great job keeping myself safe so far, and now it's looking like that will no longer be possible."

Somehow, he'd managed to effectively silence McMurphy. However, the younger agent stepped forward, apparently willing to take up where his partner had left off. "We don't have a mole," he said, his condescending tone setting Brett's nerves on edge. "Stuff like that only happens on TV and movies."

Brett decided he'd had enough. "Agree to disagree. Anyway, what do you two want? If you needed to chew me out, consider it done. Unless you have something else you want to say, I should be getting back inside."

McMurphy rolled his eyes. "You're not going anywhere. We are taking you into protective custody right here and right now."

"You can't take me anywhere against my will," Brett pointed out. "While I did agree to testify for you, unless you plan to arrest me for something, you have no choice but to let me go."

"Is there a problem?" A voice asked from behind them.

Brett turned to see Greg and the uniformed police officer. Greg appeared stern, in full-on mayor mode, while the state trooper seemed perplexed. The sight of them made Brett want to laugh, though he managed to hold it in.

Head held high, he walked over to join them, ignoring the two FBI agents. "No problem," he said. "No problem at all. Come on, let's go back inside."

Part of him half expected the FBI agents to attempt to detain him. They did not. Instead, he walked back into Mikki's, feeling both apprehensive and relieved.

"There you are!" Kenzie exclaimed, pushing a wayward lock of tangled hair away from her battered face. Someone had given her a damp bar towel and she'd made a valiant attempt to clean off some of the blood but had ended up with streaks.

He took the towel from her and gently swabbed at some of the worst spots. Though she winced a couple of times, she closed her eyes and, with her face upturned, she stood absolutely still until he'd finished.

"There," he said, resisting the urge to kiss her. "That's the best I can do for now. How are you feeling?"

"I'd like to go home and lie down," she admitted. "But first, I need to address everyone one last time."

"What are you going to say to them next?"

"They've had time to think about everything I said earlier. Now I want to ask them to make a decision."

Frowning, Jane rushed over and took Brett's arm, though she looked directly at Kenzie. "Those two FBI agents are back," she said. "They don't look very happy either."

"They're not." Brett shook his head. "They were trying to strong arm me into going with them. Unfortunately, short of kidnapping me, there's not a whole lot they can do. Come on, Kenzie." He took her arm. "Let's see if we can rally this place around us."

Her brilliant smile took his breath away. She brushed

away her long matted hair with one swollen hand. Though bruised and battered, she kept her head up and shoulders back. He thought she was the most beautiful woman he'd ever seen.

Together, they made their way to the microphone.

"Everyone?" she said, then waited for the hum of conversation to die down. "I've given you time to talk about and consider what I told you. Now I need you to come to a decision. Do we have your help? Will you guard our backs?"

Sound rose again as people started talking among themselves. Jane joined Kenzie and Brett, tapping the microphone for attention. "Everyone!" she said. "Kenzie asked a valid question. Now, we are going to put this to a vote. Everyone who feels they want to protect our new doctor and her friend Brett, please go to the right side of the room. Those of you who wish to opt out, you can either stay seated, or you're welcome to leave." She turned to Kenzie, making no move to lower her tone. "This way, you can see who is on your side. And when they come to you needing help, you'll likely remember them."

Kenzie winced and glanced at Brett, clearly finding Jane's method a bit harsh. He shrugged, trying to decide if Jane was brilliant or way off base.

One by one, people got to their feet and moved over to the right side of the room. By the time everyone had reassembled, only a few remained seated where they'd been before. All of them were men.

"Joshua Caldwell," Jane scolded, singling out a young heavily bearded man. "I know your mother raised you better than that."

"Annette's my friend," he defended, crossing his arms. "And I don't believe she actually did any of those things."

"Oh, I do," another man piped up. He wore a cowboy hat and aviator sunglasses, even though they were inside. "I dated her for a while. That woman is intense. The only reason I didn't join your group of supporters is because I'm leaving town in the morning. I'm on my way to California." He shrugged, then pushed to his feet and left the room.

Kenzie tugged on Brett's arm. "I know I need to do something, but my brain is so foggy I can't think," she whispered.

"Let Jane handle it," he advised. "It looks like she already is anyway."

Clipboard in hand, Jane had begun to move among the assembled crowd. She appeared to be taking names down and assigning various people jobs. Watching her, he couldn't help but be impressed.

Kenzie sagged against him, clearly losing her battle to stay upright. He put his arm under hers, propping her up and hoping Jane would finish up soon, so he and Kenzie could get home.

Greg wandered over, taking in the situation with a glance. "She shouldn't be much longer," he advised. "Why don't you two sit down and take a load off. Jane's setting up committees and neighborhood watch groups and all of that. She's making sure no one will be able to get to you two without a fight." He smiled proudly. "Blake takes care of its own."

"I appreciate that," Kenzie replied with a tired smile.

Brett helped her get to one of the chairs, easing her into it slowly before taking a seat himself.

After a few minutes, Jane hustled over, clipboard in hand. Looking extraordinarily pleased with herself, she took one look at Kenzie and shook her head. "We need to get you home," she said. "You look like you're about to collapse at any moment."

"I feel like that too," Kenzie responded, her tired smile making Brett's heart hurt.

"Come on," he said, pushing to his feet and helping her up. "Let's get you home." He glanced at Jane, who'd gone back to intently studying her paperwork. "Is there any way you can take us? We're without a vehicle right now."

"Of course." Jane's attention snapped to them. "Greg, are you about ready to go? If not, and you want to hang out here, I can swing back once I get these two home."

Greg nodded. "I'll stay and have a beer. There's a few more things I want to get straightened out, since I'm mayor and all." He glanced at the two FBI agents, still watching them from one side of the room. "Let me go and distract those two, and you guys make your getaway. Give me just a moment."

They all watched as Greg strode up to the men, engaging them in conversation.

"Come on," Jane said. "We're not using the front door. We'll go out through the kitchen. You two head for the sign that says Restrooms, but after you get down that hallway, go straight through the double doors into the kitchen. I'll be along right after you. Here." She pressed a key fob into Brett's hand. "Get inside and I'll join you in a minute."

Brett thanked her. Supporting Kenzie with one arm, he helped her limp down the long hallway toward the restroom sign.

Chapter Fourteen

Jane's plan appeared to have worked perfectly. Jane strolled out the side door and across the parking lot, sliding into the driver's seat a few minutes after Kenzie and Brett, and started the engine. "Get down and stay down," she commanded. "Just in case those agents figure it out and come looking for you."

But no one did. Once they'd turned off Main Street, Jane motioned at them to sit up. "Wow," she said. "Imagine those two thinking they could protect you and they couldn't even figure it out when you snuck away. Ridiculous."

"Exactly," Brett agreed. "It's almost like they have a vested interest in *not* protecting me."

Kenzie half listened to the conversation with her eyes closed. The physical effects of the accident now made themselves known, full force. She wasn't the kind of woman who cried easily or often, but she found herself wiping away tears as they leaked from her eyes.

By the time they neared the cabin, she felt as if she'd been bludgeoned by a sledgehammer. Everything hurt, from her head down to her toes. Her body throbbed, ached and she knew she needed to take a strong anti-inflammatory and get some rest. Assuming she didn't actually have a concussion, that is. Right now, exhaustion combined with pain made her feel as if she were melting, as if she could collapse into a boneless puddle if she even so much as relaxed her spine. The thought of trying to do any kind of self-diagnosis felt like too daunting of a task.

While Jane drove, keeping up what had now become a one-sided conversation with Brett, Kenzie knew she should ask about her Jeep, but she couldn't summon enough strength for that either. She'd deal with that tomorrow. All she wanted to do right now was to take a hot shower and then collapse in her bed and sleep. She really hoped she didn't have a concussion, but since there was no way she intended to ask Brett to make sure she got up every hour, it was a risk she'd have to take.

She glanced at Brett. Earlier, he'd seemed to be holding up much better than she, but now, lying back against the seat with his eyes closed, he appeared to be feeling just as badly.

Pulling up to the cabin, Jane parked and got out. She offered to walk them inside, but Kenzie declined. "Brett and I will lean on each other," she said, with a faint smile. "Thank you so much for all your help today. I'll touch base with you tomorrow."

To her credit, Jane didn't argue. She simply nodded, waiting beside her vehicle and watching until Kenzie and Brett made it inside.

"Home," Kenzie breathed, sagging with relief. "I hope you don't mind if I take the first shower."

"Not at all," he replied, dragging a bloodstained hand

across his face. Exhaling sharply, he sat gingerly on the couch. "I'll just wait here until you're finished."

She entered the bathroom. When she caught sight of her reflection in the mirror, she winced. No wonder everyone had been so horrified at her appearance. She'd thought Brett looked bad, but she had him beat.

Gingerly removing her ruined clothes, she stepped into the shower and turned the water on hot. Watching as rust-colored water swirled down the drain, she washed her hair first and then gently used soap to clean her battered body. The hot water helped ease some of the aches and pains, but she knew she would hurt for a few days. At least nothing appeared to be broken. She'd count that as a blessing.

Feeling slightly better, she dried off and wrapped her hair and herself up in towels. "Your turn," she called to Brett. "Believe me, the shower really helps."

When he didn't respond, she went into the living room and found him still on the sofa, fast asleep sitting up. She decided not to wake him, figuring he'd shower once he got the rest he clearly needed.

She poured herself a large glass of water and went back to her room. After combing out her hair, she braided it and put on a soft oversize T-shirt before slipping under her sheets and closing her eyes.

She must have fallen asleep almost instantly because the next thing she knew, she opened her eyes to see sunlight streaming in through her bedroom window.

She smelled two of her favorite morning things—bacon and coffee—and made her way stiffly to the kitchen to find a freshly showered Brett sitting at the table, drinking a cup of coffee, a heaping plate of bacon in front of him.

As she slowly entered the room, he looked up and smiled. The warmth in his blue eyes took her breath away.

"Comfort food," he said, indicating the bacon. "I can fry some eggs up too, if you want them. And toast. Whatever you need."

"Coffee and bacon," she said. "And ibuprofen. I don't know about you, but I'm still stiff and sore this morning."

"Me too, but better than yesterday." He shook his head. "I'd planned to make huevos rancheros this morning, but it was too much effort. So a simple breakfast is what we're having."

"Sounds perfect." The first sip of coffee tasted even more like ambrosia than normal. "I need to find out about my Jeep," she said. "Depending on how badly damaged it is, I might have to borrow or rent a car until it can be repaired."

He nodded. "I'm sure Jane will be calling you. She's probably just barely restraining herself because she knows you need to get some sleep."

His comment made her laugh, which hurt. She checked her watch. "I need to get in to the clinic," she said. "But I have no way to get there."

"After what happened, I'm sure everyone will understand if it's closed for a day," he said.

"True." She took another sip of coffee and grabbed a slice of bacon. He'd cooked it exactly the way she preferred, crispy. "And if there's an emergency, everyone is aware that Jane knows how to get ahold of me."

"I think we both need to take it easy today and let our bodies heal," he continued. "We can sit on the front porch and watch nature, maybe do some reading or napping. Whatever we want."

"As sore as I am, that sounds like heaven," she agreed.

Once they'd demolished all the bacon, they each made another cup of coffee and carried them out to the front porch.

"This is perfect," she said, sighing. "I have to say, I'm loving this weather. Back in Houston, it would be so hot and humid that you wouldn't be able to sit outside for very long."

"We'll revisit that sentiment come January," he told her, smiling. "By then it will definitely be too cold and snowy to sit outside like this."

January. Five months away. She liked the way he casually let her know he planned on sticking around that long.

They sat outside, enjoying the weather and each other's company, long after they'd finished their coffees.

JUDGING BY THE number of vehicles that drove by—not just down the road, but up into the driveway, parking and taking a good look at the cabin before turning around—Jane had been successful in organizing her neighborhood watch, or whatever she was calling it. They'd jokingly started counting after the second one, and after an hour there'd been three.

Shifting slightly in her chair, Kenzie shook her head. "That's the third one," she told Brett. "We don't usually get that much traffic all day. I have to admit, it feels kind of weird." She didn't tell him she couldn't help but feel nervous. As each vehicle appeared, she found herself tensing, wondering if they were friend or foe.

"I agree," he said, surprising her. "I keep wondering if the next one will be full of gang members."

"Me too!" She looked down at her half-empty cup. "Do you want to go inside?"

"Not really. Unless you do."

She sighed. "It's beautiful out here."

Another SUV came tooling up the drive. Spotting them, the driver and passenger waved as they turned around.

"I just wish all that would stop," she said. "Honestly."

"It's rough, but Jane's trying her best to keep us safe. It's only the first day. It'll probably slow down once the newness of the idea wears off. Jane means well. I honestly think she has our best interests in mind."

"I know. She might be pushy, but she has a good heart." Kenzie stretched, wincing slightly as her injuries from the previous day made themselves known. "If Jane doesn't call soon, I'm going to touch base with her. I'll need to file a claim with my insurance company before we can start on repairs."

"For now, you need to rest," Brett insisted. "I know you're a doctor and all that, but if we'd been in Anchorage, I would have driven you straight to the emergency room myself."

Since she really couldn't argue with his logic—she'd been a bit shocked when she'd gotten her first look at herself in the mirror—she simply nodded and changed the subject. "I wish they'd locate and arrest Annette. That way there'd be one less thing to worry about."

He snorted. "True. And when the gang members

show back up in town—and they *will*—I hope law enforcement is prepared. Because if they're not, things could get extremely messy around here."

Messy. She supposed that was a euphemism for bloody. From what she'd read about this gang, they tended to shoot first and ask questions later. She'd hate for any of the townspeople to get injured. Especially since Blake didn't have a full-time police force.

We protect our own, Jane had said. Kenzie sure hoped the older woman was right. After what she'd seen of the two incompetent FBI agents, she had to acknowledge she'd rather take her chances with the townsfolk.

"Speaking of law enforcement, have you heard anything from the FBI agents?" she asked, just in case they'd managed to track Brett down.

"Nope. They don't have my phone number and Jane said she didn't give them your address, so they don't have any idea where I'm staying. Right now, I imagine they're spinning their wheels, looking for me."

"That makes me wonder if they really represent the FBI. Because if they do, those two agents were certainly incompetent," she mused. "I think you should contact someone higher up and let them know you still plan to testify, but you won't be relying on them to keep you safe. You've got an entire town behind you now."

The fierceness in her voice made him smile. "I just might do that," he said. "In fact, I like that idea. It's all begun to feel a little ridiculous."

Yet another vehicle turned into her drive. Spotting it, she tensed. "I think we need to talk to Jane. I know she means well, but they need to back off on the patrols. Every ten minutes is too much. Not only do we lose all hope of having any privacy, but the townspeople are going to get burned out."

Grabbing his phone, he gave Jane a call. Kenzie listened when he explained the need to tone down the constant surveillance. "We appreciate everyone's concern," he said. "But after the day we had yesterday, we both need a little peace and quiet."

Jane must have said she understood because Brett was smiling when he hung up. "Consider it done," he said.

"Jane wasn't upset, was she?" she asked, worrying slightly.

"No," he replied. "She said she understood completely."

Despite him speaking to Jane, it must have taken a little while for the news to filter down to the self-designated neighborhood patrol. Vehicles continued to arrive like clockwork, every thirty minutes or so. Judging by the enthusiastic waves most of the drivers gave as they turned around in front of the cabin, everyone appeared to be enjoying themselves tremendously.

"It's almost like they're having a single vehicle parade every time," she mused.

Brett stretched, drawing her attention. "Since I'm making phone calls and getting things accomplished, I'm thinking of touching base with the FBI. They need to call off those two agents and understand I'll keep myself safe until the trial."

"Good idea." Stifling a yawn with her hand, she leaned back in the chair and closed her eyes. "I swear I could take a nap right now."

Just then another vehicle, this one with a loud muffler, came rumbling up the drive. She opened her eyes, grimacing. "Clearly not."

"If you want to go inside and rest, I can keep up the watch from out here," he offered.

That got her attention. "Is that what we're doing?" she asked. "If so, what are we watching for."

He grimaced. "Sorry, I shouldn't have brought it up. But it occurred to me that we have no way of knowing which one of these vehicles are friends and which ones are not."

"You have a point." She pushed to her feet. "Come on, let's both go inside. It never occurred to me that we might be sitting ducks out here in plain sight."

Once they'd closed and locked the front door behind them, she felt she could breathe a little easier. Still, feeling shaky, she wasn't surprised to see her hands were trembling. Because she didn't want Brett to see and feel responsible, she mumbled something about needing a shower and hurried down the hall to do just that.

Only once she'd stepped under the hot water did she allow the tears to fall. She'd finally started practicing medicine, something she'd trained for years to do, and on top of that she'd met Brett, a man she could love—might love—did love. While she hadn't endured a winter in Blake yet, she'd begun to feel this remote Alaskan village could be a place where she could put down roots permanently.

It all should have been uplifting and beautiful. Instead, everything had gone crazy and their lives were in danger. Sore in both body and spirit, she allowed herself to cry. Once she got that out of her system, she'd put her head up and soldier on.

As soon as he heard the shower turn on, Brett pulled out his phone and looked up the number for the Anchorage office of the Bureau of Federal Investigations and made the call he'd been dreading. Once connected, he asked to speak to the special agent in charge of the Glacier Grill case.

Immediately, the woman who answered connected him to someone named Agent Everitt. "How may I help you?" she asked, her tone both professional and made of steel.

As soon as he identified himself, she laughed, surprising the hell out of him. "I was told you managed to give both my agents the slip when they finally caught up with you," she said, her voice rich with humor.

"That's one of the reasons I'd prefer to keep myself safe," he admitted, and then went into his theory about a possible mole inside her organization.

To her credit, she listened without interrupting. When he finished, she promised to look into it. Then she asked what his plans were for the immediate future.

Intentionally vague, Brett told her he had a place to stay for the time being. He was pleased to learn that the trial had finally been scheduled for a little over four months away. Mid-January, in Anchorage. Which meant that Brett not only had to keep himself alive until then, but would have to figure out a way to get from Blake to Anchorage in the dead of winter. At least they were keeping the two head gang leaders locked up until then. A judge had denied them both bail.

He couldn't wait. Because after that, his long ordeal would finally be over.

Finishing the call, he briefly considered joining Kenzie in the shower, but afraid she was still too sore, nixed that idea. Instead, he made one more call, this time to Greg, while he waited for her to emerge. When she did, wearing a short bathrobe, her hair under a towel, she looked so beautiful his heart caught in his throat.

"I have news," he managed. "I spoke to the special agent in charge of my case. She's going to leave me alone and trust me to keep myself safe until the trial. And it's scheduled for January. We'll have to give ourselves time to get from here to Anchorage, since the weather isn't exactly favorable that time of the year."

"We?" she asked.

"Yes. If you don't mind, I'd like you to go with me. Surely, you can get a few days off."

Kenzie smiled softly. "I can definitely try. I'm glad to hear you plan on sticking around here that long. Though I think you mentioned it once in passing, when we were drinking coffee out on the front porch. But I couldn't help but wonder…"

The vulnerability in her brown eyes had him pulling her close. She smelled like soap and shampoo. He gazed down into her beautiful face, hoping she could see the emotion in his expression. "How could you think I'd leave you now?"

Before she could respond, he kissed her. Long and deep and hot. He'd started with the intention of showing her exactly how much she'd come to mean to him, but ended up becoming so aroused he could hardly think.

She took his hand and led him into her bedroom.

"Wait," he said, as she let the towel fall, exposing purpling bruises and numerous cuts. "Are you too sore?"

Her sexy smile never wavered. "Not if you're careful," she answered. "Now come here and make me forget about yesterday."

Later, in her bed facing each other, she lay with her head pillowed on his chest. "January is still a way off," she murmured. "And while I'm glad to have your help at the clinic, is that something you want to do for that long?"

"Honestly?" He smoothed her hair away from her face, marveling at the silky texture of the auburn strands. "No. I have other plans."

"You do?" she teased. "What are they?"

"I'm tired of hiding," he told her, his tone fierce and quiet. "At first, when I didn't know who I was or why I felt afraid, it made sense. But now…"

She nodded, saying nothing, simply waiting for him to continue.

"I want to get on with my life. I'm thinking about opening a business."

She sat up, so quickly she winced. "Here? In Blake?"

"Yes." Propping himself up on one elbow, he smiled at her. "I even spoke to Greg about it and he's fully on board. There are only two places to eat in town—the Café and Mikki's. I could open a small restaurant, lunch and dinner only. And along with that, run a meal-delivery service. How much I could do would depend on whether or not I can find employees to work for me."

Excitement made her eyes sparkle. "I bet you could. Now that people know us and we're not strangers, it should be easier to find help."

He couldn't help but feel relief that she loved the idea. Taking a deep breath, he continued, "That's good, because if I do this, you'll need to hire someone else to assist you in the clinic."

Even that didn't dim her enthusiasm. "That's fine," she said. "I had a feeling you wouldn't want to work there for very long. And, I honestly can't wait for the people of Blake to taste your awesome food."

Humbled by her faith in him, he kissed her, a slow lingering sort of kiss. "I'll need to buy a vehicle," he said. "I have a Chevy pickup back in Anchorage, but it's in storage."

"If I can get mine fixed quickly, we can share that."

He had to tell her the truth. "I saw your Jeep. It's pretty messed up. I think the best bet would be to see if we can buy a used vehicle off someone here in Blake. I can buy it, since I've got access to my bank accounts again."

"You do?"

"Sure." He shrugged. "The only reason I didn't access anything before was because if I did, doing so would have been a beacon letting anyone looking for me know where I was. Now, not only can I pay you back for everything you've done, but I can help you as well."

As if she sensed this was important to him, she smiled and nodded. "I really didn't spend enough for you to have to worry about repaying me."

Since he didn't want to argue, he simply nodded and pulled her close again. "How about we take that nap?" he offered, settling in so they were spooning.

She gave a contented sigh and nodded. "That sounds wonderful."

He dozed off holding her in his arms.

LISTENING AS BRETT'S breathing evened out as he fell asleep, Kenzie smiled. The thought of Brett putting down roots in Blake both thrilled and terrified her. While she knew she'd be living and practicing medicine here for the next two years, she hadn't thought much beyond what she'd do once her contract ended. She'd always pretty much figured she'd go back to Texas and either open her own small general practice or join a larger one. She still considered Houston her home, though there was a lot to be said for the wild beauty of this small Alaskan town.

As long as Brett was here, she admitted. They hadn't talked much about the future—their future—likely because they'd only been together a short period of time. Plus, Brett's circumstances, with the gang after him and needing to testify in a high profile and possibly dangerous trial, hadn't exactly provided the kind of security they needed to solidify their relationship.

And honestly, the casual approach had worked well for them so far. She wasn't sure she wanted to change anything. They were having fun and enjoying each other's company too much right now.

She must have fallen asleep too, because her stomach growling woke her. Sitting up, she smiled to see Brett still asleep next to her as she glanced at the alarm clock on the nightstand to check the time.

The red numbers blinked six fifteen. Momentarily confused, at first she thought they'd slept through the day and night until the next morning, but then she realized it was early evening.

Moving quietly, she slipped from the bed.

"Come back," he said, smiling, his eyes half closed and looking sexy as hell.

"I need food," she told him. Her stomach rumbled, as if to emphasize. "Let me make us…"

"I'll do it." Wide-awake now, he pushed up from the bed and padded, fully naked, to the kitchen. She couldn't help but eye his perfect backside.

"No need to cook," she insisted. "Cheese and crackers are fine."

Rolling his eyes, he considered. "Sit. Let me see what I can whip up."

In a few minutes' time, he'd put together a nice charcuterie board, using three different kinds of cheese, cold cuts, some fruit and chopped vegetables. He'd even made a few dipping sauces.

As he placed this on the table in front of her, she had to restrain herself from devouring it all at once. She had no idea why, but she felt as if she could eat it all without pausing for air.

Brett grinned as he passed her a plate. "Help yourself," he said.

She needed no second urging. They ate and talked and laughed, and she realized she felt great. Better than great—happy. For the first time in her life, she understood the saying *home is where the heart is*. As long as she was with Brett, she thought she could be happy anywhere.

Something of her thoughts must have shown in her face. Brett gazed at her, his eyes darkening. "Let's go back to bed," he said, his voice rough.

And they did.

The next morning, they almost managed to oversleep, since Kenzie forgot to set the alarm on her phone. Luckily, Jane called at six o'clock, which woke them on time.

Jane just wanted to confirm that she was picking them both up at 8:00 a.m. She'd drop Kenzie off at the clinic and take Brett to meet up with Greg, so the two men could go check out the available spaces for rent downtown.

Kenzie thanked her. The instant she ended the call, she glanced at Brett.

"How'd you get that set up so quick?" Kenzie asked.

Brett grinned. "I texted Greg last night, after you fell asleep. He texted back that he'd make sure he had a comprehensive list of properties. Did you know he's also the local real estate agent?"

That information made her laugh. "Around here, everyone is a little bit of everything, it seems."

By the time Jane arrived, they were both ready. When they heard the sound of Jane's vehicle outside, Brett pulled Kenzie in for a quick kiss. "I'll miss you today," he said.

Throat tight, she gazed up at him. "I'll miss you too."

Holding hands, together they walked out to meet Jane.

When Kenzie arrived at the clinic, she couldn't help but hope it would be a slow day. Her entire body ached. She waved to Jane and Brett, watching as they drove away, then unlocked the door and went inside to start her day. Jane had promised to swing back around in an hour or so to check on Kenzie and help out if needed.

Unfortunately, she barely had time to make herself a cup of coffee before the door opened, sending the bell jangling. She hurried up front, hoping it would be something quick and minor.

A tall slender man wearing a navy windbreaker and a baseball cap stood waiting in the reception area. He held a pair of mirrored aviator sunglasses in one hand.

"Can I help you?" Kenzie asked politely, wishing she weren't alone. Something about him hit her the wrong way. She didn't think he actually lived around here, and if he was just passing through, that could mean trouble.

Swallowing back her unease, she forced what she hoped looked like a welcoming smile.

"I'm Agent Dewberry," the man said, flashing a badge. "I'd like to talk to you about Brett Denyon."

She considered asking for a second look at his badge. He'd put it away so quickly she hadn't really been able to see it. But she was alone in the clinic and she couldn't help but suspect she might be in danger if she showed the slightest bit of distrust. Whoever this man might be, she felt pretty confident he was not an FBI agent.

She'd just need to stall him a few minutes. Ever since Jane had organized the townspeople, someone had taken to stopping by the clinic every hour like clockwork to check on her.

"Brett? He no longer works here," she replied, looking him straight in the eye. "He left town and didn't leave a forwarding address."

While lying had never been her strong suit, she thought she sounded confident.

"Why would he do that?" he asked, frowning. "Last I heard, he was thinking about putting down roots here."

"We broke up." She swallowed hard, aware she'd

need to do a convincing acting job. "Now that we're not in a relationship, there's nothing to keep him in Blake."

"You are aware we suspect Mr. Denyon of being part of the same gang that shot up his restaurant?" he asked. "If you're sheltering him or trying to cover for him, you could be charged as an accessory if he's convicted of a crime."

"Part of a gang?" she didn't have to feign her shock. "That's ridiculous. This gang destroyed his business and he almost lost his life. That's why he's going to testify against them."

The man's smirk reminded her again that she was alone and unprotected. "You only know part of the story, lady," the so-called FBI agent said. "Mr. Denyon only told you some of the truth. His restaurant has long been a meeting place for one of the most powerful gangs in Anchorage. The shooting occurred because a rival gang showed up to try and take them down. We now have reason to believe he was in on it this entire time."

Bewildered, Kenzie stared. "But what about the politician? Brett told me some presidential hopeful was killed in the gunfire."

"He was. As far as we can tell, that was sheer coincidence. He just happened to be eating there at the time of the shooting."

The clinic door opened just then and Jane walked in. Kenzie nearly sagged with relief. "Jane! So glad to see you," she said. "This is FBI Agent Dewberry."

Jane narrowed her eyes. "I've met both the agents assigned to this case. You're not one of them."

Kenzie gave the tiniest shake of her head, hoping to warn Jane to play along. But Jane wasn't much for

subtlety, so she either ignored Kenzie or refused to acknowledge the warning.

"And you are?" the man asked, his expression as
cold as his voice.

"I'm Jane Norman. My husband is the mayor here
in Blake."

"I see." He returned his attention to Kenzie. "As I
was saying, there is a very real chance that Brett Denyon knows more than he's letting on. That's what we're
investigating."

Jane's mouth fell open. She looked from Kenzie to
their visitor and back again.

They both ignored her.

Taking a deep breath and hoping this man would
leave soon, Kenzie shook her head. "Are you telling me
that Brett wasn't in the Witness Protection Program?"

The maybe-agent studied her. "He told you that?"

"Yes, he did. As I said, he had a bit of memory loss
for a while. Once he remembered, he told me everything."

"Except for the part about his restaurant being a gang
meeting place. And the very real possibility that he
might be part of one of those gangs."

"What?" Jane screeched. "Are you serious?"

Again, both Kenzie and Agent Dewberry ignored
her.

"You didn't answer my question," Kenzie pointed
out. "Was Brett Denyon in the Witness Protection Program?"

"He was and he wasn't," the man replied. "It's complicated. We had asked him to consider WITSEC, but
he didn't want to leave Alaska."

Which jived with what Brett had told her. Either this guy had access to inside information, or he truly was who he claimed to be. An FBI agent.

"Honoring his requests to stay in state, we were trying to make arrangements to get him to a safe house in Fairbanks. But he disappeared before we could move him."

"Disappeared?" Kenzie stared. "He told me he went to stay at a friend's place on the river."

Instantly alert, he stared at her. "Which river?"

"The Neacola," Kenzie answered. "Why?"

But the man had already taken out his phone. He walked away as he made a call.

Good, Kenzie thought. Now he could go chasing down a false path. And she'd be able to warn Brett.

"Wow," Jane said, apparently still oblivious to the undercurrents in the room. "Exciting stuff, though I'm not sure I believe any of this. I wish Greg was here. He's a much better judge of character than I am." She sighed. "I'm thinking I need to call him. I want to make sure he's safe, as well as your young man."

"He's not my young man," Kenzie pointed out for the stranger's benefit, even though she and Jane both knew he was. Keeping her eye on the man, who had his back to them while talking on his phone, she motioned Jane over. "We need to be careful," she whispered. "I don't think this guy is on the up-and-up."

"Didn't you ask to see ID?"

"He flashed a badge," Kenzie admitted. "But too quickly for me to actually get a good look at it."

"Then ask to see it again." Jane turned, as if she planned to do exactly that.

"Don't." Kenzie grabbed her arm, stopping her. "I just want him gone."

Just then, the man finished his call and walked back over to them. "Thank you for your help, ladies." He flashed a pleasant smile. "I'll be in touch. Reach out to the Anchorage office if you think of anything else."

With that, he let himself out.

The instant the door closed, Kenzie ran over and turned the deadbolt. "See," she said. "If he was an actual FBI agent, he would have given me his card so I could contact him if I had any more information."

Tilting her head, Jane considered Kenzie's statement. "But what if he's really who he says he is? There's a possibility he's right."

"No. There's not. I find it difficult to believe that Brett could be part of anything nefarious."

"Nefarious!" Jane cracked up. "I love your word choice there."

"This is serious, Jane," Kenzie said. "I had a bad feeling about that man."

"Really?"

"Yes." Kenzie swallowed, her stomach knotting. "Something about him is off. I think he's lying." She decided she might as well say it all. "I don't believe he's actually an FBI agent."

Jane gasped. "Seriously?"

"Yes." Kenzie pulled out her phone and tried Brett's number. As usual, she had only a half bar of signal and the call wouldn't go through. "Damn it! I need to get a new cell phone carrier."

Taking a deep breath and refusing to allow herself to be panic-stricken, Kenzie grabbed Jane's arm. "May I use your phone? I need to talk to Brett and make sure he's safe. I want to let him know about that guy and what he said."

Jane handed over her phone. Kenzie dialed, but the call went straight to voice mail. She left a message, asking Brett to call her back as soon as possible, then passed the phone back to Jane.

"Let me try Greg," Jane said. "He and Brett are out looking at storefronts. They were mostly going to view available ones on Main Street, but there were a couple on side streets that might be a good fit too."

But Jane's call to her husband also went unanswered. Jane too left a message. When she'd finished, she eyed Kenzie. "How about we call the FBI and verify if there actually is an Agent Dewberry."

"I don't have their business cards with me," Kenzie said. "I left them at the house."

"I think I might." Jane dug in her purse, grinning in triumph when she dug out a card. "Here we are. Let me just make a quick call and check."

But that call too went to voice mail. Jane left another message and shrugged. "We've done all we can right now. I've got a few errands to run. Do you feel safe here by yourself?"

"Not really," Kenzie admitted. "I have to admit, I'm a bit shaken up."

"Then turn the open sign to closed and let's go find Greg and Brett. If there's an emergency, they can always call you."

Kenzie wasted no time doing exactly that. After

locking the clinic up, she made sure to check out their surroundings.

"Are you looking for that FBI agent?" Jane asked, craning her neck to look too.

"Yes. I want to make sure we're not followed," Kenzie replied. "I definitely don't want to lead him straight to Brett."

They'd just made it to Jane's vehicle when Agent Dewberry appeared, a pistol pointed straight at Kenzie. "You," he said, motioning with his gun. "You're coming with me. And you." He indicated Jane with a jerk of his chin. "You go and find Brett Denyon and give him a message for me. He'd better show up alone in one hour at the bridge where he went off the road, or this little lady is going to end up dead. You got it?"

Jane gave a jerky nod. Kenzie, still trying to weigh her options, held perfectly still. She could always try to rush the guy, hitting him headfirst in the stomach, hoping the blow would be enough to send any shots he might fire into the air. Except she couldn't risk him hitting Jane.

If she went with him, she suspected she wouldn't make it out alive, no matter what Brett did.

"Come on," he ordered, moving closer and keeping the gun trained on her. "Put your hands behind your back."

Moving slowly, she stared at Jane, trying to signal the older woman to get down. But Jane, clearly scared out of her wits, stood frozen, her eyes huge, looking like a deer in the headlights.

Kenzie simply couldn't take the chance. She put her hands behind her back, wincing as the fake FBI agent slapped on metal handcuffs. Once those were on, he motioned her to a car parked in the lot next door. "Get in," he ordered.

She did as he asked, hoping she could figure a way out of this before she—or anyone else—got hurt.

Chapter Fifteen

Brett and Greg had just finished touring what Brett thought might be the perfect location for his new restaurant when Greg's phone rang. "It's Jane," Greg said. "Probably wanting to know what's taking so long." Chuckling, he let the call go to voice mail. "After all, it's only been a little more than an hour since we started looking."

Five seconds later, Brett's phone began to ring. Jane again. He also saw he'd had one missed call and a voice mail. "Maybe there's a problem," he told Greg. "I'm going to answer and if you don't want to talk, I'll say you're in the restroom."

His statement had Greg shaking his head and laughing. "She has no patience. Don't say I didn't warn you," Greg said.

"Hello?" A second after answering the phone, Brett's heart began to pound. Hysterical, Jane sounded as if she were crying and panicking, all at the same time. She screamed at him, and the only words he could make out were *Kenzie* and *gun*. "Wait, Jane. Please, slow down. I can't understand you and you're not making sense."

"Put her on speaker," Greg ordered, all traces of humor gone from his face.

Brett did as he asked. "Jane, I've put you on speaker. Greg is here with me. What's going on?"

"Greg…" she wailed. "I knew that man wasn't with the FBI."

The back of Brett's neck began to prickle. "What man?" he asked. "Jane, is Kenzie there with you?"

Audibly taking several deep breaths, Jane sniffled as she clearly struggled to compose herself. And then she told them about the stranger claiming to be an FBI agent who'd been in the clinic when she'd arrived to check on Kenzie. "I had a bad feeling about him and Kenzie did too. But we got him to leave and we locked the place up with the intention of coming to find you two. He ambushed us in the parking lot."

A chill snaked down Brett's spine. "Let me talk to Kenzie," he demanded. "Right now."

"I can't." Jane started sobbing again. "He took her at gunpoint. Kenzie's gone, Brett. And he said he'll kill her if you don't meet him in an hour at the bridge where you went off the road."

Fury warred with terror. Still holding the phone, Brett turned to Greg. "I need you to drive me," he said. "Once we get there, assuming he's up front about the exchange, I want you to get Kenzie out immediately. Don't hesitate, don't look back, just go."

"You're forgetting something." Jane's voice, from the open phone line he'd completely let slip his mind.

"What's that?" he asked, trying not to grit his teeth in impatience.

"The entire town is behind you," she said. "You're

no longer in this alone. Let me alert everyone. No worries, Brett. We'll make damn sure both you and Kenzie are safe."

"Don't—" he began, but Jane had clearly ended the call.

Jamming the phone back into his pocket, Brett cursed. "Greg, we need to go. That man who has Kenzie is likely part of a bloodthirsty gang. The longer he has her, the more danger she's in."

"We can go," Greg said. "But the instructions were to meet him in an hour. It's likely all we're going to be doing is sitting around and waiting for him to show." He placed a hand on Brett's shoulder. "We need to wait. You know as well as I do that it's possible you'll be walking into an ambush. People like that rarely honor their word."

"He has to let her go," Brett roared, shaking off Greg's hand. "Kenzie has nothing to do with any of this. I can't let her be hurt." Shaking his head, he felt as if he were drowning underwater. "I just can't."

"We won't let anything happen to her," Greg replied, the sympathy in his expression letting Brett know he understood how Brett felt. "And I suggest you take some deep breaths and calm the hell down. You're going to need to keep your wits about you if we're going to be successful."

Though he was still fired up, the rational part of Brett's brain realized Greg gave excellent advice. If he went charging in like an enraged bull, he'd likely make mistakes he couldn't afford to make.

Greg checked his watch. "I'm glad he gave you an hour. That gives Jane enough time to rally the troops."

The troops. "You don't understand," Brett said. "These people are ruthless and dangerous. They'll shoot first and talk later. You don't want to endanger innocent towns-people."

Drawing himself up tall, Greg stared at Brett. "It's not like we're going to send out our elderly or our children. We're grown-ass adults, we're Alaskans and we're tough. I guarantee you everyone who shows up will be armed and well trained in how to use their weapons."

Heartsick, Brett didn't have the fortitude to argue the point. He just wanted Kenzie safe. Once they got her away from the gang, he'd fight his own battles, thank you very much.

Instead of telling Greg any of this, Brett again asked the other man if they could drive to the bridge. "I prefer to be early. That way I can scout out the terrain."

Greg's phone pinged, announcing a text message. Checking it, Greg nodded. "Jane had the same thought. She's already setting everyone up. We've got people stationing themselves in the woods surrounding that area. We'll be ready for those bastards when they show up."

"Already?" Brett couldn't believe it. "I know Jane is organized, but seriously."

"You're forgetting, people signed up for this." Greg grinned proudly. "Here in Blake, if we sign up for something, we're ready when called on. We follow through."

Not sure what to think, Brett simply nodded. "All I care about right now is making sure Kenzie isn't hurt. Whatever it takes. Do you understand?"

"I do."

Trying to curb his impatience seemed like an exercise in futility. Brett began to pace, walking up and down the sidewalk in front of the building they'd just checked out. Finally, he gave up. "Greg, I'd feel a lot better if we just drove out to the bridge."

Greg checked his watch. "Okay. Come on."

Once they were inside Greg's pickup, Greg turned to face him. "We've got to work out a plan," he said. "Just showing up and offering to trade yourself for Kenzie isn't going to cut it. You know as well as I do that it's likely this guy will put a bullet through both of you and be done with it."

Teeth clenched, Brett knew the older man was right. "Do you have any other options in mind?" he asked.

Greg started the truck. "Let Jane get everyone in place before we go charging in there, for one. Then, when we do arrive, we need to see proof of life. I'll handle that—I want you to stay hidden at first. I've got to make him show me Kenzie."

"And then what?" Brett wanted to know. "I can't guarantee I'll stay in the truck once I see her." This was only the truth. Once he laid eyes on Kenzie, nothing on earth would be able to keep him from going to her. While Greg's plan made sense, Brett was done with hiding. Danger be damned. All that mattered was saving Kenzie.

Greg shrugged, giving Brett an uneasy smile. "Several of our townspeople are crack shots, but we have one guy who used to be a sniper in Afghanistan. We're hoping he can get a clean shot and take that guy out."

With that, Greg put the shifter in Drive and they headed out of town.

All the way there, worry gnawed at Brett. Sure, Jane and Greg seemed to have a good plan. But all he needed was for Kenzie's captor to arrive at the bridge and see fifteen or twenty parked vehicles. If that was the case, the guy would likely drive off with Kenzie and Brett would never see her again.

Just the thought sent a bolt of pain knifing through his heart. He loved her—more than that, she was his everything. The idea of living in a world without Kenzie was unbearable.

When they finally pulled up to the overlook by the bridge, there wasn't another single vehicle in sight. Relieved, Brett took a deep breath and checked the clock on the dash. They were thirty minutes early. "Do you think any of the townspeople are in place yet?"

Greg shrugged. "I imagine they are in the process. But we won't see them. A lot of us are hunters and we know how to stay hidden."

As the clock ticked ever so slowly toward the appointed hour, Brett's tension grew. Once, when he'd been younger and just starting out, he'd appeared on a televised cooking competition. The pressure had been intense. Instead of giving in to fear and letting himself fall apart, he managed to hone his attention on the task at hand, making a delicious and complicated dessert using only the assorted ingredients he'd been given.

While he hadn't won, he'd managed to come in a respectable second.

This time, the stakes were even higher. He had to get Kenzie away from this man. Without allowing one hair on her head to be harmed.

Finally, the clock showed ten o'clock straight up. Impatient now, Brett alternated between watching out the rear window and the front.

"Do you hear that?" Greg asked, sitting up straight. "Some kind of motor."

Just then, a boat came around a bend in the river, heading directly toward the bridge.

"Son of a…" Exchanging glances with Greg, Brett cursed. Instead of arriving by road, Kenzie's captor had elected to use the water. Smart. The only drawback Brett could see was how a boat made doing an exchange a lot more difficult.

Stricken, he cursed again. "He has no intention of letting Kenzie go."

"I agree." Grim-faced, Greg opened the driver's side door and got out.

A second later, Brett joined him. Keeping the body of the truck in between them and the river, they watched as the boat slowly made its way toward them.

"Now what?" Brett muttered.

But instead of stopping, the boat continued on, under the bridge and down river, until it disappeared from sight.

He briefly considered diving off the bridge into the water, but even if he were to survive the distance, he knew he'd never catch them.

Kenzie and her captor were gone. And Brett had no idea if they were coming back.

WHEN THE FAKE FBI agent had driven her away, Kenzie tried frantically to calm her pounding heart. Deep breathing exercises helped a little, but she knew she had to keep a clear head if she wanted to survive. This might be scary as hell, but she was determined she'd make it out alive.

Immediately, she started looking for a way to escape. The handcuffs hindered that a lot. If he'd used rope, she might have had a prayer of working her way loose, but metal was unyielding. Even if she turned her back toward the door, she couldn't move her hands enough to work the handle. If she could have opened the door, then what? Falling out of a moving car with hands bound behind her didn't have high odds for survival.

And then they'd turned down a long hidden driveway. He'd made her get out of the car and ushered her onto a boat.

Another surprise. Did he truly intend to meet up with Brett on a boat? Terror clogged her throat as she wondered if he intended to weigh her down and drop her into the river to drown. Heck, he wouldn't even need to attach weight. With her hands bound behind her back, she wouldn't have any hope of navigating the swift current.

She had to figure out a way to escape.

In the channel where the rustic boat slip was, the water seemed muddy, less clear and slower moving. She had a feeling it wasn't anywhere near as deep. She took quick notice of her surroundings, the other boat slips, some of them rotted beyond any hope of being used, and the older homes set back from the water.

Then she checked out the boat itself. An older watercraft, it had a small cuddy cabin and an inboard motor. Despite the peeling, faded paint and worn and cracked upholstery, she could tell it had once been a nice boat. Maybe she'd luck out and it wouldn't start.

"Sit down," the man ordered, practically shoving her onboard.

Immediately, she dropped onto one of the bench seats behind the driver's chair. Her arms had started aching and the too-tight handcuffs were cutting into her wrists. "Is there any way you can loosen these?" she asked. "Just a little, so they'd be less painful?"

"No." He barely looked at her. "Just sit there and shut up."

The motor started immediately. He quickly untied them from the dock and pulled out into the river. A few minutes later, she could see the bridge in the distance.

There! She spotted Greg's truck, and Brett and Greg standing outside, holding onto the guardrail.

Pushing to her feet, she hoped they could see her. But then her captor accelerated, and the sudden momentum knocked her back onto her seat. They were going, she realized, too fast to stop now.

Under the bridge, emerging out the other side, they continued on. "Where are we going?" she asked, looking back hopelessly. "I thought you were going to do an exchange."

"Do you have your phone on you?" he asked, ignoring her question as he slowed the boat to almost a stop. Since he didn't anchor them, they drifted with the current.

Slowly, she nodded. "It's in my back pocket."

Shoving her roughly, he got it out. "Put your thumb against it so it's unlocked," he directed.

Once she'd complied, he opened her phone contacts. "Brett," he said out loud. "I'm going to dial him and here's what I want you to say. Deviate from that, and the phone goes in the water."

"I get it," she said, inwardly wincing. Using a few words, he told her the message he wanted her to give Brett.

She listened as Brett's phone rang, aware her number would show on the screen. "Kenzie?" The worry in his voice stabbed at her heart. "Are you all right?"

"So far," she replied, her voice shaky but firm. "As I'm sure you noticed, we're in a boat. He had me call you because he says you violated his rule. I'm not sure what's going on, but you were supposed to come alone."

Then, before Brett could reply, her captor ended the call.

"Why'd you do that?" she demanded, blinking back tears. "You didn't even let him respond."

"Oh, he will," the man said. "One, two, three…"

Her phone rang. This time, the fake FBI Agent answered. "I told you to come alone," he said. "You've talked to Kenzie, you have proof of life. If you want her to stay alive, you'd better do as I say."

Brett must have responded in the affirmative.

"Good," her captor continued. "We are going back toward the bridge now. I want you to ditch your friend and walk down to the water. It's shallow close to the bank. Wade out there with your hands up and wait for our return. I'll give you more instructions after that."

Ending the call, he tossed her phone onto the bench seat next to her.

Hearing Brett's voice on the phone strengthened Kenzie's resolve. She hadn't expected this—being used as a pawn by the bad guys in order to get to the man she loved. Damned if she was going to let this man kill him.

They rounded the final curve in the river and she could see the bridge up ahead. "You aren't going to let me go, are you?" she asked.

"Of course not. You and your boyfriend are both going to end up dead. It's much cleaner that way."

Ahead, she could see the empty bridge. Greg's truck had left. And a man—Brett—had waded out into the water.

Now or never.

She took a deep breath, her path certain. Screaming at the top of her lungs, she launched herself at the man driving the boat, slamming her head into his so hard she almost lost consciousness.

The impact knocked her to the side. She struggled to stay on board, but since she was unable to use her hands to hold on, she went over. Still upright, her captor shook his head, as though her blow had been nothing more than a minor inconvenience. The last thing she heard before hitting the water was the sound of a gunshot. Who or what or where, she didn't know. She had more important things to worry about.

Like not drowning. At least she had the presence of mind to take a deep breath before going under. She couldn't use her hands, but she used her legs to kick, trying to get close enough to the surface to attempt to float and far enough away from the boat.

Her lungs ached with the need to inhale. She broke the surface, gulped in air and immediately started to sink again.

And then Brett was there, swimming with her, keeping her head above the water. Exhausted, she tried to help as he towed her toward the shore. As soon as her feet touched the bottom, she turned to look for the boat, afraid her captor would come after them.

"He's dead," Brett told her. "One of the townspeople took him out. Jane has already alerted the state police, so someone should be here shortly."

Her arms ached. "The handcuffs," she said. "He has the key."

"I'll see if I can get it," he promised. "But for now, let's get up to the road and into Greg's truck."

True to his word, once Greg arrived and could watch over her, Brett swam out to the boat, which had drifted ashore a little farther downstream. Sagging against Greg, she apologized for getting him wet.

"It's okay," Greg answered. "I'm just glad you're alive."

She tried to laugh and ended up coughing up water instead. "I am too," she managed.

They both watched as Brett reached the boat. Once aboard, he tossed out the anchor and must have searched the man's body for the key, because when he returned, he had it. He unlocked the handcuffs, massaging her wrists to help get her circulation going.

Meanwhile, one by one, people began emerging from the woods. One here, another there, most wearing camouflage and all carrying weapons.

"We protect our own," Greg said, his voice proud. "And you, Dr. Kenzie Taylor, are one of our own."

Later, after giving her statement to a very sympathetic Alaskan State Trooper, Kenzie sat wrapped in a towel in her medical clinic, thanking people one by one. They arrived in groups, filling the parking lot with their vehicles, all of them wanting to see with their own eyes that their village doctor was okay.

Brett stood behind Kenzie's chair, hand resting protectively on her shoulder, as they crowded through the door, milling about in the waiting room and talking amongst themselves. An air of camaraderie filled the place, so much more so that Kenzie had felt during her open house. She knew she'd never remember all their names, but she'd try her best not to forget their friendly faces.

"This is freaking amazing," Brett murmured. "I've never seen anything like it."

Reaching up, she placed her hand over his. "I agree." Looking out over the sea of people, she blinked back tears. "My heart is full. I think I might have finally found the place where I belong."

Jane heard this and snorted. "Wait until you make it through a winter here first, then say that. You're from the south, so this won't be anything you've seen before."

"Negative Nelly," Greg said, walking up. "Don't listen to her. You two will definitely find ways to make the snow feel cozy." He winked.

To her astonishment, Kenzie felt her face heat as she blushed. She glanced up at Brett to find him grinning down at her.

"I imagine we will," Brett drawled.

Later, after the FBI had arrived—they'd sent two completely different agents—things wound down and Kenzie and Brett rode home with Greg and Jane. After dropping them off, the mayor and his wife sat in their truck and waited until they got inside.

Once they were gone, Kenzie stumbled over to the

couch before allowing herself to collapse. A second later, Brett dropped down next to her. He slipped his arms around her shoulders and pulled her close. "Hell of a day, wasn't it?" he asked.

She allowed her head to fall back against him. "It definitely was. All I can say is that I think it'll be all downhill from now on out."

That night, they slept wrapped up in each other's arms.

In the morning, Brett made coffee and crepes and brought them to her on a tray. Smiling, she thought she must be the luckiest woman in the world.

"Aren't you going to eat?" she asked, inhaling the deliciousness before taking a sip of her coffee.

"I thought we could share," he told her, smiling. "I made plenty."

"I think I love you," she told him. The instant she spoke, she caught her breath, wondering if it might be too soon.

His teasing expression vanished. Gaze darkening, he looked deep into her eyes. "I *know* I love you, Kenzie. And I'm looking forward to spending more time together so I can prove it."

"Me too," she responded. Heart full, she thought about leaning over and kissing him. But her stomach chose that exact moment to growl, so she picked up the fork and ate a piece of crepe instead. It tasted like heaven. "That's amazing. Make sure to put those on the menu at your restaurant."

"If I do breakfast, I will," he promised. "Speaking of that, I think I found the perfect spot. Greg and I looked at a couple, but the instant I set foot in this one, I felt like it was meant to be my place. It's right on Main Street, down by the tourism office. It's far enough away from Mikki's that it shouldn't be a problem."

She thought for a moment, trying to place which building. "The red brick one with the boarded-up windows?"

"That's it!" His infectious grin had her smiling too. "Evidently, it used to be some sort of restaurant at some point in time. It's already got a full kitchen that just needs some updating. That will save me a ton of money, not having to put in a kitchen. I'm letting Greg know that I'm ready to move forward on signing the lease."

"Have you thought of a name?" she asked. "Or are you going to call it Glacier Grill like your former place in Anchorage?"

He shrugged. "I'm not sure. I was thinking of going with something simpler. Maybe just Brett's Kitchen or Brett's Grill. I have a bit more time, since after I sign the lease, I've got to get the operating permit and the liquor license in place. In between all that, I've got to decide on a menu."

"Sounds like you're going to be busy. If you need any help, I'm in."

"I might just take you up on that," he replied, the heat in his gaze making her blush.

ONCE BRETT SIGNED the lease, he began work immediately getting the building cleaned up. Kenzie helped him after clinic hours and planned to help on weekends. To both their surprise, several townspeople showed up bright and early Saturday morning to help.

Annette had been located and arrested. She'd surprisingly pled guilty to all charges, claiming she didn't want a trial, just wanted to do her time. Because it was her first offense, she'd been given probation. Instead of returning to her home in Blake, she'd gone to Fairbanks to stay with a friend. Kenzie couldn't help but feel relieved when she heard that news.

Kenzie settled into a comfortable routine in her clinic and had even hired a middle-aged woman named Sarah to help. Sarah was also a licensed midwife and had nursing experience, which was a bonus. They got along well.

With all the cleanup and repairs done, and the permits in place—Greg helped get those fast-tracked—they scheduled the grand opening for mid-September. Brett decided to call the restaurant Brett's Grill. He'd settled on a simple menu, all of which he tested on Kenzie. Everything, from the salmon to the steaks, tasted out of this world. She couldn't wait for her fellow townspeople to sample them.

She'd never been so busy—or so happy.

"You're never going to believe this," Brett told her, walking in to the clinic at the end of a busy Friday. "I just heard from the special agent in charge of my case. The DA arranged a plea deal with the gang members and they took it. They're going to testify against people higher up than them in the chain of command. Which means there's not going to be a trial."

"It's over?" she asked, almost unable to believe.

"It's over," he confirmed, pulling her into his arms.

On the morning of Brett's grand opening, she woke up to snow flurries. "Snow!" Kenzie exclaimed, delighted. "Does it always start in September? I'm so excited!"

"Believe me, that'll change," Brett teased. "It's rare that we get snow this early, but it sometimes does happen, as you can see."

"Is this going to mess up your grand opening?" she asked, worried.

"In what way?" Frowning slightly, he appeared genuinely perplexed. Then, before she could answer, he shook his head. "Are you asking if a little snow is going to deter people from going out?" He waved his hand toward the outside. "This is nothing. We're Alaskans. We're used to snow, and believe me, there'll be a lot more than this."

She stuck out her tongue. "Well, it might be nothing to you, but it's amazing to me. We don't get snow in Houston. I can only remember once, in fact. So I'm going to go enjoy it."

Grabbing the down parka she'd ordered online, along with a knitted cap and gloves, she dressed and then rushed outside. Hurrying out into the front yard, she stood and watched the beautiful white flurries drift down from the slate gray sky.

"This is amazing!" she exclaimed, her breath sending a plume of mist into the frigid air. She twirled, laughing as she spun. When she looked up, she saw Brett watching her, his gaze warm.

"You're beautiful," he told her. Crossing the space between them, he pulled her in for a kiss, his mouth warm on her cold lips.

That night, despite the on-again, off-again flurries, people started lining up in front of the restaurant an hour before opening time. Brett had decided for now to only serve dinner, though he'd said he might expand to breakfast or brunch on weekends only.

He'd hired his entire staff quickly, some of them inexperienced young people just out of high school, others who had been waitstaff or cooks in other places. The one thing they all had in common is they were excited to work for Brett Denyon. Two kids had expressed their own dreams of someday becoming chefs, and Brett had made them his apprentices, starting them out as line cooks.

By the end of the night, Kenzie knew Brett's grand opening had been a roaring success.

Later, after closing, once the place had been cleaned and restocked and all his employees had gone home, they sat side by side in the empty dining room. Outside, snow flurries continued to swirl and fall.

"Tonight was amazing," Brett said softly. "Before, I thought Glacier Grill was all I could ever ask for, but now I realize how little I knew."

Turning to her, he kissed her cheek. "It's different when you're feeding people you care about. Blake, Alaska, might be a small town, but everyone who lives here has a huge heart."

"I know," she said, leaning her head on his shoulder. "I never expected to find so much happiness when I took this job."

"Who would have known?" he mused. "All that awfulness in Anchorage would lead to this. Not only a new restaurant and town but also finding the love of my life."

She went still. "Is that what I am to you?" she asked, her voice steady, though she could barely catch her breath.

He cupped her face in his hands. "Yes. I'm all in, Dr.

Kenzie Taylor. I can picture us growing old together. Here. In Blake."

Heart full, she slowly nodded. "Me too," she said.

"That is," he continued with a rakish grin. "Assuming you still like it here after the end of winter."

Laughing, she swatted him. "As long as I have you to keep me warm, I'm sure I'll be fine."

"I'll do my best," he promised. And then he kissed her, sealing the deal.

* * * * *

COMING SOON!

We really hope you enjoyed reading this book. If you're looking for more romance, be sure to head to the shops when new books are available on

Thursday 5th January

MILLS & BOON

THE HEART OF ROMANCE

A ROMANCE FOR EVERY READER

MODERN

Prepare to be swept off your feet by sophisticated, sexy and seductive heroes, in some of the world's most glamourous and romantic locations, where power and passion collide.

HISTORICAL

Escape with historical heroes from time gone by. Whether your passion is for wicked Regency Rakes, muscled Vikings or rugged Highlanders, awaits the romance of the past.

MEDICAL

Set your pulse racing with dedicated, delectable doctors in the high-pressure world of medicine, where emotions run high and passion, comfort love are the best medicine.

True Love

Celebrate true love with tender stories of heartfelt romance, from the rush of falling in love to the joy a new baby can bring, and a focus on the emotional heart of a relationship.

Desire

Indulge in secrets and scandal, intense drama and plenty of sizzling hot action with powerful and passionate heroes who have it all: wealth, status good looks...everything but the right woman.

HEROES

Experience all the excitement of a gripping thriller, with an intense romance at its heart. Resourceful, true-to-life women and strong, fearless face danger and desire - a killer combination!

To see which titles are coming soon, please visit

millsandboon.co.uk/nextmonth

LET'S TALK

Romance

For exclusive extracts, competitions
and special offers, find us online:

- **f** facebook.com/millsandboon
- **𝕏** @MillsandBoon
- **◎** @MillsandBoonUK

Get in touch on 01413 063232

For all the latest titles coming soon, visit
millsandboon.co.uk/nextmonth

JOIN US ON SOCIAL MEDIA!

Stay up to date with our latest releases, author news and gossip, special offers and discounts, and all the behind-the-scenes action from Mills & Boon...

 @millsandboon

 @millsandboonuk

 facebook.com/millsandboon

 @millsandboonuk

It might just be true love...

GET YOUR ROMANCE FIX!

Get the latest romance news, exclusive author interviews, story extracts and much more!

MILLS & BOON
Desire

Indulge in secrets and scandal, intense drama
and plenty of sizzling hot action with powerful
and passionate heroes who have it all: wealth,
status, good looks…everything but the right
woman.

MILLS & BOON
MODERN
Power and Passion

Prepare to be swept off your feet by sophisticated, sexy and seductive heroes, in some of the world's most glamourous and romantic locations, where power and passion collide.

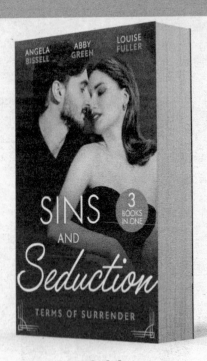